THE CHOLA

Amish is a 1974-born, India-based, bestselling and award-winning author. He is also a broadcaster, the co-founder of a video-gaming company, a film producer and a former Indian diplomat.

His books have sold more than 8 million copies and have been translated into 21 languages. His Shiva Trilogy is the fastest-selling and his Ram Chandra Series the second-fastest-selling book series in Indian publishing history. His Indic Chronicles books, which are based on medieval Indian history, are also blockbuster bestsellers.

Amish has anchored several acclaimed documentaries produced in India for many years running and is a successful podcaster. He is a graduate of the prestigious B-school IIM Calcutta, and earned a BSc in mathematics prior to that from St. Xavier's College, Mumbai.

You can connect with Amish here:

www.facebook.com/authoramish
www.instagram.com/authoramish
www.twitter.com/authoramish

Books by Amish

SHIVA TRILOGY

The fastest-selling book series in the history of Indian publishing

The Immortals of Meluha (Book 1 of the Trilogy)

The Secret of the Nagas (Book 2 of the Trilogy)

The Oath of the Vayuputras (Book 3 of the Trilogy)

RAM CHANDRA SERIES

The second-fastest-selling book series in the history of Indian publishing

Ram: Scion of Ikshvaku (Book 1 of the Series)

Sita: Warrior of Mithila (Book 2 of the Series)

Raavan: Enemy of Aryavarta (Book 3 of the Series)

War of Lanka (Book 4 of the Series)

INDIC CHRONICLES

Legend of Suheldev: The King Who Saved India

The Chola Tigers: Avengers of Somnath

NON-FICTION

Immortal India: Young Country, Timeless Civilization

Dharma: Decoding the Epics for a Meaningful Life

Idols: Unearthing the Power of Murti Puja

'{Amish's} writings have generated immense curiosity about India's rich past and culture.'

—***Narendra Modi***
(Honourable Prime Minister of India)

'{Amish's} writing introduces the youth to ancient value systems while pricking and satisfying their curiosity …'

—***Sri Sri Ravi Shankar***
(Spiritual leader and founder, Art of Living Foundation)

'{Amish's} writing is} riveting, absorbing and informative.'

—***Amitabh Bachchan***
(Actor and living legend)

'Amish is one of India's greatest storytellers, creative, imaginative, so you have to turn the page.'

—***Lord Jeffrey Archer***
(One of the highest-selling authors of all time)

'{Amish's writing is} a fine blend of history and myth … gripping and unputdownable.'

—***BBC***

'Thoughtful and deep, Amish, more than any author, represents the New India.'

—***Vir Sanghvi***
(Senior journalist and columnist)

'{Amish} is an extraordinary gift to the world from India. He has done a great service by taking ancient myths and giving them relevance in modern times.'

—***Deepak Chopra***
(World-renowned spiritual guru and best-selling author)

'{Amish is} one of the most original thinkers of his generation.'
—*Arnab Goswami*
(Senior journalist and MD, Republic TV)

'Amish has a fine eye for detail and a compelling narrative style.'
—*Dr Shashi Tharoor*
(Member of Parliament and author)

'{Amish has} a deeply thoughtful mind with an unusual, original and fascinating view of the past.'
—*Shekhar Gupta*
(Senior journalist and columnist)

'To understand the New India, you need to read Amish.'
—*Swapan Dasgupta*
(Member of Parliament and senior journalist)

'Through all of Amish's books flows a current of liberal, progressive ideology: about gender, about caste, about discrimination of any kind … He is the only Indian bestselling writer with true philosophical depth—his books are all backed by tremendous research and deep thought.'
—*Sandipan Deb*
(Senior journalist and author)

'Amish's influence goes beyond his books, his books go beyond literature, his literature is steeped in philosophy, which is anchored in bhakti, which powers his love for India.'
—*Gautam Chikermane*
(Senior journalist and author)

'Amish is a literary phenomenon.'
—*(Late) Anil Dharker*
(Senior journalist and author)

THE INDIC CHRONICLES

THE
CHOLA TIGERS
AVENGERS OF SOMNATH

AMISH

&

THE IMMORTAL WRITERS' CENTRE

In this book, the commissioned writers were
Ram Sivasankaran and Bhavna Roy

**HARPER
FICTION**

An Imprint of HarperCollins *Publishers*

First published in India by Harper Fiction 2025
An imprint of HarperCollins *Publishers*
HarperCollins *Publishers* India, Cyber City,
Building 10-A, Gurugram, Haryana – 122002, India
www.harpercollins.co.in

2 4 6 8 10 9 7 5 3 1

Copyright © Amish Tripathi 2025

P-ISBN: 978-93-6989-609-7
E-ISBN: 978-93-6989-492-5

Typeset in 11.5 pt/14.2 Adobe Garamond Pro
by HarperCollins *Publishers* India Pvt. Ltd

Printed and bound at
Replika Press Pvt. Ltd.

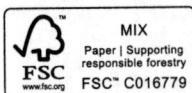

MIX
Paper | Supporting
responsible forestry
FSC
www.fsc.org   FSC™ C016779

HarperCollins *Publishers*, Macken House, 39/40 Mayor Street Upper, Dublin 1,
D01 C9W8, Ireland

This is a work of historical fiction. It draws upon real historical figures, locations and events, but the characters, dialogues, motivations and plot developments are fictionalized for the purpose of storytelling. The depictions found herein, including those involving war or warlike situations, violence, including sexual violence, religious, cultural or political themes, et al., are dramatizations and do not represent the views or endorsements of the author, publisher or any affiliated persons.

Any references to religious texts, doctrines or societal customs are included solely for narrative purposes and do not imply authenticity, accuracy or support for such ideologies. The terms used by characters are presented within the context of their historical settings and should not be interpreted as promoting hatred, prejudice or enmity towards any group.

The intention of this book is not to hurt the sentiments of any individual, community or religion. This book should be read as a creative exploration of history and not as a factual account or commentary on contemporary or historic social or religious dynamics.

Om Namah Shivaya

The Universe bows to Lord Shiva
I bow to Lord Shiva

Kandanakku aroghara, Muruganakku aroghara

Glory to Lord Karthik, the valorous Murugan, the Son of
Lord Shiva

Lead us, our Lords, unto Dharma

To my siblings,
Bhavna didi, Anish dada and Ashish

The road may get rocky,
Life may get hard,
But the whole world together,
Can't tear us apart …
If pressure makes diamonds …
Our love is a diamond by now.

We have been through a lot together,
We have been tested by Fate together,
We are stronger together.

I love you guys.

(With due apologies to Don Williams for mutilating his
divine song 'Pressure Makes Diamonds')

Acknowledgements

To the men who guided me when they were alive and still continue to inspire me now that they are in *pitrulok*. The late Vinay Kumar Tripathi, the late Himanshu Roy, the late Dr Manoj Vyas.

My young son, Neel. My greatest pride, my most sublime joy, my most cherished creation.

My wife, Shivani. She pulled me out when I was sinking. And I soar now because she is the wind beneath my wings.

To the brilliantly talented author Ram Sivasankaran and the wise writer (also my elder sister) Bhavna Roy, who worked with me on this book as part of the Writers' Centre. And Shikha, who helped with the initial edits. What a journey it has been. *Veeravel. Vetrivel.*

Anish, Meeta, Ashish and Donetta, my siblings and sisters-in-law, for their constant support and advice.

The rest of my family: Usha, Sharda, Surendra, Pankhuri and Siddharth. For their constant faith and love. The next generation of the family—Mitansh, Manvi, Nikita, Daniel, Varun, Aiden, Keya, Yash, Anika and Ashna—the future of our larger clan. May their numbers increase!

Neel's mother, Preeti, and her family, Shernaz, Smita, Anuj, Ruta, for their consistent support.

The team at HarperCollins. My publisher, Poulomi; Nandini, Shabnam, Naveen, Ameya and the entire marketing team led by Akriti; Vikas, Gokul, Shreya and the entire sales team led by Rahul; the copy editor, Rachita, proofreader, Paloma, and editor, Swati; the Harper360 team of Karen, Serena, Darren and Sinead; all led by the brilliant CEO of HarperCollins India, Ananth, guided by Charlie Redmayne, the CEO of HarperCollins UK, Ireland, India and Australia, and driven by Brian Murray, president and global CEO of HarperCollins Publishers. The partnership with them grows from strength to strength, as they take my books all over the world.

The team at Pratilipi. Gautam, business head of Westland, Karthika, the editor, Minakshi, Vidhi and the rest of the team, which brings out the Indian regional-language editions of this book. Gautam has been a friend for a decade and a half, and is one of the nicest men in publishing.

Aman, Vijay bhai, Padma, Smruti, Mehul, Krishn, Jash, Prerna, Gauri, Khushi, Dhanaji, Mitali, Anisha, Shubhangi and the rest of my colleagues at my office. They take care of the business, which gives me enough free time to write. I would also like to mention an ex-colleague Shaurya who has now moved to London.

Hemal, Neha, Vinit, Harsh, Leonard, Kevin, Shubham, Vishrruti, Anoushka, Maseera and Team OktoBuzz. They have made the cover of the book, which I think is fantastic. And they also drive all the digital activities.

Sandeep, Caleb, Isha, Manish bhai, Dominic, Neha, Meghna, Disha, Jayesh and their respective teams, who support my work with their business, legal and marketing advice.

Aditya, a passionate reader of my books, who has now become a friend as well as a fact checker.

I also wrote parts of the book at the Isha ashram in Coimbatore. My gratitude to Divyaji and Shwethaji for their kindness and support when my sister, wife and I stayed there.

And last, but certainly not the least, you, the reader. I know that this fiction book has taken time; nearly three years after my previous fiction book. My apologies. However, in my defence, I have also been busy making documentaries and podcasts for you, as well as working on a high-end video game called *The Age of Bhaarat*. I hope you have enjoyed all that too. And I promise to bring my next fiction book to you at a quicker pace. Your consistent affection, understanding and encouragement are what drive me. Thank you so much. May Lord Shiva bless all of you.

Uttaram yat samudrasya, Himadreschaiva dakshinam,
varsham tad Bhaaratam nama, Bhaarati yatra santatih

North of the Ocean, and south of the Himalaya
Lies the nation of Bhaarat, and there live the descendants
of Bharat

—From the Vishnu Purana

Some say that India didn't exist in ancient times,
That the British Raj created the nation of India.
False.
India, that is Bhaarat, was created by our ancestors.
We have existed since the dawn of human civilization.
Every other pre-Bronze Age civilization is dead.
But we are still here. We are still standing.
And we will be there till the last human lives.
For our Motherland is Sanatan. She is Immortal.
She lives in the soul of us, Her children.
Even if one of us lives, She lives.
Bhaarat. Will. Never. Die.

PROLOGUE

The Last Stand at Somnath

Somnath, India, end 1025 CE

The sun slid beyond the shimmering horizon of the Arabian Sea. Twilight gave way to night as the almost-cloudless sky glowed in vibrant shades of red, orange and purple. The rippling waves crept lovingly up the beach and gently cuddled the sands, almost like the water, serene and compassionate, was trying to soothe the tortured land. At many places the sand was unusually red, as if the ground was bleeding. The water washed off some of the red, and retreated, as though shrinking from the macabre vision. And yet, undeterred, like a lover refusing to give up on her suffering beloved, the sea returned to the shore. Again and again. Trying to wash the blood away.

The first step in healing is washing the wounds.

But no matter how hard the sea tried, the red remained. There was too much blood. Too many dead bodies.

A scream pierced the deathly still air. A Turkic soldier, pointing ahead, shouted, 'Stop, thief!'

1

Turks. Very different in looks and physique from the large-eyed, brown-skinned Indians. By any expert's analysis, the Indians should have defeated the Turks. The Indians were taller, healthier, with better nutrition and finer weapons. The Turks were fairer, shorter, leaner. They didn't look like they could be the most vicious killers the world had ever seen. But looks can be deceptive.

Turks. To Indians, they looked a little like the Chinese, with roundish faces and narrow eyes. They weren't from China, though; they were from farther north. Even the Chinese were afraid of these ruthless invaders from Central Asia, the vast rolling grasslands of the Steppes. They had been slave soldiers of their cousin tribe, the Mongols, earlier, but now they were conquerors in their own right.

Turks. Ferocious invaders known to massacre all in their path. Looting, raping, making pyramids of skulls. Revelling in their barbarism.

'Stop, you ba**ard!' shouted another Turkic soldier.

There were two Turks, one of whom was a dwarf. They were chasing an Indian who was dressed like a priest. Shaved head, with a knotted tuft of hair at the crown. Thin and wiry. Dark-skinned. Clad in a saffron *dhoti*. Tears were streaming down his grief-stricken face. He was running hard, negotiating the obstacles of dead bodies strewn all over the bloodstained sandy beach. The bodies of Indian soldiers who had perished in the battle that had just been fought.

The Brahmin was holding something in his hands as he ran. Something immeasurably precious, wrapped tightly in a saffron-coloured cloth.

'Stop!' one of the Turkic soldiers yelled again. 'Stop, you son-of-a-bi**h!'

'Bekarys!' shouted the shorter Turk, panting, to his fellow soldier. 'Bekarys ... Enough ... Can't run more ... Enough ... Knife!'

Bekarys stopped and quickly drew his knife. The Turks were expert marksmen with the bow and arrow. Or a knife. He stopped for just an instant, closed one eye, swung his arm back and flung the blade. All in a moment.

The serrated knife whizzed through the air and slammed brutally into the Brahmin's back. The force of the blow, even from a distance, was so vicious that the priest arched back, screaming in agony. Admirably, considering his frail frame, he didn't fall. Even more admirably, the immeasurably precious object in his arm did not slip from his grasp.

He was mumbling, despite the unbearable pain, 'Ganeshaaaa ... Ganeshaaaa ...'

He stumbled forward, noticeably slower now. The Turks were catching up fast. Then he tripped over a dead Indian soldier's body lying prone on the beach. He fell hard on his face, holding close the object that he carried, covering it with his body.

The Turks had finally caught up. Bekarys's companion was panting hard. 'Goddammit ...'

Bekarys growled, 'You dirty Indian dog! You tired out my friend!'

The Brahmin was howling. Desperate. Eyes wide in panic. Trying to get up. 'Please ... Please let me go. Please!'

Bekarys bent down and slowly pulled the knife out of the Brahmin's back, twisting it as he did so, letting the serrated blade lacerate more muscle and tissue. Blood burst forth in a torrent. The priest shrieked in distress. Screaming, as all men do when in intolerable pain, for his mother.

'Maaaaa … Maaaa …'

The Turkic dwarf, having caught his breath now, laughed. 'Don't call out for your mother, Indian … You don't know Bekarys's immense appetite! He is a tiger! He will violate your mother to an inch of her soul!'

Bekarys joined his friend, guffawing, 'Anyway, let's see what we got for our troubles …'

Bekarys kicked the Brahmin and forced him to turn over, till he was lying on his back, the wet sand sticking to his face. But despite the tremendous anguish he was in, the Indian refused to let go of whatever he was holding. It was still wrapped tight in the saffron cloth that was now stained with his blood. He shook his head furiously. 'No … No …'

The dwarf Turk smiled greedily. 'It must be worth thousands of gold coins if this infidel won't hand it over even now.'

Bekarys laughed at the priest. 'You stupid goat … this is *Maal-e-Ghanimat*. It's ours by right. Give it to us, and we will be kind. We will give you a quick death. Hand it over.'

Maal-e-Ghanimat, according to the interpretation of Islam followed by the Turks, translates as *war booty*. And this principle was particularly applicable in *Dar al-Harb*, meaning the *House of War*, any part of the world that was not ruled by an Islamic ruler and where laws other than the Islamic sharia were practised. According to *Maal-e-Ghanimat*, the Turks were allowed by their religion to claim the property of *kafir*s or *unbelievers*, including gold, land, valuables, and even wives and children as slaves.

It was said that many Muslims, including many Arabs who were the original Muslims, disagreed with this interpretation.

In any case, the Turks were attacking and massacring many Arabs as well. And looting from them too.

The dwarf turned back and looked at the temple complex in the distance. 'Bekarys, they are beginning to burn the smaller temples. We must rush back. There is more gold there …'

Bekarys drew his sword and bent down. 'Let it go, Indian!' he bellowed. 'Or I will chop your arm off!'

The Brahmin clutched the cloth-covered object even tighter. 'No … Please … No … Ganeshaaa … Ganeshaaa …'

'Who is this Ganesha?!' shouted the Turkic dwarf.

Bekarys had had enough. He drew back and held the sword high above his head. The priest, strangely, leaned in and enveloped the object completely with both his arms, protecting it with his own body.

Bekarys's greedy eyes opened wide. *It must be really precious!*

The Turk swung his sword down savagely, hacking through the left arm of the priest, just below the elbow, slicing clean through flesh, tissue and bone. The blow from the curved scimitar was so ferocious that it went even deeper, into the right arm of the priest that lay below the left one, cutting through half of it. Here, the blade got stuck. In the bone.

The priest howled in dreadful misery as blood flooded out in waves from what remained of his severed arms.

'Goddammit!' screamed Bekarys as he tried to yank the blade free. He wrenched it out of the priest's right arm. Finally, the object came loose. The dwarf Turk immediately picked it up, eagerly unwrapping the bloodied saffron cloth. 'What the hell is this?'

The Indian priest, on the verge of losing consciousness, pleaded desperately, 'Please … Don't … hurt … Bal … Ganesh … Don't … hurt … Bal … Ganesh …'

Bekarys stared at the idol. 'THIS IS JUST STONE!' he roared, livid beyond measure.

It was a stone idol of Ganesh, but in His form as a *bal*, or *baby*. Small childlike arms and legs. A podgy torso, with oodles of baby fat. An elephant head that was comfortably plump. One long tusk, and another that was broken. And most endearingly, an innocent and childlike smile on His face.

But unlike many other Hindu *murti*s, this *idol* had no gold plating. No diamond insets. No precious stone inlay.

For the Turks, the idol was worthless.

For the Indian, however, the *murti* was priceless. Despite being on the verge of death, the priest kept repeating, 'Don't … hurt … Bal … Ganesh … Don't … please …'

The dwarf looked back at the temple complex in the distance in a furious rage. 'We lost all the loot there … for this?'

He screamed in frenzied madness and threw the idol on the ground. The waves from the sea came in stronger around his feet.

Bekarys, meanwhile, drew his knife and swung viciously at the Brahmin, stabbing him through the heart with one ruthless blow—killing him instantly.

The dwarf Turk turned and raced towards the temple complex. 'Quickly, Bekarys!'

Bekarys followed swiftly behind his friend.

The Indian was dead, but his cleaved-off arms kept leaking blood. The kind sea waves moved in, nudging the *murti* of Bal Ganesh towards the Brahmin. The idol of the child God almost seemed to embrace the priest, consoling his tormented soul.

—·◦⧸⧹◦·—

It was late in the night when thousands stood outside the ruined boundary wall of the temple complex, roaring flames consuming the millennia-worth of history and culture inside. Hapless multitudes had been rounded up en masse. It was the culmination of the brutal rampage of a city famed for its wealth and splendour.

And a temple.

A temple that bore the same name as the great city.

Somnath. The Lord of the Moon God. One among the countless names of the greatest God of them all. Lord Shiva. *The Mahadev. The God of Gods.*

Yet, for all the grandeur of the fables and monuments peculiar to the Holy City, no help came from the immortalized heroes of yore. Som, the Moon Good, looked down with eerie placidity from the sky above. Shiva, the Benefactor, the God of Gods, remained shrouded in the smoke and dust of the temple—aloof in the face of the onslaught on His house and His people.

Was the Mahadev testing His followers? They all laboured under the same thought … *What have we done wrong, Lord? Why do you abandon us? Why have you chosen to let these barbarians win?*

The crowd was held in check by a human chain of almost two thousand Turkish warriors. They had congregated on the part of the beach closest to the temple, on the other side of where the battle had been fought earlier in the day. The height of the wall was lower here, since this beach was closer to the city. This meant the Indians clustered on the beach could actually see much of the devastating destruction being inflicted by the venomous Turks on the temple complex.

The merchant Someshwar stood at the outer rim of the huddle, his eyes pinned down on the grainy sand. Portly and balding, the fair-skinned Someshwar's face was marked with a salt-and-pepper beard and eyes that were normally kind and genial. They only held pain and dismay right now. He shivered. The wealthiest and most prominent businessman in the city—in fact, among the wealthiest in the world—the sixty-four-year-old had spent his life in the Lord's shadow. He had been named after the Lord, in the Mahadev's sanctum. At the age of eight, he had received his *janau*, the *sacred thread*, at the Somnath Temple. At fifteen, he had picked up the reins of his father's business, after dedicating land and money to the temple's coffers. Since then, every voyage to places near and far began with a prayer to the Lord at the Somnath Temple, in Whose care he entrusted his family in his absence.

Someshwar's fortunes had grown in the presence of the Lord. He had lived and breathed the Lord. His name was that of the Lord.

And now he had witnessed line after line of the city's defence fall to a ruthless enemy. The attack surpassed his imagination and boggled his mind. His faith in the divine Master stood shaken.

The Lord tests me. The Lord tests us all. He wants us to pass through the sieve of these terrible times and separate the resolute believers from the hypocrites and opportunists. I must stay steadfast. I must stay true. I must remain loyal, for there is no power in all the seven worlds that can match the might of the Mahadev, the God of Gods.

And still, that foreign invader, the monster, the Turkic beast from Ghazni, had won.

Sultan Yamin-ud-Dawla Abul-Qasim Mahmud ibn Sebuktegin. More commonly known as Mahmud of Ghazni.

Someshwar had lost track of the time that had passed since the Turks had stormed the main temple at the centre of the huge temple complex. The last battalion of Indian defenders had barricaded themselves in two layers, in a last-ditch attempt to resist the brutality of the Turks. One platoon was positioned at the small gate to the main temple, while the other, along with the temple priests, was behind the massive doors of the sanctum sanctorum.

Someshwar's youngest son Dhruv was among the brave soldiers making a last stand at the main temple. He had gone in under the command of the valiant warrior prince, Malladev of Shravasti. Dhruv was no great soldier. He was a mid-ranked officer in the city's defence corps, which largely comprised volunteers. And he had sworn his life to the service of Somnath*ji*—in a soldier's uniform.

Someshwar knew his boy. Knew his average fighting skills, his medium height and reed-thin body. But these attributes were dwarfed by his mighty heart and fearsome loyalty to Shiva. He knew his boy would fight to the death. With honour. But he didn't know if it had come to that yet.

Time passed in painful, excruciating minutes that ground forward at an agonizingly slow pace.

Someshwar and his fellow delegates from the city's trading guilds awaited a response to the proposal they had sent with Khwaja Hassan, the sultan's prime minister. Khwaja was

Persian, a more civilized race than the Turkic hordes from Central Asia, more attuned to poetry, wisdom and pragmatic business choices.

The message from Someshwar was simple and would have been very profitable to Ghazni: *Dead and destroyed, we would be of no use to Sultan Mahmud, the ruler of Ghazni. If the sacred murti, the Shiva Linga in the temple, is desecrated, you may as well consider us dead. Our Lord is the vessel that holds our souls, our very lives. Spare the temple. Spare the Linga. Spare the men guarding the Linga, and I, Someshwar, will ensure that the sultan gets his rightful tribute and revenues from this city, year after year. Both for himself and his progeny. Forever.*

Khwaja Hassan's beady eyes had gleamed with greed. And the broken businessmen of Somnath had derived hope from it.

'I will go in and negotiate with the sultan on your behalf,' the portly, incredibly fair Persian had told Someshwar and the anxious delegates. He had then scurried as fast as his heavy frame allowed, through the ranks of Ghaznavid soldiers who had parted to let him pass. They had seen him disappear through the temple's main doors.

An agonizing passage of time later, they were yet to receive a reply ...

Someshwar felt his heart contract, as if readying to burst forth from the prison bars of his enfeebled rib cage. Would the desperate plea salvage the honour of the Mahadev? Would his boy, a fragment of his body and soul, live to see another day? Would Mahmud of Ghazni relent?

And yet, for all the optimism in Khwaja Hassan's springy steps, the only sound that emanated from within the temple was a repeated and cruel rumble, like the sound of a gigantic temple bell repeatedly crashing against an immovable rock. It pulsated rhythmically, like booming thunder that had a chilling metallic twang to it.

Clang.

Clang.

Clang … clang … clang …

Again. And again. And again.

The door remained shut, while Abu Q'asim, the rabidly fierce general of Mahmud's hordes, secured the temple's premises from the outside with a battalion of five thousand men. The savages toyed with the captured members of the city's defence corps, mutilating, murdering casually, as if for sport. The sturdiest were dragged, kicking and screaming, to serve as Ghaznavid slaves. Or to be traded as slaves.

The city had already borne the brunt of Abu Q'asim's cruelty earlier in the day. Women, even children, both boys and girls, had been violated. Men beheaded, and pyramids made of their skulls. Livestock butchered. Wells poisoned. And the crimes were accompanied by a dreaded bark: *Kafir. Infidel.*

Clang!

Clang!

Clang!

Clearly, something *inside* the temple was being demolished. A solitary tear ran down Someshwar's cheek. It could only be one thing. The Turkic army had put great effort into degrading the religious beliefs and rituals of the idolaters of the city. Truth be told, they had derived zealous satisfaction from their barbarism. The mere existence of the

Somnath Temple complex, with minor temples of both Goddesses and Gods, and the main temple dedicated to Lord Shiva, seemed to offend them. The Hindus didn't have to do anything to give offence. Their mere existence as idol worshippers was offensive to Mahmud and their Turkic interpretation of Islam.

Smashing the celebrated levitating Shiva Linga *murti* of Somnath would be the climax of the tyrannical Turkic campaign in India.

The steady clangs disturbed the tense silence with morbid repetition.

Clang! Clang! Clang!

Someshwar wept as his mind flooded with the events of the terrible day. For all his hopes, he knew what he was hearing. His mind wouldn't allow him the comfort of delusion. He cried, for what else could he do? They had killed his wife, his sons, his daughter, his daughters-in-law … His grandchildren. Oh! His grandchildren. All in a day. And now he would lose his last surviving son in the sanctum of Shiva Himself.

Suddenly, the clanging sound stopped.

In a flash, the booming voice of Abu Q'asim announced the arrival of the sultan.

The monster.

Mahmud of Ghazni.

Someshwar peered through swollen, burning eyes, his vision glazed by both age and tears. Mahmud strode out of the temple complex, closely followed by his guards and coterie. He was grotesque, ugly, hateful to the eyes of the hapless people of Bhaarat. The normally affable Someshwar felt a wave of murderous rage.

'Someshwar *bhai*,' whispered Iqbal, his friend and business partner. Someshwar was like a *brother* to him. 'He is coming straight for us. He will kill us all!'

Someshwar felt his heart race with trepidation. The terrifying monster—the orchestrator of the worst day of his life—moved towards him menacingly. Flanking him on one side was the twitchy, nervous Khwaja Hassan; on the other was a stocky, clean-shaven youth of medium height and muscular arms. He had entered the temple on the heels of the sultan.

'*Om Namah Shivaya, Om Namah Shivaya, Om Namah Shivaya,*' Someshwar repeatedly mumbled. He was reciting an *ancient Hindu chant which meant that the entire universe and he, the devotee, bowed to Lord Shiva.* As the Turk came closer, the Indian merchant swallowed nervously and muttered, 'Protect me, oh Lord.'

The demon marched menacingly up to the group of Indian businessmen.

Mahmud of Ghazni. Unusually tall for a Turk. Towering above his coterie, which crowded around him, some holding fiery torches aloft, others brandishing weapons that were dripping blood. Someshwar had learnt to recognize them during his travels: *jambiya*s, *katar*s, *peshkabz* …

Mahmud spoke in a gruff growl, 'Who offered me bribes in exchange for sparing his heathen God? Step up!'

Before Someshwar could react, the corpulent Khwaja Hassan squeaked, '*This* one, My Lord!'

The Persian prime minister stepped forward and jabbed his finger into Someshwar's face. 'This *kafir*. He wanted you to sell your faith and your honour in return for paltry riches. Mere gold in exchange for the dignity of his pagan God! Ha!'

Mahmud's evil eyes pierced through Someshwar. He cowered in dread. The sultan snapped his fingers, and two guardsmen swiftly seized the merchant by the arms.

'Mercy!' cried Someshwar. 'Mercy, My Lord! Spare me! I did not mean to ask you to sacrifice your honour! I only sought your mercy!'

The guardsmen pressed his shoulders with force. Someshwar's joints buckled. He fell on his knees.

'Mercy,' Someshwar pleaded as he doubled up in terror. 'Mercy, My Lord!'

Mahmud turned to the youth beside him and laughed like a hideous hyena. 'Did you see that, Maqsud?! Did you see that?! He bleats like a goat!'

The stocky, muscular youth did not make a sound, but his hazel-coloured eyes glinted with malice, and the sides of his mouth twitched with amused contempt. Salar Maqsud. The beloved nephew of Mahmud of Ghazni. He mirrored his uncle's beastly expression, devoid of compassion and warmth.

Khwaja Hassan, the opportunist, laughed loudly in an attempt to conceal his fright. For he was the one who had gone with this offer to the sultan. An offer that had not gone down too well. He clapped his hands with glee and yelled expletives at the hapless Indian merchant, till his master quietened him with a stern look.

'This is the fate of your country. Of your heathen God. Of your women,' Mahmud barked and raised his left hand skyward. 'Of your children …'

He bent slightly and slapped Someshwar hard across his right cheek. Then the left. Then the right …

'Of your soldiers. Your sons. Your kings. Of *everything* you hold dear, you dogs!'

Mahmud continued to strike Someshwar, playfully now, on both cheeks. Drops of blood dotted the corners of the old man's lips. Mahmud looked him in the eye. 'How dare you ask me to trade with you?' he whispered. 'The defeated do not trade. They beg. I will take what is mine, whether you like it or not. I will smash your idols. I will take your sons as my slaves. I will carry away your daughters and wives to fill the brothels in Ghazni.'

The frail old man remained limp on his knees. Crying. Mahmud held his neck in a vice-like grip, like he was a sacrificial goat. He thrust the old man's chin back and traced a line with one long nail.

'*Beg* for mercy,' Mahmud hissed. 'Beg me to spare your life.' He leered with ogre-like delight and said softly, in a singsong voice, 'I just *might*. Our God, our One True God, tells us to be merciful and kind when the enemy submits. Do you submit before me today?'

Someshwar tried to look at the sultan, but his eyes rolled into his skull. He groaned.

'I cannot hear you,' teased Mahmud, cupping his ear. 'Do. You. Submit?'

'I submit.'

Mahmud released his grip, and Someshwar fell back. The tyrant sniggered. 'You idolators are not men. You are eunuchs. Meant to be hunted by us masculine *momin*s.' Then the sultan spread his arms in the air like a messiah. 'But I promised you mercy and I am a man of my word. I will spare your miserable life. I will also reward you with a parting gift. You can clutch it in your pathetic arms for the rest of your life, filthy *kafir*. May it forever remind you of my mercy … and the mercy of the *One* True God, Allah.'

Someshwar looked up apprehensively. Mahmud waved his right hand and beckoned two bulky men with large sacks slung over their shoulders. The men rushed towards their master. Mahmud snapped his fingers at one of them. He hurriedly dropped his sack to the ground, dipped a hand inside and pulled out a fistful of fragments of what looked like broken stone. He handed it to Mahmud, bowing low.

Someshwar looked down. He knew what the fragments were. They were a mix of lodestone and metal, a product of magical science and fervent devotion. Fragments of a whole that, for the Hindus, was more precious than their very lives. He wished that the earth would crack open and swallow him up, so that he wouldn't have to look at this scene. But he remained where he was. Paralysed.

The sultan of Ghazni took a broken piece of the Shiva Linga that he had demolished only a short while ago from the soldier.

'Let me clean this for you,' Mahmud murmured sarcastically. He spat on the little piece of lodestone with venom. He rubbed it against his sleeve and peered at it in mock satisfaction. The sultan then tossed the piece of stone to the ground. It landed near Someshwar's knees.

The grief-stricken crowd around Someshwar gasped. But too afraid to speak, they remained silent.

'Take it home and worship it,' laughed Mahmud. 'Or you can leave it here to be trampled upon by millions for millennia. What difference does it make? It is just a stone!' He howled with laughter. 'In any case, this is the destiny of the remaining pieces of your precious idol. I am taking them back to Ghazni, where I have built the greatest mosque the world has ever seen. I will bury your dead, heathen God, under the steps of my mosque. He will be stamped upon by the followers of the One True Faith, Islam.' Mahmud's voice had risen to a roar. 'And it will be so till Judgement Day!'

The sultan turned to his nephew. 'Torch the entire temple complex, Maqsud. And the dead *kafirs* inside. They burn their dead, don't they? Today, they will burn with their puny Gods and Goddesses.'

Salar Maqsud walked briskly away while Mahmud threw one last contemptuous look at Someshwar, kicked him and moved in the other direction. His guardsmen fell in step like shadows behind him.

The crowd surrounding Someshwar was rooted to their spots on the beach. Grief-stricken. Hesitant. Unsure about whether to be relieved or to expect more violence from the Turks. On seeing the Turks marching away finally, some Indians began to disperse while others followed tentatively. But Someshwar remained on his knees. He gently picked up the precious broken piece of Somnath's Shiva Linga and held it against his chest. Even if the Shiva Linga was broken, Someshwar still derived strength from its fragment. The tears had stopped. His heart had been scorched beyond pain. He closed his eyes, whispering repeatedly... '*Om Namah Shivaya ... Om Namah Shivaya ...*'

Iqbal crouched on the ground beside him. He placed a hand on his friend's shoulder.

'Let us go away for a while, Someshwar *bhai*,' he proposed gently. 'Let us remove ourselves from this land until it recovers. Come with me to Bengal, my homeland. It remains out of this barbarian's reach. We practise Indian Islam there.

It is nothing like what these vile Turks do. We worship both Allah and Mother Durga there. Come home with me. We will rest and heal ourselves in Bengal.'

Someshwar gently brushed off his friend's hand.

'My family may have died here, but my wealth and assets are spread over many lands, including yours.' Someshwar's voice was calm, like a heart that stills itself when faced with pain beyond the threshold of tolerance. 'I have as much wealth as that cursed sultan. I will use it all for one purpose and one purpose alone. We will *not* rest, Iqbal. We will have our vengeance. These savages will feel the wrath of *Dharma*. The anger of Mother India. We will restore our Mahadev's honour.'

Iqbal remained silent. He looked with gentle sympathy at his friend, for he believed that they could do nothing. The Turks were brutal warriors who had defeated much of the civilized world. The civilized, with their values and ethics, often do not know how to fight barbarians.

'Are you with me, Iqbal?'

'Someshwar *bhai* ...' Iqbal's voice was broken. 'Have we not seen enough? These people are monsters, the likes of which the world has never seen. We are merchants. What chance do we have against this vicious sultan when fifty thousand seasoned warriors from a dozen Indian kingdoms couldn't stop him?'

Someshwar rose and wiped the lodestone piece against his shirt. He brought it to his head with respect, then kissed it gently.

'We will be Lord Shiva's carrier pigeons, Iqbal,' he said. 'We must strike at the enemy's heart. We have travelled far and wide, and I know only one man who has the will and the power to take the fight to Ghazni itself.' Someshwar pointed to the north-west, where Ghazni was. 'The answer to this monster from the north-west lies in the south, where one of the greatest devotees of Lord Shiva lives. Come, there is much work to be done.'

Iqbal followed his friend. He didn't think that vengeance was possible. He believed that the Turks were too ruthless and brutal to be defeated by anyone who followed civilized norms. But Iqbal was a good man, a good Muslim. And a good Muslim never leaves his friend's side.

CHAPTER 1

The Gold That Bled

Gangaikonda Cholapuram, capital of the Chola empire, south India

1029 CE *(nearly four years after the attack on Somnath Temple)*

Narasimhan Gounder lay on his back, his left arm wrapped around his wife as she curled to her side, her head resting on his ample shoulder. Their fingers, entwined on his chest, rested over his heart. He slid his right hand over her shapely hip. Harini purred like a satiated Persian cat, stretched gently and snuggled closer.

Through half-shut eyes, the newly appointed captain of the city police looked out of the wooden window on the right side of their bedroom. He gazed at the recently built city, gleaming in the gentle dawn sunlight, and the many torches and lamp towers still lit along the broad streets.

Gangaikonda Cholapuram. The greatest city on earth. The jewel of the Tamils. The pride of India.

Gangaikonda Cholapuram. The grand new capital city built by the mighty Chola emperor, also known as *Gangaikondaan, the one who brought the waters of the holy Ganga* to the south.

The city from where the most powerful man on earth ruled over his vast domain that stretched from India to Southeast Asia.

Rajendra Chola.

Son of the legendary Rajaraja Chola, young Rajendra had moved the centre of power from Thanjavur, where his forefathers had reigned for long, to Gangaikonda Cholapuram. Built with careful planning and forethought, the new city was lined with broad main and side streets arranged in a neat grid, with ample tree-lined footpaths for busy pedestrians to use. The buildings were organized keeping both aesthetics and efficiency in mind. Civic offices were bunched away from residences and recreational squares. The magnificent palace of the king rose in statuesque grandeur at the north end, while the city centre was host to the grand temple of *Brhadishvara*, consecrated in honour of the *Great God Shiva*.

The mighty Chola empire held sway over the imagination of India, and its power and glory cast influence over most of the civilized world.

Narasimhan's thoughts turned to his beat constables patrolling the streets, their ears trained to respond to any cries for help or any minor crime taking place. The constables carried swords, spears and torches. Narasimhan had recently armed them with Ahom knife-axes, imported from Kamarup in the eastern part of India. The weapon had a single-edged blade on the axe side, with a somewhat recurved point.

The standard design had an elephant-head decoration that connected the axe blade to the shaft. It also featured a dagger neatly concealed in the knob of the handle. Overkill, some would say, as weaponry for beat constables policing the streets of a largely safe city. But then, the paramount duty of the captain of the city was to make his citizens feel safe. And Narasimhan believed in the state holding a monopoly on violence in a civilized society. No vigilantism or random violence would be tolerated under his watch.

The crickets shrilly sang their monotonous melody in the early-morning light, all but drowning out the irregular, abrupt sounds of the passing guards' footfalls. Narasimhan's mid-sized spartan home was a few streets away from the palace of the Imperial Chola Household. As a couple of guardsmen passed by, the light from their torches briefly sieved through the cane grills of the window and illuminated the room of the resting couple.

Shadows danced on the powerful bare chest of the thirty-eight-year-old police chief. His wife stirred and slid her hand over his right shoulder. He looked down at her. Swarthy, slender, achingly beautiful. She wore a long beige skirt and a matching blouse. Her dull-blue *angavastram* was spread loosely over her torso and shoulders. Long eyelashes skirted her large, almond-shaped eyes. Her nose was arresting in its refined elegance, with a remarkably straight bridge devoid of any humps or curves. Her dark, curly, lustrous hair was tied in a half-undone bun at the nape of her neck. Her petite bosom expanded and fell as she breathed softly in a gentle rhythm.

Harini was graceful and elegant Indian femininity at its most sublime.

Her husband's physique, on the other hand, was the embodiment of masculine virility. Well over six feet in height, his fair complexion complemented his wife's dusky skin. His neatly trimmed beard ran down the side of his face and curved to merge with the handlebar moustache that adorned his upper lip. Clean-shaven at the chin and neck, Narasimhan's boat-shaped beard hugged his cheeks like a fierce mane on his handsome, leonine face. His powerful legs were covered by the folds of his *dhoti*.

Harini was a city highborn, whereas Narasimhan was from rural peasant stock. A relationship that many believed would not last. But it had. Sometimes, character and class differences make the hearts grow fonder. And a fond heart may not cure the poison that afflicts it, but it can bury it so deep that it causes less trouble.

Narasimhan abandoned his feeble attempts at sleep for the sun would soon announce its arrival with majestic élan, as it always did. He had lain on the bed for several hours in a state of wakefulness, and yet in perfect stillness, so he would not disturb his wife's rest. He felt numbness in his limbs.

Carefully, very slowly, he touched the gold annulus pendant suspended from his neck by a long black thread. The annulus: too large for a ring, too small to be a grown woman's bangle. He felt the fire go through him as soon as he touched it.

He moaned softly.

Mahadev … Have mercy …

The captain's eyes moistened slightly. He gently moved his wife's hand from his chest and shifted her on her back. He raised her head gently and freed his left arm. He sat up on the king-sized bed and stretched his upper body, careful not to disturb Harini.

He then swivelled around and planted his feet on the cool, clay-paved floor. In a trice, he was on his feet. He threw his wife a quick loving glance before wrapping a shawl over his shoulders.

He exited his bedchamber and strode through the colonnaded walkway towards the courtyard, on the other side of which was one more passage which led to the main door. On the way, he halted by a room and peeped in. His boys. The nine-year-old slept spread-eagled, his duvet cast aside on the floor. The six-year-old was buried inside his. Narasimhan padded in and silently covered his older boy.

As he shut the door behind him, he touched the gold annulus again—and immediately pulled his hand back, as if scalded. It didn't trouble him when the annulus touched his chest, but he couldn't hold it in his hands. It brought back all the memories.

Narasimhan shook his head and walked through the open central courtyard. He wore his outdoor sandals and gently released the heavy bolts on the beam-braced teakwood entrance.

The captain stepped out into the street, carefully closing the door to his home. The guardsmen discreetly saluted him, silently thanking the stars above for keeping them awake and alert. The new police chief's wrath at his men's dereliction of duty was severe; his reputation as a fearsome former general had travelled far. Though the current peaceful, almost-Jain-like avoidance of violence by him in the present times clashed with his warrior reputation. He breathed deeply and looked at the dark shapes that were homes in his neighbourhood. Open windows and tightly shut doors. Looming in the distance was the grand palace, where the emperor was asleep. Narasimhan gazed at it fixedly.

Narasimhan was loved and respected by Rajendra Chola. He had been the emperor's right-hand man in the magnificent naval victories against the Srivijaya empire. And the Chola writ had now spread deep across Southeast Asia. Along with his already existing control over southern and eastern India, the Eastern Sea had become Rajendra Chola's pond.

This should have been Narasimhan's moment of glory. Of triumph.

For this was all he had ever wanted to be. A great warrior. Fighting to protect and serve his land, his people and his king.

He knew now. He understood now.

Maa was right ... As always ...

He remembered his mother's words. Among the greatest curses in life is to be denied what you have always desired. But an even bigger curse is to actually get what you have always desired.

He looked down again at the pendant resting on his chest. He closed his eyes.

Mahadev ... Mahadev ... Help me ...

Narasimhan had relinquished his position as the emperor's most trusted general a few weeks earlier. He had expressed a desire to return to his massive rural estate in southern Karnataka, an idyllic region where the Kaveri River flowed young, swift and deep. He would take up farming, like his forefathers. Like his brothers back home, he would sow and harvest paddy.

The emperor—his friend and confidant—had refused to let him go. Partly refused. He would not completely relieve his most trusted man from service to the Chola throne. He had asked the general to stay back in Cholapuram as the chief of the city police. A very senior role with direct access to the emperor. Also, an apparently easy job, since the city was relatively crime-free. Furthermore, violent crime was practically unheard of here.

Narasimhan had given in ... One could not simply say no to Rajendra Chola.

He felt a tiny hand on his broad shoulder, and was startled. Then he smiled. He knew that his wife knew him well. She must have let him leave the room to be by himself for a short while. And she would have known to find him here, on the street closest to the house, where the palace was visible.

'Simha?' Harini caressed him with her melodious voice, using the name only she called him by.

She held his arm gently. He crooked it instinctively and looked at his best friend, his anchor for thirteen years. Within her dark-brown eyes he found what alpha males always hanker for most from their mate—peace.

She was his shelter from the storm. His oasis in the desert-like struggle of life.

And like all good wives, she had impeccable instincts about what troubled her man.

'Please, my love,' she whispered. 'For the love of Lord Shiva, shake it off. I have never asked you what it is about this ...' Harini looked at the annulus pendant. 'Enough ... enough now ... Immerse it in Mother Kaveri. Let it go ...'

Narasimhan remained silent.

Harini believed that the pendant was bewitched. Infused with some malevolent spirit. Like a voodoo curse. A well of eternal pain that had drowned her honourable husband.

And Narasimhan did what he always did at such times. He changed the subject. 'Let's go home, my love.'

—◦❋◦—

Harini and Narasimhan were back in their house. The domestic staff had awakened and begun their morning chores. Their sons were awake, bathed and doing their yoga. Harini was a good mother, and strict about their daily schedule, as good mothers should be with boys of that age.

'Here,' said Harini, as a servant walked into their chamber with two glasses of buttermilk. She handed Narasimhan a glass and then took one herself.

'I love you,' said Narasimhan, as he took a sip.

'I know,' said Harini coquettishly, and began drinking too.

Narasimhan smiled.

Harini hesitated, and said, 'I've been meaning to ask something …'

Narasimhan smiled. 'Of course, darling. Ask away …'

'What about Vijayan?'

Vijayan had been the acting chief of police of Cholapuram for the last many years. And he had, by most accounts, done a good job. Now, for no fault of his, he had been, in effect, demoted and placed under the command of the favourite general of the emperor, simply because Rajendra Chola wanted to somehow prevent Narasimhan from leaving his city.

'It has only been a week since I was appointed, Harini,' Narasimhan reminded her. 'Vijayan is a good man. He is a great archer. And he has every reason to feel slighted. He must serve under me now—a man with no experience in his line of work.'

'You are not just any man. You are one of the greatest generals in the Chola army.'

'But what do I know of policing? I will bring Vijayan around. Don't worry. The fact that he's from Pandya territory makes things that much more complicated.'

The Chola heartland lay along the sacred Kaveri River. The Pandyas, another great warrior dynasty, were based farther south, along the holy Vaigai River. The Chola and Pandya rivalry went back many centuries. There was a time when the Pandyas had ruled, and the Cholas had been their feudatories. But over the last century the positions had reversed. The Pandyas were now vassals under their Chola overlords. The Cholas had offered senior roles within their administration to many influential nobles who had served the Pandya dynasty, to bring them into the folds of the empire. But at times, the strains of the ancient rivalry remained.

'I would prefer that Vijayan get his old job back and we leave Cholapuram for our estate. And live in peace there … Farming, rearing cattle … Maybe have some more children,' said Narasimhan.

'I would like that. Especially the part about making more children!'

Husband and wife laughed softly.

'But,' continued Narasimhan, 'I cannot leave without the emperor's permission … I will try again. I will plead with him to let me go.'

Harini looked at her husband, ensuring that the sadness she felt inside did not reflect on her face.

Her husband had fought ten campaigns for the Chola army. Won famous victories for them. But the conquest of Southeast Asia had been the hardest, lasting over four years. He had returned a changed man. Damaged, in some ways.

I gave my lion to the Chola army. To the emperor. What did they do to my man?

Narasimhan held his wife's hand. 'Don't worry … Remember, all that matters is you and me.'

Harini started crying. She took a step and embraced her husband tightly.

———

Narasimhan sat in his private office at home, leafing through the scrolls and parchments for the day. He liked to finish this boring job early in the morning, before leaving for the police headquarters. If there was one similarity between the Chola army and the police force, it was their compulsive infatuation with paperwork.

'Simha!' Harini called loudly.

'I'm here,' Narasimhan answered.

Harini came in, bearing a silver plate. 'I had gone to the temple …'

Narasimhan rose from his desk, slipped off his footwear and joined his palms together respectfully, bowing his head to make it easy for his wife. Harini dipped her index, middle and ring fingers into the earthen bowl of sacred ash on the plate. Narasimhan placed his right hand on his head. His wife drew a neat *tripundra* on his forehead—the *three streaks of ash worn by Shaivite Hindus*, those who worship the Mahadev, Lord Shiva. She wiped the remaining ash from her fingers on her throat and then on the edge of her *angavastram*.

'Go, now,' she said lovingly. 'Go to work. That is, if you are done looking over your scrolls.'

'Nearly done.'

'By the way, Vijayan was at the temple. It seemed as if he was personally overseeing security in that area today.'

Narasimhan nodded. Harini couldn't tell if this was unexpected news for her husband, or not.

—◦⚜◦—

It was late in the morning, nearly noon, when Narasimhan reached the Brhadishvara Temple complex.

He was clad in a white *dhoti*, with a saffron-coloured cummerbund tied around his waist. He had draped a white *angavastram* on his right shoulder and wrapped the end of the cloth around his forearm. On his head was a turban tied from a long red strip of cloth. He wore simple studs in both earlobes, and a religious *janau*, hung down from his left shoulder, across his torso, to the right side. He cut a dashing yet fearsome figure, with his immense musculature and height, yet simple, understated clothes.

The city was abuzz at this time of the day. Fruit and vegetable vendors lined the streets, displaying fresh produce in their stalls. Haggling customers jostled for space, while schoolgirls and schoolboys walked back home for lunch, some sprightly, others tired and morose, for the afternoon classes were still ahead of them.

On reaching the threshold of the temple, Narasimhan slipped off his sandals at a nearby stall and entered the gates. He bent and touched the first slab of stone under the *gopuram, a massive tower that was also a ceremonial gate to the temple complex.* He raised his hand and touched his forehead with respect.

'My Lord *Brhadishvara,*' he whispered to his Great God Shiva. 'Lord of the Universe. I am here. Bless me with your compassion.'

The throng of devotees was relatively sparse today. Through the crowd, Narasimhan's eyes fell on the police officer standing in the distance with his back towards him.

Vijayan.

A quiver full of arrows was slung across his taut, well-built back, while a recurve bow hung over his right shoulder. He was surrounded by policemen in the temple courtyard, all in their uniform of yellow *dhotis* and thin leather armour. A standard military-grade combat knife dangled from their waists. The officer was instructing his men.

Narasimhan forced a convivial smile and walked towards the group. The animated men sank into an uneasy silence as their newly appointed chief approached. Vijayan turned around. Narasimhan felt the animus before it was efficiently masked by contrived civility.

'Good afternoon, Sir,' Vijayan spoke languidly, executing the formal police salute. He did all the right things. The greeting, the salute. Even the slight smile. It was all polite and proper. But the crispness in the salute was missing.

Good leaders always know when a subordinate is being disrespectful, even if he is doing all the right things on the surface. Narasimhan let the insult slide.

'Good afternoon, Vijayan,' he responded with a courteous nod and a return salute.

Vijayan dismissed his men with a gesture. Although a good four inches shorter than Narasimhan, the clean-shaven, handsome swarthy face of the second-in-command of Cholapuram's police force indicated no intimidation. On the contrary, it was passively belligerent.

'What brings you here, Sir? This is not the traditional day of the week for your prayers to Lord Shiva,' Vijayan said in a calm voice as he adjusted the tautness of his bowstring. The subtle 'we-can-manage-without-you' attitude not quite so subtle this time.

'Narasimhan ...' said Narasimhan. 'You can call me Narasimhan when it's just the two of us and there are no other police officers around.'

'No,' said Vijayan, shaking his head slightly. 'I'll stick to "Sir". How may I help you ... *Sir*?'

'I need the force to check on ...' Narasimhan stopped suddenly as his warrior instincts sensed a presence closer than it should be. His muscles tensed, ready to spring into action. His eyes widened automatically. He swung around instantly, his hand moving smoothly to his side and drawing a knife. All in one smooth motion. All within the blink of an eye. Like a coiled panther reacting instantaneously to a threat.

Narasimhan's knife was right at the throat of the startled old man standing behind him.

'SIR!' said an alarmed Vijayan loudly. He knew of soldiers with post-traumatic stress disorders killing someone without meaning to.

The portly man, with a balding head and a salt-and-pepper beard, had raised both his arms in submission. As had another man, of similar age, standing beside him.

'Take it easy, Sir,' said Vijayan. 'I don't think they mean any harm.'

'We certainly mean no harm, great Lord,' said the portly man in chaste Tamil, but in an accent foreign to the Chola lands.

'I'm sorry ...' apologized Narasimhan, pulling his knife back. 'I'm sorry ...'

'No, we are sorry, My Lord,' said the old man. 'We didn't mean to disturb you.'

'You shouldn't sneak up on anyone like that.'

'I ... I did try to call out to you ...' said the man apologetically, his palms joined in a penitent namaste. 'But perhaps you didn't hear me. So I thought I would come up and talk to you. This is a temple after all, and we are all devotees of Lord Shiva.'

'That we are,' said Narasimhan, taking a deep breath to compose himself. '*Om Namah Shivaya.*'

All the others repeated the chant. *Om Namah Shivaya.*

'You're not from here,' said Narasimhan. His heart, and mind, were calm now. 'I can't place your accent.'

'Depends on what you mean by "here", My Lord,' said the man.

Narasimhan laughed softly. As did Vijayan.

'My accent may be Gujarati, My Lord, but my words are Tamil ...' said the man. 'And my "here" is Mother India.'

'Well said ...' Narasimhan laughed before continuing. 'Though I have to admit, I have never heard Tamil in a Gujarati accent before. It sounds ... different ...'

The portly old man laughed genially.

'What do you want, *anna*?' asked Narasimhan, referring to the old man as *elder brother in Tamil*. 'How can I help you?'

'We just want to talk to the warrior Narasimhan, the great general of Emperor Rajendra Chola.'

'You're in luck, for I am Narasimhan, but I am not a general any more. I am the police chief here. How can I help you?'

'I am Someshwar,' the old man said. 'A merchant from the western shores of our country; from the once-glorious city of Somnath.'

Narasimhan's face fell, his heart heavy. Tears sprang to his eyes almost instantaneously. And Vijayan's too. Seeing their reaction, Someshwar and Iqbal also teared up, remembering that most terrible day again.

'I understand your anguish, Someshwar*ji*,' said Narasimhan. 'The attack on the great temple at Somnath*ar* ...' Narasimhan added the Tamil *ar* for respect. 'It is the first thing my wife mentioned when the emperor and I returned a few weeks ago ... The emperor is also aware of it now. We ... we intend to help rebuild it ... And ...'

'We will rebuild, My Lord,' Someshwar said passionately. 'But rebuilding can be done by us merchants and priests and common people ... Rebuilding is not the task of our warriors ... The warriors have a different duty. Their *Dharma* is different.'

Narasimhan remained silent.

The tears spilled from Someshwar's eyes. His podgy fists clenched as tight as his advanced age and broken heart would allow. His body quivered slightly with righteous fury. 'They ... That monster Mahmud and his army ... They need to answer for their sins ... Our warriors need to teach them a lesson in dharmic justice ...'

'What have the other kingdoms in India been doing these last four years? What did your north Indian kingdoms do to stop Mahmud?'

'The kings of western and northern India are no less courageous than the ones in the south, Chief Narasimhan. They fought hard. They fought valiantly. The mistake they made was that they fought separately. Many tens of thousands of brave Indian soldiers and kings have died fighting Mahmud. They have attained martyrdom, but not victory. Why? Because of our usual problem, My Lord. Internal divisions. And since there is no unified empire in north India any more, it is almost impossible to get different groups to agree on one common strategy to take on Ghazni. I know, because we have tried our best to unite them in the recent past. They have fought heroically but not unitedly. And that just wasn't good enough against the Turks. We need the greatest emperor in India, Rajendra Chola, whose empire is bigger than most other kings of the country combined, to lead our fight for vengeance ... But he was missing in Southeast Asia these last few years. The moment we heard that he had returned, my friend Iqbal and I rushed here to seek his help.'

Narasimhan was aware of the plans being made by the emperor. He also knew that perfecting those plans would take time. But he did not know how much he could trust this old Gujarati man. 'You are a merchant, Someshwar*ji* ... Leave this to the Chola emperor. He is a great devotee of Lord Shiva ... Probably the greatest devotee of the Mahadev in this land ... We will ...'

'My apologies for interrupting you, great Narasimhan,' said Someshwar. 'But even Lord Ram needed the help of squirrels to build the bridge to Lanka. Only a squirrel can do what the squirrel can do.'

All Indians knew this legendary story from the Ramayan. This was when Lord Ram and his army had come to the sea, and were building a bridge to cross over to Lanka, to defeat the demon king Raavan ... At that time, a squirrel had offered to help in the construction of the bridge. Others had laughed and questioned what a tiny squirrel could possibly do. But Lord Ram, as was his wont, had seen the courage in the squirrel's heart rather than the sparsity in ability. He had accepted the little squirrel's help.

Narasimhan remained quiet.

'I was there ...' said Someshwar, crying now.

Narasimhan suddenly straightened up. He shot a glance at Vijayan, who looked equally stunned, and then looked back at Someshwar. They had been under the impression that every Indian who had seen the destruction of Somnath Temple had been killed by Mahmud of Ghazni.

'We were both there,' said Iqbal, Someshwar's friend, speaking for the first time—his accent clearly revealing his Bengali heritage.

'I must show you something ...' said Someshwar.

Someshwar turned to Iqbal, who carefully fished out a piece of polished dark stone from the bag slung across his shoulder. He gently and respectfully handed it to the Gujarati merchant.

Someshwar cupped the stone in his right hand like a delicate, fragile baby. His left hand lay below, touching the right hand—as it must always be when holding something sacred.

Narasimhan's fists clenched tight, his teeth gritted. Fury and grief blazed through him simultaneously. Vijayan stepped closer, tears flowing from his eyes. Both the Tamil soldiers sensed what the stone had been a part of.

'This is a piece from the Somnath Shiva Linga that Mahmud of Ghazni broke four years ago.' Someshwar's voice quaked as he spoke.

Vijayan touched the stone with trembling hands.

Someshwar was shaking in misery. 'That ... That Mahmud has taken ... the rest of the pieces of the sacred Shiva Linga with him ... He announced to us that he intends to bury the pieces of the idol under the steps of the main mosque in Ghazni. So that the so-called believers can step on our Lord five times a day ...'

'We will burn that scoundrel alive ...' Vijayan snarled.

Someshwar continued, 'We have been trying to meet the emperor for the last few days, My Lords. But the palace guards have turned us away, again and again. They say the noble Chola cannot be disturbed. Then we were advised to find the great General Narasimhan ... for he has the ear of the emperor. And he will fight for the honour of the Mahadev and our Mother India.'

'I will get you an audience with Emperor Rajendra Chola, Someshwar*ji*,' whispered a visibly shaken Narasimhan.

Iqbal let out a loud wail as he fell at Narasimhan's feet. Narasimhan pulled the Bengali up and embraced him. Vijayan stepped up and held Someshwar's shoulder, as the Gujarati merchant continued to bawl, cradling the broken stone in his hands.

Someshwar knew. His soul knew. All he needed was an audience with Rajendra Chola. Then the furious broken Heart of the Lord Mahadev would do the talking and remind the great dharmic warrior of his duty.

A duty that cannot be denied. For *Dharma* demands it. History demands it. Our ancestors in *pitrulok* demand it.

Because the purest of all masculine motivations is righteous vengeance.

In righteous vengeance lies the restoration of balance.

In righteous vengeance is *Dharma*.

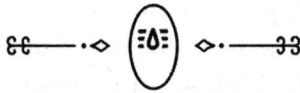

CHAPTER 2

A Brother in Chains

Guzgan, Afghanistan

Ismail detected a shadow approaching the doorway.

Allah, have mercy …

He gulped air uneasily, entwining his fingers, half closing his eyes. Almost in childlike hope that if you don't see the danger, it will disappear.

And then he saw it. The shadowy shape against the wall.

An unkempt, grey goatee that flowed down the pointy chin of the approaching man.

Ismail visibly relaxed and sighed aloud in relief.

A gaunt old man entered his chamber.

'Did you stop him in time, Talib?' Ismail rushed forward anxiously, asking his trusted confidant and servant.

The elderly Talib's aquiline features twitched. He straightened his hunched back a bit, his arms clasped behind him. His face was thoughtful. His small black eyes stared impassively at Ismail. A calm servant to a very nervous master. But before he could answer, his master continued.

'If the sultan's party saw someone so much as exit this fort without permission, it would be death for all of us. And you know what he carries ...' Ismail was clearly jittery. He wore an exquisite but voluminous fur coat which made him look bulkier than he was. For sure, Ismail was tall for a Turk. Nearly six feet. But he was slim and gangly. His eyes always seemed troubled. Despite the cold, he was sweating.

'I got to him in time, My Lord,' reassured Talib, smiling slightly to settle his master's nerves. 'Near the stables. He has received your new instructions.'

'Where is he now?' Ismail persisted, on edge because of the sudden change in plans. 'And where is the letter? I don't want it falling into the hands of my mad brother. But I intend to send it, remember that. Only our schedule has changed. Nothing else. I did not expect the sultan to return so soon.'

Ismail, the highly strung brother of Sultan Mahmud of Ghazni, changed his mind and therefore his instructions often. This made it very difficult for those who worked for him. But Talib had learned how to manage this.

'The messenger—your head chef—has gone back to the kitchens,' said Talib. 'And I am sure the letter is safely stashed away somewhere in the pantry. Rashid is resourceful. You have nothing to worry about, My Lord.'

Ismail walked to the barred window. He peered at the southern road which wound up to the great but secluded fort of Guzgan—his prison for thirty years now.

A massive cloud of dust was moving towards the citadel.

Mahmud of Ghazni. And his royal entourage.

Ismail felt the black bile rise within him. He laughed bitterly.

'Nothing to worry about, huh?' Ismail remarked, his tone resentful. 'What about that?' He pointed through the window, to the direction where, in the distance, his elder brother Mahmud was marching towards him. 'We shouldn't worry about that fraud Mahmud, should we? I was also told not to worry when I became the ruler a lifetime ago! A fat lot of good it did me. Whenever I meet that savage Mahmud, there is nothing but anguish for me!'

Ismail spat through the barred window, as if at his elder brother Mahmud, who had deposed him as the ruler of Ghazni three decades ago and put him under house arrest at the fort of Guzgan. But Ismail's abilities, confidence and destiny were such that he couldn't even spit properly. Some of the spittle splashed back from the bars, falling on his expensive fur coat. Ismail shrieked and started wiping his coat clean, tears forming in his eyes.

Talib remained where he was. Silent. Unmoving. He knew better than to react when Ismail was having one of his panic episodes.

'*Thirty years*, my friend,' Ismail continued resentfully. 'Thirty years I have spent in this godforsaken fort in the middle of bloody nowhere, while the usurper sits on *my* throne, enjoying *my* riches, ravishing *my* women!'

A quiet Talib, his head bowed, was holding back his counsel. *Now is not the time.*

'Tyrant!' Ismail spat out the final word. He was breathing heavily now. Exhausted by his rant. He walked up to his table and picked up a glass of water, gulping the liquid down in bursts. Wiping his mouth with the back of his hand, he looked at his servant and confidant Talib. 'But I am grateful that wretch visits ... Even if it is just to show off his conquests to me. Especially the last two visits … They have finally shown me the beast's weaknesses. His exploitable weaknesses.'

'Indeed, My Lord,' said Talib with an emphatic smile. *Now was the time to speak.*

'You know, it was me who planted that dangerous idea in his head …' Ismail paused briefly and looked at the copper mirror on the wall, admiring his own intellectual brilliance, which far outshone, in his opinion, the acumen of his brutishly bestial brother. He looked out the window at the swirling dust. 'I hope he is here to tell me he has taken the bait.'

Talib nodded. 'I have a feeling that he may have.'

'Come now,' urged Ismail as he began walking to his chamber door. 'Ready the guards and the minstrels. Mahmud is almost here. We better all be at the fort gates when he arrives, lest he uses our absence as an excuse to have us all executed.'

———◦✦◦———

The Ghaznavid Sultan Mahmud sat in the middle of a large, circular stone hall that served as the audience hall in the fort. His wife, Kausari Jahan, was seated beside him. The curving wall of the audience hall was lined with an array of torches, their flames feeding the space with much-needed light and some warmth. There was a fireplace in the northern arc of the room, lit with a roaring flame, which helped in substantial measure with the cold. The windows were shut, and thick curtains drawn over them to keep the icy-cold night winds out. But some chilly air still filtered through. It was peak winter in Afghanistan. A table had been laid out with food and wine, and several nobles and members of the royal family, part of the travelling court of the sultan, were gathered around it.

Mahmud was tall for a Turk, at six feet. While his facial features were like that of his brother Ismail, and he had fair skin and small eyes, his battle scars—particularly the one that ran up his right cheek to the bridge of his now-deformed nose—gave him a grisly air. But Mahmud enjoyed that, for he liked intimidating any man who stood before him. His physique was bulky, with mighty shoulders and a broad chest. He was a creature made for war, unlike his younger brother Ismail, who was better at court intrigue.

Kausari Jahan, his queen, sat proud beside her husband. Regally distant and hauntingly beautiful. Tall, over five feet nine inches in height. Slim body, with limbs that were slender and graceful. Fair-skinned, with high cheekbones that were achingly red. Sharp facial features and jawline. Wide eyes that were an evocative bluish-green. Elegant, long neck that was, just by itself, a thing of beauty. It was clear that she wasn't Turkic; her features made it evident that she was, most likely, from the crown of India—Kashmir.

Mahmud, now at the age of fifty-nine, was only five years older than Kausari. But the queen looked many decades younger than him. Some people say, how you look at twenty is determined by the genes your parents blessed you with, while how you look at fifty is a result of the life you've lived. But other people say, how you look at any age is dependent on how much make-up you put on and the witchcraft your apothecary used. Many did think Kausari was a witch. But very few said it out loud. For obvious reasons.

It was widely believed that the queen held tremendous influence over Mahmud, despite his unhidden bisexual tendencies. In fact, many suggested in hushed whispers that, if it weren't for Kausari Jahan, Mahmud would have been exclusively taking male lovers by this time. He was enslaved by her physical magnetism, ferocious intellect and a grace that was always alluring but just out of reach. And it was also unquestioningly accepted that she was deeply loyal to Mahmud.

Abu Q'asim—Mahmud's trusted general who, during peacetime, was assigned as the chief of the bodyguard corps—stood in the shadows behind his master, with ten bodyguards on either side of him. Q'asim towered over them all, including his sultan. His blunt, indistinct features framed the dark void within his deadpan eyes. Emotionless, he stood still, like a watchful gargoyle. His unblinking eyes were pinned on Ismail, who sat a short distance away. Some nobles, who had accompanied Mahmud's royal entourage, sat at tables placed around the hall.

Five tasters huddled around the main table, meticulously sampling the food before it was served to Mahmud and his wife. Tasting for poison. Kausari trusted no one.

Rashid, the *sar aashpaz*, stood at a polite distance. The *head chef* was proud of his skills.

Tasting done, the feasting began. Bending over and feeding Mahmud was a foppish young man, not more than thirty-five years of age, and of extraordinarily feminine physical beauty. He had high cheekbones and pale, almost-translucent, skin. His lean, fluid physique had the suppleness of a dancer. His fingers were long, covered with smooth, radiant skin. His elaborate attire suggested nobility, though he served the sultan with obsequious servility.

'I like this meat, Ayaz,' remarked Mahmud, biting off half the leg of lamb. 'I want more. More!' he roared with maniacal intensity.

'I am glad you like it, My Lord,' Ismail said politely, hiding his irritation that the appreciation was directed elsewhere. 'Rashid is an excellent cook.'

'Seriously, Ismail!' laughed Mahmud. 'You know the name of your cook?' Tiny drops of spit and morsels of meat flew out of his mouth. Some got stuck in his sparse, pointy beard. 'Do you know the names of these women who serve you, Kausari?' he asked, pointing to the girls who stood to her side.

In response, the queen raised her nose and snickered superciliously, before looking at Ismail. 'Not really, no.' Kausari Jahan's silken voice was like the majestic cry of aristocratic Himalayan bulbul birds on the Dal Lake in Kashmir.

Dinnertime passed, with Ismail's feeble murmurs and his older brother's humiliating banter. Soon Mahmud was talking to himself, fulminating over the far more succulent meat in Ghazni and the unoppressive weather in his capital. Ismail reddened with embarrassment and sank into silence, like a lamb who knew its slaughter was imminent.

Suddenly, the sultan shifted gears. With loud bombast, he proclaimed that he had defeated his younger brother within months of their dying father installing Ismail as the *emir*, or *governor*, of Ghazni. Mahmud reminded Ismail of his mercy. He could have had him skinned alive, beheaded and his carcass hung from the gates of Ghazni—as he had done with most of Ismail's supporters. Instead, he had allowed Ismail to live in this lavish fort of Guzgan.

'Am I not kind, brother?' asked Mahmud, bending forward, apparently drunk on wine, his eyes aggressive and taunting.

'Of course you are, great King!' blurted back Ismail almost immediately, afraid that even a split-second's delay would be interpreted incorrectly.

'Isn't it tradition among us Turks that any capable ruler massacres all the male competitors of his family? Just like lions do when they conquer a pride. I could have done that to you. Did I?'

'No, you didn't, my brother,' said Ismail, his wimpy voice sounding even more frail. Fear gripped his heart for he didn't know where this was going. 'Your kindness is beyond compare. Songs will be sung in your honour till Judgement Day.'

'I could have made you a slave. Returned you to the fate that our father once suffered.'

Mahmud and Ismail's father, Sebuktegin, had once been a slave. Many Turkic tribes had served as slave soldiers for more powerful races, like the Arabs, Mongols and Persians. But over time, many of them had, through sheer bravery and ruthlessness, established their own independent kingdoms. That's why, across the world, the first Turkic dynasties were often known as Slave Dynasties.

'You didn't do that, My Lord,' squealed Ismail. 'Your love for me knows no bounds.'

Almost everyone had stopped eating now. Nobody knew where this interaction was going. But it obviously wasn't normal. Even for the mercurial Mahmud.

The sultan turned to Abu Q'asim and nodded.

'Everyone, leave,' Abu Q'asim announced in a deep baritone that was always menacing.

The noblemen from the royal entourage, the servants, everyone immediately abandoned their food and rushed to the exit, eager to implement Mahmud's order with unseemly haste. Much to their surprise, Abu Q'asim headed to the door as well, followed by the bodyguards.

Ismail too got up uncertainly.

'Ismail. Sit,' ordered Mahmud.

Ismail collapsed into his chair. He was stripped of the comforting company of the only people he had a relationship with now: his servants. He felt raw fear seize his gut, making it almost leaden. He felt a choking sensation in his throat. His hands were cold and clammy.

Does he know? How does he know? Allah, have mercy.

Ismail looked around nervously. Besides Mahmud, there were only two other people in the audience hall now. Queen Kausari Jahan and Malik Ayaz, the recently appointed King of Lahore—the handsome man who had been fussing over Mahmud all evening. While Malik Ayaz was, for all practical purposes, a governor, he had been bestowed the grand title of king. Everyone knew why.

The queen and Malik were both looking at Ismail with a deadpan expression. Try as he might, Ismail couldn't read them. He became even more nervous.

'What can I do for you, My Lord?' asked Ismail meekly.

Mahmud looked at Kausari and Ayaz. Almost like he was reconfirming something. And then his eyes turned to a now-petrified Ismail.

'My brother,' Mahmud spoke, his voice surprisingly kind—unconvincing, since it was a tone that Mahmud didn't have too much practice with. 'I can only imagine how you must have felt all these years. In this godforsaken fort in the middle of nowhere …'

Ismail's mind was already racing. *I'm going to be killed. How will he kill me? Poisoning? Beheading?*

'… though it is a very comfortable fort …' Mahmud's voice continued in an almost monotonous tone. 'A big, beautiful fort … Not that I would have lived here …'

I hope I won't be skinned alive. Allah, make it painless. I beg you.

'But my brother, I have come to make changes … make amends …'

Ismail was jolted back to attention at Mahmud's words. *Amends?*

'Against the advice of those I hold most dear …' Mahmud glanced quickly at his wife. She pursed her lips. 'Against much of what our Turkic tradition is …' Mahmud was staring hard at Ismail's eyes now. 'I am setting you free, Ismail.'

Ismail couldn't believe his ears. *What?!*

'I'm taking you home, my brother,' said Mahmud. 'To Ghazni. I have plans. I want you to support me in carrying them out. Be by my side.'

'My … *Lord*?' Ismail squeaked, stunned beyond measure.

Mahmud stared at Ismail and spoke, 'You will be the governor of Ghazni and the grand mufti of the Jama Mosque, Ismail. How does that sound?'

The governor of Ghazni would be in charge of all the non-royal government departments of the capital city, reporting directly to the sultan. It was a senior administrative role. Even more surprising was the role of grand mufti of the Jama Mosque, the main mosque in Ghazni. This was a priestly religious role. Being appointed to both these positions gave Ismail temporal as well as religious power. A rare combination.

The news hit Ismail like a bolt of lightning. After the decades he had spent in Guzgan, he had given up all hope that he would breathe the air of freedom while his brother lived. But this? Governor of Ghazni? Grand mufti of the Jama Mosque? He couldn't believe his ears. 'I am ... I'm not sure I understand, My Lord,' he said cautiously, a nervous smile fluttering at the edges of his lips.

'I need you to come work for me, you fool!' Mahmud's voice was gruff now. Irritable. 'I have taken our father's small kingdom and made it one of the biggest and wealthiest empires on earth, with all of Afghanistan, Balochistan and Punjab, some of Iran, and most of the Kazakh, Uzbek, Tajik and Turkmen territory in my control. Now, I need to take it to the next level. I need you to fulfil your duty towards me. Will you, or won't you?'

'I am flattered, My Lord,' said Ismail humbly, his breathing ragged. He still couldn't believe the turn in his fortunes. 'I am grateful ... Grateful for all that you have done for our clan and our family. I will be eternally loyal to you. I will do all you ask of me. I will not fail you.'

Mahmud looked at Kausari and Ayaz with an I-told-you-so expression.

'But ...' Ismail spoke nervously. 'What about the current grand mufti of the Jama Mosque?'

'Dead.'

'Dead?'

'Dead. Very unfortunately, he fell down the stairs of the minaret while returning from a call to prayer.'

Ismail had gotten over his nervousness and was now thinking more clearly. Clear enough to ensure that he did not smile or voice the thoughts running through his mind. *Of course. 'Fell down the stairs.' How convenient.*

'But even before this unfortunate accident, I had spoken with him about your idea … Our idea, actually.'

Ismail knew exactly which idea Mahmud was referring to. *Our idea! He took the bait!*

'But …'

'But?' asked Ismail.

'He went about quoting various Hadiths, our secondary scriptures after the Holy Quran, to me … Apparently …' Mahmud's face screwed up in disgust as he said this, '… it must always be an Arab … It can't be a Turk … He was wrong, obviously. I just couldn't prove how he was wrong.'

Ismail held his breath. *And the penny drops. Now I know why he needs me. He knows that I have spent the last thirty years reading the Holy Quran and many of the Hadiths. I am a* hafiz, *since I am one of* those who know the Holy Quran by heart. *That's why he wants me to be the grand mufti, so that I can find the scriptural justification for him to do what he wants.*

Ismail spoke gravely, 'It cannot be ignored that the late grand mufti himself was an Arab … Maybe that clouded his opinion. How could he appreciate how much we Turks have done for Islam …'

Mahmud raised his hand and pointed at Ismail, his gesture indicating complete agreement. Then he looked at Kausari and Ayaz.

'So, what do you say?' Mahmud asked Ismail.

'To not support you would be treason,' said Ismail gravely. 'And supporting you will also be in the interest of our entire family and clan.'

Kausari Jahan watched her exhilarated husband. She hid her disagreement. This was going all wrong. She had never liked Ismail. He was too intelligent. Deviously intelligent.

Mahmud, always one for grand gestures, extended his hands towards Ismail. 'Hold my hands, my brother.'

Ismail lunged forward. And he did it so quickly that a suspicious Malik Ayaz too rose almost instantly from his chair, a protective hand reaching out in the direction of Sultan Mahmud. Ismail went down on one knee and held both his elder brother's hands, and looked up, with tears in his eyes.

'There is another problem, Ismail,' said Mahmud. 'One that I need you to solve.'

'Anything, great King!' Ismail's voice was almost too eager.

Mahmud continued, 'I had built a great mosque in Ghazni, as you know. The Jama Mosque. The grandest in all Islamdom. A mosque that would showcase the power of Islam and our One True God. I brought relics from the land of the *kafir*s—broken pieces of their heathen Gods. I had them buried under the mosque's front steps to be trampled upon five times a day by the believers. It was magnificent, Ismail. Magnificent! No better testament to my acclaim as a Ghazi, a destroyer of *kafir*s! But then ...' Mahmud paused. He took a deep breath and went into a trance.

There was silence in the room. The air felt as cold as ice.

'My Lord?' Ismail whispered.

'The earthquake struck,' answered the sultan.

'Earthquake?'

'Yes. Three years ago.'

Ismail masked his shock. *Three years? And I had no idea? How cut off have I been?*

Mahmud continued, 'It levelled much of the city, Ismail. Including the Jama Mosque. I had ordered a massive reconstruction. Much has been done. But not all obviously. You know how lazy those swine Hindu slaves are … The grand mufti—the *late* grand mufti—he did not lift a finger. No cooperation. If I have to make my big move, then, I am sure you will understand, the Jama Mosque must be rebuilt quickly. The fool told me in private that he believed that the Buddha made the earthquake happen. "Curse of the Gods," he said, almost with terror! Do stones curse, huh? Tell me? Tell me?!'

'This is preposterous!' Ismail exploded, more royalist than the king. 'The *late* grand mufti was a fool … Even worse, a *murtad*, an *apostate*! And an apostate has only one punishment: Beheading!'

Of course, Ismail did not care to explain further that according to his reading of some of the Islamic Hadiths, homosexuality was also punishable by death. But nobody was about to give the death penalty to Mahmud.

'Exactly!' Mahmud snorted.

'I always suspected that the late grand mufti had kept his old religion alive in his heart,' continued Ismail. 'I am sure you know that both his parents were Buddhist. And even he converted to Islam very late, after his teen years, if I am not wrong. But our laws are very clear. Everyone is allowed, in fact encouraged, to convert *to* Islam. But you cannot convert *out* of Islam. The punishment for that is death. And once you have converted, you cannot respect any other religion or acknowledge any other God, like the Buddha. That is apostasy.'

Most Turks were Buddhist, and their conversion to Islam was relatively recent. In fact, even Sebuktegin, the father of Mahmud and Ismail, had been a Buddhist in his childhood. This was also a reason why most Turks were especially aggressive towards Buddhists and Buddhism, the religion they had converted from. It was the easiest way to prove their loyalty to their new religion, Islam.

'But who would have believed me if I had accused the Arab grand mufti of apostasy?' asked Mahmud. 'Because he was very smart to only tell me this in private. In public, he pretended to be such a good Muslim.'

In most Islamic empires, the public considered clerics as powerful as the rulers. So it was not easy for a king to simply overrule a mullah publicly, especially if the mullah quoted any scriptures to prove his point.

'Just as well that he died after falling down the stairs,' said Ismail.

'Yes. That was Allah's punishment.'

'True. Allah's punishment. For Allah is ever wise and merciful.'

'So we understand each other,' said Mahmud, rising to his feet. The meeting was over. Kausari and Ayaz rose too.

Ismail got up like a spring chicken. He finally felt energy coursing through him. 'Yes, we do, great King. Or should I say, great soon-to-be Caliph.'

Caliph was derived from the Arabic word Khalifah, which literally meant deputy or successor. It was believed that the caliphs were deputies to the Prophet, and they ruled the entire Islamic world as politico-religious leaders.

The power of the State and the authority of Religion were both combined in that one post. The caliph was the highest possible position that any Muslim king could hope to reach. Caliphs had, from the dawn of Islam, always been Arabs. But the Arabs weren't that powerful any more. The Turks were the most powerful Islamic community now. And Mahmud had decided that it was time for a Turk, more specifically him, to become the caliph. The fact that the present Abbasid caliph in Baghdad, an Arab, had become weak and was under the control of the Persian Buyid dynasty, made the task easier in Mahmud's mind.

Mahmud smiled. 'Good. We understand each other well.'

Ismail bowed low. *I understand you. But you don't understand me, you moron. The field of war, that's your area. But this … This is the arena of intellect and religion … This is mine. My birth right will be mine … Mine …*

CHAPTER 3

A Call for Vengeance

Gangaikonda Cholapuram

Two weeks had passed since Someshwar and Iqbal had met Narasimhan. The Cholapuram police chief had brought the merchants home as house guests. Harini had welcomed the elderly men with utmost kindness. After all, in the Indian way, it is believed that *Atithi Devo Bhava*, or *the guest is God*. But she also had immense sympathy—or rather, empathy— for the suffering that the two merchants had experienced and witnessed at Somnath. And most importantly, she identified with their cause, for the fire of vengeance at the insult to Lord Shiva burned strong in her as well.

The presence of the merchant duo had also given Narasimhan a renewed sense of purpose. Harini had noticed that he was sleeping better. He could touch the pendant with his hands, briefly, without flinching. Men are simple creatures, not given to immense emotional and psychological self-analysis like women are. For most men, the best way to manage past trauma is to not talk about it; instead, they would rather commit themselves to a higher cause. And what higher cause could there be than Lord Shiva?

Vijayan's relationship with Narasimhan had also improved. His professional jealousy appeared minor compared to the objective they now had. Since the day they had encountered the two old men at the temple, Vijayan had been visiting Narasimhan in the evenings. In the beginning it was obvious that he only wished to meet the men from Somnath. But then he began to consult Narasimhan on work issues as well.

Still, for all their motivation, being experienced and well-trained Chola warriors, Narasimhan and Vijayan had carefully verified the credentials of the merchant duo before reaching out to the emperor. Narasimhan had, naturally, expected that an audience would be granted almost immediately by his king, who was more of a friend. And he was not disappointed. They were given an appointment for the very next day. A scroll had arrived. It bore the imperial seal of the Chola dynasty: a ferocious golden tiger with sharp black orbs for eyes, one paw raised, ready to maul the enemy of the empire.

They would now prepare for a private audience. With the most powerful man on Earth. Rajendra Chola.

—◦⟡◦—

'In the letter you sent … Did you mention all that I told you about what happened at Somnath*ji*, great Narasimhan?' Someshwar broke the nervous silence with his question.

Narasimhan was leading Someshwar and Iqbal down the fire-lit granite hallway of the emperor's palace. It was just after sunset, and the fading light of the sun mingled with the gleam from the torches. Four guards flanked the men as they walked down the cavernous corridor.

'I detailed all the events of what happened that day, Someshwar*ji*,' reassured Narasimhan. 'And the emperor reads all important briefings himself and in detail. A golden rule with the great Rajendra Chola: If he has agreed to meet you, he will be well prepared for the meeting. He does not waste time. Think deeply about what you want to tell him.'

The men climbed a zig-zagging flight of steps in single file, two guards in front of them, two in the rear.

Someshwar looked around. From the outside, the Chola palace was massive, ornate and grand. It had a granite core and was supplemented with sandstone and wood. The black of the granite, pink of the sandstone and the multiple dyes painted on the wood made for an extravagantly palatial residence that looked like it was straight out of a fairy tale. Like most south Indian dominion buildings—temples, palaces, universities—the palace had been covered with intricate carvings and sculptures of sages, apsaras, Goddesses and Gods ostentatiously painted in myriad colours. South Indians on average, tended to be very understated in their personal clothes, but were opulent when it came to the architecture of their universities, temples and palaces.

But within the palace, Someshwar could see none of the extravagance that was so visible on the outside. They were walking down small narrow hallways, past spartan chambers and walls.

'Is this the path meant for the personal staff and visitors of the emperor, noble Narasimhan?' Someshwar asked. 'For there is none of the grandeur inside that one sees outside. I am sure there are magnificent sections of the palace for official visitors like foreign diplomats.'

Narasimhan nodded and kept walking.

'The king perhaps uses these sections of the palace more,' said Someshwar. His nervousness was making him talk more. 'Maybe this internal architecture is for security reasons as well.'

Narasimhan just kept walking. No answer.

The trio now entered another hallway, narrow in the middle and broad at the two ends. Iqbal felt like he had walked into the insides of a massive convex *thimila*, a *percussion instrument of the people of Kerala*. There were guards stationed all along the hallway, but the largest posse was stationed at the narrow end in the middle. A natural bottleneck. A good security measure. The hallway ended at a high doorway with two giant guards stationed on either side. The imperial guards who escorted them retreated into the shadows.

The guards saluted Narasimhan crisply. The big man brought his right hand to his chest and returned the military gesture. He took a deep breath and looked at his nervous companions.

'This is it, Someshwar*ar* and Iqbal*ar*. Your time starts now.'

Someshwar and Iqbal swallowed nervously. Their legs shivered as they walked ahead.

The guard on the left side opened the massive door and the three men marched into the emperor's private meeting chamber, Narasimhan first, then Someshwar and, finally, Iqbal.

One man sat at the far end of the large hall, on the northern side.

Only one man.

Nobody else.

It was, as promised, a private meeting.

Pure electricity surged up the spines of the two merchants, as though the Goddess Kundalini had been awakened. Across the length and breadth of India, all had heard of the mighty Chola emperor, Rajendra, and his father, the late Emperor Rajaraja. The father–son monarchs were living legends, their names evocative of their stature. Rajaraja meant the King of Kings. And Rajendra meant the Lord of the Kings. The two merchants expected a dazzling divinity when they entered the room. They halted at the entrance, entranced.

Before them, the Somnath merchants saw a man of flesh and blood—just like them. The experience was more overwhelming than if they had encountered a demigod.

For he was one of them. Just like them. An Indian.

But at the same time, he was also much more. A man who exuded awesome power and unpretentious humility at the same time. A combination of attributes that was counterintuitive, and incredibly enchanting.

A man of *Dharma*.

The Gangaikonda himself.

Rajendra Chola.

Swarthy, with a handlebar moustache, and just short of six feet in height, Rajendra Chola's thick, heavy brows arched over a pair of eyes that glinted like black opals embedded with orange embers. He was exceptionally well-built, with the powerful shoulders and back of an accomplished archer, his formidable chest narrowing down to the slim waist and powerful legs of a warrior who is adept at the subtle and deft moves of a swordsman as well. The fact that he was this fit, at the age of fifty-nine years, showcased his awe-inspiring discipline. His body had numerous battle scars, a matter of pride for a warrior. One particularly extensive one was a deep indentation on his belly, with thin stitch marks on the sides; perhaps he had been stabbed in the stomach during a recent battle and the wound had only just healed. The emperor's delicately curled black hair, which had thinned a bit with age, fell over his shoulders, combed to precision. His hypnotizing eyes expressed kindness and a keen intellect.

A *janau* ran down from his left shoulder to the right side of his torso. A red *angavastram* placed over his right shoulder made its way across his powerful chest and back. It was secured with pins at either end of the cummerbund that was wrapped over his white *dhoti*. An ivory-and-gold-hilted tiger tooth dangled over his chest, held in place by a thin black thread around his neck. Except for the diamond studs in his earlobes, the mighty Chola wore no other jewellery. His head was bare. He did not wear the royal crown.

Rajendra Chola nodded his head politely and joined his palms in greeting. '*Vanakkam*,' he said, in a deep baritone that echoed within the soul of anyone who heard it.

'My Lord,' announced Narasimhan loudly from the distance, thumping his chest, clicking his heels sharply and bowing low. 'I am grateful to be allowed to meet you, and express my sincere apologies for the inconvenience caused by requesting a private audience while you are … recuperating.'

Someshwar and Iqbal remained silent. They were captivated. Rooted to the spot. Not moving. Not speaking.

Not noticing the tasteful and understated elegance of the private chamber they had walked into. A few exquisite carvings and paintings on the wall. Torches fixed along the length of the chamber, spreading light and warmth. Large picture-windows on the eastern and western walls, opening into lush gardens on either side. The subtle fragrance of flowers and the soulful chirping of birds carried in by the moist evening sea-breeze.

At the far end, behind where Rajendra Chola sat, was a giant painting covering the entire northern wall. On it, in the centre, was Lord Shiva, in his *Dakshinamurti* form, meaning, literally, the *God Who is facing the south*. To the left and right of Lord Shiva were two men, on their knees, facing the Mahadev, palms joined in a namaste, heads bowed, like they were the servants of the God of Gods. The paintings of the men were remarkably lifelike and easily recognizable. On the right of Lord Shiva was the late Rajaraja Chola, and on the left was his son, the present emperor, Rajendra Chola.

This was how the mighty Cholas saw themselves.

Rajaraja Chola and Rajendra Chola. In spite of all their earthly power, magnificence, grandeur, authority and supremacy, in their innermost chamber, they only saw themselves as mere servants to Lord Shiva.

Awesome power and unpretentious humility. A rare combination.

'Come, sit,' said Rajendra Chola kindly.

But Someshwar and Iqbal continued to stare, like deer entranced by a shooting star. Rajendra Chola knew that he often had this impact on common people meeting him for the first time. And as usual, his compassion and kindness emerged in such instances. He looked at Narasimhan and nodded.

The police chief of Cholapuram softly elbowed Someshwar to pull him out of his nervous trance. And the three began walking to the far end of the hall. Three comfortably luxurious chairs had been placed there in front of Rajendra Chola.

Narasimhan reached the chairs, went down on one knee and bowed his head again.

'Sit, Narasimhan,' said Rajendra Chola. 'Sit.'

Someshwar and Iqbal sank to their knees, and touched their heads to the ground, their hands placed in front of them, bowing completely before the emperor. Rajendra Chola looked at Narasimhan and gestured to him to make them sit. He did so.

Someshwar and Iqbal, seated on the chairs now, were still quite nervous. Both had their palms joined together in a namaste. They knew that this was the best chance they had. They had been waiting for this moment for four years. They didn't want to mess it up.

Rajendra Chola spoke once again, politely. 'I am aware. Narasimhan has written all the details to me. Of what you saw and suffered ...' The emperor took a breath. Like he was evaluating something. 'What can I do for you, noble Someshwar? What do you want?'

Narasimhan knew what Rajendra Chola was doing. He was assessing Someshwar and Iqbal. Whether they were trustworthy and reliable. One deeply necessary skill that all successful leaders have is the ability to evaluate other people quickly. Masterly leaders meet so many men, and they have so much to do that they don't have the time, like ordinary human beings do, to take years to truly judge the motivations of others. Accomplished leaders usually possess a finely tuned instinct, which speaks to them when they meet others. It is this instinct that is a key factor in their success.

'My Emperor ...' said Someshwar. He had prepared a speech for this very moment. He had practised it. Many times. But it was forgotten. Someshwar, regardless of all the emotions he was feeling at this moment, was a wise, seasoned businessman—among the most successful merchants in India, if not the world. Like most good merchants, he could read between the lines. And when you meet truly important people, you judge the situation and speak impromptu, rather than rattle off a prepared text.

'I ...' Someshwar stopped and glanced briefly at the painting behind Rajendra Chola, at Lord Shiva and the two Chola emperors bowing to Him. 'I can guess what is being planned, Sire. For no living man will doubt your devotion to Lord Shiva. And ... there is nothing that I can offer that you do not have more of. Warriors or resources. But great Emperor, I have been planning and studying the enemy for four years. I have committed all my wealth, which is not inconsiderable, to this cause alone. I have lost my family, my city, and the temple that was my soul, the temple that I was named after. I have nothing left, except this mission. Allow me, please, to be the squirrel in the hunt for this era's Raavan.'

Someshwar genuinely believed that Mahmud was like Raavan, the villain of the Indian epic Ramayan, who had fought Lord Ram. But having read all the reports, Rajendra Chola understood that this mission would not be modelled on the Ramayan. Raavan, for all his faults and monstrosities, was still circumscribed by at least some *Dharma*. Mahmud was far worse than Raavan. He was a barbarian beyond measure. And the Indian scriptures are clear when fighting such enemies: *Shathe shathyam samacharet; the wicked should be treated with more vicious wickedness.*

But that was not what Rajendra Chola focused on. He had recognized the key message that Someshwar had delivered in a very subtle way.

He has been studying the enemy for four years. That is invaluable.

Rajendra looked deeply at Someshwar's face and into his eyes. Then he turned to Iqbal. He saw the pendant that Iqbal wore on a black thread that hung around his neck. The numbers 7 8 6 were etched on the pendant in the Arabic script. It symbolically signified the saying 'In the name of Allah, the Most Gracious, the Most Merciful'. And if you added up the numerical values of the letters in that phrase, it was 7 8 6. Rajendra Chola knew that many Indian Muslims wore this exact pendant. But then he noticed Iqbal's forehead. It had three horizontal lines, running across his brow, made with grey sacred ash. Just like on Someshwar's forehead. It was obvious that the two merchants had been to the Brhadishvara Temple earlier in the day to pray to Lord Shiva.

Rajendra's instinct kicked in. He turned to Narasimhan, speaking simply and crisply. 'Bring them.'

'Yes, My Lord.' Narasimhan knew when and where he had to take the two merchants. Rajendra had decided. Someshwar and Iqbal were going to be a part of this mission as well.

Righteous vengeance. The most noble of masculine motivations.

'Thank you, My Lord,' said the two merchants almost simultaneously. They too had understood the import of Rajendra Chola's cryptic command.

Someshwar turned to Iqbal, who reached into the bag hanging from his shoulder and carefully, with great reverence, took out an object from it. Someshwar reached across and took the small black stone from his friend.

Rajendra immediately guessed what the object could be. He glanced at Narasimhan for confirmation. Seeing the emotion in his former general's eyes, the emperor knew that his conjecture was correct. He instantly took off his slippers and rose to his feet. Seeing him rise, the three men got up as well. Rajendra walked up to Someshwar, tears welling in his eyes.

Someshwar saw the misery and grief on the mighty emperor's face. He bowed his head low and raised his cupped palms, handing the shattered piece of the Somnath Shiva Linga to the emperor. Rajendra gently picked up the sacred relic. He held it to his chest, and then raised it to his forehead with both his hands, keeping it there for a long period.

One of the names that Rajendra had given himself in his official title was *Shivacharana Shekhara—One Who Wears Shiva's Feet as His Crown*.

The emperor was holding the stone so tightly that his knuckles had turned white. *Forgive me, Lord. Forgive me that I wasn't present to prevent this sacrilege when it happened.*

Rajendra always exhibited tremendous control over his emotions in public. His tears rarely had the temerity to escape his eyes in the presence of others. But this ... this was too much to bear even for the mighty Chola's heart. As the emperor closed his eyes, a tear ran down his cheek, his body shook in deep and anguished sorrow. A prominent vein in Rajendra's left temple throbbed intensely.

He breathed heavily, repeating softly within the confines of his mind.

Forgive me, Lord. Forgive me.

Only Lord Shiva, Whose expansive heart, expressing Itself through the shattered stone, could help at this time of wretched sorrow. He soothed His grieving devotee.

As the grief subsided, furious rage rose in Rajendra's heart.

A simple death will not do. It has to be brutal. It has to be harsh.

'Never forget, never forgive,' said Iqbal in his native tongue, Bengali, speaking for the first time since entering the hall. Succinct and powerful words.

'Never forget, never forgive,' Someshwar spoke in Tamil and joined his hands together.

Rajendra looked to the two merchants. *We will not forget. We will not forgive.*

'Somnathar will be avenged. Mother India will be avenged.'

Righteous vengeance. The most powerful of masculine motivations.

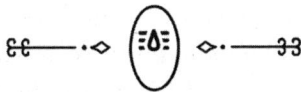

CHAPTER 4

Home at Last

The frontiers of Ghazni, Afghanistan

'You are home at last, My Lord.' Talib looked at his master, his grainy face creased with intense joy, his grey goatee that flowed down his pointy chin, waving about wildly as the wind picked up again.

The barren white landscape of Ghazni stretched on before their tired eyes.

'Thirty years … For thirty years I have dreamt of this moment, Talib,' replied Ismail as he looked at his beloved homeland, his eyes blinded by shimmering tears.

The two men stood on the craggy edge of the last bend in the mud-and-stone pathway. The late-evening light lent a sepulchral feel to the barely visible fort walls, faraway in the distance. Their meagre caravan—an army of servants and scrawny guards—had halted behind them in the narrow pass, hidden from direct view by the snowy bulwarks of the mighty Hindu Kush. It was a party of condemned men and women who had lived with their master, grown old with him, whined and schemed with him. Each man, woman and child in Guzgan had nursed, nurtured and fanned a personal animosity towards the man responsible for their isolation—their master's brother and the usurper of their power and privilege: Mahmud of Ghazni.

Ismail turned his horse around and looked at his caravan of five hundred mules, horses and oxcarts. Tired men and women on the brink of collapse. He had insisted they travel at breakneck speed.

'Let us rest, Talib. We can wait till the morning light.'

Talib's shoulders sagged with relief and his hunched back bent a bit more. The clouds had begun to sprinkle fresh snow, and they still needed to cross Dashte Nawur, the great frozen lake that separated them from their capital city. He pulled the collar of his fur coat over his ears and raised a gloved hand, signalling their intention to halt. The caravan soon began to split and disperse. The horsemen dismounted and set up camp on the bare stretch of ground to the left of the mountain. Fires were lit while untiring children scampered around exhausted adults.

Ismail slid off his horse and ground his teeth to prevent his numb jaws from chattering. A chilly blast of ice-cold wind slipped in through the gaps of his sleeves. He held the sleeve ends with his frosty fingers.

The newly appointed governor and grand mufti of Ghazni made his way to a low precipice, his gaze fixed on the city that was, against all odds, his seat of power, again. The glassy surface of the Dashte Nawur glimmered like a giant sapphire in the bleak expanse where snowflakes fell like diamonds in the dark. He focused his gaze on the bits of firelight of the capital of the Ghaznavid sultanate sparkling in the distance.

'So beautiful,' murmured Talib.

'Beyond beautiful.' Ismail smiled, savouring his freedom. 'It is indescribable. Memories, Talib. Memories. Of people and events long gone—my parents, my childhood and my ascension to the throne ... What could have been ... But for Mahmud ...'

'It shall soon be yours again, My Lord,' said Talib, casting a triumphant look at his master and savouring the prospect of vicarious power. 'You have done an exceptional job of influencing the sultan's mind. His ambition will do the rest. Till now, the missives from Ghazni to Baghdad only carried news of the many *kafir*s Mahmud had killed and the many idols he had destroyed. Their response would obviously have been joy at such news. But now, when they hear that Mahmud is coming for them too ... Well ...' Talib started cackling with laughter.

The Abbasid caliphate was based in their capital city of Baghdad. But the Abbasids weren't as powerful as they used to be. They were under the effective control of a powerful Persian dynasty called the Buyids who were Shia Muslims. The Turkic Ghaznavids and the Arab Abbasids, on the other hand, were Sunni Muslims. As was well known, most Shia and Sunni dynasties despised each other, and called the other apostates.

'We need the Buyids to think that Mahmud is coming for them because they are Shias,' said Ismail. 'And the Abbasids to think that Mahmud wants to replace them as the caliph.'

'And they will certainly attack ... You, My Lord, will be the obvious ally for them to replace the sultan with. Before long, our beloved homeland will be liberated from that ... that ...'

Ismail turned to his servant, amused. 'That *what*, Talib? Do not hold back your righteous anger!'

Talib was happy inside. He had noticed that his master's all-pervasive nervousness had disappeared. He was confident and sure of himself now, thirty years of torture quickly forgotten. He played along, for he wanted his master's continued trust and dependency. 'That ... monstrous beast ...' On Talib's face was reflected a livid anger that was more intense than what he felt inside. 'You would have been such a good king, Master. Ghazni and Islam lost a great son in you, My Lord Ismail. But now, the cruel tide of time will finally turn back. You taking your rightful place on the throne will be good for the world.'

'Yes! And we will not just stop at the title of emir and mufti ...' said Ismail. 'Mahmud wants a puppet cleric who will proclaim him the caliph. But very soon, the puppet himself will cut the strings and send the puppeteer to an unmarked grave that is his due!'

'Of course, you will, My Lord.'

Ismail stared at the frozen river. 'But we must move carefully and slowly. Many alliances will have changed over the last three decades. We must win the support of Ghazni's noblemen and clergy. It will be easy to do with this caliph escapade that Mahmud has set out on. Patience. Patience. A little more patience.'

Talib smiled and nodded in agreement, as he rubbed his hands together to generate warmth. His master had really come into his own over the last few weeks.

'Wine, My Lord?' a trembling female voice wafted in from behind the two men.

They turned around.

A wispy, small-boned maid stood holding a small sheepskin bag containing wine in one hand and two earthen cups in the other.

'Just in time,' said Ismail, clapping his hands together. 'Thank you, Reshma. You can hand this to Talib. Let us know when dinner is ready.'

The woman bowed and handed the wineskin and cups to Talib, who gave her a quick smile. She scurried away, biting the flimsy scarf that covered her ears and half her face. Ismail watched her retreat.

'We must ensure she doesn't sneak up on us like that, My Lord,' said Talib. 'I don't know how much she heard.'

'Nonsense, Talib,' said Ismail. 'She has the brains of an obtuse child who has been whacked on the head every day since she was born. She will not be able to recall what she wore yesterday, let alone our conversation.'

Talib looked down and kept quiet. *Good. He doesn't suspect anything.*

'But speaking of her, there's another benefit in returning to Ghazni,' Ismail said with a sly smile. 'I don't have to make do with skin and bones for pleasure now. I need some fat, some bounce in the women I bed. We will both make up for our lost youth now!'

'Of course!' smiled Talib. He uncorked the wineskin and poured wine into the two cups.

'Dinner is ready, My Lord!' Reshma had walked up to them, waiflike, undetected again. 'Please come. The food and wine have reached your tent.'

Ismail nodded and dismissed the woman as the two men walked towards the fully functional camp.

'Let us eat, drink and sleep. And awaken to my inevitable rise, Talib.'

'And to the fall of the tyrant, My Lord.'

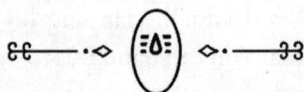

CHAPTER 5

Two Emperors and Their Lord

Gangaikonda Cholapuram

Narasimhan slowed down, allowing Someshwar and Iqbal to catch up with him. He held the flaming torch aloft. Dawn was just a short while away, and the full-moon night serenely illuminated the beautiful city of Cholapuram. But the light from the torches still helped.

This was the part of the night that the ancestors traditionally referred to as Brahma Muhurta. It was the last quarter of the night before sunrise, a time believed to be extremely potent for creativity, as the pineal gland was most active during this period. It was believed that the best thinking and inventive work could be done then. It was too early for the aged merchants to be awake, but the importance of the task at hand had encouraged them to sacrifice their sleep.

It had been five days since their meeting with Rajendra Chola at the royal palace. And Someshwar had been waiting eagerly for this morning.

They walked in silence towards the temple dedicated to *Brhadishvara*, the Great Lord Shiva, where Rajendra Chola had gathered his conclave of key advisors to plan the attack on Mahmud of Ghazni.

As Someshwar turned the last corner, the giant silhouette of the temple suddenly came into full view. It rose in massive splendour, its refined elegance rendered even more stunning in the bright moonlight.

The Brhadishvara Temple complex was built to an exquisite plan, with the courtyard formed from two squares stacked next to each other, showcasing perfect geometrical symmetry. The courtyard afforded entries through multiple gateways, each crowned by ornately carved *gopuram*s. Inside the complex were the shrines, most of which were aligned on an east–west axis. These shrines were dedicated to Gods and Goddesses from various dharmic traditions, including Lord Ram and Lord Krishna from the Vishnu tradition, Lord Ganesh and Lord Karthik from the Shiva tradition and forms of the Mother Goddess Shakti.

But the main temple, at the heart of the complex, was dedicated to Lord Shiva. This temple was gargantuan in dimensions, the platform on which it was built measuring twenty thousand square metres. There was an enormous seated bull representing Lord Nandi at the entrance to this giant platform, looking adoringly through the temple halls towards the sanctum where His Master, Lord Shiva, was present. The main temple structure had a *maha mandapa*, a *massive pillared hall*, at the end closer to where Lord Nandi's *murti* was, with the sanctum sanctorum at the other end of the structure. An *ardha mandapa*, or *partial hall*, connected the great pillared hall with the sanctum sanctorum, which was guarded by two stone-sculpted, remarkably lifelike gatekeepers measuring six feet in height. Within the sanctum was Lord Shiva in the form of a Shiva Linga. The enormous idol rose high, with the Linga soaring to a grand height of thirteen feet and the circumference of the base *yoni* measuring nearly sixty feet.

The *vimana*, or *spire*, above the sanctum sanctorum shot up to an awe-inspiring one hundred and eighty feet. One of the tallest in the world, but ten feet shorter than the Lord Shiva temple at Thanjavur, the old Chola capital. That temple had been built by Rajendra's late father, Rajaraja. Out of humility, Rajendra did not wish to surpass his father's masterpiece and deliberately made his own temple *vimana* slightly shorter. The temple spire rose nine levels, but the contours were delicately curvilinear, and slightly concave towards the top, giving the *vimana* an unusual yet striking parabolic form. The spire was capped with a traditional *kalash*, or *urn-shaped finial*, that was gold-plated, and an intricately carved lotus bud that was open to the sky.

The entire temple was an incredible combination of severe masculine geometrical forms and gracefully feminine curved towers. Truly symbolic of the Lord Mahadev, because He was also worshipped as the *Ardhanarishvara, the half-masculine and half-feminine Lord*.

Someshwar's throat constricted as he beheld once again the engineering marvel dedicated to Lord Shiva. For it reminded him of the splendid temple of Somnath by the Western Sea.

It is fitting that we meet for this mission in the abode of the Lord Mahadev, the God of Gods.

A hundred imperial soldiers stood near the tower at the main entrance of the temple complex, guarding the deserted streets of a still-sleeping city. Policemen were also perched on the walkway atop the temple complex's high walls, and all along the perimeter.

The soldiers saluted their former general Narasimhan and let him, along with the two merchants, pass, but only after a body search. Rules had to be followed, even for former generals. This was the Chola administration, after all.

As soon as they were inside the complex, the trio walked up to the large stall on the left to stash away their footwear. Narasimhan felt a hand on his shoulder as he bent to take off his sandals.

'The emperor is already inside,' Vijayan informed his chief.

'I should hope so.' Narasimhan smiled. 'I do not imagine this pomp and vigil is to facilitate *my* early morning visit to the temple.'

Narasimhan had already been informed by the emperor's staff that he planned to come in early to the temple, since he wanted to pray to the Mahadev before the meeting. Therefore, he was not surprised by Vijayan's news.

Vijayan continued speaking. 'But he saw me, Sir.' The deputy police chief could not contain his excitement. 'The emperor passed right in front of me. He nodded and acknowledged me. I was too stunned to even bow.'

Narasimhan patted him on his shoulder and smiled. It was a rare honour to be within speaking distance of the emperor, who was seen as almost divine by most of the denizens of his empire. 'Let's go.'

The party, now consisting of four people with the addition of Vijayan, began walking through the temple-complex compound towards the inner gate, which led to the main temple.

'Halt.'

Imperial guards were blocking the inner entrance, their spears crossed with each other. Their commander, Kannan, walked up to Narasimhan, recognizing him instantly. A dozen soldiers stood guard behind the commander, their spears crossed as well.

'Good morning, General,' said Kannan.

'It's police chief now,' corrected Narasimhan.

'You will always be our general, Sir.' Kannan smiled and bowed. 'You may not recognize me, General. I am Kannan, commander of the Chola Imperial Guard. You saved my life once.'

'Really?' Narasimhan was surprised.

'You have saved so many lives, General. But I will not delay you any further. I know the emperor awaits you. Papers, please.'

Narasimhan smiled. Despite the awe the Chola officer felt, he would not break protocol. Rules must be followed. Even for a general with the reputation of a lion.

Narasimhan reached into the folds of his *angavastram* and fished out an official scroll of summons with the emperor's seal. Kannan inspected the scroll quickly. All was in order, Narasimhan and his companions were authorized to enter. Satisfied, he handed the document back to Narasimhan and thumped his chest with his fist. He lowered his head with respect, executing the formal salute reserved for the military, and moved aside, signalling that the path be cleared.

The Chola soldiers parted their spears and stood aside with the graceful synchrony of an elite fighting force. They were the personal military guards of Rajendra Chola himself.

Narasimhan thumped his chest with his fist and bowed slightly, acknowledging the military salute. Just as a general, or a former general, should.

His elderly companions, Someshwar and Iqbal, followed him. As soon as he stepped inside the tower's passageway, a thought struck him. He turned around. Vijayan was watching them from the other side of the gate.

'Come with us, Vijayan,' Narasimhan said, making a quick decision.

Vijayan was stunned and understandably exhilarated, because having seen Someshwar and Iqbal accompanying Narasimhan, he could guess what was going to be discussed with the emperor. He threw a quick look at Kannan, who made no attempt to stop him. Vijayan briskly entered the gateway and nodded to his captain in gratitude.

The group of four walked rapidly forward. Their attention was diverted by a flurry of activity in the circular path on the right side. The prime minister of the Chola empire, Kathiravan, had arrived. Dressed in a milk-white silk *dhoti* and *angavastram* that contrasted with his ebony-dark skin, Kathiravan strode in, surprisingly brisk for his advanced age. His white beard, neatly trimmed, along with his waxed white moustache speckled with a few stubborn black strands of hair, heightened the luminescence of the slender lanky figure. The guards on either side of Kathiravan half-marched, half-ran as they tried to keep pace with him.

Kathiravan was the Chola dynasty's most trusted officer by far. He had served Emperor Rajendra's great father, Rajaraja Chola. And now, besides being the prime minister, he was also advisor to Prince Rajadhiraja Chola, the next in line to the throne. He had held the reins of the empire during the emperor's long naval campaigns. He was the voice of the Chola court.

Kathiravan spotted the decorated general and, turning to the left, went towards him.

'Venerable Prime Minister Kathiravan,' said Narasimhan, bringing his hands together and bowing low with genuine respect. Vijayan and the two merchants followed his lead.

'Let us proceed. The emperor awaits us,' said Kathiravan, his thin aged voice in no way lessening his magnificent aura. Kathiravan began walking and the others kept pace. Or at least they tried to.

'You have just returned from the Chera lands, Prime Minister. You must be tired,' Narasimhan said.

'No rest for the wicked, my friend,' said Kathiravan, his eyes dancing with mirth. The prime minister was known for his sense of humour and self-deprecating manner. But the dry wit camouflaged a cunning, ruthless mind that was unimpeachably loyal to the interests of the empire. 'Narasimhan, seriously speaking … My heart is with the emperor … You know my devotion to the Mahadev … But I must keep in mind the best interests of the Chola dynasty. Our army is not trained for mountain warfare. You know that. I will not allow a full-blown war that hurts the empire, honourable though the cause may be. Some other way must be found.'

Narasimhan was beginning to realize that perhaps Kathiravan running into him before the meeting had not been an accident. And of course he didn't miss the subtle mention of the Chola dynasty, rather than only the emperor. They would have to formulate a plan that would find Kathiravan's approval as well. Furthermore, the prime minister was, of course, right about mountain warfare, for Ghazni was high in the frigid Hindu Kush mountains, and the Chola army was trained for naval and flatland warfare.

Someshwar had been listening to the prime minister's words, even as he struggled to keep pace with the noble's fast strides. His heart sank. He wondered if his hope for vengeance would be realized in his lifetime. Or ever.

— ·◦·❦·◦· —

Kathiravan, Narasimhan, Someshwar, Iqbal and Vijayan were sitting in the *maha mandapa* of the main temple. Before them was the *ardha mandapa*, and farther ahead was the sanctum sanctorum. Because of the exceptionally symmetrical architecture and construction of the temple, the party had a direct view, even from this distance, of the Shiva Linga in the sanctum sanctorum, directly in front. They saw Rajendra Chola from behind, praying to the Shiva Linga. Seated next to Rajendra Chola, like a brother, was another man. Narasimhan could not recognize him from the back, due to the distance. Royal priests stood to the sides of the emperor and his friend.

'We'll wait here till the emperor calls,' said the prime minister.

'Of course, great Kathiravan,' Narasimhan said.

Kathiravan looked at the two merchants.

'Allow me to introduce them, Prime Minister,' said Narasimhan. 'This is Someshwar*ar*, a Gujarati merchant from Somnath. And that is Iqbal*ar*, a Bengali merchant from the eastern parts of India. They ...'

'Yes, I was informed,' said Kathiravan. 'They were there at Somnath*ar* on that terrible day.' The prime minister looked at Someshwar. 'Noble Someshwar*ar*, you may have heard my words. I am sorry for that. I want vengeance against the ghastly Mahmud as well. But … vengeance is not something that should be chased with an enraged, impatient heart. It must be carried out with the calm calculations of a cold, ruthless, patient mind. We will have our vengeance, but at a time and place of our choosing. Not only must the timing be perfect, but the strategy should be impeccable as well.'

Someshwar had seen enough of the world to know that the prime minister had indeed wanted his words to be heard earlier. And he understood the import of what the man was saying. He knew what he must convey. 'You are right, great Prime Minister. As it is said in our Gujarat, you must strike with the hammer only when the iron is hot. Simply put, it's best to do things at the right time. But even more importantly, it's not just about the iron being hot and semi-solid at the time of striking. What is critical to remember is that the hammer doing the striking must be cold and hard.'

Kathiravan smiled. *This Gujarati is smart.*

Someshwar continued. The time was right for his important message. 'We have a trusted contact in Ghazni, My Lord. Someone very high up. Furthermore, we have recently discovered some positive developments in that area.'

Kathiravan waited for more to be revealed. When Someshwar didn't say anything more, he smiled even more broadly. The prime minister liked nothing better than speaking with those whose intelligence rivalled his own. He knew why Someshwar was waiting to reveal more. 'We'll wait for the emperor.'

Kathiravan turned to Vijayan and smiled.

'This is Vijayan, Prime Minister,' said Narasimhan. 'The man I will soon relinquish my office to if I am allowed to go.' Vijayan bowed again, hesitating and uncertain. 'He has had years of distinguished wartime service in the Pandya territory before coming here,' explained Narasimhan. 'I thought he could offer valuable insights to help in our planning.'

Vijayan remained quiet, grateful to Narasimhan for the kind words.

'I know who he is, General,' Kathiravan said to Narasimhan. 'You are forgetting that it was I who appointed him police chief when the emperor and you were away conquering Srivijaya. He is a good man.'

'My Lord.' Vijayan bowed low with his palms joined in a namaste.

—◦⋅✦⋅◦—

Rajendra Chola was ready to see them.

The imperial guards crisply positioned themselves around the five men, ready to escort them to the emperor. They guided the five from the *maha mandapa* of the main temple to the *ardha mandapa*, where the meeting would take place. The talented architects and engineers had built the structure such that the sound of the ocean waves crashing against the shoreline wafted into the *ardha mandapa*, but it was inaudible in the much-larger *maha mandapa*. Maybe they wanted the devotees to hear the sound of the sea before they went in to worship Lord Shiva in the sanctum sanctorum.

The sound of the ocean brought tears to Someshwar's eyes, as they reminded him of that gruesome day. All he could hear that terrible evening was the sound of the sea crashing in outraged pain against the shore, as Mahmud burnt the Somnath Temple to the ground. He shook his head and focused on the present.

The same ocean sounds also brought tears to Narasimhan's eyes. Not for what he had seen, but for what he had done. The violent waves, the sea foam thick with blood, the floating bloated lifeless bodies, the severed limbs, the guttural screams of pain and misery …

And that one voice. The voice that had scarred his soul. *I hope this victory was worth it.*

Narasimhan gripped the golden annulus pendant strung around his neck, feeling the flames of guilt and torment on his skin.

I hope this victory was worth it, because your soul is now cursed.

The voice got louder. And louder.

And then, in a flash, the vision and the voice were gone. Narasimhan looked around. No one had noticed. He furtively wiped the solitary bead of sweat from his forehead and let go of the pendant.

They finally halted and the escort guards dispersed. To the left and right edges of the hall, the pillars were lined by the emperor's elite guards. They stood like statues, unmoving, their sword hands on the hilts of sheathed blades, their shields slung over rippling shoulders. Two of the pillars had a wall connecting them, both on the left and the right sides. The left wall was engraved with a stunning rendition of a relief sculpture: the coronation of Rajendra Chola by Lord Shiva Himself, while His consort, Goddess Parvati, stood to His left. The Mahadev sat on His rocky throne on Mount Kailash, while the youthful Chola knelt before Him. Lord Shiva held a simple wooden crown over the neatly combed hair of a young Rajendra, bestowing the right to rule the earthly realm in His stead to the Gangaikonda. Carved within a flat stony surface, the chiselled images were embedded within the wall. It made the artwork antifragile. It would last, signifying that Rajendra's right to rule was derived from the blessing of Lord Shiva Himself. This was a copy of a larger version on the outer northern wall of the main temple complex.

Rajendra Chola stood beneath the relief sculpture, his back to the approaching men. His friend stood to his right. They were speaking softly with each other.

The men walked to their emperor and halted behind him in silence. Kathiravan stepped closer and whispered gently in the emperor's ear, 'Everyone is here, Your Highness.'

Rajendra Chola turned around. As did his friend, Bhojadev Parmar, the emperor of Malwa in central India.

Bhojadev Parmar, known across India as a scholar-king, was a dear friend and ally of Rajendra Chola. He ruled most of central India across eastern Rajasthan, Madhya Pradesh, Chhattisgarh and small parts of northern Maharashtra. Rajendra and he had formed an alliance to defeat the Chalukyas of northern Deccan and also the Palas of Bengal. The lay of the Indian land was such that the Chalukyas were the immediate northern neighbours of the Cholas. And the Parmars, in turn, were the immediate northern neighbours of the Chalukyas. To the east of the Parmars lay the kingdom of the Palas.

The ancient Indian scholar Chanakya had said that for an expanding empire, their immediate neighbour would always be an enemy. And the neighbour of that enemy would be a potential ally. It was logical, therefore, that the Cholas and Parmars would be allies, to jointly attack their immediate neighbour, the Chalukyas. It helped that Bhojadev was roughly the same age as Rajendra, and that the south Indian emperor was a genuine admirer of Bhojadev's ethereal poetry and plays. This further strengthened their bond of friendship. Bhojadev had accompanied Rajendra on the conquest of Southeast Asia as well. So the emperor of Malwa first looked at Narasimhan and nodded. Narasimhan bowed low, for they had met before on the sea journey to Srivijaya.

'*Vanakkam*,' Rajendra Chola greeted the men.

'Namaste,' said Bhojadev Parmar.

All present bowed in respect to the two emperors.

'As I was telling my friend Bhoja ... When I had commissioned this relief sculpture,' said Rajendra as he gestured towards the wall, '... I had intended for it to serve as a lasting reminder to myself and my people that I would always be the servant of the Lord of Kailasam, the mountain that Bhoja's people call Kailash. All my achievements so far, the lands I have conquered, the upstarts I have quelled, the wealth I have gathered, the city I have built—they have merely served my pride and my ego. I had the opportunity to serve my Divine Master only as a builder of temples and charitable institutions. It is only now that I ... no, *all of us* ... have been given the opportunity to personally serve Lord Shiva, as warriors.'

Rajendra looked at Bhojadev.

'My friend Rajendra, I echo your thoughts,' Bhojadev said. 'I have conquered territories, built a new capital, established a Sanskrit university, constructed dams and water canals ... Like you, I know that this is simply our task as kings. It is our duty to our people. But now, it is about our duty to our Lord, our God, the Mahadev. We have been given a mission as fellow devotees of Lord Shiva.'

The men looked at the emperors and listened attentively.

'We will avenge Somnath*ar*,' said Rajendra Chola, his voice calm but the fire visible in his eyes, adding the Tamil *ar* for respect. Glancing briefly at Prime Minister Kathiravan, Rajendra continued, 'I don't want to hear the logic about why we should not attack that barbarian from Ghazni, Mahmud. All I want to hear from all of you is how we should do it.'

'Yes, Your Majesty.' Kathiravan's response was immediate. 'Let's sit.'

Some soldiers quickly brought in comfortable cushions and spread them on the floor. Rajendra Chola, Bhojadev Parmar and the five men sat down, all of them careful not to show their backs to the Shiva Linga in the sanctum sanctorum.

'First, how many soldiers can we raise and how soon?' Rajendra began crisply. 'Second, how do we reach the Ghaznavid capital since whatever route we take, there will be many Indian kingdoms on the way who may not let our army pass since they would be scared of us conquering their lands.'

'In answer to your first question, we have fifty to sixty thousand soldiers in our standing army, My Lord,' Kathiravan said. 'Including five thousand imperial guards. We could perhaps double that number if you issued a call to the other territories and your vassal states, but those forces will take many months to arrive. And of course, from what I know of Malwa, your great friend and ally Emperor Bhojadev Parmar can bring in another fifty thousand soldiers.'

Bhojadev smiled as he glanced at Kathiravan before turning to Rajendra Chola. 'I can understand why you like your prime minister. His intelligence network is good. His assessment of the strength of my Malwa troops is correct.'

Rajendra Chola smiled as well. 'However, if I know him well enough, there is a "but" coming ...'

Kathiravan laughed softly. 'It is an important "but", Your Highnesses ... We can bring together large numbers of troops but we must also bear in mind that our standing troops have just returned from a brutal four-year campaign. As have many men in the Malwa standing army. The troops are exhausted, and new recruits must be hired and trained. That will take time. My estimate is that it will take at least a year to be ready to march. And then, to set up the logistics chain for food and supplies for such a large army all the way up to the lofty mountains of Ghazni will be a challenge. We will have to work that out too. But I am only speaking of recruitment and logistics, My Lord. Brave Narasimhan understands military strategy and tactics much better than I do.'

Rajendra turned to Narasimhan.

'I agree with the prime minister, My Lord,' Narasimhan said. 'Mobilizing our full army, including vassals, will take time. But that's not the real problem ... The real problem will be getting all our troops to Ghazni.'

'Yes,' agreed Kathiravan. 'All direct paths are blocked.'

Narasimhan continued, 'If we take the western route, we will come across the Chalukya kingdom of Karnataka, Maharashtra and Telangana, and then the Solanki kingdom of Gujarat. They may not be strong enough to defeat us, but they do have the power to weaken our army and kill many of our soldiers. We will be sapped of strength even before we reach Ghazni. Emperor Bhojadev would also have to fight through the Solanki kingdom to get his troops across …'

'Both the emperors have already fought battles with these kingdoms,' said Kathiravan. 'So even if we tell the Chalukyas and Solankis that we just want to pass through their territories to Ghazni, they will not believe us. They will assume we have come to conquer them.'

Vijayan cut in, 'And even if we do get past the Solankis, we will have to contend with the Thar Desert, where supplies will be strained for such a large army before we even reach Sindh, let alone the core Ghaznavid territory. There are too many obstacles.'

'Agreed,' said Rajendra. 'The western route is not a good one.'

Vijayan puffed up his chest slightly at having given a worthy insight.

'What are the other options?' asked Bhojadev.

'How about the naval route?' asked Iqbal.

'We can't take such a large army on ships … There are logistics and, more importantly, coordination issues,' said Narasimhan, who had immense experience with naval battles. 'Communicating at sea across a large number of ships is very difficult. You could have separate parts of the army making landfall at different times, and that too in the enemy Ghaznavid territory in Gwadar. They would be easily picked off in small contingents by the enemy. Remember, the battle with Ghazni will primarily be a land battle, unlike our battles in Southeast Asia which were fundamentally fought at sea.'

Rajendra Chola said with barely disguised irritation, 'You are all listing out the problems. Find me solutions!'

Kathiravan knew what Rajendra Chola was doing. He could guess what the emperor's plan was. But he always believed in having discussions so that others bought into his plans—they would come to believe that the final plan was their own suggestion. Let the obvious wrong choices be discussed first and get shot down by all, and then the logical option emerges. And Rajendra expected the logical course of action to come from one person.

The emperor looked at Someshwar.

'Your Majesty,' said Someshwar, speaking for the first time. 'I am no military strategist. But I have been thinking and planning this assault for four years now … If I may make one suggestion: this attack does not call for a soldier's broadsword but a surgeon's scalpel.'

Rajendra continued to look at Someshwar, seemingly non-committal, but Narasimhan was aghast.

'Are you suggesting sending assassins?' asked Narasimhan. 'That is against the principles of war. We fight like men. We fight open battles against enemy soldiers who have every chance to fight us fair and square. And then we defeat them. There is honour in victory earned that way—through blood, sweat and raw courage. There is no honour in slyly slinking up, hidden like cowards, and slitting our enemy's throat when he's sleeping.'

Narasimhan looked to Rajendra Chola for confirmation. But his emperor did not say anything.

'Brave Narasimhan,' said Someshwar, 'have you read Acharya Chanakya's writings?'

Bhojadev Parmar, the scholar-ruler who had studied many of India's ancient texts, including the works of Chanakya, smiled slightly.

Chanakya was universally considered across the Indian subcontinent to be among the greatest political, economic, governance, warfare and social theorists ever. Everyone had heard of him, for Chanakya had guided and midwifed the birth of the largest empire in Indian history, and one of the biggest ever in global history—the Mauryas—nearly one thousand four hundred years before Rajendra Chola's and Bhojadev Parmar's time.

'Of course, I know who Acharya Chanakya is,' answered Narasimhan.

'Have you read his books, noble Narasimhan?' Someshwar asked.

Narasimhan remained silent. Sadly, most Indians had heard of Chanakya, but very few had actually read him.

'One of the things that Acharya Chanakya had said,' continued Someshwar, 'was that open war is the most honourable option, but it should always be the last option. Because open war is too unpredictable. One can never be sure of victory or defeat. And that, too often, in open warfare, there is collateral damage. Innocents get hurt, right?'

Narasimhan froze. *I hope this victory was worth it.*

Rajendra looked at his friend Narasimhan as well, but he had the grace to not say anything. Narasimhan shook his head slightly, exercising tremendous self-control to not reach for the annulus pendant hanging around his neck.

'So what are the options *before* we try open war?' continued Someshwar. 'According to Acharya Chanakya, these are *saam, daam, dand, bhed—diplomatic negotiation, bribery, punishment and creating rifts in enemy ranks.* There is no point in *saam*, because Mahmud is a barbarian who doesn't understand diplomacy. I tried bribery to save Somnath*ji* then, but

Mahmud refused. He told me that his holy texts tell him to destroy idols and kill *kafir*s. So the only options left are *dand* and *bhed*. Assassinate him, but in a way that we trigger a civil war within Ghazni. Let the rabid dogs fight each other, so that they won't have time to attack us.'

Rajendra Chola leaned forward, interested.

'And on the question of honour,' said Someshwar—he was looking at Rajendra Chola and Bhojadev Parmar, but it was obvious that his words were meant for Narasimhan— 'a soldier has courage, no doubt. But in a battlefield, he is surrounded by his buddies. He knows that if he wins, he will be rewarded. He knows that if he dies, songs will be sung of his bravery. But think of an assassin or a spy. He is alone in enemy territory. He knows that if he is caught and killed, his king cannot even acknowledge him. He knows that even if he succeeds, he cannot be openly lauded and given a medal, because that destroys the entire point of the assassination. So why does an assassin or spy do what he does? One reason, and one reason alone. A reason that is higher than even honour.'

Kathiravan was fascinated by the Gujarati merchant.

Someshwar continued, 'And that reason is patriotism. Love for our Motherland. That is the only reason why a nation's spies and assassins do what they do … It's not just about honour. They know that their deeds skirt the line between *Dharma* and *Adharma*. They know that they may end up cursing their own souls because of the work that they do. They know that they will never be publicly thanked for their work. They know that they can't even be acknowledged for it. But they go ahead and do it anyway. Why? For the good of their Gods, people and the Motherland. I believe that spies and assassins are noble warriors, as much, if not more, than soldiers.'

There was silence all around.

'And equally importantly,' continued Someshwar, 'with assassinations, the chances of collateral damage—which is so common in open war—are extremely rare. A surgeon's scalpel does not cut extra flesh unnecessarily.'

This last point hit Narasimhan hard. Very hard.

'What is your idea, Someshwar?' asked Rajendra. 'I understood the assassination bit. That we can plan. But creating *bhed*, divisions and discord, among the Ghaznavids … How will we do that?'

'Just killing Mahmud will not be enough, My Lord,' said Someshwar. 'The vast majority of the Turks follow a radical interpretation of their religion. These people are the greatest killing machines the world has ever seen. They have no remorse, no guilt, no hesitation. Barbarism beyond belief. They genuinely see all outside their fold as animals to be tortured and killed. They have no sense of honour when it comes to dealing with us … They have mutilated and misinterpreted a very nuanced concept called *al taqiyyah*; they say that their religion allows them to lie to and mislead *kafir*s when their own positions are weak. So, a peace treaty with them means nothing, because it will only hold as long as they are weak. As soon as they become strong, they will break that peace treaty, even if it has been sworn to in the name of their God. They are like a bunch of rabid dogs. There is no permanent peace possible. You have to constantly keep fighting them.'

Rajendra and Bhojadev both looked at Iqbal, uncomfortable with such talk in the presence of a Muslim.

'My friend Someshwar *bhai* is right, Your Highnesses,' said Iqbal. 'These Turks have twisted my religion beyond belief. I practise Indian Islam, which is a very different interpretation from what these Turks follow. My Islam teaches me some very different lessons. The Holy Quran in chapter 109, verse 6, says, *Lakum deenukum wa liya deen.* It means, *To you your religion, and to me mine.* Moreover, for us Indian Muslims, our word of honour is everything. We will never break our promises because we think that Allah is watching us, and He will punish us on Judgement Day if we behave immorally. The Turks clearly only use the great religion of Islam as a tool for their conquest and barbarism. Their promises, even those made in the name of Allah, mean nothing to them. They are an embarrassment to Islam itself. They are truly like rabid dogs.'

'I understand your pain and anger towards the Turks, Iqbal,' said Rajendra Chola. 'Islam came to our Chera territories through traders. And it has been a peaceful and positive addition to our lands. The Chera Muslims honour our traditions, and we honour theirs. That is the way it must be. These Turks are insulting the noble religion of Islam with their barbarism.'

'So what do we do, Someshwar?' asked Kathiravan.

'The best way to deal with rabid dogs is to make them fight each other. And keep them busy fighting each other.'

'And how do we do that?'

'Fortunately, the Arabs and Persians also see the Turks as rabid dogs.'

'But aren't they also Muslim?'

'Yes, the Arabs are the original Muslims. But they are a much more cultured bunch. They are interested in science, music, literature and other civilized pursuits.'

'What does this have to do with Mahmud?'

'The caliphate.'

'The caliphate?'

'Many Indians have heard of the term Khilafat. They think it means Opposition. Actually, it is one of the ways to pronounce caliphate. And the caliph is, technically, the head of all of Islamdom. In every Islamic kingdom, the clergy and the royalty are separate. And the tension between them always remains, because both are powerful in Islam. But the caliph is different, since he has powers both as a royal and as clergy. There can only be one living caliph in the entire Islamic world. That is apparently the law.'

'Do you believe in this?' Bhojadev asked Iqbal.

Iqbal answered immediately, 'In this part of the world, we only believe in the first four rightly guided caliphs who followed Prophet Muhammad, peace be upon him. These are Caliph Abu Bakr, Caliph Umar, Caliph Uthman and Caliph Ali. We don't follow anyone else. Nobody living now can be a caliph, according to us.'

Rajendra asked Someshwar, 'So how does this give us an opportunity?'

'Since the dawn of Islam, the caliph has always been an Arab. The present one is an Abbasid caliph, with whom the Chola empire trades as well. He is much weaker than his ancestors, and the Persian Buyid dynasty effectively controls him.'

'And?'

'And Mahmud wants to declare himself caliph.'

Rajendra Chola straightened up, finally putting two and two together. 'The clergy and the royals fighting each other in Ghazni. And the Persians, with their Arab allies, fighting against the Turks. All being triggered by the assassination of Mahmud.'

'Yes, that is the plan. If all goes well, we could get even the Seljuk Turks on the side of the Arabs against the Ghaznavid Turks. That way the civil war will not end anytime soon.'

'How sure are you of Mahmud's plans to become a caliph?'

Someshwar turned to Iqbal, who reached into his bag and pulled out a scroll. Someshwar bowed low and presented it to Rajendra Chola. And he also handed over a sheet, saying, 'The message is in code, Your Majesty. This cryptographic key sheet is needed to decode it.'

Rajendra Chola gave the scroll and the cryptographic key sheet to Kathiravan.

Kathiravan was an expert multilinguist and adept at different scripts. He was also well versed in the principles of code-deciphering. But this was easier since the cryptographic key was available. It was also, mercifully, a short message.

Kathiravan decoded the short message in no time. 'Mahmud wants to be caliph. This is the opportunity.'

'Hmm,' Bhojadev Parmar murmured.

'And I recognize this seal,' continued Kathiravan. 'It is the royal Ghaznavid seal. But I don't know the other one.'

'That,' explained Someshwar, 'is the seal of the grand mufti of the Jama Mosque in Ghazni.'

Everyone was stunned into silence. This conspiracy went all the way up. To the apex of the Ghaznavid power structure. Someone from within the royal family and the grand mufti were both involved in the conspiracy.

Someshwar had planned this exceptionally well.

'Hmm. This is ... very interesting.' Rajendra Chola looked at Bhojadev, who nodded. He turned back to the five men sitting before him. 'Give us a week to think it over,' said the Chola emperor, calling the meeting to an end.

Someshwar nodded and bowed low. Rajendra Chola and Bhojadev Parmar would want to check all the information through other sources. That was understandable.

CHAPTER 6

A Wife's Counsel

Ghazni

Kausari Jahan, queen of Ghazni, glided through the corridors of Mahmud's winter palace, surrounded by her ladies-in-waiting and eunuch guards. Her delicate, long fingers were interlocked over her flat belly, and her long, diaphanous pale-blue gown swept the floor made of Persian marble. Large Basra pearls strung together in an almost-invisible rose-gold chain adorned her slender neck, and her ears were hidden by lush waves of auburn hair. The queen walked briskly, her expression pensive. She unclasped her hands and clutched the pearls around her neck with one hand, as if to yank them off in anger and have them roll on the alabaster floor. Or maybe she felt the fear of losing what she had given so much to achieve. In any case, the pearls remained where they were, around her exquisitely beautiful neck.

The winter sun had slid behind the mountains. It had been a fretful morning and a tiring day. Ismail, returned from exile, had been formally installed as the governor of

Ghazni and the grand mufti of the Jama Mosque. The court was in full attendance by the appointed time of noon, with delegates from across the Ghaznavid sultanate gathered in the mosque complex. Mahmud had addressed the assemblage with pomposity and flair, aided no doubt by the Kandahar opium he had smoked earlier in the day.

By late afternoon the chaos was appalling to her eyes. The sultan had abruptly left for his palace, no one noticing his vanishing act. It was not lost on the queen, though. She watched like a kingfisher eyeing a small fish, unmoving, as her husband slipped away with his lover, Malik Ayaz. Ismail, meanwhile, went around mingling with the nobility, reconnecting old bonds and friendships.

Kausari had sat in the court for another hour, wordless, repressed rage flowing through her. Still as a statue.

Idiot!

The queen reached the arched doorway of her husband's bedchamber. It was no longer hers. The door was open, but the curtains were drawn. Kausari Jahan heard the muffled voices and laughter of Mahmud and his lover.

She commanded her retinue to halt ten yards from the door. They stayed in formation. Polite. Non-threatening. But ready for action.

She ignored the salutes of the two guards. One of them gathered the courage to extend his arm, holding his pike at a slant and barring Kausari's way. The queen stopped dead in her tracks and turned her head slowly to face the man who dared deny her passage into what was still, technically, her bedchamber.

'Stand aside, wretch,' Kausari breathed softly.

The guard's blood ran cold and his hair stood on end.

'Now! Before your face is set in my memory.'

The hapless guard was aware of her brutal reputation and now found himself caught between the devil and the deep sea—his sultan and the queen. In a blink, he chose which side to take and stood his ground. His mind grappled feverishly for exit routes.

The voices in the room had lapsed into silence. Mahmud and Ayaz were aware of her presence, no doubt.

'A thousand pardons, great Queen,' apologized the unlucky guard. 'And a thousand more. I am acting under direct orders from the great sultan. I was instructed to not let *anybody* in. He is attending to some urgent matters of state with the King of Lahore.'

The other guard nodded vigorously in agreement, clearly relieved that his colleague had taken up the gauntlet. He had no intention of imprinting his face in the queen's mind. She was known to crush the subordinates who crossed her like troublesome flies.

Kausari Jahan's lips broadened in a sinister smile, distorting her elegantly bewitching face.

'Urgent, I am sure. Clandestine as well,' she said. 'Now, I am going to walk in. Straighten your pike, you fool. If you care for your family, you will let the queen of Ghazni pass. If you don't, I will scrape myself against this spear of yours. My blood will be drawn … What do you think will happen to you?'

Kausari looked back at her retinue. 'Hakeem?' she called softly.

'Ready, My Lady,' answered a large eunuch, clearly of African origin. He placed his hand on the hilt of his sword and looked the frightened guard in the eye, then took a large step forward. Eight massively built eunuchs, each towering over six feet in height, stepped up behind Hakeem. Some held swords, others thin daggers made from Damascus steel.

The sultan's guards stood like statues. Not stepping back, not advancing. Terror had arrested their muscles and their minds. Hakeem and the eunuchs took one more step. And waited.

'Have mercy, My Lady,' begged the courageous guard, sinking to his knees but holding the pike in place. His partner followed his lead. 'Allow me to announce your arrival to the sultan. I cannot disobey your order without risking my life, I understand. But I cannot disobey the sultan either.'

'That will not be necessary,' a man's musical voice interjected, smooth as butter. The speaker had emerged from the sultan's bedchamber like a stealthy cat.

Malik Ayaz.

Rumoured to be among the most influential voices in Mahmud's court. Second only to his formidable rival, Kausari Jahan. At times, his influence could best hers too.

Tall and slender, his fair skin gleamed like white sillimanite. His thin lips were parted, displaying a row of milk-white, flawlessly aligned teeth. The young man wore a rich, crimson velvet robe. He looked like a Turkish nobleman, but without the Turkish features. With wavy hair that was an ethereal golden-brown, slim and sharp facial features, and hazel eyes that were a hypnotic combination of brown and green, many felt that when it came to dazzling onlookers with beauty, Malik Ayaz, the former slave from Georgia, competed with none other than the exquisite Kausari Jahan herself. It was no wonder that Mahmud was besotted by him.

Ayaz took off his feathered headgear with a flourish and bowed low to the queen of Ghazni.

Kausari Jahan narrowed her large eyes into slits and locked her venomous gaze on her husband's lover.

The dandy returned the look with a sardonic smile. But the metaphorical daggers were drawn. Ayaz and Kausari glared at each other, and it seemed for a moment that a vicious catfight was about to break out between two jealous lionesses bickering over their control on the lion, the source of their power.

But it was Ayaz who stepped back this time. 'In you go, My Queen,' he said with a slight snigger. 'My work here is done, at least for tonight.'

Kausari Jahan didn't deign to respond. As Malik Ayaz left, she turned and ordered her eunuch guards to relax. She then strolled into the bedchamber like the freezing winds of the North Pole on their way to douse the steaming Steppe summer.

The room was very large, yet it felt warm and cosy. In the centre was a huge bed, its ruffled sheets wet with sweat. Plush floor cushions lined the right side of the room, facing the bed. Between two cushions lay jewelled smoking pipes, filled and ready for use. A stunning round table made from wood and alabaster sat in solitary splendour on the left side of the room. On it was placed a ceramic jar of wine surrounded by used cups. Metal oil lamps were placed on stone pedestals in the four corners of the room. Two were unlit. A large window was opened to a narrow slit to allow some relief from the room's suffocating confines. It did not help.

Mahmud stood in the middle of the room with a grin on his face. Warmly wrapped in his fur nightrobe, he scratched the skull-cap-shaped bald patch on his head with his long, dirt-filled fingernails. The sultan invited his wife to sit on a blue velvet floor cushion, no trace of embarrassment in his jaunty demeanour. Far from it, he seemed rather delighted to see her.

The queen remained standing where she was.

'Kausari!' Mahmud drawled happily, spreading out his arms, his right hand holding a wine glass. Some wine spilled on the floor as he stumbled forward. 'My dearest friend. My most trusted advisor. My wife.'

The queen stood still, icy. She did not lose her civility, though.

'My Lord,' she greeted, with a courtly bow.

Mahmud took a sip of wine from the misshapen silver goblet and walked towards her. He had smashed that goblet on someone's head once to kill him—he couldn't remember who—and it was therefore one of his favourite cups.

'I'm certain you have forgiven me for my sudden departure from the celebrations, My Queen,' he slurred, halting two inches away from her, swaying. 'Ayaz ...' he said, pointing towards the doorway. 'Malik Ayaz ...' he repeated. 'He and I had some important things to discuss.'

His breath was foul. Kausari did not recoil. Instead, she held her husband's raised wrist gently in a gesture of reassurance. Mahmud took a small step back. Her eyes scanned his body from head to toe, noting that he was clearly intoxicated, and smelling of fornication. His beard was knotted and sodden with spilled wine. And the hair on his head, whatever remained of it, stood on end and made him appear clown-like.

The queen ran her fingers through his wet beard, unknotting the strands with care. She swallowed back the bile that rose, unbidden, to her mouth.

The things I need to do …

'You do not owe me an explanation, My Lord,' she whispered kindly, tightening the belt around Mahmud's robe and pulling his collar in to keep him warm. 'You are my lord and master. Your word is the law, and your actions are beyond question.'

Mahmud grinned like a pleased child. He touched her cheek and ran his index finger over her upper lip. 'I do not know what I would do without you, Kausari,' he said, his drunken voice a high-pitched twang. 'You have always watched over me with utmost devotion.'

'*Someone* must look after the man who looks after the empire,' answered the queen, directing a maternal gaze his way with her evocative bluish-green eyes. 'My Lord, I have always spoken my mind with you, and you have always extended me the liberty to advise you as I see fit.'

Mahmud's expression turned petulant. He was the absolute master of his realms and his destiny, except when it came to this woman. His wife. His queen. Standing before him was the only person capable of influencing him with impunity. She said things that others would tremble to say.

Spellcaster. Witch.

He was infatuated with her, entranced from the moment he had laid eyes upon her.

Mahmud had made his distaste for late-night sermons known on many occasions. But he knew full well she would not be dissuaded.

'It has been a long day for both of us, Kausari,' he groaned. 'The ceremonies in honour of my brother have drained me, and you must be tired as well. If you are here despite that, this must be important. So speak, my love. What can I do for you?'

The queen lowered her gaze to the floor, carefully plastering her face with pained reluctance. Like a marionette the sultan responded, raising her face slowly with a hand on her chin. He looked into her eyes indulgently and raised his bushy brows. Kausari Jahan shook off his hand with the slightest shake of her head and pretended to walk away defeatedly.

Mahmud swiftly brought the pantomime act to an end and grabbed the queen by the wrist, pulling her back roughly. She banged into his chest, winced, then glowered at Mahmud, shocked.

'Tell me, what is the purpose of your visit,' he snarled, tightening his grip around her wrist. The queen's eyes clouded with fear. She knew too well that Mahmud was a predatory animal, even as he was gentle to her with his words. She had weathered too many brutal beatings from her loving husband to overlook that.

'No one turns their back on me, never forget that,' barked Mahmud, looking at the woman with a strange cocktail of lust and rage shining in his eyes. 'You are here, are you not? Now talk to me.'

'It is nothing new.' She threw back the words, fighting her instinctive fear with what the Jews called *chutzpah—extreme audacity*. She twisted her arm to loosen his grip. He let go of it, intrigued by her temerity.

'Speak before I start beating you!'

'I warned you about this. And now it is upon us, the arrival of your brother. It bodes ill for us, Mahmud. All of us—me, your children and heirs, and you too,' Kausari spoke sharply. 'Do not forget that before you made him the governor of Ghazni and the grand mufti on a whim, Ismail was an exiled traitor. He should have been left to rot in that Guzgan hell and not brought back to the capital with pomp and ceremony.'

Mahmud stiffened with irritation. He threw the wine cup down. It landed on the blue velvet cushion. Kausari watched the elegant Andhra velvet fabric darken with spilled wine, diligently controlling her obsession to keep all her surroundings clean and hygienic. The sultan wiped his mouth with the back of his hand and stared at the queen.

'The decision was mine, Kausari,' he reminded her, fighting his inebriation to sound articulate. 'We have talked about this. Whatever may have happened in the past, he is my brother. He is my blood. And I need a mufti of unquestioning obedience, a puppet … Ismail will proclaim me the caliph. He is beholden to me now, and too scared to betray me.'

Kausari walked wordlessly to a stone pedestal on which was placed an open metal lamp. Mahmud followed her.

'My Lord,' she said, turning her pained face towards him as she warmed her hands over the flames. 'Forgive me for not sharing your optimism. You may look upon my discomfort as the worries of a paranoid but loyal woman, if you like. Indulge me—you know I am nothing without you.'

Mahmud brought his hands close to the fire, self-involved. He edged Kausari's hands away. The queen pulled back and left the warmth for Mahmud.

'Have I ever *not* indulged you, my dear?' he turned and asked his wife coyly. He gathered her hair and ran a finger around the back of her long neck and then down to the small of her back. 'It has been a tiring day, but the night is young. Be done with this silly conversation and we can catch some action. I've missed you!'

Mahmud turned Kausari around, wrapped his hands around her and pressed into her back. Kausari pressed back, for she knew how he liked it, quickly calculating that she had precious few moments left before she would have to submit fully to his violent, voracious sexual appetite.

'I know we have discussed this, my love,' said Kausari as she covered his hands with hers and intertwined the fingers. 'But I'm convinced this title of caliph will do us no good. You should stay away from it, regardless of what that snake Ismail has said to you. He has planted this foolish fantasy in your head.'

Clearly stunned by her impertinence, Mahmud pulled back with a frown. Kausari had touched a raw nerve. The sultan's ego was hurt.

'And *why* do you think I am not fit to be caliph?' he demanded, indignant and bruised. 'I pointedly announced my annual *jihad*s against India, like a good follower of the Faith. I have plundered and destroyed the cities of the infidels many times over, like a good follower of the Faith. I have brought back untold wealth and relics of the heathen Gods from their country to display as trophies of the One True God's many victories, like a good follower of the Faith. I even constructed the great Jama Mosque as a tribute to the One True God. All this I have done as a follower of the Faith. My exploits are announced regularly in the caliphate in Baghdad.

And they certainly don't mind the money I send them. Why, then, Kausari, am I not fit to become Allah's prime servant in this world? Why must I not be the caliph?'

'It is not about being a good follower of the Faith, My Lord. You are clearly the greatest living devotee of our religion. Your services to it are unparalleled, even the man who currently calls himself caliph cannot measure up to you.'

Mahmud scowled, unmollified.

'Nevertheless,' Kausari continued, undeterred, though her demeanour had subtly shifted from firmness to the pleading of an ardent fan. '*Must* you pursue a title as dangerous and fiercely controversial for a non-Arab as this? You became the sultan with the support of the Abbasid caliphate, and you promised them that you would expand *Dar al-Islam* into the lands of the *kafir*s. The caliph and the Buyids sent their own armies to assist you when you fought that usurper—your brother. Why do you not see that Ismail is merely pitting you against your strongest ally?'

'My Queen, I appreciate your worry. But when the Buyids and the Abbasids helped me, I was the weaker one. Now, I am far, far stronger than them. Titles should catch up with reality. Even Ayaz thinks this is a good idea. It will cement my legacy in Islamdom for all time to come.'

Kausari rolled her eyes. 'Ayaz has his uses, I know, My King. And I am not jealous of that. But he is a sycophant. If you tell him to sit, he won't even search for a chair; he will sit wherever he is!'

'You are overthinking, Kausari. I do not see any cause for alarm. Not with Ismail. He is an old man, like me. He has no heir to fuel his ambitions. Why would he plot against me?'

'My King ... Please listen ...'

'This is the destiny Allah has set for me. I can feel it. I know it.'

'Well, if your mind is made up, My Lord,' she conceded. 'I want an assurance from you about the safety and security of our family. I believe there is a snake in our backyard, and his name is Ismail. Prove to me that his intentions are pure—to a wife who loves you and your children, whom she treats as her own.'

'Of course!' Mahmud laughed and wrapped his arms around her waist, yanking her close. He knew that Kausari could not have children, and was happy that she loved and cared for his twin sons from his first wife, whom he had had to unfortunately kill. 'So tell me, how can we ... how do we gauge Ismail's *true* intentions, hmmm? How can we test him?'

Kausari smiled shyly and melted into him. 'Why don't you give him six months to restore the Jama Mosque to its former glory?' She ran a finger over Mahmud's wrinkled cheek.

'Six months!' Mahmud exclaimed, and then buried his nose in her neck, her mass of hair covering him like a pile of auburn silk threads. He breathed in her rose fragrance and then bit her hard. She winced quietly. 'Six months is impossible. It is a massive structure that was felled by the great quake, you know that. We have not been able to reconstruct it in three years. How do you expect poor Ismail to do it in six months?'

'My Lord,' the queen purred as she withdrew teasingly from him and looked at Mahmud with her hypnotic bluish-green eyes. 'Six months is *plenty* of time for a man to prove his loyalty to the throne and to the Faith. A lot has already been done under your supervision to return the mosque to its former glory. Besides, you cannot declare yourself the caliph with the greatest mosque in your capital city being anything less than perfect, can you?'

'And what if my brother is not able to achieve this objective, despite his best efforts?' questioned Mahmud, beginning to undo the strings on the back of the queen's diaphanous dress. She turned around, making it easy for him.

'If he does not complete this task on time, then he fails to prove his commitment to you, My Lord,' Kausari Jahan said as she felt Mahmud press into her back again. 'There is no reason why your brother should not complete the task within six months, with the right attention and resources. It was the previous mufti who was sabotaging your efforts to rebuild the Jama Mosque. Ismail should be better than that. The sultan has every right to demand the impossible from those who love him. And they have to deliver. Haven't I always delivered whatever you demanded from me, My Lord?'

'Hmm.' Mahmud was constrained to agree, even as he started pulling Kausari's dress apart.

'And if I can deliver, so should your brother Ismail. If he fails, you may be rest assured that Ismail has neither the capacity nor the intention to be useful to you, especially when you become the caliph. It is my duty to caution you ... counsel you ... as your wife, mighty Mahmud Ibn Sebuktegin of Ghazni.'

—◦✦◦—

Gangaikonda Cholapuram

Iqbal sat stony-faced, for he genuinely did not know what to expect. Narasimhan and Kathiravan sat opposite him, calm and relaxed, like they knew what was about to happen. They knew their emperor. Someshwar was calm. The Gujarati merchant had seen enough of the world to know that if he had been called back for a meeting, it meant that his information had been double-checked and fully verified. But he wasn't sure exactly how Rajendra Chola and Bhojadev Parmar would want to proceed—for Police Chief Narasimhan, who had now become a friend since he was living at his house, had been taciturn on what to expect from the meeting. Vijayan shrank back in his chair, instinctively keeping his seat slightly behind the others, he seemed almost surprised that he had been invited back to this august gathering. And this time to Rajendra Chola's private chamber at the royal palace; he had never been inside the private section of the royal palace before.

It had been a week since the meeting at the Brhadishvara Temple. Rajendra Chola and Bhojadev Parmar had substantiated all that they had wanted to. Rajendra had the backing of the best spy system in the world; one week of engaging them had been more than enough. And the reach of Bhojadev's intelligence services, too, went deep into the Ghaznavid territories.

Soon, the guard announced the arrival of the emperors.

'Sit, sit,' said Rajendra, as he seated himself on his throne.

Next to Rajendra was a second throne of equal dimensions, for Bhojadev Parmar. The great Chola knew how to treat his friends with respect.

As the party of seven settled down, the emperors' bodyguards marched back to the end of the chamber. Out of earshot. But within their line of vision.

Rajendra glanced at his friend Bhojadev, and then looked at the men sitting in front of him, resting his eyes for an extra moment on Narasimhan. He began speaking suddenly. 'So here's what we will do ...'

Everyone leaned forward.

'We will dispatch an assassination squad into the heart of Ghazni. I will assign forty of my best men from the Chola Imperial Guard for this mission. Emperor Bhojadev will allocate ten men from his personal bodyguard corps, which is already here. This task force—this *mandalam*—will be small enough to escape detection and will not be tracked easily by a conventional army. But it *will* be large enough to be a lethal force with support and backup. It can storm a decent-sized palace, if needed, and drive a blade into the heart of the enemy.'

Everyone nodded in agreement, including Prime Minister Kathiravan, for this plan would achieve the objective without hurting the long-term interests of the empire. But to be effective, the group needed a leader. Who would be the leader of this assassination squad? The emperor had the answer.

'Just yesterday I received a request, which I was happy to comply with,' said Rajendra. He turned to Narasimhan and continued, 'Police Chief Narasimhan has volunteered to lead the squad, and I was happy to honour his request.' The emperor beamed at Narasimhan with a proud almost-fatherly smile, the unspoken message clear: *My greatest warrior has returned.*

Someshwar was genuinely surprised. He looked at Narasimhan.

Narasimhan felt the need to explain. He looked at the merchant. 'You were right, Someshwar*ar*. Assassinations rarely have collateral damage ... and killing an indisputable monster ...' Narasimhan held the annulus pendant before he continued, 'Maybe after torturing him the way he did to many ... That will cleanse the soul.'

Someshwar smiled and reached over to hold his friend's hand.

Rajendra turned to Someshwar and Iqbal. 'Please share all your information and intelligence reports with Narasimhan and my men. We will take it from here. We will get the butcher of Ghazni.'

Someshwar's face fell. He almost seemed hurt. 'We want to come along on this mission, Your Majesty. Please don't take this away from us.'

Bhojadev Parmar cut in, for he had expected this reaction from the Gujarati merchant. 'Don't misunderstand us, Someshwar. But both Iqbal and you are old. And while Emperor Rajendra and I respect your courage, you are not warriors. This will be a dangerous mission. Many may not survive. Narasimhan will have to take tough decisions at times, perhaps even leave people behind when he has no choice.'

Someshwar responded almost instantly, his voice ringing loud. His mind was crystal clear. 'I, Someshwar, with all of you and Lord Shiva as my witness, am giving General Narasimhan permission to leave me to die at any point during this journey if I end up threatening the success of the mission.

I'd rather die on this journey than live an unfulfilled life here till I am a hundred. For even a day of service to Lord Shiva is worth more than decades of an easy life.'

Iqbal nodded, showing his assent as well. While Someshwar had given an emotional answer, Iqbal pitched in with logic. 'We will make ourselves useful as guides and interpreters in the foreign land, My Lords. We are well acquainted with their local languages since we have traded there, and we are reasonably familiar with their customs and habits. Besides, we have been in contact with a clandestine rebel group there. They trust us. We will be of great help.'

Rajendra Chola and Bhojadev Parmar's eyes had moistened a bit. Great emperors and fierce warriors that they were, they expected valour from other warriors. But to see this raw physical courage from elderly businessmen was another thing altogether. This old, portly, vegetarian non-violent Gujarati merchant, and his devotion to the Lord Mahadev and the Motherland, and his friend, the Bengali Muslim, an achingly skinny, aged man, with thinning grey hair, who knew in his heart exactly who his own people were and loved them dearly.

Rajendra nodded his assent. 'Alright. Both Iqbal and you can go, Someshwar.'

The prime minister turned to Narasimhan. 'Have you started choosing your men, General? I guess I can call you "general" again?'

'Yes,' said Narasimhan with a smile. 'I will have a list ready in a few days, My Lord. And Vijayan here will finally get back the post he so richly deserves. Police chief of Gangaikonda Cholapuram. And not just the acting chief as he was earlier, but the *actual*, fully appointed chief.'

Vijayan finally understood why he had been extended the invitation today. He looked briefly at the painting on the wall. Of Lord Shiva, with Rajaraja and Rajendra at the Mahadev's feet. He knew now … He knew why he had been called. But he realized immediately that his calling was different. 'General, Sir,' he said to Narasimhan. 'I don't want this post.'

'What?' Narasimhan was shocked. As were all the others in the chamber. They had all assumed that becoming the police chief of the city was Vijayan's ambition.

'I want to come with you. To Ghazni.'

Rajendra cut in. 'You don't need to do that, Vijayan.'

'A thousand apologies for disagreeing with you, Your Majesty. I know I don't need to. But I *have* to,' said Vijayan, his voice quivering slightly. 'As Someshwaran said so correctly, I'd rather die on this mission than live an unfulfilled life here till I am a hundred. With all due respect, My Lord, the Cholas may be the dominant power on these lands now, but only the sons of the Pandya lands—of Madurai—are breastfed with the milk of Goddess Shakti Herself, Lady Meenakshi … We are Her sons. Her Husband, and our Father, Lord Shiva, has been insulted. The sons must honour the call of the Mother's righteous vengeance.'

The emperor stared at brave Vijayan, emotions choking his words. He understood something that his father had told him once. What a nation always needs for its survival, and to ensure that foreign barbarians don't claw, mangle and hack it to death, is only one thing: people willing to die to save it. India has never had a shortage of such men. They leave their families in poverty, their bodies in immense pain, their souls scarred, all because of their devotion to Mother India. All that they needed to be effective was committed and selfless leadership.

'Brave Vijayan, I, Rajendra Chola, with the powers vested in me, immediately raise you to the rank of brigadier in the Chola army.'

Vijayan was stunned. He got up, stepped up to the emperor, went down on one knee, and bowed his head.

'Rise, Brigadier Vijayan.'

Vijayan bowed again and sat back in his chair.

'I know that lives will be at risk,' continued the emperor. 'I also know that none of you are afraid of death. But everyone worries about their families. I am assigning the revenue of five villages for the families of the fifty soldiers accompanying you. Whether they return alive or dead, the Chola empire will take care of their families. Forever. Brigadier Vijayan, I am setting aside the revenues of one full village for you and your family. General Narasimhan, I am setting aside the revenues of five villages for you and your family. The Cholas will take care of you and your families for as long as the Chola dynasty rules.'

Rajendra Chola turned to the old men. 'Someshwar and Iqbal, you are already far wealthier than what many villages are worth. Riches will mean nothing to you. Therefore, I, Rajendra, son of Rajaraja, promise both of you that your statues will be carved in your exact likeness and placed within the inner temple complex of Brhadishvara, next to those of the members of the Chola dynasty. Through that stone image, may both of you look at the divine form of the Lord Mahadev, for eternity.'

Bhojadev Parmar added, 'On behalf of the Parmar dynasty, I promise a similar grant to all the soldiers going on this mission. For as long as the Parmars live, none of these men or their descendants will want for anything.' Turning to Someshwar and Iqbal, Bhojadev continued, 'I am building a new temple in Bhojpur, great merchants. It will be called Bhojeshwar Temple. I vow that when that structure is complete, your statues, in your exact likeness, will be placed in the inner complex of this temple as well.'

An emotional Someshwar and Iqbal bent down to touch Rajendra Chola's and Bhojadev Parmar's feet. But the emperors immediately pulled back. 'You are older than us. Please don't do this.'

'And one more thing, General,' Bhojadev Parmar said to Narasimhan, 'there is a deep asset I have in Ghazni. A long-term agent. The motivations are different, but the desire of this person for vengeance is no less than ours. You will receive help from this agent.'

'How do I contact him or her?'

'You cannot. You will be contacted by the agent at the right time. A message has been sent already. You just need to know the operative name of the person. The Caucasian.'

'The Caucasian?'

'Yes. I saved the Caucasian's life once. And trust me, any help from this person will be invaluable.'

Narasimhan nodded at Bhojadev. 'Thank you, Your Majesty.'

Rajendra Chola rose from his throne. Everyone else stood up too.

The final order from the Tamil emperor was simple. 'Go get him, my tigers. Mission Ghazni starts today.'

CHAPTER 7

Plans and Pilgrims

Chera territory, Kerala, India

Narasimhan and Vijayan trekked across the slopes of the sacred forests of the Sabari hills in Chera country. Barefoot. It had been a little less than two weeks since Rajendra Chola had given his final approval for the assassination squad. Fifty soldiers—led by Narasimhan, with Vijayan serving in the role of deputy commander, accompanied by Someshwar and Iqbal, and other suppliers—had set off immediately. It was the night of *Makara Sankranti*, what the Westerners call the Winter Solstice. *Lord Surya*, the *Sun God*, had transited to the zodiacal field of Capricorn, beginning His journey north—Uttarayan, a most auspicious time for the dharmic religions of Hinduism, Buddhism and Jainism.

The light of the late-evening winter sky struggled to penetrate the thick tree cover of *Poongavanam—Forest of Poonga*—as the duo wound their way forward. Scattered groups of devotees walked in clusters among the dense shrubs, surrounded by orange, jackfruit and banana trees. They moved as a giant self-organized body in the direction of the abode of *Lord Ayyappan, Son of Lord Rudra and Lady Mohini.* The youthful Bachelor God had settled in the Sabari hills a very long time ago.

'I don't believe this, Sir. We rode all the way to Kollam just to ride back inland again!' Vijayan was fuming—though even in his irritation, he did not forget Narasimhan's instructions to not refer to him as general in public. He tugged at the belt that fastened his quiver of arrows to his shoulder. 'Old man Rajasinh should have kept a ship ready at Kollam! We were at the Chera port capital! We could have set sail for Ghazni immediately. Instead, here we are, on pilgrimage. Forgive me, Lord Ayyappan!'

The dark silhouettes of devotees, clad in the traditional all-black garb of pilgrims here, glided through the forest like an assembly of spirits, chanting with gusto the cry of glory dedicated to God Ayyappan.

Swamiye sharanam Ayyappa! I take refuge in Lord Ayyappan!

'*King* Rajasinh, Vijayan. You are talking about the Chera ruler and trusted vassal of Rajendra Chola,' corrected Narasimhan. 'Also, it was my decision to come here. Lord Rajasinh's logic was sound.'

Rajasinh had convinced Narasimhan to redirect his Chola squad to the Sabari hills. His reasons were nuanced, but important.

The Chera ruler, being on the western coast, had traded with many Arabs, who employed Turkic soldiers on their ships for protection. The Turks were fantastic warriors but awful sailors. Rajasinh had admitted that from all that he had seen, Someshwar and Iqbal had very good knowledge of Muslim culture and the Turkic way of life. But they were restricted from putting it to use because of something the merchants could do little about—their appearance. They looked very obviously Indian. And the Turks had huge biases against darker-skinned people, even if they were Muslim. They called African Muslim converts *abd*, meaning *servant* or *slave*. And they derided the Indian Muslim converts as *pasmanda*s, meaning *those who are meant to be left behind*. Only fair-skinned Persian and Arab Muslims were allowed to rise to the highest levels in Turkic courts. The other Muslims who were darker-skinned, unless they were capable warriors, were usually assigned jobs like toilet cleaning, drainage maintenance, road building, and so on.

Therefore, Someshwar and Iqbal, for all their understanding of the enemy, and of course their obvious motivation, would not be as useful as one would hope. So Rajasinh had arranged a meeting with someone who looked Turkic but whose heart was loyal to India. They were set to meet this guide at a rendezvous point in the Sabari hills.

Narasimhan and Vijayan had travelled with their squad to the pilgrimage spot. They had then set out on their own for the rendezvous, leaving the rest of the group in a guest house at the foot of the hills. A huge band of powerfully built and heavily armed men would draw unnecessary attention in a pilgrimage spot.

Having said what he had, Narasimhan understood Vijayan's frustration and impatience to press on. Despite the requirements of secrecy and risk of exposure, he had told his wife, Harini, about the mission. She had already bonded with the two men from Somnath, and he felt compelled to share with her the mission they would embark upon. The general had experienced the benediction of a tearful farewell. His wife had insisted on a promise that he come back safe and sound, even if it took longer than they anticipated to complete the mission.

However, it was different for men like Vijayan, whose families lived away from the Chola capital. No goodbyes or even the exchange of cryptic letters was possible. They were eager to complete the noble duty entrusted to them quickly. For that would mean returning home faster.

Vijayan still seemed unmollified about their detour into Chera territory. He genuinely thought that this was an unnecessary distraction. Further, he always harboured doubts about the loyalty of the Chera king towards the Chola ruler. 'I'm not so sure about this Amal person …'

Amal was the 'Turkic-looking but India-loyal' person whom the Chera king, Rajasinh, had insisted that Narasimhan pick up. Also, the astute Chera had recognized the risks involved in sailing from a militarized shipyard like Kollam, which is idle and empty during times of peace, like the present time. If they sailed from there, the Chola squad would get noticed by others. Instead, he had advised Narasimhan to transport his troops on an inconspicuous merchant ferry from the busy and usually crowded commercial town of Kochi. The merchant ferry would also arouse no suspicions in the Arab Navy that patrolled the Arabian Sea close to the Balochistan and Arab coast. Narasimhan had decided to pick up Rajasinh's proposed agent Amal from the Sabari hills on the way to Kochi.

'Come now, my friend,' urged Narasimhan, taking long strides up the slope with his deputy. 'Rajasinh has done us a favour by pointing us to Amal. He is one of the custodians of the Vavar shrine, and I am sure you are aware that the shrine is the sister-house of the Lord Ayyappan Temple. Amal is also apparently a Muslim scholar and a master of languages, including the Ghaznavid Turkic tongue. And because he is Tibetan, he can pass off as a Turk as well. He will prove invaluable to us.'

Vijayan nodded. He was still unconvinced. But like a good soldier, he would not argue with his commander beyond a point.

'This will be a simple rendezvous,' said Narasimhan. 'We will be in and out before you know it. Besides, let us take advantage of our good fortune in being here during *Makara Sankranti*. It is a good omen, and I want to pray to the Lord for our success.'

Vijayan nodded more convincingly this time, and the duo proceeded in silence. They stayed close to the other pilgrims, watchful, as any soldier should always be, yet seemingly unperturbed. They left enough room between themselves and the nearest groups of devotees to enable them to weave around the clusters of people in case of any disturbance.

'We are being followed,' Vijayan said suddenly in a casual voice, looking ahead, his expression unchanged, almost like he was discussing the weather with his commander.

'I think I know who is following us,' whispered Narasimhan. 'These men have altered their course to align with ours too many times for it to be a coincidence.'

Vijayan nodded in acknowledgement. 'I know. They were at the rest house this afternoon too, when we moved in with our men.'

Narasimhan did not answer. He walked on, looking straight ahead.

'Rajasinh, you think?' The Pandya's suspicion of the Cheras was amply evident.

'No,' Narasimhan's answer was immediate. 'If he had wanted us killed, he would have done it at sea. No suspicion would have fallen upon him. He wouldn't do this in his own territory. This is someone else.'

Vijayan was regretting having left all the Chola soldiers back at the rest house. He had of course heard of the fearsome warrior-reputation of Narasimhan earlier. But since he had met the general at Gangaikonda Cholapuram only in the relatively recent past, he could not see how the reputation matched reality. Vijayan had heard of many great soldiers who had grown sick of the violence and taken a one-hundred-and-eighty-degree turn to become completely peaceful, non-violent vegetarians. He had even seen Narasimhan hesitate to step on a cockroach once. While, like all Indians, Vijayan admired men of non-violence, at this time, when a threat appeared imminent, Vijayan would have liked the warrior incarnation of Narasimhan by his side. He knew that Narasimhan's old form would return when confronted with the brutal Turks. But against those who looked just like his fellow Indians? Maybe not. But he kept these thoughts to himself.

'What are your orders, Sir?' asked Vijayan. 'Should we confront them?'

'No,' replied the Chola general firmly. 'We are on a secret mission. We cannot attract attention. We will mirror them. If they engage, we engage.'

'As you say, Sir.'

The pair walked in silence for a while longer but encountered no surprises. They finally reached the summit, facing the giant stone gateway to the Lord Ayyappan Temple.

It was a massive granite structure flanked by tall elephant-shaped pedestals crested with great bowls of fire. The gateway was crowned with a beautiful *murti* of the temple's presiding deity—Ayyappan, Who stood tall beside a roaring tiger, His mount. His head was held high with pride and grit. He held a bow in one hand and three arrows in the other.

Temple guards on horseback flanked the perimeter of the temple complex. The guards patrolling on foot shepherded the devotees respectfully into an orderly line. The two men from the Chola lands noted that they were discreetly questioning the devotees before letting them in through the gates. A live elephant stood by the gateway and, as instructed by its mahout, raised its trunk and rested it gently upon the head of every devotee, blessing them as they entered.

'We are almost there,' whispered Narasimhan, jostling for space among the throng of devotees who clogged the entrance to the ancient temple. 'Let us first seek divine grace. Afterwards we will head to the Vavar shrine.'

The pursuers seemed to have fallen behind. Maybe it was a false alarm. But Narasimhan's instincts still kept warning him.

'But we cannot climb the eighteen holy steps, obviously,' said Vijayan. Only those who had done the strict forty-one-day *vrat* were allowed to climb the eighteen steps to the sanctum sanctorum. And Narasimhan and Vijayan had not done the *penance*. Vijayan noticed a shiny copper pillar as he passed.

'Of course, no climbing,' said Narasimhan, who was looking at the same shiny copper pillar, so shiny that it afforded a good reflection of the scene behind them. 'And it appears that our friends have …'

'… found some buddies,' said Vijayan, completing Narasimhan's sentence, while quickly counting the number of pursuers. 'They are in a huddle. Fourteen of them.'

'Hmm,' said Narasimhan.

Vijayan narrowed his eyes. 'I don't think they will attack us in this crowd and around those burly temple guards.' He suddenly straightened his back. 'What if one of them is Amal? What if the one we seek is seeking *us*? And sizing us up?'

'Possible …' conceded Narasimhan. 'But he was supposed to meet us at the Vavar shrine, not here. So let's not let our guard down …'

'Yes, Sir.'

Vijayan did not like the idea of disappearing into the crowd and waiting for something to happen. But they had little choice.

The two men pressed into the serpentine line of pilgrims and slowly inched forward towards the temple gate. Many devotees were armed, a common practice in this thickly forested region which was home to tigers, leopards and other animals of prey.

Have we walked into a trap? Narasimhan shook his head. He trusted Rajasinh, for a simple reason—Rajendra Chola trusted the Chera king. And the Chola emperor was an exceptional judge of men. Also, Rajasinh was a great Shiva devotee, as everyone knew, and would naturally support the mission targeting Mahmud of Ghazni. Most convincingly,

Amal's occupation was symbolic of the friendship, harmony and brotherhood that prevailed between common followers of all faiths in India. He came from a line of Muslims who had been serving Lord Ayyappan with the utmost loyalty and commitment for generations. He was descended from Vavar, the famous Muslim devotee of the Lord of Sabarimala. Vavar had defended this temple from that terrible Arab naval invasion three hundred years ago. Amal came from a line that was sworn to defend the Hindu faith, even while adhering to his own Islamic one. Amal might share the enemy's faith, but he was a son of India.

Maybe this is about something else …

'*Swamiye sharanam Ayyappa! Swamiye sharanam Ayyappa!*' The crowd was in a frenzy now, and the guards at the gateway were still several yards away.

'It's a bit slow this year, isn't it?' A tranquil voice came from behind them. The men from Cholapuram looked over their shoulders, their muscles taut. Standing behind them was a tall, burly devotee wearing a pleasant smile that bordered on a smirk. He was not part of the group that had been trailing them. His clean-shaven face was weather-beaten. Almost as tall as Narasimhan, the man wore a black *dhoti* and a mass of beaded *rudraksha* necklaces around his neck. Like the other pilgrims.

'Usually, there are no guards at the gates,' said the newcomer, offering an unsolicited explanation. He spoke affably, so affably that it was unsettling. 'People just come and go as they please.'

Narasimhan looked him in the eye genially and smiled, then turned away. The Chola warriors had sensed imminent danger. They rested their hands on the hilts of their swords. Ready.

Perhaps this man was also working with their pursuers … So now, there could be fifteen adversaries.

Narasimhan frowned, trying to place the man's accent. It sounded strangely familiar. But the words the mysterious man spoke next, shocked the two men … Acidic words, delivered in a sinister yet serene voice.

'Are you not offended? How dare these guards make Narasimhan, the rabid hellhound of Rajendra Chola, wait like a street mongrel? Will you not walk up and butcher these men in one of your infamous fits of rage?'

The two men were stunned. Their cover was blown. With feral speed and stealth, they whirled around in unison. Narasimhan wrapped a powerful arm around the man's shoulder. The friendly gesture drained the colour from the stranger's face and his smirk was replaced by a surprised frown. He pulled the dagger tucked in his cummerbund, but Vijayan immediately seized his arm and twisted it in a nimble move, forcing the flat, cold steel of the knife against the intruder's back.

'Perumal, my friend!' exclaimed Narasimhan with a grin, using a random name as he pulled the man away from the teeming crowd. 'Fancy meeting you here, after so many years. Let us catch up!'

If their cover was blown, he needed to know how and also find out who was responsible.

'Yes, Perumal,' Vijayan hissed from between gritted teeth as he tightened his grip around the man's wrist and twisted it. The dagger dropped. Vijayan buried it into the moist earth with his foot.

The men zig-zagged through the surging crowd, dodging the captive's comrades. Leaving the multitude behind, they soon entered the dense, impenetrable forest. Behind them, the subdued man's accomplices hurriedly searched through the sea of devotees. But the captors and the captive had disappeared into the night.

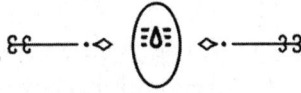

CHAPTER 8

Regret Is a Blade

Forest of Poonga, Chera territory

Away from the faintest of temple lights and the pilgrim footpath, the men halted on a grassy patch, surrounded by dense trees through which some slivers of moonlight filtered in. Vijayan pulled off the man's *angavastram* and used it to tie his hands securely around a tall, thin mootti pazham tree. The bitter juice of the rose-coloured berries, which dotted the main trunk of the tree, soaked the intruder's *dhoti*, giving the macabre impression that blood was leaking from his legs. The way the man had fought, even when disarmed of his weapon, had made it clear to Narasimhan and Vijayan that he was a trained soldier. But certainly not a Chola one. And he was no match for one of the fiercest warriors alive: Narasimhan. Particularly now that the Chola general had recovered his fighter mojo.

Narasimhan thrust his powerful forearm against the intruder's chest and pinned him to the trunk. With his hands tied behind him, around the tree, the enemy was immobilized. The Chola general drew his dagger and held it against the accoster's throat, while Vijayan drew an arrow from his quiver and nocked it on his bowstring. He turned around and stood guard, scanning the forest for their enemy's mates.

'Speak,' Narasimhan said menacingly. 'Who are you? And how do you know my name? Why were you and your men following us? Are you Amal? Do you work for Amal?'

The prisoner grinned insolently. 'Who the hell is Amal?'

Narasimhan delivered a backhanded blow to the man with the hilt of his knife. 'How do you know my name?'

The man spat out some blood. He glared at Narasimhan, hatred and rage pouring out of every pore of his body. 'Who doesn't know your name? Who doesn't know of your savage bloodlust and sadism?'

Vijayan did not turn to look at their prisoner. His eyes were focused forward, to see from where the accomplices of their enemy could charge. But he had heard of the kind of brutality Narasimhan had once been capable of. Though he had seen none of it since he had known the general.

Narasimhan stared at his enemy, his eyes steady and ruthless, his tone menacing. 'Your insults mean nothing. Give me some useful information, wretch, before I chop and mince you up like a pesky rat that needs to be exterminated.'

Vijayan's blood turned cold. It wasn't just the words. It was the tone. He had never heard his general like this. Now he understood why Chola's enemies feared Narasimhan so. But like a good soldier, he kept his eyes trained in the right direction. Towards the trees ahead, where their prisoner's comrades would be searching for him.

The accoster continued, 'You will die today, Narasimhan. Vatapi will rule! Sathyashraya will be avenged!'

Narasimhan was stunned.

Sathyashraya … Chalukyas … So deep in our lands?!

The Cholas and the Chalukyas had been at war with each other, off and on, for over two decades. The first set of battles were in 1008 CE … The then crown prince, Rajendra Chola, had fought the Chalukyan emperor, Sathyashraya, in a series of devastating battles through the year, the final one being at Toanur on the Krishna River. Rajendra Chola had killed Sathyashraya in hand-to-hand combat, and one of the most violent conflicts plaguing the region had ended with the defeat of the Chalukyas. They had licked their wounds for over a decade and attacked the Cholas again in 1019 CE. Rajendra Chola had fought hard, and his general had led a brutal rampage through the southern Chalukya lands, in a bloody shock-and-awe campaign, suppressing the enemy once again into surrendering. The Cholas had annexed large parts of the then Chalukya kingdom. The Chalukyas had then retreated to their capital in Vatapi, and peace reigned for another decade.

These series of battles enforced a decisive Chola hegemony over the southern region of the Indian subcontinent. It also heralded the rise of a fierce young Chola warrior called Narasimhan, who had fought bravely and fiercely against the Chalukyas, first in 1008 CE as a mere lieutenant, when he caught the eye of Rajendra Chola. And then again in 1019 CE, when he led the Chola army as general, during a bloody onslaught through Chalukya lands. No wonder they hated Narasimhan.

The thought that struck Narasimhan was clear. *A decade has passed since their last defeat. Are the Chalukyas planning another war against us? Who told them about my squad? And revealed our location?*

The Chalukyan soldier answered at least one of Narasimhan's questions of his own accord. 'It is Lord Ayyappan's blessing that we saw you at Kollam. I can never forget your face. You killed all my mates brutishly. You left me alive … You taunted …'

I remember…

'Yeah …' interrupted Narasimhan, snarling. The blood-thirsty warrior buried deep inside, under layers of guilt and regret, was slowly emerging again. Emerging because, after a long time, there stood in front of him a man that he believed was worth killing. 'I remember … I had said—I think I had said—that I don't kill rats while they are still wetting their beds … Maybe you are worth killing now.'

The Chalukyan soldier gritted his teeth in rage. *He finally remembers … Now is the time to kill him.*

Just at that time, Narasimhan hit the Chalukyan hard on his Adam's apple. In a savage blow with the hilt of his knife. The Adam's apple is a protrusion in the throat, made from thyroid cartilage. It protects the walls and the frontal part of the larynx, including, most crucially, the vocal cords. These had all been crushed viciously.

'You were planning to shout for your comrades, weren't you, rat?' Narasimhan smiled cruelly.

The soldier was writhing in pain, trying hard to make some sound. But his destroyed voice-box was incapable of doing anything.

'Kill him, General,' Vijayan hissed softly. 'He said that it was Lord Ayyappan's blessing that he saw us in Kollam. It was just a coincidence that they found us. They don't have any intelligence information about our squad. Our mission is safe. We should kill him quickly and get out of here.'

'Perhaps ...' whispered Narasimhan, never once taking his eyes off the Chalukyan.

'General ...'

'This piece of vermin cannot talk any more, in any case,' said Narasimhan.

Narasimhan pushed the Chalukyan's forehead back against the tree with his brawny left hand, giving himself an unobstructed space to strike. Then, very slowly, with the incision skills of a surgeon, he sliced through the throat of the enemy with his knife. From the right edge of the neck, in an immaculate circular cut, all the way to the left. Deep. So deep that not only did he slice through the jugular veins but also the carotid and cervical arteries. Both the left and the right ones. Blood burst forth in a fountain, bathing Narasimhan's face a deep red colour.

Vijayan turned and saw the gruesome sight. A bloodstained, indeed blood-drenched, Narasimhan. For the first time in his life, he felt intense fear. 'General ... Let's get out of here ...'

Narasimhan pulled the *angavastram* cloth loose. The one that had been used to tie the Chalukyan. The lifeless body crumpled to the ground. Then he used the same *angavastram* to wipe his face and blade. His voice was calm. 'No. We need to hunt down the rest of them. And we need answers. How much do they know?'

'General …'

Narasimhan shot a withering look at Vijayan.

'As you command, Sir,' said Vijayan.

—◦❊◦—

They had been hunting for over three hours. Fifteen Chalukyan soldiers comprised the group that had discovered and tracked the Chola squad, including the one who had accosted Narasimhan in the queue at the temple. Only two of the team were alive now.

Narasimhan had taken down thirteen men, one by one, methodically. Separating the herd from each other through feints and animal calls. Moving in at the right time, with the speed of a cheetah and the silence of a panther. Killing, and retreating into the darkness. Vijayan had helped a few times, as ordered by his commander. But he had mostly been slinking behind in the shadows, staring at Narasimhan, sometimes in awe, at other times in dread, never having seen killing skills so fine they could be called a work of art.

'General …' Vijayan said softly.

'Hmm.'

'The two surviving soldiers are up ahead.'

'I can see them.'

'General, may I speak freely …'

'Hmm.'

'We have not asked any questions, except to the first one. We've just killed them all. What is the point? Thirteen of them are dead now. And we still don't know anything more about them … I mean …'

'We can't ask questions when we know someone can shoot us from the back. All of them are carrying bows and arrows.'

Vijayan remained silent.

'In a scenario such as this,' whispered Narasimhan, 'we could have either asked questions to the first one, when the others didn't know where we were. Or we can ask the very last one, when the others are all dead.'

Vijayan nodded.

'I'm moving far to the left. When I make a birdcall, shoot the Chalukyan to the right. Through his throat.'

'Yes, Sir,' Vijayan said. He could see in the faint moonlight that the Chalukyan to the left was the one giving instructions. So killing the one on the right seemed logical, for he would know less.

Narasimhan slipped away without a sound. It fascinated Vijayan how a man as enormous as his commander could move with such stealth. He gently pulled an arrow out of his quiver, without making a sound. Nocking the arrow to his bow and pointing it towards the target, he waited.

And then it came. The birdcall. But it was too perfect. Maybe it was a real bird. Vijayan was confused. He waited. What if his general had not reached the correct location yet? He strained to hear more. He could see the Chalukyans in the faint moonlight, looking at each other. The one on the left was whispering something to the soldier on the right. They looked like they were about to move. There was another birdcall, which sounded more impatient than the last one. Immediately, Vijayan drew the bowstring and released the arrow, flicking the fletching as he did. The missile flew in an unerringly straight line, spinning on its axis, and slammed into the throat of the Chalukyan soldier on the right. The arrowhead emerged on the other side of the poor man's neck, the shaft buried deep inside. The soldier collapsed, holding his throat, beginning to drown in his own blood.

The Chalukyan soldier to the left immediately fell to the ground, on his haunches. The knife held high in his right hand as a logical defence against enemy arrows. Offer a smaller target. And cover the vital organs with the legs and hands.

Very logical.

But not so logical against an enemy coming in close with a knife.

Narasimhan burst forward with blinding speed. With knives in both his hands.

In Southeast Asia, there is a knife-fighting tactic called 'defanging the snake'. It means targeting the opponent's limb to destroy its structure and function. Symbolically, the weapon is the 'fang' and the arm wielding it is the 'snake'. Removing the fang from the snake immediately eliminates the primary threat from the defender.

Narasimhan slashed ruthlessly, slicing through the Chalukyan's flexor tendons at the wrist that connected the muscles of his right forearm to the fingers. A simple surgical strike that immobilized the fingers of the Chalukyan's sword arm and caused the knife to fall from his hand. The snake had been defanged. Before the enemy soldier could even wrap his head around where the attack had come from.

In the same smooth movement, Narasimhan rolled on the ground and shouldered the Chalukyan down. As the soldier screamed in agonizing pain, Narasimhan sliced with his left hand, cutting through the patella tendon, which connected the bottom of the kneecap to the top of the shinbone. As the Chalukyan continued to shriek miserably, Narasimhan casually cut through the patella tendon of the other leg. In just a moment, Narasimhan had executed what, in knife fights, is called a mobility kill.

The Chalukyan soldier couldn't move, as the 'connection' from his thigh muscles to the lower legs had been severed. He couldn't pick up his knife either, for the muscular link from his right forearm to his fingers had been severed. All he could do was writhe in pain. And screech expletives at Narasimhan.

Vijayan came running up, mouth agape at how quickly Narasimhan had reduced the last Chalukyan soldier to a helpless cripple.

'Finish him off,' Narasimhan ordered calmly, pointing to the soldier that Vijayan had shot just a few seconds back.

Vijayan drew his knife, bent down and stabbed the Chalukyan soldier through the rib cage, deep into his heart, putting him out of his misery.

As he turned to his general, he noticed that Narasimhan was wiping his blade clean. 'Pull this one up and tie him against the tree, Vijayan.'

'Yes, Sir.'

—·◦✦◦·—

'You can scream all you want,' snarled Narasimhan, not feeling the need to whisper any more. 'Nobody is coming to save you. We are very, very far from the temple. But if you talk quickly, we will make the suffering go away.'

The Chalukyan kept screaming and shouting in pain. His arms were tied around the Ashoka tree behind him, with his *angavastram*. His fellow soldier's *angavastram* had been taken under his armpits and tied to the branch just above, to keep him from falling, since his legs were practically useless now. He had been tied at eye level with Narasimhan.

The Chalukyan kept cursing and shrieking. But nothing he said was intelligible.

Narasimhan stepped forward and stabbed the soldier's right shoulder, digging the knife in deep. As the Chalukyan wailed once again in delirious pain, Narasimhan thundered, 'Speak! And you will have mercy. What do you know about our mission? How did you know I was coming here?'

The Chalukyan didn't answer. He just kept spitting curses at the Chola general.

Narasimhan turned to Vijayan. 'Let's sit for some time. Let this one tire himself out. Then he'll talk.'

'Yes, Sir.'

—◦❦◦—

'Wake him up,' ordered Narasimhan.

The Chalukyan soldier had lost consciousness from bleeding and being forced to stand despite the grievous wounds on his legs. With a few slaps from Vijayan, and some water thrown at his face, the soldier awoke.

'Step back, Vijayan.'

Vijayan did as ordered. He looked up and noticed that dawn was breaking. Daytime meant more travellers in these hills, which also meant that they could be discovered. Whatever they had to find out, they must find out quickly.

'Feel like talking now?' Narasimhan asked.

The Chalukyan looked crestfallen, like he had surrendered. 'His name … was … Vikram.'

'Whose name was Vikram?'

'Our leader … the man who accosted you at the temple … the first man you killed.'

Narasimhan remained silent.

'You killed … all his friends … in the Chalukya–Chola war.'

'It's war. We are soldiers. We know how it works. If I hadn't killed them, they would have killed me. This is ancient history now. You have to learn to move on.'

'Do you deny … a man … his right to vengeance?'

Narasimhan kept quiet. For even his mission to Ghazni was about vengeance.

'Do … you?'

Narasimhan didn't feel like talking about it. 'How did you find out about my mission?'

'What … mission …?'

Narasimhan stared into the Chalukyan soldier's eyes. He could sense that he was telling the truth. 'Then how did you track us all the way down here?'

'We were here … protecting … a trade delegation … We saw you … in Kollam. Captain Vikram … changed … our mission objective and decided … to track you down … And … kill you.'

Narasimhan looked at Vijayan. His deputy was right. This was just a coincidence.

The Chalukyan looked at Vijayan. 'We have nothing against you … We only want … Narasimhan's head.'

'Well, you aren't getting it,' Narasimhan said.

'We had hired some … Arab mercenaries … to hunt you down at sea … in case we missed you … But we thought we got lucky … when you and your party … turned back inland. We planned … to get you here.'

Vijayan took a deep breath. *Arabs mercenaries. In the seas. Paid to hunt us down … Damn.*

The Chalukyan seemed to be collapsing. He mumbled something. Very softly.

Narasimhan leaned forward to listen more clearly. That was the first mistake that the Chola general made that night. A costly one.

The thing with deep wounds on tendons, particularly on wrists, is that the blood doesn't coagulate quickly. The injury just keeps leaking blood. Almost continuously. That blood was trickling onto the *angavastram* that was used to tie the Chalukyan's hands behind the tree. As blood seeped into the cloth, it made the fabric slick and slippery. As a result, the Chalukyan, struggling slowly through the night, had managed to free his uninjured left hand. Where the fingers were still connected to the forearm muscles. They could still grab and hold.

As Narasimhan leaned close, the Chalukyan almost instantaneously pulled an arrow from his cummerbund, yanked his left arm loose and stabbed straight at Narasimhan's abdomen. Narasimhan noticed, and in that split second, took evasive action. Slipping down and swerving left. But it was too late. He couldn't avoid the blow entirely. The arrowhead cut fiercely, going deep into Narasimhan's right trapezius muscle, in the region of the upper back and right shoulder. Vijayan cried with horror, rushed forward, and held the Chalukyan's arm.

'General!'

It seemed like an exiguous wound. Surely, the formidable Narasimhan would not be felled by a mere arrowhead injury on his upper back.

The Chalukyan was laughing loudly now. 'Captain Vikram! I got him! I got the monster! We are avenged!'

A furious Vijayan drew his sword and stabbed the Chalukyan right through his chest. Deep into his heart—killing him instantly.

'General!'

The mighty Narasimhan crashed to the earth, like a giant invincible teak tree that had been chopped viciously down to its roots. The world dissolved into an abyss of darkness for the magnificent warrior.

'General!'

Vijayan tried to pick up Narasimhan. But he was too bulky and heavy for the leaner Pandya. He guessed that the arrow tip must have been laced with a very potent poison.

'Don't sleep, General! Open your eyes!'

He knew that falling asleep was the worst thing to do when poison was involved. Particularly those that didn't have an odour. He kept shaking the general desperately, feeling sheer panic rise within him.

Stay alive, General. Please stay alive.

And then he heard it.

The sound of many horse hooves slamming on the soft ground.

Have mercy, Goddess Meenakshi.

People were riding towards them.

Vijayan drew his sword and turned to face the fresh threat. Ready for the new attack. He whispered the war cry of his people. 'By Meenakshi of Madurai ...'

The light in the jungle was slowly increasing as the sun rose.

Vijayan could clearly see the uniformed horsemen in the distance, weaving through the gaps in the trees.

The temple guards.

He let out a long, exhausted breath.

'Help! Here! Help!'

Vijayan pushed his sword tip into the mud and sank to his knees. To signal that he presented no danger to the mounted soldiers. He waved at the approaching guards riding towards him.

'Over here!' cried Vijayan. 'Over here! This man needs help!'

The horsemen were led by a slight, lean rider in civilian clothes. An incongruous headgear, with a hanging cloth tied across like a mask, obscured most of his face. The leader reined in his horse as he reached Vijayan.

The Pandya soldier remained on his knees, keeping his hands raised and away from the sword's hilt. He didn't want there to be any confusion that he meant no harm. For the guards would have seen the many dead bodies already.

Another guard, mounted on his horse next to the slight, lean leader, spoke with barely disguised rage. 'So much killing! Around this holy land! This is preposterous, noble Amal! How can we allow this? You said they were your guests?!'

The slight, lean leader, Amal, gestured with his hands, appealing for calm from his comrade.

'Listen, my General Narasimhan needs help,' cried Vijayan, pointing to his commander. 'He has been stabbed with a poisoned arrow. He needs medical attention right now. In the name of the mighty Chola emperor, I demand that …'

'You will demand nothing!' shouted the angry guard. 'You and your general have broken laws here. We are temple guards. We don't answer to the emperor. We answer to our Gods.'

'You have a duty to help him!' Vijayan knew that he had little time to save his general.

'Quiet!' screamed the mounted rider they had addressed as Amal.

Vijayan fell silent. For many reasons. Firstly, at the plainly commanding tone of the slight, lean leader, Amal. But even more, at the clearly feminine voice of the leader.

Amal, the deputy, and the eldest child of Ahmadullah, the sitting custodian of the Vavar shrine. The eldest child was not a son, but a daughter.

The cloth covering the leader's face had come loose, revealing a delicate, pale face with small eyes, a tiny, pert nose and thin lips that glowed in the early-morning sunlight. Crowned by straight silken hair that fell to her shoulders. Amal, the daughter of Ahmadullah, a Keralite Muslim, and Tashi, a Tibetan Buddhist. Her Tibetan heritage clearly dominated her appearance.

'My sincere apologies for all this, great Chief Guard,' Amal said politely to the temple guard next to her. 'I am deeply ashamed at the pain and embarrassment caused to you. Please allow me to handle this situation.'

Evidently, Amal had tremendous credibility. The chief guard took a deep breath to control his outrage and let Amal handle the situation.

CHAPTER 9

The Pretender's Plot

Ghazni, Afghanistan

Ismail looked into the oval mirror and moved from side to side. Made from burnished copper, the mirror reflected a pleasing image. He raised his chin and stared at himself. Hard. He did not smile.

A servant boy placed a large fur surcoat around his shoulders and outstretched arms.

Not bad. Not bad at all.

He scanned the plush bedroom in the mufti's mansion and, at last, smiled. His valet and manservants withdrew with a bow. He looked again in the mirror.

Poor Ghazni! Dealing with a grotesque monster with delusions of Godhood all these years, when it had already experienced this fine gentleman as a ruler. No worries ... I am back now ...

Ismail had been here for a little over a month and had settled in well. The grand mansion of the second-oldest male of the Ghazni Royal House was second in splendour only to the sultan's palace, and the governor-mufti had spent the last month savouring the comfort and his newfound freedom.

Ismail barely spent his waking hours indoors. He had had enough of closed walls and confined spaces in Guzgan. He woke up well before sunrise, and itched to be out in the open. Every morning, he cleaned and groomed himself, ate breakfast and rushed to the tower of the Jama Mosque to personally give the *azan* for *fajr, calling the faithful for the dawn prayer.*

He then spent the remainder of the day visiting people and places. He sometimes visited the Garden of Jannat-e-Adan, frequented by the nobility. At other times he chose the Khalid Bazaar, packed to the gills with the hoi polloi—peasants who swarmed and haggled all day. Ismail gradually acquainted and endeared himself to the common people he was determined to rule one day. It was easy.

The noblemen were more difficult to please, on the other hand. They were less eager to accept him as a new figure of authority in Ghazni.

The *azan* from the Jama Mosque was answered only by a few of the faithful. Most kept away, fearing an inevitable collapse of the hastily repaired temporary structure, built to meet an unrealistic deadline. The original mosque had cleaved into two during the terrible earthquake three years earlier. The entire landmass had in fact been torn apart.

In a morbid instance of divine comedy, the splendid buildings of the rich and mighty, made of marble and other expensive stones, were reduced to dust, including the sultan's palace, while the humbler homes of the poor, made of mud and tears, had escaped nature's wrath. In the aftermath of the natural disaster, the wealthy cruelly cocked a snook at the will of divinity by rebuilding their plush homes using underpaid labour drawn from the city's peasantry. They weren't given fair wages, despite being impoverished as they already were, due to the earthquake. Why? Because they could always be replaced by the numerous Hindu–Buddhist slaves captured during Mahmud's regular raids into India, who obviously worked for free and barely subsistence-level food rations. Therefore, ironically, the presence of slaves, much like in the case of illegal immigrants, enriched the nobility, but impoverished the common citizens of Ghazni.

The sultan had led by example, exercising first claim over the resources and people of the land for his own needs and luxuries.

The deputies of the sultan came next. And then their subordinates. The chain of command had descended, step by step, till the hapless workers, stripped of their livelihoods and pulled into a vortex of reconstruction efforts, rued the day they had survived the cataclysm.

The elite enclaves of Ghazni had regained their former glory within two years, owing to this coerced frenzy of reconstruction and reparation. Most of its infrastructure was restored, except, ironically, the Jama Mosque. It failed to exercise precedence over the mansions of the powerful and the wealthy, despite the self-proclaimed piety of Mahmud of Ghazni.

The pious old previous grand mufti had, apparently, paid with his life for the delay and shoddy reconstruction of the mosque. Surreptitiously blaming the pompous sultan, the petrified populace desisted from freely voicing their contempt for Mahmud's impiety and debauchery. But they quickly warmed up to the austere religiosity, at least outwardly, of the new grand mufti, Ismail, who also doubled up as the governor of Ghazni city.

Ismail had the people in his pocket. He just had to convert the nobility. But gaining both at the same time wasn't easy. He knew that, behind his back, the nobility called him what they thought were insulting words, like 'populist'.

'The guests are here, My Lord,' Talib, his faithful head-servant, whispered from the doorway, interrupting Ismail's musings. 'The council of the sultan, led by the prime minister, Khwaja Hassan, is growing impatient. The prime minister wants to know if he can be granted an audience soon so he can leave and get on with his other duties.'

'His duties,' scoffed Ismail, still admiring his reflection in the mirror. 'The first thing that far, effete racketeer will do is go back to his house, quaff a jug of wine and fall on to his bed with some whores. Let them wait, Talib. They would have waited patiently without complaining if it were the sultan, or even the queen, wouldn't they?'

'Of course, My Lord! Let them wait.'

Ismail picked up his feathered headgear and brought it down slowly upon his neatly combed locks of grey. He checked his teeth in the mirror. 'Today, they will learn to wait for me. Tomorrow, they will wait *on* me,' he murmured.

'So it shall be, My Lord,' agreed Talib, saluting his master and withdrawing from his presence with a bow. Ismail walked to a *divan* by the wall. He plopped down on it and reached for a smoking pipe placed on a low stool. Bringing it to his lips, he inhaled deeply, taking in the dense opium fumes to calm his nerves. The governor-mufti's mind scanned the topics he hoped to discuss at the august gathering he had arranged.

Twenty minutes later he made his way to the audience hall. As he neared the area, he heard the chattering of six senior councillors of the sultan, and of the seventh, their leader, Khwaja Hassan. They were laughing, mocking him with the cruellest words.

A sudden silence descended as Ismail drew aside the translucent pink curtains. He stepped into the chamber and interlocked his hands behind himself. Seated in a crescent before the governor-mufti were the seven men he had invited. Some held cups of *sheer chai* while others smoked hookahs that had been set up for them.

None rose in respect. Seconds passed. And then one man rose to his feet: Khwaja Hassan. He bowed perfunctorily and then shuffled forward, his girth jiggling like a badly made *masghati*, a *soft jelly-like Persian sweet*. He halted close to the governor-mufti and kissed his hand theatrically, then embraced him.

The two men broke the embrace and held each other by the elbows. Hassan spoke first.

'It is good to see you at home and not bump into you in odd places, My Lord,' he said with an unmistakable air of haughtiness. 'Some of us were beginning to think your kindness is reserved only for the peasants.'

Ismail smiled cordially and looked at the other men. Without rising, they lazily brought their hands to their foreheads in a salaam. None had shown courtesy. Affronted though he was, Ismail knew that the sultan's men were only mirroring his brother's utter disregard of him over the decades. The governor-mufti took his seat while the prime minister waddled back to his *divan* and sat down. He looked at Ismail with his beady eyes, entwined his long-nailed fingers and rested them on his ample belly.

'My Lord,' said Khwaja Hassan. 'Thank you for inviting us home. As the prime minister of the Ghaznavid sultanate and the leader of these men, allow me to introduce this honourable assembly.'

Hassan spared no effort in displaying to the governor-mufti his authority while carefully adopting affected humility, bordering on servility.

'This is Farzad, My Lord, the Master of the Treasury,' said Khwaja Hassan, pointing a pudgy finger at a short, portly, balding, middle-aged man seated to Ismail's left. Farzad, the treasury man, nodded casually at the governor-mufti and shifted his glance respectfully towards the prime minister. Ismail hid his rage with the ease of a confidence trickster. He had perfected the skill of hiding his emotions and aggression when necessary, having learnt this art as a defence against his elder brother, Mahmud, who had taunted and belittled him for as long as he could remember.

But the opium helps as well, thought Ismail.

'My Lord,' continued Khwaja Hassan, indicating the man seated next to Farzad. 'This is Jaleel, the sultan's chief diplomat. Next to him is Qahhar, the supreme judge.'

Each man fleetingly nodded in the direction of the governor-mufti.

'Yazdan is the head of the city guard, and Baghish is controller of trade and commerce. And lastly ... umm ...'

Hassan faltered. Narrowing his eyes, he looked at the person seated to his left without recognition. The embarrassed young man leaned into the prime minister's ear and whispered.

'Badid, Minister of the Arts!' declared Khwaja Hassan jubilantly. The Turks were trying to show that they could be as civilized as the Persians and the Arabs, by promoting or at least pretending to promote the arts.

Badid looked at Ismail and bowed. 'Apologies, My Lord,' he spoke respectfully. 'I am new to the council.'

Ismail softened. He smiled at the young man.

Khwaja Hassan looked expectantly at the governor-mufti.

'Welcome, all of you.' Ismail smiled genially, pinning his eyes on the prime minister. 'I am honoured by your presence.'

'Oh, My Lord! Don't mention it!' Khwaja Hassan purred, pompously waving his hand. He leaned into the soft cushion behind him. 'I apologize that all my councillors are not here. One is missing …' He quickly scanned the group. 'Aah! Of course! Ashtaq is not here—the minister for religious affairs.'

Ismail's eyes became slits.

'A forgivable mistake, I'm sure,' Khwaja Hassan continued airily. 'The offices of Ghazni have changed a lot since you last held command over them, My Lord.' He smiled benignly.

The governor-mufti did not return his smile. It made the prime minister abandon the comfort of the soft cushion and straighten his back.

'We will get to Ashtaq momentarily,' assured Ismail. He savoured Khwaja Hassan's fleeting look of confusion and reached for the winecup offered to him on a tray by a wispy attendant. He took a sip and sloshed it around in his mouth. 'You are right,' Ismail continued. 'A lot has changed. A lot of garbage must be cleaned up. A lot of broken things need fixing.'

Khwaja Hassan raised his eyebrows.

'Tell me, Prime Minister,' Ismail said slowly. 'All of you survived the earthquake that ripped through the heart of Ghazni three years ago, did you not?'

'Evidently so.' Hassan smiled and looked around. 'Surely, we are not reanimated corpses here!'

The men laughed like triggered toys. Except for one.

'Seriously, though,' continued Hassan. 'Yes, we survived, by the grace of Allah. Those who did not … they were replaced expeditiously by the sultan. Why do you ask?'

'I have been doing some reading,' Ismail said. 'And I have been talking to people. They told me the largest buildings were the most affected and took the longest to rebuild. Official records detail the event and the reconstruction efforts that followed.'

'Pardon me, My Lord,' said the prime minister. 'I am not quite sure where this interrogation is going. My men and I have duties to attend to, much as we enjoy your company. The demands on our time are quite formidable. But I assure you, the largest buildings took the longest to rebuild. The sultan's palace was fully repaired in two and a half years. Half the subjects of the capital worked on it.'

'Interesting,' remarked Ismail, and then spoke slowly. 'The sultan's palace took two and half years to repair, and the Jama Mosque is almost the same size as my brother's home. I wonder what made him decree that I restore it to its former glory in six months. A bit ambitious, don't you think?'

'I am afraid I cannot offer any opinion on this, My Lord,' replied Khwaja Hassan sweetly. 'You are closer to your brother than I am.'

Ismail's expression froze.

'Did *you* put that preposterous idea into my brother's head?' the governor-mufti demanded, cutting to the chase. 'I received the sultan's deadline for the mosque reconstruction from *your* office, on a scroll with *your* seal.'

Khwaja Hassan turned red. 'You are accusing me of something that was not my doing,' he replied shakily, trying to muster sternness into his voice but sounding squeaky. 'You're accusing your brother, the sultan himself, of mischief. Excuse me, My Lord, but I must cut this conversation short.'

He edged forward on the *divan*, quite nimbly for a man his size.

'Oh, and by the way,' the prime minister continued, 'the grains of sand are flowing down the hourglass even as we speak, My Lord. If I were you, I would get on the job immediately. You know how fate punished the previous grand mufti …'

Khwaja Hassan began to rise from the *divan* but stumbled. The heavy gold chains around his neck yanked his head farther down. He straightened himself up with all the decorum he could muster, while the other men quickly put aside their smoking pipes and winecups. They came to their feet and followed him, like puppets.

Ismail remained seated, unfazed.

'Wait, My Lords.' He was humming, sonorous, an apologetic smile playing on his lips. 'Are you offended? Oh, but I was merely venting my frustration at this difficult task. I do believe I am in the company of friends. Aren't I?'

'Goodbye, My Lord,' Khwaja Hassan said brusquely. 'As you well know, if you want any support on the mosque reconstruction, you will have to discuss it with my deputy,

Ashtaq. He is in charge of providing all the administrative support for your Religious Affairs department responsibilities. He is the one you did not invite to this little morning party.'

Khwaja Hassan began walking away. Like chickens, the other ministers fell in line behind him.

Ismail smirked as he placed his cup of wine on the side table and rose to his feet. 'But I doubt Ashtaq will be of much help to me, dear Prime Minister. I am afraid he was picked up by my *Jundiin-ul-Din, the religious police who directly serve the grand mufti of Ghazni* …' His voice was soft and mellifluous, but the menace in it was clear.

Khwaja Hassan stopped in his tracks. As did the men behind him.

'I think,' the governor-mufti continued, 'they unearthed some disturbing evidence. Ashtaq was embezzling funds that had been collected as *jaziya*, which is a *religious tribute paid by non-Muslims to our Islamic state*, and therefore comes under the jurisdiction of the religious police. You would agree that this cannot be condoned by decent and pious men like us.'

The governor-mufti's words dramatically transformed the room. The men of the council stood rooted to their spots. Paralysed. Some had panic displayed clearly on their faces. The religious police had never dared to go after one of them; it targeted only the powerless. Khwaja Hassan remained outwardly calm, staring at Ismail. He was too seasoned a courtier to lose control and display an unnecessary reaction. But there was a hint of a bead of sweat on his temple.

Ismail noticed and savoured the moment. *The fat blob also has his hands in the till, it seems … Time to strike the hammer …*

'My men presented the evidence to the sultan before you slithered out of your bedsheets this morning,' Ismail said. 'Ashtaq's life is in my dear brother's capable hands now. I have a feeling he will ask me to further investigate this embezzlement issue. And all those who benefited from it.'

Khwaja Hassan continued staring at Ismail, his expression stoic. But more beads of sweat appeared around his temples.

'Perhaps you can help me, Farzad. Together we can get to the bottom of this strange case, hmmm?' The governor-mufti threw a mischievous look at the master of the treasury, who shifted his gaze to the ground. 'Let us see how deep this rot runs. Or should I say how *high*?'

'My Lord ...' Khwaja Hassan spoke slowly, his podgy face red, his expression an intriguing mix of anger and nervousness. 'I was not aware of this at all. Happening under my very nose! That swine, Ashtaq! I trusted him, gave him his opening in the court! We can never trust those oily Arabs. Locust-eaters, I tell you. His punishment must be most severe. He must receive only one penalty. And that is ...'

'Death,' completed Ismail ominously. 'The penalty for any embezzlement from the sultan is death. As is the penalty for trafficking infidel slaves in an underground market without giving the State its share of property tax. Now, I wonder, how could this be happening under your nose, dear Prime Minister? Many other embezzlements come to mind, really ... The distribution of the war booty ... The purchase of supplies for the army ... The acquisition of horses from Tajikistan ... The list just goes on and on. Sometimes, I think that there are so many scams, maybe even you aren't aware of all of them, great Khwaja. Or are you?' The last line was delivered perfectly by the governor-mufti. Slow and severe.

His attack had the intended effect. Khwaja Hassan was smart enough to know when he had been beaten. He controlled the look of shock on his face.

How does he know so much in such a short time? Who from the nobility is informing him?

The tension in the room was palpable, suffocating all but the placid governor-mufti.

Khwaja Hassan knew. He knew the information he had to reveal. To save his obese hide.

'It was not my idea, My Lord—this six-month deadline to repair the mosque,' the prime minister broke down, bowing low, bleating like a lamb being led to slaughter. His philosophy was clear: When you surrender, surrender completely—so that the enemy may show some mercy. 'I had nothing to do with it. I was only the messenger, My Lord; I was the arrow that was let loose.'

The governor-mufti walked to Khwaja Hassan and placed a hand on his shoulder. 'You were the arrow, yes,' Ismail said. 'My brother was the bow. Who was the bowman?'

The prime minister looked at his men with pleading, drowning eyes. They transferred their gaze to their feet, or the wall.

Rats!

Khwaja Hassan turned to Ismail.

'It was a bow-woman, My Lord,' whispered the prime minister.

I knew it! thought Ismail, but he remained silent. He wanted to hear the name spoken aloud. That would signal the prime minister's complete surrender.

'The queen, Kausari Jahan ...' Khwaja Hassan continued, in an even softer tone, afraid that the walls may hear. 'She summoned me to the sultan's winter palace in the morning, four weeks ago. The sultan was asleep, but the queen was waiting for me in the antechamber of the royal bedroom.'

The prime minister stopped, hoping this revelation would satisfy his tormentor. He had already revealed too much. For when two elephants fight, it is usually the grass underfoot that gets trampled first.

'Go on,' the governor-mufti urged. 'Your life hangs on this information,' he added sinisterly.

The condemned man continued.

'She conveyed to me the sultan's desire to test your faith and devotion to the family, My Lord. She asked that you be informed that you had six months to complete the repairs on the mosque. I told my men to draft the order that very day, but I lost track of getting it delivered to you. I assure you, My Lord, I dispatched the communique as soon as I remembered my lapse.'

'Which was four days ago,' Ismail reminded icily. 'I received a time-sensitive order almost a month after it should have reached me. Now I am left with *five* months to finish the task instead of six.'

The prime minister hung his head. 'I am sorry, My Lord. It was a careless mistake. I was …'

'Busy, no doubt.' Ismail smiled, tapping Hassan's shoulder in camaraderie. 'Things are about to get a lot busier for you and your men, I am afraid. As you are well aware, I have … limited resources … with which to take on a task such as this. The Jundiin-ul-Din are good enforcers of the Holy Law but they are lousy stonemasons. I will need help to clear this web that has been woven around me.'

As he spoke the words, Ismail scanned every man in the room. Minutes back, they had treated him with scant respect. They stood now with bent bodies, fearful and submissive. Completely submissive.

'I will need your help, my friend,' Ismail said, pinning his eyes on Khwaja Hassan again. 'You and your fine men will find the money and the workers to begin repairs on the mosque immediately.'

'Anything you say, My Lord.' Khwaja Hassan eagerly jumped at the reprieve offered. 'What would you like me to do?'

'Find the architects, engineers, stonemasons, water carriers … Everyone and everything needed in this endeavour. Build me a workers' city around the mosque and see that we work overtime, round the clock. I will meet the sultan's deadline. Our collective good depends on it, does it not?'

'Of course, My Lord,' Khwaja Hassan said eagerly, bobbing his head up and down like a baby elephant. 'I will do all I can, I assure you. Right away.'

'Right away,' repeated Ismail, wagging his index finger like a schoolmaster. 'And from now onwards, I expect you to protect my interests with the sultan and the queen. I hear you are particularly close to the queen. I will expect first-hand information about anything that transpires in your meetings with the royal couple. I want to be well informed in *all* matters, at *all* times. Is that understood?'

The prime minister struggled with his words when the extent of Ismail's newfound strings of manipulation dawned on him. But he knew when he had been beaten.

'My Lord …' the prime minister whispered. 'As you command …'

There will always be opportunities in the future to pull back. Life is long … Khwaja Hassan kept his thoughts to himself as he bent forward to kiss the back of Ismail's outstretched right hand. The other council members also lined up and kissed Ismail's hand one by one.

Having got what he wanted, Ismail suddenly whirled around and walked towards the curtains leading to the private chambers. The subjugated prime minister and his deputies stood rooted like lifeless statues.

'You are dismissed,' he boomed as he disappeared behind the curtains. 'Let me not keep you from your duties.'

The governor-mufti's voice dispersed slowly in the thick air.

—◦ৡ◦—

'That was perfectly done, Sire.' Talib beamed from ear to ear. He had been listening carefully to the conversation from the secret spyhole that Ismail had installed in the mansion. While the idea for the meeting was Talib's, the execution of the plan by the governor-mufti had been flawless. The manservant smiled. This was his master's domain. Court intrigue. He was made for it. Not for battle and violence, an area in which his brother Mahmud was far superior, and where his master's loss was not a matter of surprise.

Talib was happy. For if the master did well, the loyal servants prospered too.

Ismail didn't react to the compliment. 'Kausari Jahan … That Kashmiri witch … She got it done.'

But my master's tendency to panic still remains.

'You have solved the problem, My Lord,' Talib said reassuringly. 'Khwaja Hassan is resourceful, like most of these Persian bureaucrats. He will find all the resources you need to complete the mosque in time.'

'But how much does Kausari know?' Ismail shrieked. Anxiety tended to make his voice shriller. 'Do you think she knows about the letters we have sent out?'

'No, she doesn't, My Lord. Our men are trustworthy. I think she is just playing her normal womanly games since she knows that you are the biggest threat to her control over the sultan. Her relationship with Sultan Mahmud is her only source of power. She will defend it like a wounded she-wolf.'

'I want to keep an eye on her. I want to hear about everything she does.'

'But the prime minister said that he would …'

'Khwaja is a peacock. He only knows what the family allows him to hear. They only use him to carry out their orders. The information that Khwaja Hassan will give me will always be second-hand. I need more. I need what only an inside man is privy to.'

'My Lord, that has risks … I wouldn't use …'

'I want to keep an eye on her! You tell him. He will never say no to me!'

Talib nodded. He knew whom to speak with.

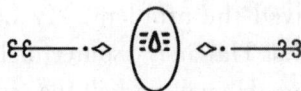

CHAPTER 10

Blood and Belonging

Somewhere in the Arabian Sea

Vijayan stood on the foredeck of a small schooner as it slipped into the waters from the coastal village of Alappuzha, some thirty miles south of Kochi. He wrapped his palms around the wooden rail and stared at the North Star gleaming in the velvet black sky.

The deputy commander of the Ghazni-bound assassination squad closed his eyes as his mind flooded with the memory of the storm of events that had blindsided the Chola squad in the forests around the sacred Sabarimala Temple around two weeks ago, during which Narasimhan had been grievously injured.

Luckily, the poisoned arrow had not penetrated any vital organ of the brave general. But the wound was deep. By the time Amal's troops had taken him to their infirmary, his breathing had become shallow, and his pulse rate was extremely low. His body had felt cold and clammy, and his skin was soaked with sweat. The muscles around the wound, particularly on his back and shoulder, twitched spasmodically. His eyes were shut, though his eyelids throbbed with perturbation.

It was quite unusual for someone of Narasimhan's size to be knocked unconscious and develop such serious symptoms just because of one arrow lacerating his upper back. Evidently, the poison was extremely potent.

But Amal was descended from a long line of priests and mystic healers. She understood the secrets of Ayurvedic medicine better than most. At the shrine infirmary, she had quickly identified the poison and saved Narasimhan's life. However, the effects of the venom were so severe, it had practically paralysed the Chola general's right shoulder and arm. His sword arm. For a warrior, this was worse than death. He had also been weakened deeply and was mostly bedridden.

Vijayan opened his eyes and snapped out of his recollections of that fateful day. He turned around and leaned against the wooden rail of the schooner, looking vaguely at the fading lights from the coastal village of Alappuzha.

His mind went back to the aftermath of the event. They had rejoined the rest of the Chola assassination squad and lain low, with help from Amal. Along with her trusted men, she had expeditiously captured and killed the Arab mercenaries that the Chalukyans had met in Kollam, to ensure that there would be no attack on them at sea. But one could not be sure who else the Chalukyans, or indeed the Arab mercenaries, had conspired with. Maintaining the secrecy of the Chola squad and their mission was of supreme importance. Therefore, the rest house at the foot of the Sabari hills, where the Chola men had stayed, had 'accidentally burnt to cinders'. Amal had arranged to buy the rest house with funds from the Vavar shrine treasury and then packed it with the bodies of the dead Chalukyans as well as unclaimed corpses from the burial ground. She had clothed the unclaimed bodies in Chola armour and set the building ablaze. Thus, an elaborate smokescreen was created. It appeared as if the Cholas and Chalukyans had wiped each other out in an orgy of vengeful violence.

Amal, Someshwar and Vijayan had decided to not inform the Chera and Chola headquarters about the ruse and that the men were safe. The risk of interception of a message far outweighed the peace of mind of their benefactors. Just one secret encrypted communication, in a private code privy only to Narasimhan and Rajendra Chola, which the general had briefed Vijayan about, was used to inform the emperor directly, through one simple note: *Mission still on. Will update further when appropriate.* The news of Narasimhan's serious injury had not been revealed to Rajendra Chola. Both Narasimhan and Vijayan felt it would be an unnecessary burden on the emperor.

Despite all these precautions, the ever-suspicious Vijayan decided to not set sail from the well-known merchant port of Kochi and, instead, departed from the nondescript Alappuzha, a fishing village thirty miles south of their original port of departure. The backwaters of Alappuzha had access to the open sea.

Amal had family in the village that owned a small fishing schooner. It would suffice.

Secretly, they had set out for the coast of Balochistan.

'Valeed?'

Amal's mellifluous voice floated in from the side. Vijayan turned and looked at her heart-shaped face glowing dimly in the moonlight. Valeed was the name that Vijayan carried now, to enable him to blend into life in Ghazni when they arrived there. Amal had suggested that they start practising with the name immediately, so that Vijayan could fit into his assumed identity credibly.

'Yes, Amal?' Vijayan asked.

'It is time for the *namaz*,' Amal reminded him softly. 'The movements should come naturally to you so that nobody suspects you in the Ghaznavid lands. And then, of course, we need to arrange Arabic lessons for you. Followed by coaching in Turkic courtesies. Come on. Everybody is waiting.'

Vijayan remained quiet. He still hadn't come to terms with the fact that Amal was a woman. A woman capable of administration, strategy and navigation. Even more shockingly, capable of violence, when necessary.

Amal stared at Vijayan. She crossed her arms across her chest and stepped forward.

'Listen ... Valeed,' she repeated, using Vijayan's assumed name with emphasis. 'I am not here because of an emperor's decree, nor am I here because the king of the Chera lands wants me here. I am here because it is my own duty to my land and my faith. When I tell you to do something, the only objective in my mind is the mission.'

Vijayan was immediately contrite. 'I am sorry, Amal. You misread ...'

'It is my responsibility to get all of you to Ghazni safely. And hopefully prepare you better for the mission ahead. So outside of any battle that we are forced into, you have to follow my instructions. I might be a woman, but you will need to follow my orders on this ship.'

'I am sorry,' said Vijayan. 'I mean no disrespect at all. It's just that we had all expected Amal to be a man.'

'Well, Amal is a woman,' she said. 'Deal with it.'

'Yes, Ma'am.'

Amal turned and stared into the distance, holding the ship balustrade. Still fuming.

Vijayan changed the subject, ending the awkward silence. 'Why is it your duty to your land and your faith?'

Amal looked at Vijayan, frowning in confusion.

Vijayan clarified further, 'You said that you had agreed to come on this mission for your land and your faith ... I didn't understand.'

'You didn't understand because ... Because my faith is Islam? Apparently, the same faith as that barbarian Turk Mahmud?'

'Yes.'

Amal took a deep breath. 'You know ... The news of the desecration of Somnath*ar* Temple reached us on the day of *Makara Sankranti* many years ago—you visited the Sabari hills with your men on the same day, only weeks ago ... Ever since I was a child, I have adored Ayyappan more than anything or anyone else ... I have adored Him even more than my own parents. That is the way it is with us followers of the Vavar shrine. We are Muslims, yes. But we are Muslim devotees of Lord Ayyappan. There is no contradiction in that.'

Vijayan nodded. He understood. He was a devotee of the Goddess Meenakshi. His sister was a Buddhist. His mother was a Jain. His father was a follower of the formless Nirgun

Nirakar. This is the way it has always been with Indians. Respect for all forms of the Divine.

Amal's voice faltered. 'And Lord Ayyappan's Father had been insulted … In such a brutal manner …'

As all devotees of Lord Ayyappan knew, the great Bachelor God was the son of Lord Shiva and Goddess Mohini.

'I was distributing water to the devotees of the temple,' she continued. 'It was *Makara Sankranti*. The zenith of the pilgrimage season in Sabarimala. And do you know how many devotees came that day?'

Vijayan shook his head. *No.*

'*Fifteen* pilgrims!' exclaimed Amal, roughly tucking her silky, straight hair behind her ears. 'Fifteen—that's it! And these fifteen men were there because they were probably the only people in south India who had not yet heard of what had happened in Somnath*ar* Temple—in the Temple of my Lord Ayyappan's Father, Lord Shiva. My grandmother had told me once that Hindus do not visit temples for a period following a death in the family. And a death in the family there was … The people mourned that day, Valeed. They mourned the slaughter and desecration of our God's glory, our honour, our pride and unity as the sons and daughters of the great soil of Mother India.'

'It was the same in Madurai,' said Vijayan. 'The temple bells at the Meenakshi Temple did not ring for days in mourning.'

'I was with my parents when we heard the news,' Amal said. 'The streets were deserted for days. People living in the same homes did not talk to each other that day. In our earlier wars, the victors had only taken over the administration of the places of worship they conquered. But this, this return of barbarism that we had last seen when the Huns had attacked some centuries ago ... It shattered our soul ...'

'But I was surprised at how quickly people moved on ...' Vijayan said softly. 'Getting back to regular life. Within just a few months.'

Amal took a sharp breath. 'Yes ... We Indians have a strength that is also our weakness. We let go of our past hatred and grief. Like Gautama Buddha had advised us to. We move on ...'

'*Charaiveti, charaiveti.*' Vijayan quoted a famous mantra from the Aitareya Upanishad, which translated as *keep walking, keep walking*. Essentially, one must move on from the past, so that you can rebuild.

'It works many times, this attitude ...' said Amal. 'I will not deny that. We don't wallow in past enmities and grief. We pick ourselves up and move on. But many people from other nations are unlike us Indians. They refuse to move on. That's why you find so many communities across the world blaming the descendants of those who oppressed their ancestors. Wanting reparations and vengeance now, many centuries after the crimes had occurred. On the other hand, we Indians usually move on and rebuild our lives. That is why we always bounce back. That is why we are always successful. We don't become prisoners of the past.'

'True.'

'But ...' said Amal. And as a wise man had once said, what is truly important in a long monologue, is what comes after the 'but'. 'But, while many of us Indians may forget, some of us have to remember. We have to remember, and we have to avenge. So that our enemies learn a lesson: they cannot commit crimes against us and then pretend as if nothing has happened. So many of our enemies want to trade with us and make money off our economy, telling us to let past crimes be for now. Our enemies then win both ways; they can attack us when they want to, and yet make money from us too. They don't like Indians, but they like Indian money. That cannot be allowed to continue. That is why some of us Indians have to remember. We must bide our time if we have to. But we must remember. And we must strike back. Maybe not immediately, maybe some time later. Maybe even five hundred years later. But we must strike back. So that a clear message is sent to our enemies: If you want to mess with us, factor our guaranteed vengeance into your calculations for we will hit back. Hard.' Amal looked directly into Vijayan's eyes. 'But this stubborn refusal to forget and the desire for vengeance requires focus and discipline.'

Vijayan started laughing. 'And that is precisely what many of us Hindus don't have. We have many other strengths, creativity, passion, an ability to forgive and move on ... But yes, we don't do focus and discipline. At least, most of us don't ...'

Amal smiled. 'I agree ... That is why you need us Indian Muslims. Because we are very focused and disciplined. We don't have some of the strengths that you Hindus have. But we have other strengths ... And among them are certainly focus and discipline.'

Vijayan smiled.

Amal continued, 'And that is the responsibility of the Indian Muslim devotees of Lord Shiva ... We must remain focused and disciplined. We must not forget. We must make these foreigners feel the pain for their crimes. So that they never dare to do it again. That is why I fight. For Lord Ayyappan and his Father—the Mahadev.'

Vijayan nodded. His fists were clenched tight. 'By Meenakshi of Madurai, that is precisely why I fight as well.'

'I am grateful that Allah Himself has given me this opportunity to contribute to my Motherland. I will do my duty.'

'I know you will,' Vijayan smiled.

Amal smiled back and playfully boxed Vijayan lightly on his shoulder. 'Now you need to learn the ways of Valeed so that you can blend in while we are in Ghazni.'

'May I be frank?' asked Vijayan.

'Of course,' said Amal.

'I don't have a flair for languages. I cannot learn an alien language in a few days or even a few weeks, no matter how hard I try,' admitted Vijayan.

'You no try,' came a feeble voice from behind. It was Iqbal, Someshwar's usually silent friend. He had arrived undetected and was now attempting to speak Tamil, which he had picked up from the Cholas.

'Sir.' Vijayan bowed to the older man and brought his hands together in a respectful namaste.

'I learn your language. At least somewhat. In very small time,' continued Iqbal, gesturing with his fingers to emphasize how much he had accomplished in a short time. 'You can learn language too. But you no try.'

'I will push myself, Sir,' assured Vijayan, relenting.

'Good, Valeed,' said Iqbal, using Vijayan's assumed name. 'Get used to your new identity so that you can fulfil our mission in Ghazni.'

'Right … I promise,' said Vijayan, though he couldn't think of how to fulfil his mission without his general. 'How is General Narasimhan?'

Iqbal smiled and shook his head. 'He is a special man, that general of yours.'

'Still practising?' asked Vijayan.

Once at sea, Narasimhan's weakness had abated and he regained some strength, which allowed him to move. But his right shoulder and arm remained paralysed. Amal and her talented physicians had only been able to extract parts of the arrowhead. Some splinters embedded in the wound had been impossible to remove. The arrowhead had, somehow, shattered within Narasimhan's back when he was stabbed by the Chalukyan. It was a bizarre alloy of various metals. Perhaps made from cutting-edge, experimental technology. It was, in a way, a metallic alloy which should have been a scientific disaster—a metal that fragments on impact is of little use for most traditional uses of the material. But it was very important in an arrowhead since it made the removal of the offending projectile very difficult for a surgeon. And this material continued to slowly poison Narasimhan.

But the Chola general's warrior spirit had been reawakened by the clash with the Chalukyas. And for a warrior, mere paralysis is just a roadblock to be negotiated, not a cause for retirement. Narasimhan had been practising below deck regularly with his Chola soldiers. Every day. Learning to wield a sword with his left arm. He was, in effect, starting from scratch again, but he had already made decent progress.

'Yes, he is still practising,' said Iqbal, answering Vijayan's question. 'I have never met a soldier as capable as General Narasimhan.'

'Narasimhan's name is Nasrullah from here onwards, Sir,' said Amal. 'Let me remind you, Someshwar is Salman, and you … you remain Iqbal, of course. As I was explaining to *Valeed* here,' she added, looking pointedly at Vijayan, 'we *must* get invested in our new identities. We are travelling to a country of fanatics, Sir. Our performance must be immaculate when we arrive in Gwadar. Even minor mistakes can be costly. Like if someone calls your assumed name, and you don't even respond because you are not used to that being your name.'

'Nasrullah, Salman and, of course, I remain Iqbal,' said Iqbal, smiling warmly at the young woman.

'You know, I don't mean to be rude,' said Vijayan, 'but it just feels strange when you call me by a name which is not mine. My identity and my faith are sacred to me. I flinch every time I am called "Valeed" and made to follow customs alien to my faith.'

Amal stepped closer and looked straight into his eyes.

'Valeed … or Vijayan, if it pleases you,' she said, 'I am not trying to convert you to a new faith. Any customs that you follow will only be those that don't contradict your own faith. Nothing more. And you do not need to master a new language. You just have to learn a few crucial words and phrases, and practise a few rituals. Adopt the customs of the Turkics for a short time … a very short time. This mission is not about changing who we are. On the contrary, it is about fighting for the beliefs you—and we—have held all our lives. Trust me on this. I beg you.'

Iqbal chimed in cheerily, in Tamil, 'Learning new name and language no big deal. Only bridge to cross to destination. Once bridge crossed, go back to old identity.'

'And thank you for growing the *beard*. It is called the *lihyah*,' Amal said, her voice trilling with playful mirth. 'It looks good on you.'

With that, she turned and walked off.

Vijayan felt the blood rush to his face. He touched the rough hair of the young stubble around his chin. And smiled ever so slightly.

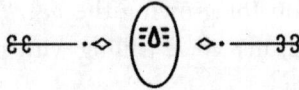

CHAPTER 11

Among Strangers

Ghazni, Afghanistan

The slave girl stumbled out of the emir's bedchamber, barely able to walk. Her dishevelled hair struggled to hide her swollen lips and bruised jawline. Coagulated blood under her thin skin appeared like a bloody map that bridged across her left blackeye and disappeared into her hairline. She let out a barely audible but achingly desperate sob.

This latest instalment of her ordeal had made her fear for her life. She was terrified.

Spotting Talib walking towards her in the passage, she pulled her scarf across her chest and face. Shame and inexplicable guilt made her close her eyes.

Talib came closer. He immediately recognized the slave girl. Yazadeh. A thirteen-, or at most, fourteen-year-old girl. From the Yazidi tribe. Her father was a slave of Governor-Mufti Ismail as well.

Talib looked down. Almost like not acknowledging what was happening would make the crime disappear. A little girl.

A child. Suffering which no child should have to endure. Talib shuddered. But he had learnt over many years to keep his mouth shut and pretend to ignore the crimes of his master. He continued to look down. 'Go … Please go to… Reshma …'

The little girl, Yazadeh, did not answer. She stared at the wall blankly. Fearful.

'Go to the main servant's chamber,' said Talib, still staring at the floor, his eyes averted from the girl's. 'Reshma … Reshma will help you dress your … your wounds …'

The girl forced herself to nod, avoiding eye contact with the head of the governor's household. She wiped a drop of blood from her upper lip with a trembling finger. Then scampered off and disappeared down the hallway.

'Talib?' Ismail's voice sounded from within the bedchamber. 'Is that you?'

Talib took a deep breath and shuddered again. But he had a strong sense of self-preservation. That is the only way he had survived for so long. He composed a smile on his face and entered his master's bedchamber.

The air inside was thick with the excessively sweet aroma of opium. Coughing, Talib waved a hand before his nose in a vain effort to clear the air.

Ismail sat half-dressed on the plush floor cushions in the left corner of the room, inhaling from a snake-shaped opium pipe. 'Come, old friend. Take a seat.'

Talib bowed low and walked to his master. He kneeled, kissed the governor-mufti's hand ceremonially and sat on a frugal cushion beside his master.

'You look tired this evening,' Ismail said jauntily. 'Is everything alright?'

'You can read me like an open book, My Lord,' answered Talib. 'A lot more servants to manage here than in Guzgan. And the royal court ...'

Ismail shook his head. 'Yes, the court ... It really drains one out.'

'Yes, My Lord. Too many moving parts to manage. And all of it has to be done so carefully.'

'Do what I tell you to do, and we will soon have complete control. Then we will manage the court as easily as we manage my household.' Ismail laughed.

Talib laughed along politely.

'We must celebrate. I have received good news,' said Ismail, holding up a letter.

Talib looked at the circular black seal stamped at the bottom. The seal was broken.

Ismail continued, 'The caliphate—the *real* one—and, more importantly, their Persian Buyid allies, have dispatched men by sea to *deal* with the sultan, if you know what I mean.' Ismail winked. 'Share a smoke with me. Enjoy!'

The governor-mufti gestured towards a hookah to his left and bade his servant to smoke.

'Thank you, My Lord,' said Talib. 'Indeed, this is good news ... Things are going exactly as you planned. Who would have thought that these pretentious and soft Persians would have been of use against lion-like Turks ...'

Ismail laughed softly. 'Sometimes, water can be used to erode stone.'

'Undoubtedly. You are the wise ruler that Ghazni deserves, My Lord.'

'So true,' agreed Ismail.

'My Lord,' Talib continued cautiously, 'I know you are always careful. Appearances have to be maintained so that we can take control of the court. But we should keep our habits within the household, where they can be managed.' Talib was talking as carefully as he could for his own sake, of Ismail's addiction to beating women. 'If we bring in any outsider, then it may be difficult for me to control leaks.'

Ismail was in a good mood, having just gotten his fill of Yazadeh. So he was willing to listen. 'Alright, fine! Don't bring that stunning African slave girl from the market! Happy now?'

Talib bowed low. 'My only objective is your success, My Master. Your success is my only goal in life ...'

'I know, I know ...' Ismail was in an expansive mood. 'I only wish this Yazadeh girl would fight back so I could subdue her some more. She is a bit dull ... no reciprocation of my passionate and deeply felt love.'

'I will try to instruct Yazadeh, Sire,' said Talib. 'Or maybe we can get someone else? Someone older?'

'No. Speak to that Yazadeh girl. Or maybe ... You know I have a fondness for ebony skin. Is there anyone else?'

'It's a matter of a few months more ... You will soon have the throne of Ghazni in your grasp. Then there will be nobody to stop you from taking what is rightfully yours. For now, we just have to be careful.'

'Alright ... alright ... But let us not celebrate too soon,' said Ismail, his expression turning serious. 'That crazy shrew—Kausari Jahan—has been making it very difficult for me to complete the mosque reconstruction. She first tried to prevent me from recruiting manpower from the city, so I had to appropriate Hassan's slaves. She then blocked some of the funding for the purchase of the building material ... The deadline approaches like the swing of an executioner's sword.'

Talib nodded, grimly, this time.

'Have you met my son?' asked Ismail. 'Only he can solve this money problem.'

Unknown to all, Ismail had a son. To be fair, his existence had been kept a secret from Ismail himself till relatively recently. By good fortune, his son was very well-placed to help Ismail.

'I have asked for a meeting, Sire. I will be speaking with him later today.'

'Every moment's delay is a risk for us.'

'I understand, My Lord.'

'Also, plan to leave for Gwadar quickly. I need a trusted man to welcome the Abbasid caliph's ambassadors.'

Gwadar was the main port in Balochistan. It served as the naval trading hub for the largely land-focused Ghaznavid empire.

'Yes, Sire.'

—◦✦◦—

Ismail stood in the portico of the great mosque of Ghazni in the late afternoon, Yazadeh and Talib a few discreet steps behind him. Against Talib's repeated advice of not displaying Yazadeh in public, Ismail had insisted that she be brought along to the mosque construction site. Talib had realized that his master, Ismail, was getting increasingly obsessed with the Yazidi slave girl.

Ismail watched the Jundiin-ul-Din flog six hundred slave labourers into a disciplined line. The dreaded religious police walked with precision, lashing the whip and swinging the baton with relish.

Farther in the distance was a collection of cages crammed with children and the elderly. On Ismail's orders, the children and elderly were used for less arduous work, such as cleaning, watering the stones and feeding the main workers. Guarded by a sparse bunch of the Jundiin-ul-Din, the prisoners clung to their cages and watched their loved ones with eyes drained of hope and the will to live.

Over the course of the past week, the lives of the infidel slaves had taken an unexpected turn. Imprisoned by Khwaja Hassan in a safe house at the outskirts of the city, the thousand men, women and children had been surviving in captivity like animals ever since they had been brought to Ghazni's black market.

The slaves belonged to various religions spread across the lands in and around the Ghaznavid sultanate. These were faiths that had held on to their practices with remarkable tenacity, faced with the hostile forces that now controlled those regions. Among them were Yazidis, Jews, Zoroastrians, Christians … But the largest contingent among the slaves, due to the sheer population in their native land, was of the Hindus and Buddhists.

After receiving the governor-mufti's ultimatum, Khwaja Hassan had desperately scrambled to retrieve the slaves he had sold off, offering their aggrieved owners double and sometimes triple of what they had paid him. He had then diverted all available manpower for the urgent task of repairing the Jama Mosque.

The governor-mufti had refused to take any of these new slaves as his personal staff. He only wanted the ones who had served him over the years in Guzgan to be in his household. The misery they had collectively suffered during the incarceration of the governor-mufti had created a loyal band of people who would not betray the conspiracies being hatched in the household against the sultan. Of course, the reason given for not taking in any slaves was that the governor-mufti desired no extra help for himself and wanted all manpower to be dedicated to the reconstruction of the mosque—an act which only burnished Ismail's public image further.

'The task is virtually impossible, Sir. We cannot clear out the ruins of the old, partially repaired mosque and rebuild a new structure within this tight deadline,' explained Butrus, a Christian slave the governor-mufti had placed in charge of the mammoth reconstruction effort. Before his enslavement, the slave had been an architect and engineer. 'We will need to fuse the structure along the cracks—the great split in the ceiling and on the floor,' said Butrus.

Ismail listened intently.

'For this, we must chip off the loose pieces in the recesses and then fill them with molten iron. That will reinforce the structure. We will then seal the remaining imperfections with mortar to provide a continuity of colour and texture. And this will only be the beginning ...'

There was a sudden commotion in the periphery of the mosque premises. It distracted the governor-mufti from the briefing being provided by the knowledgeable Christian. He looked at the crowd separating like the sea in front of Moses. The sultan and his queen had arrived.

Ismail was expecting them. He waved aside the Christian and looked at Mahmud's private guards and Kausari's eunuch soldiers tightly surrounding the regal couple, parting only at the base of the mosque steps. Mahmud stomped forward while his wife glided gracefully up the broad treads and tiny risers. Behind the royal couple was Malik Ayaz, the Georgian former slave, the King of Lahore and, most importantly, the lover of the sultan.

Ismail bowed to welcome the royal couple. Butrus quickly stepped back and joined Yazadeh and Talib. The two slaves fell to their knees, their heads bowed low, while Talib remained standing.

On reaching the portico, the guards and eunuchs formed a perimeter around the group. Ismail walked up to Mahmud with outstretched arms. Mahmud smiled and embraced his brother, who broke the embrace and kissed his brother's cheeks and then his right hand. The governor-mufti looked at the queen and bowed briefly without bending his back.

Kausari Jahan looked carefully at Yazadeh and Butrus, her expression severe, unsmiling. Her eyes lingered on Yazadeh and then shifted back to Ismail. She didn't even notice Talib.

Ismail returned the gaze. The queen's exquisitely flouncy gown, embroidered with fine gold and silver threads, was held together by a silver silken belt around her slim waist. A large black stone shone on her bosom, held in place by a sheer gossamer thread around her long, unblemished neck. Her piercing blue-green eyes glared at him with unmistakable but magisterial hostility.

'Why are those children and old people caged and displayed?' the queen asked imperiously. 'They wallow in blood and excrement like filthy pigs. This is against what I have learnt of Islam.'

'Slaves are our property, noble Queen.' Ismail smiled condescendingly. He did not miss Mahmud looking towards his wife and rolling his eyes. 'To do with as we wish … The stronger ones work every waking moment. The weaker ones are kept in cages till they are brought out for cleaning duties and any other auxiliary work that may be required. And the ones in the cages … they are better off … they do less work. Our Turkic mercy, as the entire world knows, is boundless. These slave vermin get their food on time and are not whipped while they carry heavy masonry. And … wallowing in blood and excrement? You do me grave injustice with that exaggeration, My Lady. My men wash the slaves and their cages with pails of water every morning, before sunrise.'

'Ah, of course! Pails of *freezing* water thrown over these malnourished elders and children every icy Ghazni morning.' The queen laughed mirthlessly. 'Freezing to death can be a kindness sometimes, I admit.'

'Stop it, you two!' snapped the sultan, extending his arms with the palms facing out, as if holding them apart. 'I am here at the governor-mufti's request to deliver a message of compassion to the slaves. I must motivate them to get this job done on time so that more important tasks can be accomplished.' He looked pointedly at Ismail, and spat on the floor as his energy wilted under the strong sun. 'These slaves drop like flies every day, and the work proceeds at a tiresome pace.'

The alternating extremes of piercingly cold nights and baking hot days were taking their toll. Mahmud didn't care for the slaves' comfort. But dead slaves cannot build mosques. At least that's what Kausari had pointed out to him. Perhaps motivation would work where fear and the bullwhip hadn't.

'How many have died over the last week, Ismail?' asked Mahmud. 'Twenty?'

'Twenty-two,' Ismail updated morosely. 'And yes, My Lord, indeed it would help if you made the announcement and sanctified what we discussed recently. Your words will preserve the slaves' will to survive and their passion to work.'

A flattered Mahmud smiled and patted his brother's cheek.

'We will take this world and rule it together, my brother,' he said. 'Help me formalize my position and we shall bring everyone—*everyone*—to heel under Ghazni and the One True Faith.'

Ismail glanced at the queen and lowered his head humbly. As she looked away, her eyes fell again on the kneeling slave girl Yazadeh. Kausari's eyes narrowed, almost like realization was dawning on her.

Mahmud stepped to the edge of the first step, cleared his throat and began to speak to the assemblage.

'By the grace of Allah, the Most Beneficent and Most Merciful,' boomed the sultan, 'I extend to you a unique opportunity. Living in blasphemy and sin, you are lucky—very lucky—to get this chance to get to *Jannat*.'

The slaves and their handlers watched the sultan with unwavering attention. They knew that *Jannat* was the *heaven promised to Muslims after death*. But since they were infidels, they had no chance of going to heaven and had to prepare for hellfire. At least that's what they had been told by their Islamic overseers.

'Although I am duty-bound to slaughter you, my Great Faith also teaches me to be merciful and rewarding, when required,' said the sultan, raising his hands towards the clear-blue morning sky. 'Rejoice, for I come bearing a gift … A gift that was insisted upon by your benefactor—my brother, the governor-mufti!'

Mahmud pointed to his brother with a theatrical flourish. Ismail bowed humbly. The sultan unfurled a scroll and held it aloft.

'I, Mahmud, sultan of Ghazni, exercise my right as the chosen protector and propagator of the One True Faith in this world of men and make this promise before you today.'

The slaves strained to listen as Mahmud's voice reached a crescendo.

'On this day, I decree that you will be set free from your bonds of slavery and admitted into the Faith of the sultanate upon the timely completion of your holy task. You will also be given sufficient compensation for the same, four months from today.'

Mahmud the Sultan rolled the scroll and held it aloft. The crowd remained deathly silent.

'Work hard, you *kafir*s, because you have a rare opportunity for redemption,' urged Mahmud with a smile. 'I leave this official decree in my brother's custody.'

A few men cheered in vain hope. Most stood still, perturbed and sombre. Everyone knew the task was almost impossible. They were doomed. Death wasn't a punishment, it was freedom. What they really feared wasn't death, but the relentless torture while they were still alive.

'What the hell …' snarled the sultan, his irritation rising at the slaves' lack of enthusiasm for his benevolence.

'Long live the sultan!' a hurried cry resounded from the audience. Fear works much better than incentives. 'Long live Mahmud of Ghazni!'

'Long live! Long live! Long live!' chanted the slaves, exuberantly displaying their enthusiasm, clapping as if their lives depended on it.

Mahmud handed the scroll to his brother, shooting a quick glance at Kausari with a snigger.

'Happy?' asked the sultan. 'If that does not motivate these scoundrels to meet your deadline, nothing will. I *want* you to succeed in this task, my brother.'

'I am eternally grateful, My Lord,' said Ismail.

'You better be. Failure is not an option.'

The governor-mufti bowed low, his expression obsequious and servile. As he raised his head, he began explaining the scriptural justifications he had begun to find for Mahmud's goal. Kausari too listened intently.

Unseen by the royal couple, Malik Ayaz had strolled over to Talib. The two were out of earshot of the Ghazni royal family ahead of them and the slaves behind them.

Ayaz looked down, like he was studying the floor, and muttered quickly, his tone clear, firm and deep, very unlike his usual dandy manner. 'It's done.'

'Thank you, My Lord,' whispered Talib. 'I will inform the governor-mufti.'

'Ten thousand gold dinars.'

Talib was surprised, but for only a moment. He had thought that, considering the relationship involved, Malik Ayaz would have been able to arrange for some more money. In fact, a lot more. But perhaps, Talib reasoned with himself, it had to be done slowly so that it would not raise suspicions.

The work at hand was very difficult and dangerous. And Talib knew how critical it was. He also knew that he was authorized to take decisions on Ismail's behalf in this matter.

'This is good for now, Sire,' said Talib.

Malik Ayaz looked at Talib. His usual cavalier-cad countenance had returned. He whispered with a voice that cracked a bit with emotion, 'Tell my father I love him.'

Saying this, Ayaz walked away.

Talib's face did not betray any emotions. He looked towards Ismail in the distance and then turned his eyes back to the ground. The loyal manservant had come to like Malik Ayaz, the King of Lahore, the lover of the sultan … But also, the son of a Georgian slave woman and a father who …

A father who only sees how useful his long-lost son is, not how much the son loves him.

CHAPTER 12

The Price of Escape

Narasimhan stood on the foredeck of the mighty Chola flagship
Chandrahaasa. *His men reloaded and fired the marine trebuchets*
with no let, no break.

No mercy.

The Srivijaya naval fleet, the ships of the powerful empire
that controlled most of the land and ports of the Southeast Asian
nations of Malaysia and Indonesia, lay in tatters.

'Load!' ordered the Chola general, raising his sword. The
imperial sailors placed spear-shaped bolts dunked in oil in the
slings of the war machines.

'Ignite!'

The projectiles that were loaded on the trebuchets were set
ablaze.

'Loose!' roared Narasimhan, waving his sword in an arc.
The long arms of five trebuchets hurled their shells into the night
air. The other Chola vessels followed the lead of the flagship and
catapulted the flaming missiles, their smoking tails writhing like
grey-black snakes against the inky sky.

The enemy ships retreated in a chaotic melee.

'General!'

Narasimhan turned to his right. It was the imperial messenger. Conveying information in the fog of war, and that too during a naval war playing out in the moonlight, was extremely difficult. Often, navies which didn't manage communication well ended up fighting as independent ships, rather than as part of one unbreakable armada. The Cholas, accomplished soldier-mariners for long, had in place a sophisticated system of communication between ships, facilitated through an arrangement of code flags hoisted on their main mast and bugle relays sounded out from the crow's nests. By its very nature, commands conveyed through code flags or bugle relays had to be simple, such as 'attack portside' or 'board starboard-side'. Complex messages needed messengers to row up in fast cutter boats. The expense and risk of doing so during a naval battle meant that this system was rarely used. It also meant that when a messenger was sent, particularly an imperial messenger, the message was considered to be of the utmost importance.

'Approach,' ordered Narasimhan.

The messenger marched forward, saluted, reached into the sling bag tied across his shoulder, and pulled out a sealed scroll.

'It's from the emperor, great General.'

Narasimhan stared at the messenger, irritated at him for stating the obvious. Who else would the imperial messenger bring a message from in the middle of a battle? Narasimhan looked towards the back of the naval convoy, where he had asked Rajendra Chola's ship to remain, for the emperor's safety.

He turned to his lieutenant. 'One more volley!'

As his warriors prepared to fire one more set of missiles on the hapless Srivijayans, Narasimhan tore open the seal and read the scroll.

'Narasimhan, my lion, you have done well. The Srivijayan navy is in disarray despite its superior numbers. The flames of Lord Agni eat their sails. The battle is over, my friend. Call off the assault.'

Narasimhan stopped reading, holding his breath in anger, but careful not to show his disagreement with his lord and master to others. He believed that Lady Fei Lin, princess of the Song royal family of China, among those who had impelled his emperor to initiate this campaign, was influencing Rajendra Chola for her own ends. The Srivijayan fleet was fleeing towards the Bay of Panai, the second-largest port city in the empire, when they were attacked by the Cholas. Panai port had served as the base for the biggest Southeast Asian trade federations, all controlled by Indian trader guilds before the Srivijayans had confiscated them. The Songs had allied with the Cholas to restore the old trade networks, but Narasimhan believed that China's game wasn't as transparent as they claimed.

The general continued reading his emperor's letter.

'We don't need to kill them all. We have won the war. We need to win the peace as well. We need to negotiate. For that, I need someone on the other side to negotiate with. The Srivijayan Emperor Rama Vijayavarman is on one of those ships you are hammering. Brave men keep fighting long after it is rational to continue. Vijayavarman is courageous, there is no doubt about it. He will not realize, on his own, the correct time to show the white flag. Remember that I cannot legitimize my rule over these islands without an accord with the ones the locals recognize as authentic rulers. Our goal is to bring lasting peace and stability to the region, not anarchy and turmoil. You have done well, soldier. Now, allow me to perform my task as a king. Get me Vijayavarman. Ideally, he should be alive when you bring him to me.'

'What should I convey to the emperor, General?' asked the messenger.

'The Srivijayan emperor has the option of raising the white flag. We are Hindus. He is a Hindu. I'm sure he knows that we will follow the rules of war if he offers to surrender.'

The imperial messenger kept quiet. He knew of the general's aggressive approach to war. He would have liked to finish this battle. As he said often, a naval battle is only over when the last enemy ship has been sunk. But the messenger also knew that Narasimhan rarely disobeyed a direct command from Rajendra Chola.

'Tell the emperor that his order will be followed.'

'Yes, General.' The messenger saluted and rushed back to his cutter boat.

Narasimhan looked at the helmsman.

'Command the fleet to hold fire,' he ordered. 'Move in towards the Srivijayan flagship. Get the grappling hooks and melee weapons ready.'

'The flagship is headed to the open sea, Sire,' the helmsman answered. 'It is fleeing.'

'We will take him alive,' growled Narasimhan, his eyes narrowing as he focused fiercely on the enemy flagship. The wind blew his lionlike mane in the air. 'Full sail. Ramming speed.'

'Full sail,' repeated the helmsman. 'Full sail! Ramming speed!'

He ran to pass on the command to the section chiefs.

'Full sail! The general has commanded the pursuit of the enemy flagship. The Srivijayan emperor is fleeing!'

The string of dreams snapped as the ship suddenly lurched because of the strong waves lashing against it. Narasimhan was again at sea. This time, though, he was less forceful than he used to be. Right arm and shoulder paralysed. Still weak and not at his peak strength. Lying alone in the sick bay, given medicines to induce sleep. And unaware of what was happening on the top deck, where the crew was gathered, facing a potential calamity.

In the dream, a remembrance of a time past, Narasimhan had been the hunter. In the present moment, he was among the hunted.

The Chola schooner moved as quickly as it could in the waters, as dense sea-fog surrounded it, obliterating visibility to just a few feet. But it was not enough to hide them from the stalking danger. The alien ship had pursued them for the better part of the night.

It was close to dawn now.

The fog, essentially condensed water vapour that behaved like a dense liquid, flowing and ebbing in unpredictable ways, had forced the crew to slow down the ship, for fear of running into an obstruction. But it had also protected them by obscuring the ship from the enemy.

'The dhow has fired again!' said Vijayan softly but urgently as a bolt of fire sliced through the thick, opaque white mist. 'Down! Now!'

The Chola men on deck crouched immediately. The flaming metallic bolt flew low overhead and crashed into the wooden railing. It reduced the banister to splinters and then crashed into the sea.

A close shave.

'We cannot keep this up,' whispered Someshwar. A giant spray of salty seawater wet him to the bone. 'They have someone who can aim based on sound. There is no other way they can get this kind of accuracy in this visibility!'

Vijayan did not say anything. But he knew Someshwar was right. That's why he was keeping his voice low. But he also knew that this tactic was useless beyond a point. A ship at sea made noises. Naturally. Something that could be picked up by a trained bolt-master, particularly if he was aiming based on sound.

Someshwar continued, 'One of those bolts will crack our hull like an eggshell anytime now.'

At Alappuzha, Amal had decided that the Chola squad would travel in a merchant schooner. A naval military ship, with noticeable weapon holds and trebuchets, would obviously draw the attention of the Arab navies that dominated the routes of the Western Sea. And she had assumed that they had taken care of the Arab mercenaries who had been contracted to kill Narasimhan. It appeared that they hadn't. There was perhaps a backup team in addition to the Arabs they had killed in Kerala. And the Chola squad was now in their crosshairs.

'I thought we would lose them by heading into this risky fog-ridden patch in the sea, but they called our bluff,' whispered Amal, keeping her voice low, since their enemies could use loud sounds to their advantage. 'They followed us … And now, between these bolts and the near-zero visibility, we are truly caught between the devil and the deep sea. We must do something.'

The wind suddenly quickened its speed. The waves opened their arms and collapsed like wanton lovers in the vile throes of passion. The tiny Chola schooner was tossed around like a discarded prayer flower.

Vijayan gritted his teeth. *The last thing we need now is a storm. Goddess Meenakshi, have mercy.*

'What can we do?' asked Vijayan. 'Turn around and fight with our bows and arrows?! They have heavy-duty marine weapons.'

Amal fell silent. *Obviously not. That would be suicide.*

Vijayan ordered his men, 'Raise the white flag and blow the bugle in the standard tune to signal surrender.' Then he turned to Someshwar, using the assumed name of the merchant. 'Salman, you will lead the conversation with the Arabs when they come aboard. You know their language best.'

'Yes, Valeed,' replied Someshwar.

'Good,' said Vijayan. 'I will stay close at hand for your protection, along with a few other men. Employ any method you like, but your job is to convince them that we have no Chola general called Narasimhan on this ship. We are simply traders on our way to Ghazni lands.'

Whoosh!

Another bolt flew overhead and ripped a hole through one of the sails. The rain fell hard, and the men were drenched. As was the only woman aboard.

'I have an additional idea, Brigadier,' Ansar, Amal's brother, spoke with confidence. Amal's younger brothers, all three of them, had accompanied her on this mission. Ansar was the youngest.

Vijayan knew that Ansar had served on Chera naval expeditions. He had experience with sea-battle tactics.

'Always open to ideas,' said Vijayan.

'I suggest we drop the lifeboat suspended along our starboard,' said Ansar. 'It is a dinghy. I will board it. I could circle the enemy undetected in this fog and weak dawn light. Their ship should slow down as they prepare to board our vessel, making my task easier. I can disable the enemy dhow's rudders, rear ballasts and stabilizers.'

'Will it do enough damage to the dhow to stop their pursuit?' Someshwar asked.

'A pointy-bowed ship with large sails cannot maintain its intended direction and balance without its rudder,' explained Ansar. 'Especially if the winds and rain pick up. It will likely capsize.'

'But it's not easy to do this while the ship is sailing at sea,' said Vijayan. 'Some would say it's impossible.'

'It is difficult, but not impossible. Not for me, at least.'

Vijayan smiled. 'It is settled, then, It must happen very, very quickly, and with immaculate synchrony among us. We will cut the dinghy loose. You and two other men will take it and disappear into the fog. The sea is becoming rough. Hold your balance while we lay the bait and draw in the dhow. After that, circle your way to the rear of the enemy ship and sabotage their vessel.'

'I will not fail, Brigadier!' Ansar said.

Vijayan turned to two soldiers with him. 'Accompany Ansar. Cover him with your bows and arrows. He must remain alive, for only he can damage their ship without the Arabs realizing it.'

'Yes, Sir!' said Dasarna, a Parmar army captain, and a Chola soldier in unison, bowing their heads.

'I too will go with my brother,' said Amal.

Vijayan looked concerned and relieved at the same time. Concerned because he knew the mission with the dinghy was risky. If the sea turned choppier, as it did in these parts, even the strongest of swimmers would find themselves pulled down by the currents. But at the same time, he was relieved. He knew that Turkic soldiers considered *kafir* women as fair game for rape and assault. And even Muslims from India were considered *kafirs* by the Turks. If the Arabs had Turkic soldiers in the ship, which was quite likely since the Turks were the best warriors among the Islamic groups, it would be better if Amal was not caught on board.

Vijayan did not speak. But his face said it all.

Amal smiled slightly. The Almighty has blessed women with far superior intuition than men. They don't need words to be spoken. They can just read it on the face.

She looked intently at Vijayan as he averted his gaze. The moment was not lost on Ansar. He grinned and cleared his throat.

'We should be on our way, sister,' said the young man, taking her arm.

'Complete your task without …' said Vijayan, '… without being exposed. I want you back alive. All hands at the ready when we get to Ghazni.'

'I am not easy to lose, Valeed,' said Amal. 'We will be back, all four of us.'

The crew lowered the dinghy into the fog, judging by sound and instinct how much lower the water was. And then they helped their braves board. Vijayan turned to his soldiers.

'Raise a white flag on the mast,' he said. 'Blow the bugle to signal surrender. Send a guard to the general's cabin. If there is a fight and we are on the verge of losing, instruct him to sink a dagger into Nasrullah's heart.' Vijayan used the assumed name for Narasimhan. 'He, too, must die honourably. I want the other two brothers of Amal sent down as well. Only the soldiers will remain on deck.'

Vijayan's clear orders were efficiently executed. Amal's brothers Aamir and Altaf accompanied a guard to the lower decks.

Meanwhile, in the sea below, Amal and her three companions glided silently beneath the dense low-hanging fog and gushing winds. Their small boat held steady as their oars propelled them away from the starboard side of the schooner.

—◦✦◦—

'Heave to.'

The order rang out. The sails were lowered. The Chola schooner was brought head to wind. It slowed down.

The crew on board was ready.

The dhow had stopped firing as soon as the bugle was sounded. Perhaps they had seen the white flag, despite the fog. But the message from the bugle was clear.

We surrender.

Vijayan watched the dhow slowly approach and stop at a distance on the port side to avoid colliding with them. Vijayan felt his vessel list to the left. He squinted his eyes and looked at the dhow through the slightly cleared fog. Men stood with raised scimitars, blades and machetes along the rails of the deck of the Arab ship. Much closer now, Vijayan could see the flag at the ship's mast. He recognized it almost immediately. This wasn't just an ordinary Arab vessel—it was an Abbasid ship! Chartered by the caliph's administration.

These aren't Arab mercenaries contracted to kill the general. This is about something else. What could it be? Goddess Meenakshi, have mercy.

The lusty chanting of the Arabs added to the din of the elements.

'*Allah hu Akbar!*'

'What are they saying?' Vijayan asked.

'It is an Arabic chant. They are proclaiming that *God is Great*,' said Someshwar.

'All Gods are great, but their celebration is a little premature, I would say.' Vijayan smiled. The warrior within him had awakened.

Someshwar smiled back.

The Arabs lassoed two grappling hooks towards their ship rigging. Both held. Someshwar stepped forward, Iqbal to his side.

'You better go take your place among the men at the back, Valeed,' Someshwar said. 'Remember, you are a hired hand. No more, no less. Do not speak unless spoken to. Do not overact. A simple "yes" or "no" in your own tongue will suffice when necessary.'

'Understood.' Vijayan nodded.

'And remember the names Amal gave us,' added Someshwar. 'I will only use "Valeed" to address you. Be alert. This is a trial by fire. We don't win by fighting the fire. We win by keeping the fire away.'

Vijayan nodded and retreated, leaving the task of diplomacy to the elderly merchants.

Six Arab men slid across the grappling lines in quick succession, the leader arriving last. He was a brawny man with a bushy beard and heavy brows that almost fell over his eyes. They glistened with the moisture in the air. He had no moustache.

The sails of both ships had been let down. The wind was strong. Vijayan noted his crew's numerical advantage on board their own ship.

They have the heavy weapons. But most of their soldiers have remained on their own ship. They have an advantage but at a distance. In close combat, we have an advantage, since on our own ship, we have more soldiers.

He threw a quick look at the enemy ship floating alongside. It was teeming with men at the rails, alert and keenly observing.

Good. Their attention is on us. This will help Ansar and Amal.

—⋯⚔⋯—

A hundred yards away, Ansar gave the signal to turn the boat around. They had covered enough distance to come back, unnoticed, towards the stern side of the Arab dhow.

'Make for the aft of the Arab ship,' Ansar whispered to the oarsmen. 'Quickly.'

The sea waves picked up pace as the waters suddenly became choppier, the winds abruptly becoming more squall-like.

The challenge for the little dinghy just became tougher.

'Don't worry about rowing hard,' Dasarna said, laughing. 'Any noise we make will be drowned in this mini storm.'

Soldiers considered it a sign of bravery to laugh when facing the risk of death.

Amal braced as the tiny boat lurched ahead.

—◦✴◦—

The Arab leader walked up to Someshwar on the bridge of the Chola–Parmar ship, assuming he was the leader. His steps were heavy, and the damp floorboard creaked underneath.

'Peace be upon you!' The large man greeted in Arabic. He loomed over the two relatively diminutive elderly merchants. Iqbal looked carefully, unacknowledged by the Arab who wore a heavy silken coat that smelled of the sea. Hanging around his neck was a circular golden medallion emblazoned with the round, black seal of the Abbasid caliphate. His simple headgear was at odds with the grimy plushness of his attire and jewellery.

'And to you, Sir,' Someshwar said in response and bowed low in an elaborate show of respect. Iqbal followed suit. 'I am Salman Shah and this is my friend, Iqbal,' said Someshwar, introducing himself. 'We are merchants from the Gujarat region of India. To what do we owe the pleasure of your visit?'

'You are of the *Din*, then?' the Arab asked, surprised by the chaste Arabic of the small Indian man. *Din* was the *Arabic word for their religion.*

'Indeed, Sir,' replied Iqbal eagerly. 'Although you must forgive our Arabic, it is not our mother tongue. All our crew members are *momin*s. Most are servants and hired hands, converted recently from their pagan religions.'

Pleased at the mention of conversions, the Arab leader twirled his bushy beard and smiled. He pointed towards the black flag with Arabic lettering on it, fluttering over the mast of his ship.

'You recognize that flag, don't you?' he asked quizzically. 'Why were you running away from us?'

'Forgive us, Sire, but we were scared,' explained Someshwar, smiling sheepishly. 'The dark night and the dense fog prevented us from recognizing your flag. We thought you were pirates and, fearful for our lives, we tried to escape. But the moment we got a good look at your flag, we sounded the bugle of surrender and ordered for the sails to be lowered. It was a relief for us to know that you are from the administration of the caliph, our lord and master!'

Vijayan detected subtle tension in the air. The five other Arabs scanned each of them suspiciously while their leader spoke to the two old men.

—·◦⚜◦·—

About a hundred yards away, the dinghy had reached the tail of the caliphate ship. The aft deck appeared deserted, although the dense fog made it impossible to be certain.

'The fog is on our side, Ansar,' Dasarna said softly. 'Even if there are caliphate soldiers on the aft side, they wouldn't be able to see us. Small mercies. The three of us will hold the boat steady. How long will you take to cut that rudder line?'

Ansar laughed grimly as he peeked into the bag near his foot and carefully reached for a tool. He pulled out a large, sharp saw-file, perfect for sawing through wood. 'I am not sure, brother. Cutting the line would have been quick and easy had it been a rope. However, as you can see, it is not a rope but a solid iron chain that is going down to the rudder.'

'This is impossible to cut through,' said Amal, worried. 'We should head back.'

The protective instincts of the elder sister came to the fore.

'No,' her brother said firmly. 'We will improvise. The lives of our friends and brothers … our country's honour depends on us, *aapa*,' Ansar said to his *elder sister*. 'I will saw off the stem of the rudder itself. Wood is easier to work with than iron. Besides, the way I intend to do it now, it will break the connection to the keel as well, which will quicken the death of this Abbasid ship. Since most of the rudder is submerged under water, I will need to dive. That's alright. I can do it.'

Dasarna knew enough about naval tactics to understand the enormous risk that Ansar was taking. He held the young man's shoulders and whispered, 'Go with Allah and Shiva, my brother.' His voice shook with admiration.

Amal looked stricken with pain. She did not like her brother's idea. But she remained silent.

Ansar spoke. 'I must ask you to row back to the blind side of our ship and sneak onboard, since this mission here will take much longer than we had earlier anticipated.' He looked pointedly at Amal. 'I will complete the task and find a way to return to you, *aapa*. But I cannot focus on my work if I am worried about your safety. Please listen to me. You will be safer back on our ship. Out here, all of you will be exposed in the open for too long.'

Ansar reached out and stroked Amal's cheek lovingly. She pushed his hand away.

'Ansar,' Amal hissed. 'We are all in this *together*. We came together and we will go back together—*after* the job is done.'

'*Aapa*, this is too risky,' the brother replied stubbornly. He stood up and removed his clothes till he was clad only in a cotton loincloth. 'We are lucky we got here unnoticed, but let us not stretch our luck. This was supposed to be a short and quick mission. It will clearly not be one. I can hide myself underwater. But the boat is a conspicuous target if it remains here too long.'

Ansar's logic was sound. But his sister's heart needed time to accept it. Dasarna waited patiently.

Brave men deserve the honour of patience from other brave men.

Amal, the soldier, saw the logic. But Amal, the sister, only saw her brother. She finally took a deep breath, stood up and embraced Ansar, her heart pounding like a stone hammer in her bosom. She closed her eyes and whispered his name.

'I am an excellent swimmer, you know that, *aapa*,' he spoke softly in his sister's ear. 'I will see you on the starboard side before you bat your pretty eyelids! Be there to haul me up!'

'I will be waiting, Ansar … Don't disappoint me.'

Ansar raised one eyebrow, a crooked smile hovering on his face, 'Have I ever, *aapa*?'

Amal stroked his hair. 'I love you, kiddo.'

'I love you, too.'

The young man broke the embrace, moved to the edge of the boat and tested the water with his toe. He then slid in, the saw file held tight in his right hand.

'We are turning back,' announced Dasarna, taking the oars in his hands. He rowed from the back end of the boat, while Amal and the other Chola warrior rowed from the front end, navigating their way back to their schooner through the thick fog.

A solitary teardrop escaped Amal's left eye and blended with the chill dampness on her face. She looked back.

No sign of Ansar.

—⋅◦⟜⟝◦⋅—

Back on the deck of the Chola–Parmar ship, the Arab leader spoke to the two old men.

'Let me introduce myself. I am Sayyad Al Nabhani, a commander in the army of the caliph of Baghdad,' he said. 'Salman Shah of India, tell me what you and your men are doing in these waters.'

'We are on a pilgrimage, Sire,' Someshwar answered with no hesitation. 'Our destination is Mecca.'

'You are sailing in the wrong direction, then,' said Sayyad, his voice ringing with suspicion. 'Mecca is towards the west,' he added, pointing with his thumb. 'You were sailing north when we encountered you. It is possible that you lost your way in this weather. Or you could be misleading me wilfully.'

Iqbal's gut wrenched with fear, but Someshwar held his cool.

'Allow me to make amends for the incompleteness of my words, great Lord,' he elaborately decorated his words. 'Mecca is our *final* destination. We *are* pilgrims, I assure you. We hope to land in Gwadar and continue our journey on the backs of beasts of burden. We will stop at many shrines on the way. *Inshallah*, we will begin with the magnificent Jama Mosque in Ghazni built by Sultan Yamin-ud-Dawla

Abul-Qasim Mahmud ibn Sebuktegin. We will then travel to Persia and, from there, go to Arabia. We are retracing the steps of our Faith, right back to its birthplace.'

Vijayan understood some words: Sultan, Mahmud, Ghazni …

I hope he did not tell the Arabs where we are headed. The last thing we want is for them to offer to make the journey with us.

'So you will land in Gwadar,' said Sayyad, raising his bushy brows and smiling with delight. 'And then travel to Ghazni. That is where *we* are headed too. Perhaps our ships can sail together. You could do with our protection, I'm sure. Of course, you can pay us for our assistance. Though the Muslims of India don't have to pay *jaziya* since they are not *kafir*s, they should nevertheless contribute to the caliphate and pay for the honour of Arab protection.'

Someshwar and Iqbal shuffled their feet uncomfortably. Silent. How would they get out of this? They were willing to pay, but they didn't want the Arabs accompanying them.

'Of course,' continued the Abbasid leader, eyeing Vijayan and the others intently, before bringing his attention back to Someshwar, 'if you ask me, Ghazni and Persia are a waste of time. You should head straight to Mecca. You will find real Muslims there. Others are imposters who will be dealt with in the manner they deserve. Of course, to go straight to Mecca, without any hindrance, you will need a permission note from me.'

Sayyad flashed a cruel smile and left the obvious condition unsaid—'for a payment without a receipt'.

Relieved that the Arab himself was providing them a way out of their predicament, Iqbal turned to Someshwar.

'See, Salman *bhai*!' he said, feigning jubilation. 'I *told* you we should go straight to Mecca. And now this advice is from the army of the caliph! It is a message from Allah. We have enough provisions to make course adjustments and sail directly to the Holy City.'

Someshwar scratched his chin and pretended to give Iqbal's improvisation some reluctant thought.

—·◦⚜◦·—

The boat carrying Dasarna, Amal and the Chola soldier returned to the portside of the schooner. It was the blind side. Vijayan had expressly instructed his men to keep an eye on the waters below. They helped the three come aboard noiselessly, away from the drama on the starboard side.

'Where is Ansar?' a crewman asked.

'He will return shortly,' answered Dasarna curtly. He cast a sympathetic look at Amal. 'My Lady, the brigadier had instructed us to go to the cabins below. It seems our party is engaged with the Arabs on the other side.'

Amal nodded mechanically and allowed herself to be escorted to the safety of the cabins, her eyes fixed on the sea.

Ansar …

—·◦⚜◦·—

Back on deck, Someshwar continued the charade in an attempt to escape from the clutches of the caliph's men. Besides, if the saboteurs succeeded in their task the crippled Arab ship would not follow them anywhere.

'I would listen to your man if I were you,' said Sayyad. 'I am supposed to go to Ghazni for some business, but I'll leave as soon as I can. It is a wasteland ruled by a pretentious despot. I tell you, there is no ruler in this world who can surpass the Grand Caliph. He has God-given authority over all the earthly realms. Trust me as his representative, men of India. You should go straight to Mecca.'

'I would be a fool to not heed your well-intentioned advice, Sire.' Someshwar laughed nervously. 'Perhaps we *should* change course after all.' And then he opened the negotiations. 'I would be very happy to contribute to your great ...'

Barely had the words escaped his mouth when Sayyad lunged at Someshwar and grabbed him by the shoulders. He seized the old man's earlobe. Someshwar had removed the studs when he had set off from home weeks ago, but he could not hide the piercings, enlarged by age and a lifetime of adornment.

'Your ears are pierced!' the Arab snarled. 'You are no follower of the *Din*! You are a *kafir*, filthy old liar!'

'Sire, I'm a recent convert,' pleaded Someshwar. 'My pierced lobes are a relic of my earlier life.'

'You're lying!' roared Sayyad.

'No, My Lord! Why would I lie? You must believe me. Indians cannot be born as Muslims. Obviously. We have to convert. You cannot punish us because we converted later in our lives.'

The Arab seemed unsure. He couldn't tell if the Indian was telling the truth. Or whether there was subterfuge aboard. But subterfuge certainly seemed to have begun on the deck of the Arab ship, which distracted everyone on the small Chola–Parmar schooner. The men on the caliphate ship were running helter-skelter in panic and confusion. Soon, they disappeared from sight. They had run to the aft side of their vessel, yelling about a different form of treachery.

Armed with bows, they showered arrows on the face of the raging waters off the stern of their ship. The Arab men on the Chola schooner stared at their own vessel in confusion. Sayyad's grip on Someshwar loosened.

'Attack!' Vijayan roared, seeing the opening and drawing his sword. 'Chop them to pieces. Cut the grapple lines!'

The Chola–Parmar soldiers drew their swords instantly and stormed into action.

Sayyad turned around, stunned. Iqbal and Someshwar had faded into the background while the fierce brigadier of the Cholas had taken back control of his vessel and command. The Pandya pounced on the Arab leader and yanked the chain off his neck. Sayyad lost his footing and teetered precariously.

'Why don't you snarl at someone your own size, big man?' Vijayan thundered. He grabbed Sayyad's neck and thrust his sword into the Arab's belly.

The commander of the caliphate ship howled in agony. But displaying an extraordinary will to survive, he grabbed Vijayan by the throat and pushed him away with surprising strength. The Indian crashed on the floorboard, holding the Arab's broken chain in one hand and his bloodied sword in the other. Sayyad roared, turned around and staggered toward the grappling lines. They had not been severed yet in the melee.

Someshwar and Iqbal had been taken to the lower deck by a Chola warrior, while the rest battled the Arab soldiers zipping down from the enemy ship, even as a few Indians furiously cut the grappling lines between the two vessels. Arrows fell like stormy raindrops on the deck of the caliphate vessel.

Hell had broken loose.

Sayyad, his strength fading with the enormous loss of blood, concentrated on getting back to his ship.

'Commander!' shouted an Arab.

He reached for the handrail and grabbed the rope thrown to him.

'*Kafirs*!' Sayyad cursed, roaring loud enough for his men to hear in the other ship, screaming in rage despite the immense blood loss. 'Load … scorpions! Destroy … ship!'

Unfortunately for the Abbasid commander, Vijayan had other plans. The brigadier of the Cholas threw his sword aside and picked up his bow. He nocked the arrow and let the missile loose.

Thwack.

It shattered the Arab commander's atlas bone in the neck. His head flopped forward, and he began to drown in his own blood. Sayyad's eyes closed and his body tumbled into the sea.

Meanwhile, the Chola soldiers had managed to cut all the grappling lines. Their schooner was free!

A streak of lightning lit the storm clouds with a ghostly glow.

Vijayan looked at his men. 'Hoist the sails!'

Two Chola men raised the surviving sails as others desperately fought the remaining Arabs on their ship.

Amal rushed to the deck.

'Ansar!'

Vijayan grabbed her in his arms.

'Let me go! Let me go!' She thrashed helplessly in his powerful embrace. 'Ansar!'

'Shush, Amal!' Vijayan soothed, his heart leaping with relief upon seeing her.

She was distraught. She would not calm down.

'Amal!' Vijayan cried as she writhed in frenzy, her eyes frozen on the enemy ship.

A powerful gust of wind unfurled the sails to their full capacity. The Chola schooner began to move rapidly away, escaping from the clutches of the Arab dhow.

But Amal continued to struggle in Vijayan's arms, trying to break free.

'Amal!' Vijayan shouted, trying to calm her down. 'What is the matter? We are safe …'

Amal wailed in response. She pointed towards the enemy ship receding in the distance. The caliphate dhow had also unfurled its sails. Poised to give chase. The same mighty winds powering the Chola schooner filled the sails of the Arab ship too. And suddenly, the caliphate vessel shook like a ragdoll in the midst of the roaring sea.

The vessel's controls had been lost. Not just the rudder, even the keel seemed disconnected. A rogue wave crashed on the starboard side, and the vessel heeled heavily as it broached-to. Another cruelly powerful wave struck, just as the wind roared deeper into the sails. In simple terms, it was a perfect storm for a ship with no rudder control. The great dhow keeled over, flipping to its side. Lightning flashed and thunder cracked across the sky. Blinding rain hid the calamity from further view.

Amal collapsed in a heap. Crying.

He did it ... My little angel did it ...

Realization dawned on Vijayan as he looked around. He saw Dasarna and the other soldier he had sent. Dasarna was staring at the keeled-over Arab dhow, tears in his eyes. Then he stood at attention and executed the formal Parmar military salute, towards the sea behind the Arab dhow, bowing his head deep.

Vijayan finally understood what had happened. He whispered in misery, 'Ansar ...'

He kneeled and held Amal's shoulders gently.

Swim well, little brother. Swim well for eternity ...

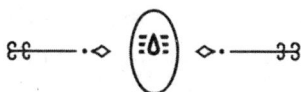

CHAPTER 13

Snake under the Pillow

Ghazni, Afghanistan

The dark starless night was alive with sleepless chatter. The slaves were awake, the labour camp abuzz with activity. The Jama Mosque in Ghazni loomed in the centre, the torch flames from the surrounding tents casting a spectral glow on the House of Prayer.

The earth shivered, as if seeking warmth, failing which it rent the air with a vehement rumble. Another. And then another. Yazadeh clung to her threadbare blanket, seeking comfort. The tremors increased as screaming men, women and children ran helter-skelter in terror.

BOOM!

The earth split in two under the House of Prayer.

People ran in all directions, away from the widening rift. Yazadeh rose and stood on the spot, unmoving. A dim blue light emerged from the abyss. Hypnotized, she moved towards it.

Yazadeh stood at the edge of the precipice and peered into the darkness. She held her breath. Three gigantic almond-shaped slits of blue watched her ... Eyes. Two eyes were aligned horizontally,

placed next to each other. The third one was above them but
vertical. They were beautiful, enticing. Yazadeh swayed ...

'Wake up, child!'

Yazadeh squealed as if she had been slapped.

'Wake up!'

She rolled on the rough mat and opened her eyes. She sat
up with a start, bracing against the chilly wind that leaked
through her flimsy blanket. Her heart sank, out of habit.
It was dawn. The night was over; it was the only time her
people were free of the brutality of their circumstances—only
somewhat, for the Jundiin-ul-Din also patrolled the slave
camps all night, like a pack of hungry wolves.

Home to the slaves working on the great mosque of
Ghazni, the goat pens had rough fabric canopies erected
overhead, as decreed by the 'merciful' grand mufti. Coarse
bedding and blankets riddled with holes kept up the pretence
of protection from the wind and sleet.

A few weeks back, she, along with her father, had been
transferred here by Ismail. Publicly, it had been presented
as the governor-mufti contributing his own personal slaves
to the mosque-rebuilding project; it was a sacrifice that
enhanced Ismail's public image further. But Yazadeh was still
whisked away by the mufti's men every few days, whenever
Ismail ordered it. She would be returned to her people in the
evening when the work on the mosque wound down. Yazadeh
deplored her own circumstances but understood they were
slaves with no rights. They had become the personal property
of the marauding Ghaznavid slavers from the day their village
was raided.

She blinked. The earth was pulsing with the frenzied
footfalls of slave men and women, clearly alarmed. Screams
pierced the air.

'What is happening, Father?' Yazadeh wailed.

'Some men have attacked the Jundiin-ul-Din!' said the old man. 'They broke the locks and hacked the chains off each other. Hurry, girl, the nightmare is over! Up, up! We are getting out of here!'

Stunned, Yazadeh scrambled to her feet. Father and daughter clung to each other and ran towards an opening in the pen, flanked on either side by the renegade band of slaves who'd taken the Jundiin-ul-Din by surprise.

'Move, move, quickly!' ordered a man. He seemed to be leading the slaves' daring escape. The tall man, with curly long hair that many weeks of unwashed dust had turned into dreadlocks, hurried along tide upon tide of freed prisoners funnelling through the breach in the fencing, Yazadeh threw him a grateful glance as she and her father crouched through the opening ... into freedom.

'Hurry!' the rebel leader called from behind. 'And stay together, all of you!'

—·◦✧◦·—

A deeply distraught Ismail burst into the corner room of the Ghazni palace. Mahmud had called an urgent private conference. Ismail scanned the space. Khwaja Hassan was surrounded by his ministerial coterie and the dreaded General Abu Q'asim. To the left of the sultan's empty seat sat his nemesis, Queen Kausari Jahan. The sultan agitatedly paced the length of the room like a frenzied wild elephant straining to charge at anyone who fell in his path.

'Ismail!' roared Mahmud as soon as his rabid eyes caught sight of his brother.

His brother's voice made Ismail's blood curdle. He threw himself at Mahmud's feet.

'Brother!' cried Ismail, clutching Mahmud's legs. 'My men kept watch every hour of the day,' he wailed fervently. 'This could not have happened without outside help. No way!'

'And yet, thirty of your men are dead and three more are grievously injured,' barked Mahmud, kicking his brother off him like a grimy mongrel. 'How did slaves—mere *unarmed* slaves—manage to overpower your guards and get away like this?'

Ismail rose to his feet, unable to articulate a response. His brother's wrath had paralysed him. He glared at Kausari Jahan furtively as she sat smug and cold.

Malik Ayaz, the King of Lahore, who spent very little time in Lahore, sat a bit farther away, a bored expression on his face.

'Is this how you repay me for freeing you from that rathole in Guzgan and bringing you here?' Mahmud asked. 'Was this treachery already on your mind when you came here, or did you plan it with the sycophants who surround me?'

The sultan scowled at Khwaja Hassan, who shrank like curdled milk in a mass of sweaty whey.

'Did you have anything to do with this, you fat buffoon?' Mahmud boomed, directing his wrath at Khwaja Hassan now. 'Did you orchestrate this escape to pit me against my brother and regain control over your pathetic infidel slaves?'

'My Lord, no!' the prime minister gasped. 'May Allah strike me down if ...'

'I knew I should have executed you when Ismail told me about your underground business and tax evasion, you worthless slime!' roared Mahmud.

'My Lord!' wheezed Khwaja and fell to the ground. 'I assure you, I had nothing to do with this! Absolutely *nothing*. I was determined to help complete the mosque repairs as fast as possible, so that you could assume your rightful place in the world. A matter of collective pride for us all!'

'Khwaja Hassan speaks the truth, My Lord.' Kausari Jahan's voice was silken and delicate. She rose, glided over to her husband and laid a hand on his chest. Mahmud's mercurial rage appeared to quieten to mere anger.

Kausari continued her ministrations of Mahmud. 'I would humbly submit, great Sultan, that your brother and you, your hearts so full of mercy, gravely misjudged the slaves' capacity for loyalty. After all, they are prisoners. They have only done the expected. They have fled from their captors '

'Are you taking the side of the slaves, great Queen?' Malik Ayaz asked.

'Stay out of this, Ayaz,' said Mahmud, glaring at Malik Ayaz. He knew of the animus between Kausari and Ayaz, who fought over him like jealous paramours. He was in no mood to witness another catfight.

'My Lord,' spoke Ismail, his voice still quivering in fear. 'It is too early to be certain, but I conducted an initial investigation into the disappearance of the *kafir*s. We have found tracks in the muddy snow that suggest an ambush on my Jundiin-ul-Din. They were attacked from *outside* the slave camp first and then the slaves broke free.'

'Is that true?' Mahmud raised a brow. 'How can you be so sure?'

'I had over fifty heavily armed men guarding the labourers,' said Ismail. 'Now there are thirty dead and three wounded, while the rest are missing …'

'What is your point?' Mahmud interrupted his younger brother impatiently. 'Do not speak in riddles. Your Jundiin-ul-Din are useless warriors. They can only bully women and children, not fight real men. I know all that already. Tell me why you think someone from the outside helped the slaves escape. Tracks in the mud are not conclusive evidence.'

'My Lord, my brother,' Ismail spoke hurriedly, afraid that the sultan didn't have too much patience left. 'The slaves could not have overpowered our men by themselves. My men had weapons. The slaves did not. Yet these slaves massacred my men and escaped with almost no casualties. How?'

Ismail hastily beckoned a servant who stood frozen at the door. The old man rushed in with a sword held horizontally in both hands. He went down on his knees and held the sword up for Mahmud to inspect.

The sultan grabbed the weapon by the hilt. The servant cowered as if about to be beheaded. Mahmud squinted his eyes and examined the rusty blade. He looked at Ismail, shocked.

'What is this?' he asked. 'How could this happen? This is a standard-issue weapon of the city guards. The Jundiin-ul-Din do not use them!'

'Precisely, My Lord!' exclaimed Ismail. He waved the servant away. 'The slaves were helped by the city's official machinery, I am sure of it!' the governor-mufti declared, sweeping a look across everyone in the room, but resting his gaze noticeably longer on Kausari Jahan, before returning to the sultan. 'I would contend, My Lord, that my men were assailed by no less than some rogue faction of the city guards! Perhaps, they were instigated by someone …'

The queen's complexion turned a shade lighter as the blood drained from her face. Her fleeting discomfort did not escape Ismail.

'Yes, My Lord,' the governor-mufti added, keeping his eyes on the queen, 'we have a traitor among us. Not literally at this moment in this room, of course, but *someone* has been trying to sabotage your plans. To delay the reconstruction of the Jama Mosque. Do you know anyone averse to your becoming caliph, My Lord? Who would brazenly go to this extent, just to prevent you from rising to the holy seat you were born to occupy?'

'This is absurd!' The queen spoke coldly. She briefly touched the black pendant hanging around her neck. 'Here is an incapable man trying to hide his failure with a ridiculous conspiracy theory. Is there anyone in this kingdom who would dare to stand up against you, My Lord?' she asked, turning to Mahmud.

The sultan looked squarely at his wife.

'This was a daring escape, with no living witnesses to tell us what exactly happened,' continued Kausari Jahan. 'Also, as the governor-mufti himself said, there were fifty Jundiin-ul-Din soldiers. Only thirty-three are accounted for—and they are all either dead or seriously wounded and cannot speak. Where are the other seventeen Jundiin-ul-Din? It's convenient that they are missing, isn't it?'

Mahmud pursed his lips. But did not say anything.

Detecting hesitation in her husband, the queen pressed on.

'Also, it is not impossible to lay hands on the weapons of the city guard,' she said more confidently. 'Many soldiers and guardsmen frequent brothels and illegal liquor dens in the city. Even a Jundiin-ul-Din could have chanced upon and stolen the weapon. Whoever brought this sword to the governor-mufti no doubt wanted to mislead his master and cover up the ineptitude of a colleague.'

'This sword was drenched in blood when it was brought to me,' Ismail protested, feeling enraged and impotent.

'The blood of a man or a goat? And who can be sure where the sword was …'

'Enough!' Mahmud roared, interrupting his wife. 'Ismail, you will investigate this matter and prove your claims. Return to me with evidence against the conspirators, if any.'

'Yes, My Lord,' said Ismail.

'And the same goes for you, Kausari,' said the sultan, turning to his wife. 'I know my brother makes some serious accusations, but it is not impossible that a few city guards went rogue. You and Khwaja Hassan manage the city guards. Crack down on them. I want to know if any weapons were provided to attack the Jundiin-ul-Din. I also want you to help Ismail so that work on the mosque can resume. I must be declared caliph before Eid-ul-Fitr. We are running out of time.'

The queen nodded and traded a quick glance with the prime minister. Khwaja Hassan bowed low.

Mahmud looked at the savage man standing in the shadows near the curtain. Across his face ran a scar like a tiny knotted *Abdi* braid. It was from an ancient street scuffle.

He was known as *Turk Kasap-e-Hind. The Turkish Butcher of India.*

'Abu Q'asim,' said Mahmud. 'Step forward.'

Abu Q'asim walked to his master and went down on one knee. Anticipating a soul-satisfying assignment, he felt a thrill run up his spine.

'Find the slaves,' ordered the sultan. 'Take two hundred mounted soldiers from my elite corps. Hunt down those *kafir* animals. I want a pyramid of heads in front of the mosque. Decorations for my consecration ceremony.'

'Your will, My Lord!' boomed Q'asim the Turk, his hand planted firmly on his chest.

'Kill them all!' Mahmud roared in anger. 'Men, women, babies. No one escapes from Mahmud of Ghazni! Let this message resound throughout the world, like your holy work in Somnath!'

'And ... General!' Ismail said to Abu Q'asim. 'I want one slave girl alive. Unspoiled, if possible ... Her name is Yazadeh. She will not be easy to miss. She is probably fourteen years old. Long brown wavy hair and green eyes. She would be the most beautiful among the filthy animals.' His words caught everyone by surprise. Seeing the confounded look on his brother's face, Ismail apologized, 'I am sorry for troubling you with this, My Lord. I am certain the girl was taken against her will. I beg your kindness, My Lord, I need her back alive. She is my personal attendant.'

Malik Ayaz cut in, 'From what I know, great Sultan, Governor-Mufti Ismail has transferred many slaves from his household staff to the construction group to help with the mosque-rebuilding project.' Looking pointedly at Kausari Jahan, the King of Lahore continued, 'Not many are willing to make personal sacrifices to help the mosque's reconstruction, My King.'

Mahmud rolled his eyes, suspecting that Ismail and Malik Ayaz may have become allies in their mutual hatred for Kausari Jahan. 'I'd said earlier, stay out of it, Ayaz.' Turning to

Ismail, Mahmud said, 'Don't make a show of your sacrifices. It would be better if you just got the job done.' Finally, the sultan looked at Abu Q'asim. 'So it shall be, Q'asim! Kill the others but bring this girl alive *and* untouched. It appears my brother needs her to work in his home.'

Ismail remained silent at the obvious sarcasm in Mahmud's voice as he uttered the last statement.

Abu Q'asim rose, an evil smile plastered on his face.

'I shall not disappoint you, My Lord,' promised the fearsome man. He bowed to his master and walked out of the room, the spring in his steps belying his size. His demeanour akin to that of a child rushing outside to play.

Mahmud looked sternly at his brother. 'Those slaves are as good as dead, Ismail, all but your plaything. But work on the mosque must go on. Do *not* fail me again.'

The sultan walked towards the door without waiting for a response. The queen followed close behind. As did Malik Ayaz.

'Yes, My Lord.' Ismail bowed to the retreating figures. As soon as they had left, he turned to Khwaja Hassan. The prime minister looked like he would swoon and fall. Ismail walked towards him and stopped within an inch of the prime minister's face.

'Hassan …' he hissed. He glanced over his shoulder to check if they were alone. He then pinned his eyes on the quivering mass of jelly. 'I said the slaves had help from within. Did you understand that?'

'I did, My Lord,' said Hassan, his head bobbing like it was placed on a spring. 'Someone wanted the reconstruction to fail and make the sultan execute us in a fit of rage. I was *this* close to losing my head.' The prime minister squealed, bringing his index finger and thumb together theatrically.

'As was I,' said Ismail. 'And we both know who that "someone" is. The sultan has ordered that I investigate this matter and produce proof. I intend to do *exactly* that. Meanwhile, Kausari Jahan is now duty-bound to provide labour for our work. I will make her in charge of the security of the slaves. Any further mishaps will lie squarely on her shoulders.'

'Good idea, My Lord.'

'I need more funds. Arrange for them.'

'I will, My Lord. I will,' assured the prime minister, bowing low.

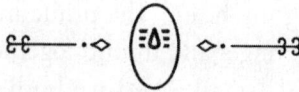

CHAPTER 14

In the Enemy's Backyard

Somewhere in the Arabian Sea

'I have to see it to believe it!' Vijayan exclaimed as he charged up the staircase and burst onto the main deck, followed closely by Amal.

And there he was on the bow of the main deck. His paralysed right arm was tied tightly to his torso, with a shoulder sling that also doubled up as a cast. His incapacitated sword-arm was now less than useless. Not only could it no longer wield a weapon but it also flopped around ineffectually and without any control as the body moved, increasing the chances of injury. In fact, if this arm was injured, he wouldn't even feel it. A warrior without his primary weapon—his sword arm—was like a horse without its primary powerhouse: its hind legs.

But this was no ordinary warrior. This was Narasimhan. Their general.

He had got a shield secured to the front of his restricted right arm and a large metallic shoulder-guard attached to his right shoulder. The shield and shoulder guard served two functions. They prevented injury to his paralysed arm and also allowed it to be put to use, serving the purpose that a shield arm did for any sword fighter. An immobilized shield arm, but a shield arm nonetheless, which Narasimhan was now using adroitly to deflect blows.

More importantly, throughout his confinement in the sick bay, he had trained rigorously, ensuring that his left arm was almost as good as his right arm in swordplay.

On the bow deck, now, he was fighting Dasarna, the Parmar army captain. And very audaciously, they were not using wooden training swords, but real weapons. Sharp swords made from the best steel known to man—Wootz steel from south India. Steel that could slice a fine silk cloth in two and cut through a human bone just as smoothly.

Narasimhan and Dasarna had been thrusting and parrying for over ten minutes already.

The Chola general was fighting an opponent who had use of both his arms. Dasarna held a shield in his left arm and a sword in his right. Having practised for years, all his movements had been stored securely as muscle memory. His skill had been finely honed through training into instinct.

But Narasimhan had converted what was a disadvantage into an advantage.

Statistically, only one in ten men is left-handed. Assuming that warriors follow the proportions of the society they emerge from, nine out of ten warriors would have been trained to battle with their right arm. Dasarna was one of them. The ten per cent of swordsmen who fought with the left hand had the advantage of attacking from unorthodox angles. But they could never know, deep in their muscle memory, how right-armed swordsmen fought.

To know the enemy movements beforehand is to know how to win.

Narasimhan knew, since he was right-handed.

But now, he was fighting with his left.

Dasarna thought he would try something different, since the traditional sword-fighting with Narasimhan had been inconclusive. The general was surprisingly adept at the sword with his newly trained left arm.

Dasarna swerved sideways, pumping his left hand forward, pushing hard with his shield. He used his defensive guard as a weapon, much like a boxer would jab forward with his left, trying to attack Narasimhan's weak and paralysed right arm, to force the general onto his back foot and allow space for the swinging sideward blow he was planning. That would have been a kill strike.

No quarter was to be given for Narasimhan's handicap. That was the order given by the general.

Narasimhan stepped back as he felt Dasarna's shield bang ferociously against his own. He winced in clear discomfort. Dasarna hesitated for just a moment but then swung from the right.

He was following the general's orders. No mercy—for a real enemy wouldn't show it either.

But Dasarna didn't know that a trap was being laid for him.

Narasimhan suddenly stepped back, allowing his right shoulder to disconnect from Dasarna's body. A surprised Dasarna stumbled forward and his sideward sword-swinging action lost direction. Narasimhan pirouetted smoothly out of the way and brought his left arm up in a brutal stab, in an upward angle. Completely unorthodox. An angle that was utterly unexpected for a right-hander, and almost impossible to defend, since there was no shield on that side.

And Narasimhan stopped just in time. The tip of his sword was touching the leather armour of Dasarna at the lower-waist level. If he hadn't stopped, Narasimhan's blade would have gone through Dasarna's belly, slicing most of the organs in the abdominal cavity. It would have been a kill wound.

'What the …' Amal was staring in awe.

Vijayan too was stunned by the remarkable swordsmanship on display by one whose natural sword arm was paralysed. 'How in Goddess Meenakshi's name did the general do that?'

The soldiers watching broke out in spontaneous applause. It wasn't flattery for their senior but genuine admiration for a masterly warrior's rare skills.

Narasimhan dropped his sword and banged his chest forcefully with his closed left fist, exuding the exultant vigour of a dry riverbed receiving a fresh burst of glacial meltwaters. He roared thunderously, '*Senani Skanda!*'

Skanda was *another name for Lord Karthik, the son of Lord Shiva and Goddess Parvati*. And *Senani* meant *commander-in-chief*. Skanda was the General of the Army of the Gods. The greatest warrior to ever walk the sacred land of India. For practically all Indian soldiers, remembering that greatest warrior in a moment of courage and heroism was most natural. What a heroic soldier seeks most is inspiration.

All the soldiers around drew their swords, raised them in the air and bellowed loudly, '*Senani Skanda!*'

Vijayan and Amal drew their swords and pumped the air. As did Dasarna. '*Senani Skanda!*'

Vijayan sheathed his sword, ran up to Narasimhan, picked up the general's sword and, holding it high with both hands, offered it back to his commander with respect. Narasimhan smiled, took his sword back and effortlessly slipped it back into the sheath.

Vijayan was overcome with emotion. He stepped forward and embraced Narasimhan, who hugged Vijayan back warmly.

'Welcome back, Sir,' said Vijayan, stepping back, smiling from ear to ear.

'Good to be back, my friend,' said Narasimhan.

—◦✦◦—

The excitement of the duel was over and Narasimhan was exhausted. Vijayan escorted him back to his chambers below deck. And the general instantly fell asleep on his bed.

'The general needs to rest for the remainder of the day,' said Aamir, Amal's brother. 'The herb extract that had been given to him had numbed his pain and made him much more alert. But any more will not be good for his heart. He must rest to recover. He cannot push himself beyond a point, not till the poison's effect remains.'

'Shouldn't the poison be out of his body by now?' asked Vijayan. He looked at Narasimhan sleeping at the far end of the chamber with concern. 'I don't understand why the Chalukyan arrow is still affecting him.'

'As you know, we extracted many of the arrowhead's shattered pieces in Sabarimala. But it was not a clean extraction,' said Aamir. 'Several tiny shards remained inside. Those splinters probably hurt all the time. And maybe those metal shards had been chemically treated with a slow-release poison, which keeps counteracting the medicines we are giving the general.'

'Can't you extract the remaining pieces?' Vijayan asked.

'We couldn't find them then. They are tiny. Too tiny. And I would not want to risk it now, when the flesh is finally closing up. Also, the strength of the counteracting medicines and the general's own resilience have ensured that he has fought this potent poison quite strongly and remained alive. It's a fine balance we need to strike—the counteracting medicines give him strength against the poison, but too strong a dosage of the medicines may cause a heart attack. Ultimately, we can only hope that the poison in those metal shards will run out. Or we can perform a surgery with better equipment when we are back in Gangaikonda Cholapuram, and can take out those remaining shards ... That is the only long-term solution. For now, we must keep fighting the poison on a daily basis, since it still remains in his body.'

'Alright,' said Vijayan. His general was back, but not completely, yet.

—·◦❦◦·—

Vijayan knelt before the general and looked him in the eye.

'Look at you, Sir,' said Vijayan, his voice suffused with happiness.

It was late in the evening. Narasimhan was lying on his bed. Still feeling tired after the exertions of the duel earlier in the day. Only Vijayan was close by. The others stayed at the far end of the chamber, near the door.

'How …' rasped Narasimhan. He cleared his throat and continued, 'In the Abbasid raid, I heard that we lost twelve men?'

'Yes, General,' said Vijayan grimly. 'Twelve.'

'Nasrullah is not a general,' corrected Narasimhan.

'Of course, Sir. I mean Nasrullah *anna*,' said Vijayan.

'Were all the funeral rites conducted properly?'

'Yes. We buried them at sea with all the customary rites. We lost brave Ansar too, Amal and Aamir's brother. He was the one who destroyed the Abbasid ship.'

Aamir's eyes filled with tears. The men looked away. They did not want to embarrass their comrade by witnessing his tears.

'*Inna lillahi wa inna ilayhi raji'un,*' said Narasimhan.

Narasimhan had quoted an Arabic phrase from the Holy Quran. It meant that *all Muslims belong to Allah, and to Him they shall return*. A prayer uttered out of respect for the valiant Ansar and the Faith he followed.

Everyone else repeated, '*Inna lillahi wa inna ilayhi raji'un.*'

Someshwar and Iqbal touched Aamir's shoulders. Commiserating with their friend for his loss.

There was silence.

'My body burns like a flaming torch.' Narasimhan broke the silence, changing the subject to ease Aamir's discomfort. 'My back is riven with pain. I am nauseous all the time. Perhaps I shall learn to live with it, like one learns to live with a wife.'

They all laughed together.

Men are simple creatures.

When confronted by pain and grief that one can do nothing about and that is beyond one's ability to bear, women like to talk about it with their friends. Sharing their pain reduces the weight of the burden. On the other hand, men like to *not* think about their grief and pain. Instead, they usually like to change the subject, often using humour as a shield. That is why the style of comedy called gallows humour is popular largely among men, not women. To laugh at one's own plight, in irony and humour, even as one is being led to the gallows to be hanged until death, is among the most masculine of traits.

Men are simple creatures.

'Now *that* will be the first thing I tell Harini *anni* when we set foot back in our Motherland, Nasrullah *anna*,' warned Vijayan, using the *Tamil words for elder sister-in-law* and elder brother, laughing uproariously.

Narasimhan laughed along good-naturedly, as did the other men.

'You should take back the command now, Sir,' said Vijayan.

'Not yet, Valeed,' said Narasimhan, straining to get up. 'Not yet …'

Vijayan tried to help Narasimhan to his feet.

'You heard young Aamir,' continued Narasimhan, holding up his palm and dissuading his brigadier from assisting him. 'I am on some kind of herb that keeps me alert for a short time. That is good. But the boy exaggerates the pain relief, believe me. I feel as if molten iron is flowing in my veins, releasing itself from a focal point in my back. From the injury. The pain will come under control soon, I'm sure. But perhaps I need more time. Perhaps, for now, I can continue to be an advisor to you. But you have the command.'

'As you say, Sir,' said Vijayan. 'I will keep the command for now ... But only for now ...'

Narasimhan smiled.

'Salman*ar*,' said Vijayan, turning back to Someshwar. 'Can you get a kaftan for Nasrullah *anna*, like you gave to the rest of us?'

'Of course,' said Someshwar. 'In fact, Nasrullah*ji*'s kaftan is ready.'

'Wonderful. We must also trim his *lihyah*—like mine.' Turning to Narasimhan, Vijayan continued, 'It means beard. Apparently, it is compulsory for an orthodox Muslim man.'

'The *lihyah*,' Narasimhan repeated slowly. 'Well, yours is rather well-kept. It looks good. Our dharmic ancestors had neatly manicured beards and moustaches. Too many of us are clean-shaven now. Perhaps we should bring facial hair back into fashion.'

'Perhaps we should.' Vijayan smiled, stroking his goatee.

Narasimhan shielded his eyes with his left hand. The sun was out strong this day, the sky devoid of any cloud cover. But the winds were kind, as they blew powerful, cool and moist, reducing the scorching force of the lone star of daytime.

'Valeed and Amal,' he said, 'I don't know if you are aware that the heads of the three southernmost dynasties in India—the Cholas, Pandyas and Cheras—are known as the *Moovendhar*, the *Three Kings*.'

Narasimhan, Vijayan and Amal were standing on the main deck of the ship. Leaning against the railing. It was late in the day, close to noon. And the coast of Balochistan was not too far away.

'Yes, Sir,' said Vijayan. 'I do.'

Narasimhan continued, 'Representatives from all three dynasties are here on this boat. I am from the Chola lands, Valeed is from Madurai, the Pandya capital, and Amal is from the Chera highlands of Sabarimala. These dynasties represent the three eyes of Lord Shiva. And we are going to avenge the insult to our Lord.'

'Yes, we will,' said Vijayan. '*Har Har Mahadev.*' This was a cry made by all those who were loyal to Lord Shiva, meaning *all of us are Mahadevs. All of us are Gods.*

'*Har Har Mahadev,*' repeated Narasimhan and Amal.

The trio smiled and looked into the distance. Land was visible now. The vast Ghaznavid empire began from these shores.

'We have been told that Mahmud's capital city, Ghazni, is in the land of Kandahar in the mountains,' said Amal.

Narasimhan and Vijayan nodded.

Amal continued, 'But of course, the Turks came to these lands recently, just a few decades ago. Their original homeland is much farther north, in the Steppe lands of Central Asia. And we all know that their simple Turkic language, the tongue of nomadic barbarians, has limited pronunciation options and syntax. Maybe their language will improve over time. For now, the "g" in our language is pronounced as "k" in their language. So the original name of the land we are going to was not Kandahar but Gandhara.'

Vijayan did a double take. 'This is the land of Maa Gandhari? Of Mahabharat?'

'Yes,' answered Amal.

'Also, Shakuni,' said Narasimhan, smiling.

Amal shrugged. 'Also, yes. Almost every family has someone to be ashamed of ...'

Narasimhan and Vijayan laughed softly.

'We Indians have lost so much. What was Maa Gandhari's land is now ruled by that barbarian Mahmud,' said Vijayan.

'Hmm ...' said Narasimhan sadly.

'The point that you made earlier, Nasrullah *anna*,' said Amal, 'on the three great dynasties working like the three eyes of Lord Mahadev ...'

'Yes?'

'Among the symbols of Lord Shiva,' said Amal, 'are not just His three eyes but also the crescent moon.'

'Yes. Which is why He is also called *Chandrashekhar. The One Who holds the moon on His head.*'

'Do you know that the crescent moon is a sacred symbol for us Muslims as well?' asked Amal.

'Really? I didn't know that.'

'Yes, it is.'

Narasimhan smiled.

Amal continued, 'We are also His. And He is also ours. Lord Shiva is not just Divine for the Hindus. He is Divine for all of us Indians as well.'

'That is Indian religiosity,' said Narasimhan. 'Built on mutual respect for each other's faiths. Something that brutes like Mahmud Ghazni do not get.'

Vijayan looked at Amal and smiled softly. Narasimhan noticed the tenderness.

'We are stronger together,' continued Amal.

'Stronger together,' said Narasimhan.

'Stronger together,' repeated Vijayan.

The port city of Gwadar loomed ahead in a brilliant haze.

The Indians were coming. United.

To the land ruled by the Turkic defiler, Mahmud.

The Indians were coming. And they would have their vengeance.

—◦•〜•◦—

'Come back with us, *aapa*,' urged Altaf, the youngest among the surviving Vavar siblings, to his elder sister. Aamir silently looked at his sister, his expression echoing Altaf's.

Amal looked at the boys and smiled. She turned to face the sea. Squawking gulls glided overhead, eyeing the people bustling around on the top deck of the Chola ship.

Their schooner was close to docking at the Gwadar port.

The chill in the air was replaced by a gentle nip under the midday sun. Thirty-eight Chola and Parmar men—survivors of the encounter with the Abbasid sailors, along with their commanders, were readying to disembark and climb down the rope ladders extending from the ship's railings to the boardwalk.

'You have played your part and laid the ground for our countrymen on this mission,' Altaf said. 'Your job is done. Return with us, *aapa*. Father needs you … Ansar …'

Altaf's voice faltered as his emotions got the better of him.

'I cannot return with you, little brother.' Amal touched her younger brother's cheek lovingly. 'I did not come here just to train and guide the Cholas and Parmars. I will participate in our country's vengeance. Time will decide whether I play a significant role, or not, but I will only leave when the great tyrant has received the punishment he deserves.'

Vijayan, standing a slight distance away, watched the lady. He was torn by conflicting emotions. He knew that if she wasn't a part of this mission, she would live a long life. On the other hand, if she remained a part of it, they might die young, but they would die together. However, thinking with a calm mind, he knew the correct thing to say.

'You must go back, Amal,' said the Pandya, stepping up to her. 'We have already had two dangerous encounters. We have lost twelve men and our leader is injured. And now we are in the enemy's backyard. Altaf is right. Go back with your brothers. Your purpose has been served.'

Amal turned and faced Vijayan fully.

'I am coming with you, Valeed,' she stated firmly. 'I have no doubt you will protect me when needed.'

Vijayan smiled. 'Actually, I was counting on you to protect me, My Lady.'

Amal smiled back. And Vijayan's face lit up. The moment was not lost on Amal's brothers.

'Take care of her, my friend,' said Aamir. 'She means the world to her brothers. She is the collective apple of our eyes.'

'I know …'

Aamir laughed softly and embraced Vijayan.

'Sail back safe and head for the port at Kochi,' said Vijayan. 'Stay close to the shoreline and within reach of our country.'

Aamir nodded in agreement.

Narasimhan approached the group. He handed a sealed scroll to Aamir.

'Aamir, take this and deliver it to the *Gangaikondaan*. He must be informed that we have safely arrived at the enemy's doorstep. And also assured that we are here to succeed.'

Aamir took the sealed scroll and placed it in his sling bag. He placed his hand on his chest and saluted Narasimhan.

'And Aamir, bring your boat back to Gwadar exactly four weeks from now,' Vijayan added. 'Stay docked for another four. If we do not return by then, consider us lost and sail back.'

—◦·❦·◦—

Narasimhan, Vijayan and Amal were the last among the emperor's lionhearts to climb down the rope ladders and join their mates on the harbour dock. Narasimhan had repeatedly refused anyone's support, using his powerful left arm to steady himself as he climbed down. He had taken some of the healing herbs in the morning to gain strength. They waved goodbye to the men standing on the ship deck and then looked around at the bustle.

The harbour wasn't as big as the ports in other parts of the Indian subcontinent. But it was big enough. There were two piers, with berthing possible for ships on both sides, and one quay against a rocky escarpment to the west, with berthing, obviously, only on one side. In all, the two piers and one quay could accommodate around fifteen ships. The rocky escarpment also worked as a breakwater, reducing wave action on the port, and gave a clean slipway for ships to go out to the open sea. There was a tall lighthouse, slightly east of the port, guiding ships to the Gwadar harbour at night. Warehouses stretched along the entire length of the port. And along a few streets leading inwards as well.

Narasimhan had seen far bigger ports. But this one was reasonably sized. The general looked around at his soldiers. He didn't say anything. He didn't need to. The message was clear in his eyes. *We're in the enemy's backyard now. Always stay alert.*

The cries of traders and sailors loading and unloading merchandise from their vessels filled the air.

Someshwar fished inside the pouch tied securely to his inner vest. The medallion from the Abbasid captain was in it. Vijayan had given it to him for safekeeping. It was a precious asset—it could be very useful in sticky situations.

Narasimhan signalled discreetly to the left with his eyes. Someshwar followed his cue and spotted some men walking briskly towards them. Port officials.

Three men walked up to the party. Vijayan noticed that their clothing and grooming were similar to theirs and felt a deep sense of satisfaction. Amal had done well. They blended in with the locals completely.

'Peace be upon you,' said an elderly port official as he approached Someshwar. From his accent, it was evident that he was Persian. Behind him stood a wiry young man with a piece of parchment in one hand and a quill in the other, a record keeper. The third, also senior in age, stood apart and observed the Chola–Parmar party.

'Peace be upon you too, Sir,' replied Someshwar pleasantly. Behind him, on the boardwalk, the Indians stacked their crates containing food, weapons, clothes and sundry supplies. The port officer curiously observed the busy men.

'What is your purpose in Gwadar?' he asked. 'What is in those crates?'

Someshwar casually looked behind and turned back to him. 'Nothing much, really,' he said. 'Food and clothes. We are on a pilgrimage to the great mosque of Ghazni. We are recent converts from the heathen lands of India.' Someshwar had decided to say this so that he could explain the piercings in his ear.

The port officer scowled. But there was clear greed in his eyes. He had learnt over time that Indians, on average, were very wealthy, and those who had recently converted to Islam were usually very eager to prove their loyalty. So a lot of money could be made from them. 'What's your name, Indian?'

'I am Salman,' answered Someshwar, bringing his hand to his chest. 'Iqbal and Nasrullah, my assistants.' He gestured towards Iqbal and Narasimhan. 'And this one here is Valeed, my nephew, and Amal is his wife,' he concluded, pointing at Vijayan and the Vavar scion from Sabarimala.

Amal felt her heart skip a beat with the improvised introduction. She looked discreetly at Vijayan and smiled.

'As for our purpose,' continued Someshwar, 'we wish to see the great mosque that Sultan Mahmud Ibn Sebuktegin has built as his victory monument. We will offer our prayers and then leave for Mecca by road. I wonder if you could guide us in buying camels and horses ... Also, a couple of carriages for our goods?'

The port official smiled warmly, like a fisherman who has been handed free fish without having to worm a hook, throw out a line and reel one in. He turned around and had a quick exchange with the curious old man behind him, who shook his head and sighed in exasperation. Someshwar listened attentively, holding his cordial smile in place. He had traded in ports around the world for many decades. He knew exactly how the game was played.

The port official finally turned to look at Someshwar. 'Salman from India. Can we step aside for a moment? To discuss the paperwork.'

'Of course, Sire,' said Someshwar obsequiously, bowing low. He knew exactly what 'paperwork' needed to be discussed.

—◦⚡◦—

Someshwar returned a short while later. Narasimhan could see the port officials walking away, looking rather pleased.

'All handled, Sir?' asked Narasimhan, sticking to character as an employee of Someshwar.

'Yes, Nasrullah,' said Someshwar, also playing his role. Then Someshwar turned to Iqbal and whispered, with a jovial smile, 'Never question the Simple Rules. Always follow the Simple Rules!'

Iqbal laughed softly. 'Always follow the Simple Rules.'

Narasimhan frowned. 'What are the Simple Rules?'

'It's a private joke between Salman *bhai* and me,' said Iqbal.

'Make it less private,' said Narasimhan. 'What are the Simple Rules?'

Someshwar clarified, 'So it's like this, Nasrullah. While bribing corrupt bureaucrats, we follow these simple rules. And they always work. First, read the officer well. Don't offer an amount so low that they get offended. And not so high that they get suspicious of what your actual game is. And let them have the pleasure of "winning" against you as they negotiate you up on the first offer. Most importantly, always be servile when talking to them. Very servile. Their ego is very dear to them.'

Narasimhan, himself a government employee, though an honest one, was offended. He regretted asking for the clarification. But Someshwar's strategy had worked smoothly, so he didn't comment further.

'Where do we go now, Sir?' asked Narasimhan.

'To the other end of the town. To meet a very specific merchant.'

Someshwar pulled out a paper from the pouch attached to his inner vest. It was a torn *hundi*, worth only one rupee. Narasimhan frowned at the small-valued *promissory note* in Someshwar's hand. It was damaged in any case since the unique identification number that was on all *hundi*s was also torn through. This *hundi* was not a valid tender any more. It was useless.

Someshwar clarified, 'He has the other half.'

Not so useless then.

Narasimhan smiled. *This Gujarati merchant is very smart. If he were younger, he would have found a place in our Chola army.*

'Let's go.'

'As you say, Sir,' said Narasimhan.

Someshwar turned to the Chola–Parmar soldiers, still in character as the merchant directing his workers. He nodded and the men began lifting the crates.

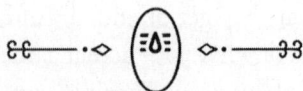

CHAPTER 15

The Only Hope

Somewhere in the Hindu Kush Mountains, Afghanistan

'Our people are falling behind, Pula. We are not prepared to deal with the hardships brought about by this escape. First the hunger and thirst, and now this weather.'

Pula, the leader of the band of escapee slaves, looked back without breaking step. A serpentine column of slaves-turned-fugitives trudged silently behind him. Their heads bowed. Occasional raspy coughs and desolate groans broke the chilly monotony of falling snow.

'This late-season snow is unexpected,' said Pula.

The sun had sunk behind the white snow-covered mountains and iron-grey clouds covered the gloomy sky. Over the past many days, a freak blizzard had battered the central regions of the Ghaznavid sultanate.

'We may have to deal with disease as well,' continued the deputy. He blew into his palms for warmth. 'The snow has brought fever and frostbite.'

'How many people have we lost so far, Dhruv?' asked Pula to his makeshift deputy.

'Four fighting men, ex-soldiers like us,' said Dhruv, pulling his blanket tight over his shoulders. 'The rear guard has reported no casualties so far, although I think it is only a matter of time before they do. There will be deaths from exhaustion, hunger and injury. Our foraging parties are returning with less food every day. These cold, arid lands are not exactly nurturing, Pula, especially for an ill-equipped rabble like us.'

'Time is a luxury we do not possess,' said Pula. 'If anyone dies, we cannot burden ourselves with the last rites, nor can we carry the fallen on our shoulders. But the corpses would be like a trail of breadcrumbs for our pursuers to track us down …'

Dhruv listened in tense silence as he walked alongside his leader.

Pula clutched the hilt of his sword. 'I am sure the sultan has sent a hunting party after us. I wonder …' Pula's words trailed off. He didn't want to worry his deputy.

Someone had sneaked in the weapons that night to Pula and his men. Initially, he had assumed that someone in Ghazni wanted to help them. And you don't look a gift horse in the mouth. Pula had promptly used the weaponry to plot the escape of his followers and of the other slaves. But now he had begun to suspect that the entire thing had been an elaborate trap. *Who helped us in Ghazni? And why?*

'Sir, with all due respect …' said Dhruv, breaking Pula's train of thought. 'Should we …'

'Out of the question,' interrupted Pula. 'That is not what we Indians do. We are better than those barbaric Turks. How will we face our Gods and our ancestors after death, if we don't act with *Dharma*?'

Dhruv fell silent. The suggestion that he had wanted to make was obvious. That the escaping party should break up. There were around fifty fighting men under Pula's command. And a few hundred slaves from many religions and nations—Hindus, Buddhists, Jains, Christians, Zoroastrians, Yazidis. And some Indian Muslims too, for they had refused to abandon their fellow Indians of other faiths. These slaves could not defend themselves or even provide for themselves. They were simply mouths to feed and bodies to protect in case the Ghaznavid soldiers caught up with them. The rational thing to do would be to split up, with the fifty Indian soldiers speeding out of Ghaznavid territory, to later return stronger to fight. And each slave could fend for himself.

Abandoning the former slaves may have been the prudent thing to do. But it wasn't the dharmic thing to do. And so, it could not be done—certainly not by one who follows the path of *Dharma*.

Dhruv was a good soldier. He did not question his commander any further.

'Pula!' cried a young man as he ran up to the two men in the lead. 'Pula! Wait!'

Pula and Dhruv stopped and turned around, triggering a reaction through the moving mass of miserable people, who instantly came to a halt. Some sank to the ground, while others broke rank and wandered off. Somewhere near the end of the caravan, Yazadeh, the rescued slave girl, helped her father, Arif, seat himself beside a group of men.

'What is it, Zayn?' questioned Pula, raising an eyebrow. 'Has someone fallen ill?'

'If only it were that simple,' answered Zayn Husayn, panting. 'A group, around ten men and women, have broken away from us. They have deserted us.'

'Deserted us?!' repeated Dhruv in disbelief. 'Deserted *us*, their protectors? In this crazy, violence-ridden land?'

'I am afraid we *imposed* freedom on some of them, Dhruv,' said Zayn. 'We herded them out of their comfort zone. They did not want it. Among them is that Christian engineer, Butrus, and his family and friends. Butrus was always grumbling about his children not having enough food to eat. And all of them had been complaining incessantly about our ruining their shot at a better life. The sultan had promised them citizenship once the work on the mosque was completed.'

'And of course, they would have to give up their beliefs and legacies—their Jesus—in the process,' Pula said contemptuously. 'Sacrifice their souls in exchange for the liberty and dignity they know will likely not come their way.'

'They lost their liberty and dignity a long time ago, Pula.' Zayn shrugged. 'For many, being a *dhimmi*—a *second-grade citizen*—is better than being raped, tortured and killed by these Turkic beasts.'

Pula shook his head. *How do you save people who don't want to be saved?*

But the problem wasn't just about saving those slaves.

'How did they get away without your knowledge?' Pula asked Zayn. 'You were tasked with keeping an eye on everyone and preventing anyone from straying.'

'Have mercy, Pula. We are just fifty soldiers, tired and hungry, and we guard nine hundred terrorized and quivering men, women and children. It is an impossible task. Butrus and his partisans are gone. The snow must have helped them vanish. Let us just accept it.'

'I hope the deserters have some shame and don't head back in the direction of Ghazni,' said Dhruv worriedly. 'The snow has been a bane but it has also covered our tracks. These deserters can undo our advantage and even send the hunters directly to us.'

'We must pick up the pace,' ordered Pula. 'There is no time for rest now. Do we have enough rations, Zayn? Will they last a while?'

'Yes, they should,' said Zayn. 'John has been doing a good job foraging with whatever little help we have available.' John was another Indian soldier under Pula's command. 'But we are running out of drinking water.'

'Well, it is snowing,' reminded Dhruv. 'Let everyone walk with their tongues hanging out, if necessary, to catch the snowflakes. Pula is right. We must keep moving.'

Zayn Husayn nodded and turned around.

'Get up!' he hollered as he zigzagged down the line, startling the slaves who were ready to set up camp. 'Get up, all of you! The enemy is at our heels. We need to keep moving. No resting! Keep moving!'

Towards the end of the line, Yazadeh rose, instantly ready to move. 'Get up, Father. Come on …'

'*Melek Taus*, have mercy …' groaned Arif, calling to his *Yazidi God*, as he struggled to his feet. 'We had just sat down …'

Yazadeh looked back. And shuddered.

—◦✦◦—

'Hakeem, I need an audience with her for five minutes. Even less, maybe. Please, please, my brother,' begged Khwaja Hassan.

The head of the bodyguard corps of Kausari Jahan looked at the prime minister impassively. He stood like a great teak tree at the entrance to the queen's private chambers. Stoic. Unmoving.

Khwaja Hassan pleaded pathetically, his eyes watery.

'The queen cannot be disturbed now,' said the eunuch firmly. 'She is resting.'

Khwaja Hassan refused to budge. 'Please, Hakeem ... Please ...'

'Are you mad, Hassan?' asked Hakeem, finally losing his patience. The mighty warrior-eunuch, who had the ear of the powerful queen, felt no need to be polite to the Persian prime minister. 'Why do you always arrive at this ungodly hour? Sunrise is three hours away!'

'It is the only time when I have complete secrecy,' said Khwaja Hassan. 'You understand that. So does she. As a true loyalist to the sultanate, I can help her!'

Hakeem looked at him with feigned disinterest. The eunuch had been rejecting Khwaja Hassan's audacious late-night requests—three hours after midnight and three hours before sunrise—to speak to the queen for a week now. Oddly enough, he made no attempt to seek an audience in the daytime.

Either there is a conspiracy afoot—or there is a genuinely terrible secret that Khwaja Hassan seeks to share.

'I cannot disturb her now,' said the eunuch resolutely. 'She is resting. Either leave the message with me or come back at a time when you will not need to go through me.'

'Leave the message with you?' Khwaja Hassan scowled. 'Absolutely not! My business is strictly confidential, and it can be conducted *only* with the queen. Are you sure she is resting, though? I can hear her voice from beyond the curtains. It almost sounds like she is … talking to someone in her chambers,' he said loudly, hoping his voice would carry beyond the curtains into the room.

As if in response, the faint voice from inside the room died abruptly. An awkward silence prevailed. Thick with tension.

'Our babbling may have disturbed the lady and made her mumble in her sleep,' hissed Hakeem. 'Or she may be praying. None of your business! You can leave the message with me or just leave. The choice is yours.'

'Fine!' The prime minister gave up. 'Fine! I shall go. But I will be back, I assure you. One of these nights, you will let me in. I bet that you have not even told the queen that I have been coming here to see her. She would have understood the gravity of the situation and met me.'

Khwaja Hassan turned and waddled out of the antechamber as fast as he could with a pace that was more penguin-like, instead of his usual slow walrus-like gait. Hakeem rolled his eyes and shook his head with a sigh.

'He is gone,' he whispered through the curtained doorway.

The curtains parted. The queen stepped out. Her wavy auburn hair framed her face and cascaded down her back, touching her hips. Dressed in a warm pink nightdress, with a woollen shawl draped across her torso, she felt a shiver run up her spine. Her face was ashen, save the ruddy bruise that began above her left brow and disappeared into her hairline.

'Why does he not get the message?' she whispered worriedly. 'Why does he keep coming here at this time? Particularly *this very time* every night! Could it be ...'

'He is a fool, My Lady,' reassured the eunuch. 'He knows nothing. Perhaps his intentions are genuine too, despite his rumoured allegiance to ... you-know-who.'

'I know about that,' replied Kausari Jahan, wrapping her shawl tightly around her. 'That is why I have refused to see him, night after night. I know the keeper whose cage this bird keeps escaping from.'

'But what if he is trying to help us, My Lady ...' suggested Hakeem. 'What if the bird truly resents its captivity and is trying to buy its freedom?'

'Whatever song this bird intends to sing, I would not trust it, Hakeem,' said the queen resolutely. 'Khwaja Hassan is a survivor. He was here before both you and I entered the picture, and here he will remain well after we are gone. He would betray anyone to survive. *Anyone.*'

—◦✦◦—

Khwaja Hassan mounted his horse with the assistance of two slaves. A third man waited on the side, also on horseback, impatiently observing the amount of time and backbreaking exertion it was taking for the two slaves to help the profanely rotund prime minister clamber onto his horse.

Khwaja Hassan finally settled on his overburdened stallion, then looked back at the dim glow of yellow light emerging from the queen's window, high on the second floor of the palace, and shivered in the dark.

Kausari Jahan was awake.

The Persian prime minister's teeth chattered like the Spanish castanet. He wrapped his fur muffler tightly around his ears and pressed his heels into the horse's belly. The three men rode with him, one in front and one at the back.

The third rode close, right beside him. The governor-mufti, Ismail.

'What did you see and hear?' Ismail asked.

'I have failed again, My Lord,' Khwaja Hassan whispered, still panting from his horse-mounting exertions. 'That foul eunuch refuses to budge.' He straightened his back. It is common for obese people to have severe back problems, and riding a horse wouldn't have helped with that. 'And why should that terrible half-man Hakeem help me? Seeking an audience with the queen at this hour is foolhardy, even dangerous. The sultan will skin us alive if he finds out we are disturbing his wife in the middle of the night.'

'Hassan,' Ismail said, 'we have learned a lot over the past week. Something fishy goes on at this time of the night in Kausari Jahan's bedroom. Did you hear her voice again?'

'As clearly as I did on the other nights,' said Khwaja Hassan. 'What do you think she is doing, My Lord? The eunuch says she mumbles in her sleep. Or she could be praying ... Praying at this hour?! What is she is *actually* doing? Meeting a spy? A conspirator? A lover?'

'This is not the time of day for prayer,' said Ismail. 'Whatever she is doing, it is dodgy. This is the perfect opportunity to bring the witch down. You have done well to bring the queen's late-night activities to my attention, Hassan. Very well indeed.'

'Your profound and incisive wisdom has revealed the dodginess of her pursuits to me, My Lord,' Hassan said with affected humility, his face and voice a near-perfect depiction of servile deference.

But not perfect enough.

Ismail was getting irritated by his constant flattery, which was too obvious for even an imbecile to not notice. 'Forget this nonsense about my profound and incisive wisdom,' barked Ismail.

'Forgotten already, Sire.'

'Just get me the information on what goes on in her chamber every night at this hour.'

'If you could just guide me on how to go about it, great Governor. I have tried all my tricks, I am at a loss.'

Ismail didn't have an answer. He looked ahead and gripped his reins tight—even more irritated.

Khwaja Hassan seized his chance. When an intelligent animal is cornered by a far more powerful predator, the best tactic is to deflect the predator's attention towards another target.

'Perhaps there is a secret entrance ...' whispered Khwaja Hassan. Almost like he was suggesting something to himself.

And the prime minister could see from the corner of his eye that the deflection had worked. Governor-Mufti Ismail was clearly thinking about what he had said. The attention would now be on someone else.

Khwaja Hassan smiled, just a little. *Thank God.*

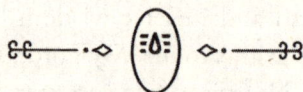

CHAPTER 16

The Price of Justice

Somewhere in the Hindu Kush Mountains, Afghanistan

Butrus the engineer looked at his wife trailing behind him, surrounded by his children. Severely exhausted, they dragged themselves along the ground covered with a thick layer of snow. Patches of ice had formed from the quick cycles of thawing and freezing. The air was frigid.

'Come on! Come on!' Butrus urged his friends and family. 'The snowfall has stopped. God is great! Come on!'

The motley crowd of ten—all deserters from the party of the escaped slaves—was headed back to Ghazni. Butrus had convinced them that this attempted return, however dangerous, would be worth their efforts. After all, Mahmud had promised them freedom once the mosque was rebuilt. It was better to go back and surrender to the governor-mufti.

Butrus was motivated by the good impression he had built with the governor-mufti. The mosque assignment had come as manna from heaven, and he would not spoil his prospects

246

of stability and a good future for his children with the rash cravings of a few freedom-loving desperados. He greatly regretted being herded by the mad bunch into rushing away from the safety and security of Ismail's custody.

The governor-mufti needs me to ensure that the mosque's architectural designs are fit and proper. He will protect me.

'I think I see a village ahead. We will get some food and rest soon,' Butrus said.

The group picked up the pace. Suddenly, they saw a grey mass emerging from the horizon.

Horsemen.

Riding hard.

They were headed straight for the small group.

Butrus's wife ran up to him and clutched his hand, crying loudly, 'Oh Lord! Save us. Jesus, save us.'

Butrus yanked his hand away and shaded his eyes to reduce the glare of the sun. He looked ahead.

The horses were approaching rapidly. The colours that the riders wore were now visible.

'Butrus!' shrieked the architect's wife, falling to her knees. Panic gripped her heart as she stared at the dreaded colours and pulled her twins towards her. The seven-year-olds cowered in her bosom. She bowed her head and began praying, hard. Praying for a quick, painless death.

More and more from Butrus's party could now see the colours the warriors were wearing.

A wail erupted among the people. 'Run!'

But nobody moved.

Strangely, though, Butrus was smiling.

He too could recognize the colours. The ordinary soldiers of the Ghazni army wore green tunics, but these mounted warriors were different. In peacetime, they normally wore white. But when they went into battle, they would be dressed all in black, with the image of a roaring lion embroidered on their sleeves in white thread.

These were Sultan Mahmud's personal guards, elite warriors handpicked by him. They were chasing the escaped slaves.

Butrus whispered softly, 'Abu Q'asim.'

Turk Kasap-e-Hind. The Turkish Butcher of India.

Butrus's wife was howling loudly now. 'The butcher has found us, Butrus! We are dead! My children are dead!'

The tattered bunch of deserters were frozen into paralysis.

'Run!' People were screaming at each other to escape. But nobody was actually moving. Where would they run? There was no way these tired, hungry slaves could outrun the horses. And even if they ran, there was nowhere to hide.

'Butrus!' his wife shrieked. 'Butrus! We are dead!'

'Quiet, Jessica.' An unfazed Butrus tried to calm his wife down. 'Can you not see it? We are *saved*! We will tell the sultan's men that we never wanted to escape. We were forced to. They will *have* to believe us! We are walking towards Ghazni, are we not?'

For sure, Governor-Mufti Ismail must have given them instructions to ensure the safety of my family and me. It's good that I am not with the other escaped slaves—I can prove my loyalty to Ismail.

His wife seemed unconvinced. Still agitated. 'We might convince the sultan's men to spare our lives, but they will question us about the others. What will you do? Will you betray them? There are many who would rather die than fall into the hands of their tormentors again.'

Butrus shook his head. 'Those silly people don't have a hope in hell of making it. Pula is being brave to the extent of being foolhardy ... But I will *never* rat on them. Jesus Christ is watching me. I will never rat on them.'

The architect waved his hands frantically at the Ghaznavid horsemen. Some around him joined in, waving with pathetic hope. The rest sank to the ground, defeated. Butrus's wife held her twin girl and boy and muttered the Lord's Prayer.

Two hundred Ghaznavid horsemen slowed down and parted into two neat columns as they approached the ragged bunch. They formed two circles around the scared escapees and broke into a low rumble, chanting glory to the sultan. On and on they rode playfully in opposing arcs, like two great vipers spiralling around a piece of meat. Butrus and his people watched in complete submission.

Three riders broke from the arcs and trotted towards the group. Butrus held his ground with a confident smile. He addressed the brutish leader of the Turkish horsemen.

'Greetings, Sire!' he cried, falling to his knees and prostrating before the mounted giant. The other escapees followed suit, including his wife and two children, in abject surrender.

'Up, you pigs!' roared Abu Q'asim.

The architect and his companions promptly sprang to their feet, their hands clasped in supplication.

'You are the slaves who bolted.' Q'asim grinned. 'But why so few? I was told there were close to a thousand.'

'We escaped those renegades, My Lord,' squeaked Butrus as he cautiously approached the brute. 'There are many more. They forced us to stay with them. But we managed to escape and were on our way back to Ghazni. We played no part in

the massacre of the Jundiin-ul-Din in the labour camp, Sire,'
he said vehemently. 'We were taken against our will.'

'Damned coward,' Q'asim spat, trading amused looks with
the men around him. 'He thinks he can escape death with this
ridiculous story. These must be stragglers who fell behind and
got lost in the blizzard.'

The Turkish warriors laughed in delight.

Butrus's heart began to pound in alarm. His decision had
perhaps been a bad mistake. 'Please, Sire,' he begged. 'I assure
you our intentions are honourable. I am Butrus. You can ask
the governor-mufti when we get back to Ghazni. He knows
me well. I am the chief architect and engineer of the repairs
on the Jama Mosque. My loyalty to the sultan is absolute!
And I have already pledged myself to Islam. I am of the One
True Faith now.'

*How will the Turks know I worship Jesus Christ in private? I
am sure that Jesus will understand. I am doing it for my family.*

'Silence, you dog!' roared Abu Q'asim, jumping off his
horse. Many of his soldiers followed him and dismounted.

Abu Q'asim casually strolled up to Butrus. He looked at
his fellow Turks, exchanging sniggers. When he was close to
the Christian, Abu Q'asim suddenly reached out and grabbed
him by the throat. The architect's wife whimpered and fell
silent. She pressed her children's faces into her body, almost
suffocating them. They squealed. She pressed harder.

'Who is Yazadeh?' growled Abu Q'asim. 'Is she here?'
He looked at the shivering mass with feral eyes. 'I don't see
a pretty wench.' He looked at Butrus's wife and spat on the
ground.

'No …' Butrus gasped. His face had turned blue. Abu
Q'asim released his grip. 'Yazadeh is not … with us … Sire!'

'I have no use for you then, scum,' the Ghaznavid general sneered.

The Turkic Butcher of India remorselessly twisted Butrus's arm, while the architect howled in desperate agony. With strength that was almost superhuman, Abu Q'asim wrenched and jerked Butrus's arm so hard that the poor Christian's arm fell free of its socket.

Butrus collapsed on the ground. His right arm hung like a loose pendulum, falling at an unnatural angle. He shrieked incoherently in pain, almost on the verge of unconsciousness. He was a simple intellectual man. Not a warrior. Not built to tolerate pain. His wife, Jessica, was on her knees, a short distance behind her husband, screaming like a banshee.

Abu Q'asim looked at Jessica. And then turned to his soldiers. 'Bring that woman here.'

The risk to his wife and children suddenly brought Butrus back to life. Most men do everything they do solely for their wives and children. They will sacrifice it all, only for their wives and children. Their health, their bodies, their minds, their souls. And even their morals. They will sacrifice it all. Only for their wives and children.

'Let my … wife and children … go … Sire,' Butrus pleaded. 'And I will … tell you where they are … Where Yazadeh … the governor's woman … is …'

The Ghaznavid general grinned. 'Finally.' He looked towards his lieutenants. 'What did I tell you about these *kafir*s? No strength. A few strong blows and they surrender completely. They are born to be slaves. We *momin*s are the only real men in the world.' Turning back to a cowering Butrus, Abu Q'asim continued, 'So tell me. Which way did they go? How far away are they? How many of them are trained military men? Tell me everything.'

'Westward ...' bleated the architect, pointing with his intact left arm. 'They are heading for Persia ... They may have broken ... into smaller groups ... Only around ten are ex-soldiers ... Sire.'

The architect's wife let out a soft breath. Her bosom swelled with quiet pride. Her husband was a good man. She always knew that. He was a man of honour. He did all that he did, only for the children. Only for the children. But at this crucial time, he had not revealed the truth: that the escapees were headed south, towards India.

He had been loyal. He was a good man.

Jessica sighed quietly. They would die with honour. They would not be embarrassed when their Saviour returned. Jesus Christ would receive them with love.

Abu Q'asim continued staring at Butrus. Silent for a little while. When he spoke, his voice was scarily calm. 'You're sure you're going with that?'

'It's the truth ... Sire ...'

The butcher pulled out his scimitar from its scabbard.

'Pity,' he spat, making a theatrical expression. 'Pity that you lie in your last moments. I hope your Christ forgives you. Because my Allah will not.'

Butrus closed his eyes and waited for the inevitable.

'Don't you want to know how I know that you lied?' asked Abu Q'asim.

Butrus remained silent. Breathing heavily. The pain overpowered his senses.

'Butter, Bugger, Butrus or whatever the hell your name is, you may be an architect, but you are not very smart. The tracks you and your party have left in the snow come from the *south*. Clearly, the people you began your journey with could not have gone west. You and your party of stragglers, deserters, escapees, whatever—you have actually helped me. This cursed incessant snowfall had covered your tracks. I thank you now for the fresh ones. They will lead me to my prey.'

Butrus was shivering in sheer terror.

'You dared to lie to me? Lie to *Turk Kasap-e-Hind*?'

Abu Q'asim swung his sword viciously. The blow was so ferocious that it cleaved Butrus in two from the shoulder down to his lower waist. Almost. Even as horrified screams rent the air, Q'asim pulled out his blade and struck again. And again. And again. Like an earnest butcher carving and dissecting meat. The cries of Butrus's wife and the other hapless pile of people found their macabre echo in the triumphant roar of the joyful Turks. Some prisoners dashed wildly and crashed into the circle of gleeful horsemen. Others were rooted, waiting for their own terrible end.

But Abu Q'asim would not stop. He hacked away at the architect's body in a mad fit of bloodlust. Other Ghaznavid soldiers dismounted and walked to the cowering men and women. Drawing their swords. Killing all in their path. The rest broke into a circular gallop in a haze of snow and thunderous hooves. Whooping loudly, as they often did in celebration while on a killing spree.

Butrus's wife, Jessica, pinned her children to the ground and covered them with her body like a mangy shield. Even as she was stabbed and cut brutally, she did not move. She protected her little children till her last breath.

It was soon over. The cleaving stopped as the twisted mass of human flesh and bone that had once been Butrus, lay in a massive red puddle, framed by crimson snow. Abu Q'asim shoved the mangled corpse aside. He looked around. Every one of the adult slaves was dead. Most of them had been sliced so many times that they were unrecognizable.

In that pit of grisly flesh, bones, sinew and blood, lay the young terrorized twins. Just seven years old. Just seven.

The boy and girl stared at Abu Q'asim with round shellshocked eyes. No tears. No crying. What they had witnessed went beyond the limits of imagination. Beyond any possible scope of reaction. The little children sat catatonic. Petrified into paralysis.

The Turkish general savoured the terror on their tender, innocent faces. He really enjoyed that. He bent and grabbed them by the scruff of their necks and hoisted them up like blood-washed kittens.

'Look!' he cheered, a wide grin splitting his face. 'They have left us little playthings! Come and collect your rightful dues, my brothers. Remember, it is not a sin if you do it to a *kafir*. All is fair in our war with *kafir*s. All is fair!'

—◦✦◦—

Ghazni, Afghanistan

'Governor Ayaz, a moment of your time, please,' said Ismail.

The governing council, including Khwaja Hassan and the other junior ministers, had gathered at the mansion of the governor-mufti to review the progress on the reconstruction of the mosque. The meeting had just got over, and all seemed satisfied with the progress. More slaves were going to be arranged, some even through Kausari Jahan. So despite the escape of some of the slaves under the leadership of Pula, the construction work for the mosque was going apace. The only issues were the architectural and structural designs. Ismail knew that he needed Butrus to ensure that the designs of the mosque were fit and proper. Architects and engineers from the more educated parts of the Islamic world, such as Arabia and Persia, were no longer coming to Turkic Ghazni. The tension between these two parts of the Islamic world, the Arab and Persian on the one hand, and the Turk on the other, was increasingly becoming evident to all. Furthermore, it was difficult to find good architects and engineers among the Turks, for they mostly specialized only in the fine art of killing. Fields like education, even in architecture and engineering, were left for those that the Turks considered sissies and pansies. Now, with Butrus gone, Ismail had decided that as long as the mosque stood for a few years, it would be more than enough. He would have gotten rid of Mahmud by then. Butrus or no Butrus, the construction of the mosque was moving fast.

Ismail was, rightly in his opinion, focused on the immediate, rather than the long term.

'Stay? Why?' asked Malik Ayaz.

'I just wanted to speak on a few other urgent matters, great King of Lahore,' said Ismail, polite and gentle.

Ayaz rolled his eyes and sighed loudly. He shrugged visibly and flopped back on his seat. 'Aaalriiiiight.'

None of the other ministers thought much of this as they walked out. But Khwaja Hassan looked at Ayaz and smiled to himself.

The dandy thinks that Ismail is only going to plead with him for some more money. But the King of Lahore doesn't know that he is going to be given a much more difficult ask ... Kausari Jahan ...

Khwaja Hassan kept his thoughts to himself. He had transferred the problem from himself to Malik Ayaz. *God is kind. In fact, God must be Persian, because He has blessed us with all the brains.*

Ayaz waited for a few moments after everyone had left, including Khwaja Hassan. Particularly that snake, Khwaja Hassan. Only when he was sure that he was alone with Ismail did Ayaz's expression change. Gone was the jaunty, uninterested, callow look. His face suddenly became warm and soft, and a broad smile appeared on it. His voice turned deeper as he rose and walked up to Ismail. 'Father.'

Ismail smiled and opened his arms as Ayaz embraced him. Their relationship had been kept a secret from all for obvious reasons. Ismail, having a publicly acknowledged heir in Malik Ayaz, would cause Mahmud to kill the King of Lahore to protect the ascension to the throne of his own sons. Turkic royal families followed the Steppe land tradition of violent dog-eat-dog competition.

Ismail had admitted to his manservant, Talib, that he genuinely had no recollection of the Georgian slave woman through whom, Malik Ayaz claimed, he had sired him. This, despite the childishly enthusiastic son, Ayaz, showing paintings of his mother to his long-lost father. But Ismail genuinely hadn't recalled the woman in the painting. There had been so many of them. For so long. As Ismail had asked Talib later, how could he be expected to remember all the women he had taken by force? It was unfair and unreasonable to expect him to remember.

However, Malik Ayaz was now a powerful, and useful, man. So Ismail had done the logical thing and had, of course, pretended to remember his long-lost son and his mother, who he claimed to miss dearly. He had also complained about being forced to be separated from them due to his imprisonment at the hands of Mahmud.

They say that love can lead to war. However, an oncoming war can also lead to love. Or at least declarations of it.

'My son,' murmured Ismail, holding Malik Ayaz in a tight embrace.

'I know the money is a little delayed, Father,' said Malik Ayaz. 'But the sultan has grown much more suspicious these days. Just give me a few days. I will ensure that nothing comes in the way of the mosque's construction. I know how crucial that is for you.'

'I would expect nothing less from you, my son,' said Ismail. 'Together we will rule Ghazni.'

'Together, we will … God is great.'

'But my request today is not about the money …'

'No? Something else troubles you, Father?'

'Yes … Kausari Jahan …'

Malik Ayaz breathed irritably. 'That witch has a demonic hold on the sultan. I simply cannot get him to shake it off. I am at my wits' end. She blocks all my schemes. I wanted some reforms in Lahore to help …'

'She is a witch, my son, no doubt about it,' interrupted Ismail. He wasn't really interested in the plans that Malik Ayaz had for Lahore. 'But I think I have stumbled onto something that may help us take her out of the picture.'

'Really?' asked Malik Ayaz, intrigued. He leaned closer to listen to his father. And to hear what was expected of him.

Talib was watching and listening to the entire meeting from the secret spyhole that Ismail had installed. His master wanted him to watch all the meetings and provide feedback and advice. He felt bad for Malik Ayaz, and not for the first time. He had really grown to like the King of Lahore. Someone who had once believed himself to be an orphan, desperately seeking the love and approval of his long-lost father. Unaware that his father doesn't even remember his birth mother, whom he had used and discarded. Unaware that his father was just using him because it was profitable. And also unaware that his father would probably discard him just as rapidly if he stopped being useful to him.

The fact that Malik Ayaz had risen from a slave's status to become one of the most powerful men in the empire also gave Talib a sense of identification with him.

But Talib was simply a servant. His task was to serve his master, Ismail. In Ismail's growth was his survival. He wouldn't let his emotions come in the way. He shook his head and focused again on the conversation.

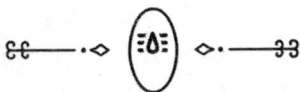

CHAPTER 17

Shadows at the Pass

Rajendra Chola sat on the green-and-red royal throne in the well-lit private court chamber of the royal palace of Panai. The capital city of the Srivijaya empire was Palembang, located farther south-east. However, Panai was the second largest port city of the empire and therefore a royal palace had been built there as well, serving as a guest house whenever Srivijayan royals visited.

Next to Rajendra Chola, to his left, sat his great ally and close friend, Emperor Bhojadev Parmar, the ruler of Malwa, on his own travelling royal throne.

Opposite Rajendra Chola sat Emperor Rama Vijayavarman, the proud king of humbled Srivijaya. Sitting on his traditional throne. The protocol advisors had suggested that, as the defeated king, Vijayavarman sit on a smaller chair rather than on a throne. But Rajendra Chola was dharmic. He believed in being defiant when defeated, but gracious and magnanimous in victory. He had insisted that Vijayavarman also sit on his own throne. And had waited patiently till the protocol officers had made the changes in the arrangements.

Arrayed alongside the rulers, to their left and right, were the generals and admirals of the two armies. The Srivijayan

259

contingent was almost two-thirds smaller than that of the Chola one with its allies. The former had lost too many brave military leaders in this decisive defeat.

The military losses were so severe when it came to personnel and equipment that the Srivijayans would not be able to rise against the Cholas again, at least for a generation or two.

Narasimhan, the Chola general, sat to the right of Rajendra Chola, in a place of honour, as was his due. In a chair that was noticeably smaller than the thrones of the three royals, obviously, but a grand chair nonetheless.

To the left of Bhojadev Parmar, and two places left of Rajendra Chola, sat a diminutive lady resting her hands daintily on her lap. Her inky black hair was combed back severely and tied in a neat bun at the base of her neck. A line of hair fell neatly over her forehead and cut above her bow-shaped brows in a fringe. Her small eyes were capped by unlined eyelids. A pert nose sat above a thin upper lip, below which, in startling contrast, was a lush, fulsome lower lip. The exquisite ensemble of features came together on a heart-shaped alabaster face. Princess Fei Lin, Rajendra Chola's enigmatic Chinese ally, observed the men in the room in subtle triumph.

The Indians in Rajendra Chola's camp had had suspicions about Fei Lin. They knew that she had encouraged Rajendra Chola to attack the Srivijayans. Perhaps a diplomatic solution could have been found for the imbroglio of the Srivijayans confiscating the properties of Indian trading guilds and handing them over to the Chinese. They knew that Fei Lin belonged to the branch of the royal family that had lost the recent Chinese civil war. Maybe she wanted her own enemies, within her own empire, weakened at the hands of Rajendra Chola. The Chinese had as sophisticated a culture as the Indians, but it was incredibly difficult to read them. Nobody could be sure what their actual game was. Fortunately, thanks to the bravery and ruthlessness of Narasimhan, the war had gone well for the Chola empire, so there was no permanent loss in this expedition.

Rajendra Chola looked at his opponent, a kindly smile on the Indian emperor's face.

The Srivijayan emperor of Indonesia, Rama Vijayavarman, was roughly the same age as Rajendra Chola, on the verge of turning sixty. He was as fit and muscular as the Indian emperor was. Though, at this time, he sat hunched, with his head slightly bowed. 'My Lord and Master, I have stamped my seal on the treaty.'

Rajendra Chola had been magnanimous despite his almost-complete victory. The Chola emperor had insisted that Vijayavarman retain the title of emperor of Srivijaya as long as he acknowledged the overlordship of Rajendra Chola and sent a nominal tribute of one hundred thousand gold coins to the Chola court every year. He had returned many territories seized from the Srivijayans, save a few ports that controlled trade along the Strait of Malacca. The Chola administration would manage those ports and pay fair rent for them to the Srivijayans. The warehouses, trade systems and berths in these ports, which the Srivijayans had seized from Indian trade guilds, had been returned to the Indian traders. The debilitating licence and control restrictions that the Indians and their allied trading guilds had been subjected to by Srivijayan bureaucracy had been removed. But it had been promised by Rajendra Chola that the Indian trading guilds would pay fair taxes and customs duties to the Srivijayan courts, provided none of this was sent to the Song emperor in China.

Considering the totality of the Chola victory, this was an astonishingly generous peace offer. Rajendra Chola believed that speaking kindly and softly, while wielding a big fearsome stick, got the best response from his opponents. And he had been repeatedly proved right.

What surprised Rajendra Chola, therefore, was how downcast Vijayavarman looked. He had lost in the battlefield, but in real, strategic terms he had not lost much. In effect, the money that had been going to China would now go to India. The Srivijayans would not be any poorer.

'I thank you for that, great Emperor,' said Rajendra Chola, nodding his head and smiling. 'And consider me your elder brother, rather than a master.'

Vijayavarman bowed his head and joined his palms in a namaste. For even he knew that Rajendra Chola had been extraordinarily benevolent in victory. But he did not smile. 'You are a great man, Chakravarti Emperor Rajendra Chola. As Gautam Buddha is my witness, I, Vijayavarman, follower of the Shakyamuni and the emperor of Srivijaya, swear in public that neither I nor my descendants will ever raise the banner of revolt against a Chola emperor.'

The Srivijayan emperor and his family were practitioners of Buddhism, which, along with Hinduism and Jainism, comprised the dharmic group of religions. Most of his common subjects in Srivijaya were Hindu, but much of the elite, particularly the trading elite, were Buddhists.

'As the Mahadev is my witness,' said Rajendra Chola, 'I, Rajendra, servant of Lord Shiva and son of the peerless Rajaraja, swear in public that I will respect and take care of your daughter, Onang Kiu, as one of my chief wives.'

Vijayavarman looked at Rajendra Chola in surprise. It was one of the terms of the treaty to establish marital relations between the two royal families, so that war may be avoided in the future. For that, Vijayavarman's daughter, Onang Kiu, was to be given in marriage to Rajendra Chola. That had been decided. But what had not been decided was that Rajendra would honour Onang as one of his chief wives.

Vijayavarman nodded gratefully. And still, he did not smile. His eyes held tremendous grief and sadness in them. This wasn't just about a military loss. There was something else.

Rajendra was staring carefully at Vijayavarman's face, trying to guess what was going on in the mind of the Srivijayan emperor. For the long-term stability of the peace treaty, he needed Vijayavarman to fully accept the new arrangement with complete satisfaction. He couldn't figure out what more he could do to ensure that.

Then Vijayavarman himself offered something. 'My Lord Rajendra Chola, with your permission, I have something more to give.'

Rajendra Chola didn't know how to react. This was unorthodox. Everything had been decided and closed already. And the treaty had been stamped with the seals of both sides. But he did not show any adverse reaction. Rajendra kept his face stoic. And very correctly, nodded his assent.

Vijayavarman turned to his priest, who had been waiting patiently at the door. At one nod from his liege, the Pandit turned around and the two guardsmen opened the massive doors. There was a man outside, holding what looked like a standard-sized jewellery box, made entirely of gold. And behind him, a posse of six men carrying a large ornately carved trunk. The men started marching up to the centre of the chambers. They were chanting something—very softly. The priest chanted with them.

Rajendra Chola recognized the hymns instantly. They were from the Garuda Purana. Hymns that are normally sung by followers of the dharmic way—Hindus, Buddhists and Jains— during funeral ceremonies.

Rajendra touched the hilt of his sword lightly. As did Bhojadev Parmar. Per the terms of the arrangement, only the Chola side had the right to bear arms. The Srivijayan side was not allowed to carry any of their weapons into the chamber. Rajendra Chola was kind, not stupid.

Vijayavarman rose from his throne and looked at Narasimhan. 'Brave General, I have a gift for you.'

Narasimhan stood up immediately. He had to. He was only a general. And there was a king, who was now an ally of his emperor, standing up to talk to him.

'Emperor …' said Rajendra Chola, also getting up. Bhojadev Parmar stood up too.

'There is nothing dangerous for the body in these boxes, Your Highness,' said Vijayavarman. 'You have my word of honour. But this is something that I must give to the general who destroyed my army and navy. It only has what he deserves.'

Narasimhan didn't know how to react. He held his hands together in a namaste, offering respect to the Srivijayan emperor, for he didn't want to jeopardize the peace treaty.

'I was on the naval admiral ship, General, during the battle,' said Vijayavarman.

Narasimhan was confused. Then who was on the royal flagship, with the royal colours flying high?

Narasimhan had attacked the royal flagship, assuming that the Srivijayan emperor was on it and was escaping like a coward.

He had also assumed that the attacks he was facing from the naval admiral ship were coming from a brave naval commander putting his own life at risk by drawing fire to himself, so as to save his fleeing emperor.

But in fact, it seemed that Emperor Vijayavarman himself was on the naval admiral ship, putting his own life at risk, drawing the Chola attacks on himself, so that the royal flagship could escape. But why?

It was Rajendra Chola who understood first. Oh Lord Mahadev!

A good man will do anything for his family, even sacrifice his own life, particularly for those who cannot defend themselves.

Vijayavarman confirmed the suspicion. 'I lost precious members of my family that night.'

Narasimhan glanced briefly towards the right of Vijayavarman's throne, where his grown son was sitting. Yes, he had lost two sons, but one was still alive. His heir was still alive. And as for his other sons dying … Narasimhan was thinking exactly how any other warrior would. This is war … It's about men killing … And men dying … We all know what we signed up for.

What Narasimhan hadn't guessed was already clear to Rajendra Chola.

This was about Vijayavarman's second wife.

The Cholas had received intelligence reports that the Srivijayan emperor had sailed with most of his navy to Ilamuridesam, at the northern tip of the Sumatra Island, not too far from the Chola naval base on the Nicobar Islands. The Cholas had expected to battle the Srivijayans in the larger port city of Panai, farther south-east on the island of Sumatra, which had a much more defensible harbour. But they had received intelligence that the local governor of Ilamuridesam was using the confusion caused by the Chola attack to mount his own rebellion. Perhaps Vijayavarman had gone to crush that rebellion. The Cholas were planning their war strategy in light of this new situation, when they received surprising information that Vijayavarman had hastily left Ilamuridesam. The Cholas had decided to give chase while the emperor of Srivijaya was still at sea. Narasimhan had always been a brilliant reader of ocean winds. And a fantastic tactical organizer of naval assaults. He had surprised the Srivijayans with the speed of the Chola advance, and had caught up with Vijayavarman's fleet before they could escape into the safety of the Panai harbour. That had sealed the Srivijayans' fate.

Rajendra Chola had always wondered why Vijayavarman had gone to Ilamuridesam to quell the rebellion. He could have sent one of his admirals instead.

From what I have heard, his second wife was from Ilamuridesam. Perhaps, it was a rescue mission rather than a campaign to stamp out rebellion, *mused Rajendra Chola.*

'*The royal ship was flying the flags in reverse, great General,*' *said Vijayavarman.*

Narasimhan knew what that meant. There was a family aboard that ship. Therefore, do not attack.

But it was night-time ... Visibility was low ... We couldn't be sure of the arrangement of the flags ... *he thought helplessly.*

Vijayavarman beckoned the bearer who was holding the first small jewellery box. The priest walked up with the bearer and opened the box.

'*This is from that royal ship that you had shelled with your trebuchet machines, great General.*'

'Emperor … I think that …' *Rajendra Chola tried to intervene.*

'Please allow me this, My Lord and Master,' *Vijayavarman insisted to Rajendra Chola.* 'I will never ask for anything else from you ever again. I will always be your loyal servant. But please, allow me this.'

Rajendra Chola fell silent. Troubled.

Narasimhan looked at the open jewellery box. There was a gold annulus inside. Slightly elliptical and not perfectly circular. It was too large for a ring, too small to be a grown woman's bangle.

The Chola general was even more confused.

Rajendra Chola saw it too … Oh Lord Mahadev … Have mercy … He had a child from his second wife

A solitary tear escaped from Vijayavarman's left eye. The side of the body where his heart lay. 'This is my daughter's anklet. My daughter Odiratna's anklet.'

Narasimhan's mouth fell open in shock. Mahadev! Forgive me … Forgive me …

The anklet was too small to belong to a grown woman. Judging from its size, the wearer of the annulus anklet would have been no older than four or five years of age.

I killed a child … Oh Lord …

Rajendra Chola once again tried to step in. 'Ask whatever you want from me, noble Emperor,' *he told his Indonesian counterpart.* 'I will not say no. But do not ask for my general's life. He didn't know … None of us knew …'

'Great Emperor …' *Bhojadev Parmar said.* 'Listen to me, please … This was a terrible mistake … But it wasn't intentional …'

Narasimhan had been too stunned to react till now. But hearing Rajendra Chola's and Bhojadev Parmar's words, he spoke up. 'I will give up my life for this heinous crime, Emperor Vijayavarman. You have the right to ask for my execution.'

'I don't want to take your life,' said Vijayavarman to Narasimhan. 'You are not a Turk.' For the ruler of Srivijaya knew what Dharma *had taught him. That the best punishment for immoral creatures, such as the Turks of Ghazni—who felt no guilt at hurting even children—should be death. The fear of death would make them behave. But for civilized men, such as his opponents from India, who would naturally feel immense remorse at killing a child, the worst punishment would be a long life of guilt, rather than a quick death. 'All I want is to give you this anklet. Odiratna's anklet.'*

Narasimhan held his breath. His hands were shaking. In the epic Mahabharat, Lord Krishna had punished the warrior Ashwathama with an unending life full of pain caused by the divine gem on his forehead, for the crime of killing children. For Narasimhan, this anklet would be like that divine gem. It would cause pus and blood to ooze out constantly from his infected, festering soul, in a never-ending cycle of pain.

'In the name of eternal Dhamma,*' said Vijayavarman, using the* Pali-language word for Dharma, *'I want your word of honour, General Narasimhan, that you will keep this anklet on your person at all times, till the moment that the tortured soul of my daughter forgives you.'*

Narasimhan, paralysed and stunned by the enormity of the crime he had committed, even if unknowingly, still found the strength to nod his agreement. He had to be man enough to accept his punishment.

Vijayavarman picked up the anklet and placed it on Narasimhan's open right palm. The Chola general flinched as he felt the annulus burn his body, his mind, his soul. A man who had not winced at even the mightiest of enemy swords striking him was being felled in front of all, by a child's ornament.

But Vijayavarman was not done. His grief was still burning. He beckoned for the men standing behind, holding the large trunk, to come forward. They did. Vijayavarman gestured to his priest to open the lid, looked at Narasimhan, and whispered, 'I hope this victory was worth it, General.'

Narasimhan, brave Narasimhan, who had never stepped back even from the greatest of dangers, was cowering. For he could guess what was inside the trunk.

Rajendra Chola and Bhojadev Parmar, too, were shedding tears.

The trunk lid was opened completely.

Narasimhan held the sides of his head and wailed in misery and horror. He could hear his heart, his soul, his immortal ancestors cursing him for what he had done.

It was the completely burnt body of a child. By her size, she was no older than four or five years of age. A remnant of a spear-shaped bolt was buried in her. The projectile had, clearly, brutally rammed into the little girl's back, at the lower end of her waist. It had blasted all the way through to burst out in the front, where her intestines were. Narasimhan remembered well: these spear-shaped projectiles were dunked in oil and loaded into the slings of the trebuchet war machines, set on fire and then launched incessantly at the fleeing Srivijayan royal ship. One of these flaming projectiles had viciously pummelled this innocent little girl. It had burst through her abdominal cavity.

This wouldn't have been a quick death. If it had hit her heart or head, the little princess would have died instantly. But this … this fiendish bolt … it would have caused her to bleed copiously while also setting her on fire. She would have been burned alive, while bleeding out, over many minutes. It would have been a horrible, painful death for even an adult, powerful warrior. And this was a little girl. Just a little girl.

No more! *Narasimhan's mind screamed in agony.* No more killing!

Narasimhan woke up suddenly. He looked around, feeling groggy. He was on a palanquin, being carried by four Chola soldiers. His left hand was clutching the annulus pendant tightly. It was burning his hand, his conscience, his soul. He closed his eyes again. *I'm sorry, Odiratna. I'm so sorry.*

'Are you alright, Nasrullah?' asked Vijayan.

Vijayan was riding a horse right next to the litter, no more than a portable bed, that carried Narasimhan. The wild contrast in the weather in these parts, with the immense heat during the day and the freezing cold at night, had weakened Narasimhan. Amal was giving him medicines, but rest had been advised.

Narasimhan shook his head. 'I'm okay.'

The Chola–Parmar platoon was on its way to Khuzdar, which was a quarter of the way between Gwadar and Ghazni. A few days ago, Someshwar had met his contact, the merchant at Gwadar. The Gujarati merchant had shown his torn one-rupee *hundi* note. And his counterpart, a local merchant, had shown his own torn half of the note. It was a perfect match. The local Gwadar merchant had informed Someshwar that his next stopover would be in the town of Khuzdar, where he would meet a man named Firdaus.

Someshwar had already heard of Firdaus. His contact in the royal Ghazni court had informed him that Firdaus was the man to get in touch with. What he didn't know was where he could meet Firdaus and what the passcode would be for establishing safe contact. Now he knew.

And the Indians were on their way to Khuzdar. Snaking slowly through the rough hilly terrain.

—·◦❦◦·—

Khuzdar was a dusty little town in the middle of nowhere. Located at a height of over four thousand feet, surrounded by the Shashan mountains, its sole purpose for existence was to be a way station on the road to Quetta. Quetta was the largest city between Ghazni and the Gwadar coast, and served as a crucial staging point on the journey to Ghazni.

If one wanted to hide in plain sight within the Ghaznavid empire, there was no better place than Khuzdar. No important people lived there. But most important people had to pass through the place either on the way to or from Ghazni. In essence, if you lived in Khuzdar, you would never be in the eye of the powerful, so you were safe. But you could always overhear the conversations of the powerful in the restaurants, inns and mosques of Khuzdar, so you could find out what was going on.

It was the perfect place for a spy or double agent to hide in plain sight.

It had not taken Someshwar too long to find Firdaus's farm. The directions given were impeccable. The independent farm was a few miles north of Khuzdar, outside of the town, on the way to Ghazni. Far enough for practically all

Khuzdarians to not come there often, thus keeping the place secluded. But it was close enough for Firdaus to zip into town if he had to. His cover within Khuzdar was that he was a dry-fruits trader.

Perfect.

Firdaus, the agent of the Ghaznavid royal rebel, was oldish. Someshwar estimated that he was between fifty-five and sixty years of age. Firdaus was frail and ill-tempered. His hair was sparse, grey and patchy, while his beard was full, white and flowing. His aged face was lined in tune with his crabby personality. Deep downward lines at the edges of his lips, no laugh lines near the eyes. The wrinkles on his forehead were so extensive and deep that it almost seemed like the Almighty had personally taken a hammer and chisel to carve them into the man's face. It appeared as though Firdaus was constantly grimacing, in a continuous battle with his inner demons.

'Well, will you answer me?' asked Firdaus rudely. 'What do you want?'

Firdaus had only let Someshwar and Iqbal into his very humble and surprisingly clean cottage. The rest had been summarily asked to wait outside. The Gujarati merchant noticed that a traditional Islamic prayer mat was neatly rolled and kept on a clean ledge built into the wall.

'I have come from Gwadar, my friend,' said Someshwar.

'I am not your friend. And everyone who comes here from the south comes from Gwadar. There is no other place to come from. State your business.'

Someshwar couldn't place Firdaus's accent. It did sound Indian, but nothing like he had heard before. The Gujarati dispensed with the polite small talk and got down to business. 'Where I come from is heaven on earth.'

Firdaus suddenly became silent for a while. His face visibly softened. 'Everyone thinks their homeland is heaven.'

Someshwar continued, saying the next line in the passcode, 'Well, I speak the truth. My homeland has everything. Wealth, beauty, intelligence, courage and passion.'

Firdaus smiled slightly for the first time. 'Sorry, my friend, but you lie. Maybe unknowingly, but you lie. Because the only people who tell the truth, when they say that their land is heaven, are my people.'

Someshwar grinned broadly. 'I'd like to visit your homeland someday, my friend.'

Firdaus frowned. 'That line is not a part of the passcode.'

'I know. I just threw that in there. I'd really like to visit your homeland.'

Firdaus smiled, widely this time, and embraced Someshwar. 'Finally, we take the fight to the monsters.'

'We will, my friend.'

'What is your name?'

'Salman.'

Firdaus stared at Someshwar. His left eyebrow went up. 'Really?'

Someshwar remained silent.

'You want me to trust you? Then you have to trust me. Once again, what is your name?'

'Someshwar.'

Firdaus smiled. 'Now you speak the truth.'

'And what is your name?' asked Someshwar.

Firdaus frowned. 'Firdaus. Why would I lie to you?'

Someshwar laughed softly.

Firdaus looked out of the window, towards the open area where the Indian soldiers had gathered. 'You don't seem to have enough people, Someshwar.'

'Salman. Only use Salman,' said Someshwar. 'I cannot afford a mistake even by accident.'

'You're right. My apologies,' said Firdaus, penitently. 'But my point remains. You don't have enough people, Salman.'

'We have the perfect number of people. Not too few. And at the same time, not too many. We are not fighting an open war. We are going to assassinate him.'

'Your soldiers … most of them don't look Turkic, except for that woman. I hope she has trained them well, and that they understand the Turkic language.'

Someshwar nodded in assent.

'Who are they? Where are they from?'

'I think it's best if you don't know that for now, Firdaus,' said Someshwar.

Firdaus stared at Someshwar for a short while. Then shrugged his shoulders. 'Well, if you are trusted by the one that I would give my life for, then I will trust that you know what you are doing. Come with me.'

—◦⊱✦⊰◦—

'Where are we going?' asked Someshwar, as the trio exited Firdaus's cottage.

Firdaus was leading the way, holding a lantern as the sun was slowly setting behind the high mountains. 'To the pigeon coop.'

Someshwar grinned. He was beginning to like this Firdaus. He did not waste any time. The message would be sent by bird courier to his contact in Ghazni right away. He must have been planning the attack on Mahmud and his family for a long while. And the time had finally come.

'Does your contact in Ghazni respond promptly?' asked Someshwar, a seemingly innocuous question.

Firdaus glanced back with a twinkle in his eye. He was beginning to like this smart Gujarati. If a person answers carelessly about someone else, then the first thing they do is give away the gender of the person in question. On account of the fact that most languages have gender built into them when you talk about someone else, you will end up using he or she or some variant if you speak carelessly. And if Someshwar had a clue about the gender of the contact in the senior levels of the court, he would immediately narrow down the field to identify the rebel. 'Nice try,' answered Firdaus.

Someshwar stayed silent and smiled. He was impressed by how careful Firdaus was, even while apparently distracted.

Firdaus turned towards the Indians in the distance and spoke loudly, 'You can make yourselves at home in the barn. There is more than enough space there for all of you.'

Vijayan looked towards Someshwar for confirmation. Someshwar nodded, playing the role of the leader of the pack. Vijayan immediately set about organizing a camp within the large barn on the farm.

Firdaus walked ahead quickly, followed by Someshwar and Iqbal. 'To answer your question, when I send a message to Ghazni, they tend to respond when they can. Sometimes it's just a day. Sometimes, it takes even a few weeks.'

'They?!' Someshwar had caught on to the key bit of information—at least in his opinion. And he was surprised.

Firdaus continued walking. Silent.

'There is more than one rebel at the top levels of the Ghazni court?' asked Someshwar.

'When did I say that?'

'You just said "they".'

'Yes, "they" identify as "they/them". But they are one person.'

Someshwar was thoroughly confused now. 'I don't understand.'

'You're not supposed to.'

Someshwar kept walking, panting slightly, struggling to keep up with the lean and swift Firdaus.

'I haven't received news from Gwadar in a few weeks,' Firdaus remarked casually.

'Hmm,' said Someshwar.

'You haven't heard of any Abbasid ship coming into port there, have you? It would apparently have the caliph's colours.'

Someshwar didn't hesitate at all. 'No, I haven't.'

He would speak of the Abbasid ship later to Firdaus. Once he was sure about the man. But clearly, the ship from the caliphate was coming in for some mission that had to do with the royal court in Ghazni. Firdaus's contact in Ghazni may have informed him about it. Someshwar glanced back at Iqbal. He could see from his friend's expression that Iqbal had come to the same conclusion.

They had reached. Firdaus pushed open the wooden door to the pigeon coop. It was dark. The lantern Firdaus was carrying would be especially useful here. 'Come on into the messaging centre.'

—·◦✦◦·—

The sun had long set. It should have been pitch-dark. But it wasn't. Because the moon spread its soft light everywhere.

Furthermore, the thing about snowy mountains is that they reflect a lot of light. As a result, there was still quite a bit of visibility.

The camp had been set up in the barn, which was quite comfortable, considering the circumstances. A filling dinner had been eaten. Relatively soft beds had been made out of straw and jute—a delight compared to how the platoon had been sleeping the previous week, out in the open, on frozen, craggy hillsides. The Indians had all turned in early. The golden rule during army marches was that if you get the chance to eat and sleep at any point of time, then you should take it. Sentry duties and watch schedules had been established, and the appointed watchguards would be switched every two hours. This way all would have a fair chance at sleep, and the security of the camp was ensured.

Comfort and safety were guaranteed for all the warriors under his charge. What more can a commander ask for?

Vijayan could afford to relax now. He sat on a fur rug spread on the ground, just outside the northern fence, at the edge of the large farm. He should have been enraptured by the beauty of the landscape, the snow-capped mountains rising in the distance, the sound of the distant waterfall, the lush vegetation along the area. Khuzdar was among the few valleys in the region with an abundance of water. A speck of green, in a land dominated by arid brown and frigid white.

Sublime. Alluring. Gorgeous.

But Vijayan was taken in instead by the ethereal beauty sitting next to him.

Amal.

The Pandya warrior held her hand for a moment and then released it. He rubbed his palms together and blew into them.

Amal stared at the strappingly masculine and yet incredibly shy man next to her, smiled, and then looked up at the sky, taking in the countless constellations scattered across it.

'It is breathtaking,' she whispered. 'I have never seen anything like this in my life. This frozen desert enhances the beauty of the sky somehow.'

'Yes,' said Vijayan. 'I have never seen snow until now. At night, it makes the land shine brighter than the sky.'

'It's my first time as well, Valeed,' said Amal. She combed her hair with her fingers and pushed the waves behind her ears. The moonlight, amplified by the snow, reflected on her flawless face, making it glow. The Almighty had created this beautiful face without any blemish at all. 'Mother Nature is coaxing us to set aside the dangers we face. Set it aside … And enjoy the moment …'

Amal looked at Vijayan and smiled shyly.

Yet, he hesitated.

The inhibition would have been achingly attractive if it weren't so frustrating.

'Valeed …' whispered Amal.

'Hmm?'

'Vijayan …'

Electricity coursed through Vijayan's body as he heard Amal say his name. It had been a long time. She had been calling him Valeed for so long. He didn't mind anyone else using his assumed name. But from her lips, he wanted to hear his own name. Her lips …

He bent forward. Slightly. Still hesitant.

Amal didn't draw back. She smiled, her lips quivering in the cold. Her eyes looked back at him tenderly. They warmed him with a fire as old as time. She raised her chin in expectation, her heart pounding frantically.

Vijayan held her face gently and brought his face closer.

Heaven alone knows what he was waiting for.

Amal had had enough. She closed the distance and kissed Vijayan. Softly. Then passionately, coaxing his lips apart. She moaned and wrapped her arms around him, drawing him close.

Vijayan awkwardly withdrew. And looked away. Amal sat up straight, averting her gaze. She touched her burning cheeks.

'Sorry … Sorry …' the Pandya mumbled.

'I am not sorry, Vijayan,' Amal said with clarity, addressing him by the name he preferred.

Vijayan stared at her, stunned into inaction. But a broad smile lit up his face. It was as though he had just touched heaven, ever so briefly. He moved his head closer to hers. And then he hesitated again.

The normal fear of any man who thinks he has a woman who is too good for him … *I will wake up and realize that this was all a dream.*

Now, most women would get supremely irritated with a man who was so inhibited and nervous. But not Amal. She knew that, awkward as it was, she would have to take charge. This man was worth it. His simplicity was worth it.

'Vijayan, it is obvious to everyone. It is obvious to me. It is obvious to you. But someone has to say it.'

Vijayan continued to stare at her. The great warrior, who could fight multiple enemies at the same time, seemed to be struggling to find the courage to say the obvious words.

'So let me state the obvious,' said Amal, smiling. 'I love you. And I know that you love me.'

Vijayan's face turned red as he blushed deeply, which was visible despite his dark skin.

'So,' continued Amal, almost laughing now. 'Do you have something to say?'

'I love you!' Vijayan suddenly found the valour to speak. And he wanted to say it all before his bravery deserted him again. 'I love you so much … I can't stop staring at you. Looking at you takes my breath away. Not looking at you makes me feel like I am not breathing … If we both survive this crazy mission, will you … I mean … Will you consider … I mean … Will you marry me?'

Amal was surprised beyond measure. First, he wasn't speaking at all. And now, he had said so much!

'I will marry you, my shy warrior,' she said, and laughed.

Vijayan couldn't believe his ears. He grinned from ear to ear. Like the proverbial cat that got the cream. 'I … Wow … I mean … I am … Ummm … That … That is … awesome …'

Amal was laughing helplessly now. She patted him on his chest. He felt alive. More alive than he had ever felt. He reached for her and then froze. He squinted, looking into the distance. Amal's ears perked up as well. They exchanged glances. They heard a dull drone from the north. A hazy mass came into view. Barely visible due to the fading light. Very far away. Cresting the mountain in the distance. Moving towards them like a giant wave.

They were still very far. At least half an hour to forty-five minutes away. It was a deathly quiet night, and the stillness in the mountains allowed the sound to carry over a massive distance.

Vijayan and Amal stood up immediately.

'What is that?' asked Amal. 'A herd of some kind?'

Vijayan, the nervous, lovesick man, had disappeared instantly. Vijayan, the sharp, fierce warrior had re-emerged.

'There isn't enough light to see into that distance,' said Vijayan, his tone steady and sure. 'I cannot tell. Rush to the barn. Rally our soldiers. Some horde approaches from the north.'

'Wait!' said Amal. She cupped her right ear. 'Can you hear that? They are human beings, certainly.'

'They seem to be yelling,' said Vijayan. 'Amal, we don't have much time. Run and warn the others. These people will soon be upon us. Warn Someshwar, Iqbal and Firdaus as well. They are in the pigeon coop.'

---·◦❧◦·---

Firdaus had just finished composing the letter to his contact in Ghazni. It had taken a long time because the letter had to be encrypted. And the encryption was more robust than anything Someshwar had ever seen, including the ones that royal families used. Firdaus and his contact changed the encryption code regularly; a fresh cryptographic key sheet would arrive like clockwork, on the first Friday of every month.

They were a very careful bunch, these conspirators against Mahmud of Ghazni. No wonder they had evaded capture or discovery till now.

Firdaus had shown the letter to Someshwar and Iqbal, who also seemed happy with it. He carefully rolled the tiny parchment that had the message written on it in a small font, and slipped it into a capsule, which he then fastened to a pigeon's leg.

Holding the bird, Firdaus nodded towards the door. Someshwar pulled it open.

'Godspeed, noble bird,' said Firdaus, as he released the bird into the night air. 'Carry our message to Ghazni.'

'Godspeed,' said Someshwar. 'Get our message across to they/them.'

Iqbal and Firdaus looked at Someshwar and smiled. They turned to look at the bird as it flew higher and higher, a small grey ball that soon merged with the darkness.

And then they saw Amal racing towards the barn. Gesturing to them urgently, she beckoned them to join her.

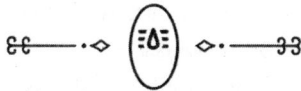

CHAPTER 18

A Storm before the Strike

Outside of Khuzdar, Afghanistan

The Chola Parmar soldiers had quickly readied for war. They tightened their *dhoti*s military-style and put on their torso armours. Affixed their arm protectors and shin guards. They wore their weapons and helmets. Checked the blades on their swords and knives. Fixed their shields on their back-holds. Strung their bows. And got into formation. Within the barn.

Narasimhan walked up to the assembled warriors. Much against Amal's advice, he had taken a double dose of the medicines that dulled his pain and gave him energy. His paralysed right arm was tightly bandaged to his torso, with a shoulder sling that also doubled up as a thick cloth cast. His shield was secured to the front of his bound arm, and a large metallic shoulder-guard was attached to his right shoulder. Shin guards were tied to both his shins and an arm guard was secured on his good left arm. His scabbard was tied to his right side. He pulled the sword out smoothly, checked it and sheathed it. He checked the four knives secured in his shin guards. And the two knives secured on small scabbards tied to the left side of his waist.

Then he began inspecting his soldiers.

In short order, they started hearing loud noises outside.

'Nasrullah Sir!'

It was Vijayan's voice.

Narasimhan nodded and one his soldiers opened the barn door. Narasimhan and Amal stepped out.

Vijayan walked up. He was followed by a flood, a massive rabble of a little less than one thousand hungry, tired, dishevelled and panic-stricken men, women and children. Though not all were panic-stricken. Around fifty of them stayed disciplined, organizing and herding along the gaggle of people.

'What's going on, Valeed?' asked Narasimhan, using Vijayan's assumed name.

'Escaped slaves from Ghazni, Sir,' answered Vijayan. 'Among them are Africans, Yazidis, Coptic Christians, Zoroastrian Persians, but the majority of them are our fellow Indians—Hindus, Buddhists and Muslims. They somehow managed to break out and flee. There are around nine hundred slaves. But they also have fifty fighting men, who are all Indians. And they are being chased by Mahmud's hordes.'

'Mahmud's fighters are riding up here?'

'Apparently so.'

'How far away are they?'

'Maybe six or seven hours away. They will probably arrive here by daybreak tomorrow.'

'That far back?' asked Narasimhan. 'How did they see them, then?'

'I asked the same thing.'

'And the answer was?'

'In the mountains back there, if you are at a height, you can see a horse many hours before it actually reaches you. Because of the amount of time it takes to climb down a mountain and climb up the next one. Also, they cannot be too quick at dusk, or they'll slip to their deaths.'

'How many are there?'

'Two hundred Ghaznavid horsemen,' said Vijayan.

Narasimhan narrowed his eyes. *Just two hundred. And we have a thousand of us. Of which around one hundred are trained warriors. This is an opportunity.*

'They are led by a man called Abu Q'asim,' continued Vijayan, 'who styles himself as something called *Turk Kasap-e-Hind. The Turkish Butcher of India.*'

'Well, we need to turn the butcher's knife on him then,' said Amal.

Vijayan agreed. 'By Meenakshi of Madurai, there are few better things in life than killing those barbarians.'

'Who is the leader among you?' Narasimhan asked the slaves.

'I am,' answered Pula.

Narasimhan looked at Pula. A tall man, almost the same height as the Chola general. Dark-skinned, with a handsome bearded face, Pula's body was muscly, lithe and sinewy. But the stretch marks on his skin showed that his muscles had been even more magnificent earlier. Lack of nutrition had weakened his body. But even in that diminished state, Pula moved nimbly, showcasing his natural warrior skills. In terms of age, he appeared to be in his mid-to-late twenties. And despite the years spent in slavery, there was a natural glow on his face. This was a man used to leading. A man who was accustomed to taking on responsibilities for those around him who were weaker.

'What's your name, my friend?' asked Narasimhan.

'I am Pula. Pulakit, if you prefer,' answered Pula. 'I am the youngest brother of the Chalukyan emperor, Jayasimha, son of Sathyashraya of Vatapi. Several years ago, my brother sent me with some troops to defend Somnath*ji* alongside the Solankis and other Indian dynasties. My men and I, and several other defenders of the city, were captured by the Ghaznavids. We have been slaves ever since.'

A stunned Vijayan and Amal stared in disbelief. They glanced at their commander, Narasimhan, and then back at Pulakit.

A Chalukyan royal!

They were well aware of the legendary Chola–Chalukya animosity. They had fought many wars with each other. And Narasimhan's master, Rajendra Chola, had personally killed Pulakit's father, Sathyashraya, in hand-to-hand combat many years ago. Pulakit would have been a little child then.

Most incredibly, a Chalukya vigilante squad was responsible for the state Narasimhan was in, with his right arm paralysed.

They had a brief respite before the Turks would reach them. Narasimhan didn't want to waste time. 'Do you recognize me, Prince Pulakit?'

Pula nodded. 'I know that Nasrullah is not your actual name.'

Narasimhan hesitated for a moment. And then spoke up. 'Your father was a great man. I am still loyal to my emperor.

However, that does not detract from the fact that your father was a great man. And I am sorry for what happened.'

Pula took a deep breath. 'It's war. It's what happens in war.'

Vijayan spoke up next. 'In the great war of the Mahabharat, there were some good people on both sides. On the side of the Pandavas and that of the Kauravas.'

Pulakit looked at Vijayan and then back at Narasimhan. His words were soft but clear. 'The Kauravas may have been a hundred. And the Pandavas may have been five. But if an outsider attacked, they were a hundred and five ...'

Pulakit had quoted the great King Yudhishthira, also known as the Lord of Dharma. Simply put, the message was that when a barbarian outsider attacks, all the people of *Dharma* must unite.

Narasimhan smiled and extended his left arm forward in a gesture of friendship. 'We are a 105!'

'We are a 105!' said Pulakit, as he held Narasimhan's left arm with his right, in the way brother-warriors held each other.

'We are a 105!' repeated Vijayan, adding his hand to the bond of fellowship.

Amal stepped up and held the arms of the three men. 'We are a 105!'

'You have the command of my troops, General,' said Pulakit to Narasimhan. He knew who the more experienced and fiercer campaigner was. There was no dishonour in handing the leadership to him.

Narasimhan nodded and bent forward. 'We have the element of surprise. They expect to be chasing nine hundred slaves and fifty soldiers, all tired, all hungry, all despairing.

They don't expect us to be fed, which we will be. They don't expect us to have forty more trained warriors, which we will have. They don't expect the approximately one thousand of us to be armed, but we will be. Because Firdaus has a hoard of weapons here. They don't expect us to be ready and waiting for them with traps and feints. They expect to charge in and massacre us all. They don't expect us to fight back. We must capitalize on this element of surprise.'

Pulakit, Vijayan and Amal nodded.

'So here's what we'll do.'

— ·◦⟫⟨◦· —

It was late in the night. The escaped slaves and soldiers were working on the plans that Narasimhan had drawn up. Working in shifts, giving everyone the time to get some sleep as well. Furthermore, Firdaus had opened out his massive trading stock of dry fruits for all. Perfect. Dry fruits don't spoil easily and therefore even old stores were completely edible. And they give a tremendous boost of energy. Precisely what the defenders needed.

Fires had been lit within the large barn where many were sleeping. But there were no fires lit outside. They didn't want to leave a beacon on for the Turks to find them in the night and surprise them.

Dhurv had been put in charge of the preparations for the front-gate defences, and Someshwar was with Firdaus managing the food and weapons horde, at the other end of the farm, behind the barn. That's why they had not met each other. And there were, to be fair, a little less than a thousand people in the farm now. But Someshwar's work was done, and he had come to the hedges, closer to the front gate. That's where he saw him. Or thought he did, because the years of slavery and hard labour had changed the look of the young man.

'Dhruv?!' asked Someshwar, stunned beyond belief.

The lack of light and his tiredness made Someshwar think that his mind was playing tricks on him. But he had to ask. He had to …

Dhruv turned around. The young man looked at the Somnath merchant, shock writ large on his swarthy youthful face. 'Father?!'

'Dhruv!!'

It was the son he believed he had lost during the attack on the Somnath Temple. The son who he believed had died defending the great Mahadev.

My boy is alive?

He looked different, like his face had aged a decade in these few years. But his medium-height lean body had rippling muscles now, because of the years of battle and strenuous work. There was a proud battle scar running down his left cheek. And another on his chest, running down to the right side of his torso. Noble marks proclaiming that his boy had become a man.

My boy is alive!

Someshwar's voice rang like a temple bell in the silence of the night. 'Dhruv! My son! Dhruv!'

The men hugged each other, like the Ganga and Yamuna *rivers merging into each other* at the Prayagraj *sangam*. It was as if fate had conspired and pulled Dhruv back from heaven, just so that he could embrace his father once more. It was as if King Bhagirath, just like the legends say, had coaxed the sacred Ganga River down to earth from the heavens above.

Tears flowed out in a flood.

Hearing the loud voices, others gathered to see what was going on. Pula looked at his trusted lieutenant, bemused. Narasimhan and Vijayan stared at their genial old friend crying like he had just been given a second lease of life.

His son was alive. Mahadev be praised. His son was alive.

------◦✧◦------

Narasimhan had worked with his team and the escaped slaves all night, making them keep guard and sleep in shifts.

Through his key lieutenants Pulakit, Vijayan and Amal, General Narasimhan had ensured his plans were implemented rapidly.

First, he had got perimeter security set up two kilometres north of Firdaus's farm, with a system to relay information about incoming enemy, to ensure his troops were not taken by surprise.

Firdaus's large storehouse of weapons had also been opened. He had been preparing for a fight against the Ghaznavids for a long time. All ninety soldiers were armed to the teeth. Swords, shields, at least five knives per person. And most critically, all of them had bows and arrows. They could shoot at the Turks from a distance.

The freed slaves were also given weapons. Knives for close-range stabbing, and long spears and pitchforks for attacking the Turks from a distance. The slaves were told that their primary task was to attack the Turkic horses from a distance. Once the Turks were unhorsed, they would be easier prey.

The Chola–Parmars had come with their horses, around forty of them, which they had bought in Gwadar. A joint contingent of some of the Chola–Parmar soldiers and some of Pulakit's men was ordered to mount these horses and remain in hiding behind the goat pen and the large cottage. Once the Turks were caught in a melee at the farm, the team would attack from the flanks and kill as many Turks as they could before the enemy realized what was going on. The Ghaznavids certainly wouldn't expect the slaves to have cavalry that would ride to their rescue.

There was no need for a speech. The motivation levels among the escaped slaves couldn't have been higher. Cornered prey, with nowhere to run, can transform into ferocious fighters because they have nothing to lose.

Everything was set.

All they had to do now was wait.

—◦—⋙—◦—

Someshwar's heart pounded like a wild animal hellbent on breaking out of the cage that was his chest. He could barely sleep. He watched the scene with excitement.

He turned to his friend. 'Iqbal, my son is alive …'

Iqbal smiled and touched Someshwar's shoulder, still calling him by his assumed name, because of the recent circumstances. 'Salman *bhai*, from the looks of it, your son is a trusted officer of Prince Pulakit now.'

Someshwar nodded vigorously, his pride shining through.

Dhruv, accompanied by the escaped Arab slave Zayn Husayn, had been working near the hedges at the entrance, under the directions of Narasimhan and Pulakit. The tall hedges formed a natural bottleneck from the gate to the inner farm as they ran along two sides of the long and circuitous pathway. Furthermore, the path was just wide enough for a large cargo cart to pass through. The Turks would have to ride in along this path, in lines of two horses abreast. Or at most three horses, if they squeezed in together. Either way, they would be hemmed in by the tall, almost-two-metre-high hedges on the left and right, which would block their view beyond. It was the perfect place to maim or kill their horses. Tiny apertures had been made in the hedges, on both sides, through which the freed slaves would be able to thrust their spears and pitchforks. It was Dhruv's responsibility to supervise this part of the upcoming battle.

Someshwar's chest filled with pride.

Perhaps the greatest grief for any man is to see his children die before him. Someshwar had experienced that with practically his entire family.

Among the greatest, albeit unexpected joys is to see one's child return from the dead. Someshwar had experienced that the previous night.

And an even greater than greatest joy was to see your son being respected and trusted by other achievers.

Someshwar couldn't be prouder.

'Who would have thought, Iqbal,' said Someshwar, 'that a non-violent vegetarian Gujarati businessman like me, who has never even killed an ant, could sire a warrior who would take on the Turks!'

Iqbal laughed softly. He joked, 'I think Dhruv has gone on his mother, Hetal *ben*.'

Someshwar laughed uproariously and hit Iqbal playfully on his back.

Iqbal continued smiling as he said what was in his heart, 'And finally, finally, we will see some of those monstrous Turks being killed. Our vengeance begins now. And your son will be one of India's avengers.'

'*Har Har Mahadev*,' whispered Someshwar.

Har Har Mahadev meant that all of us are Mahadevs …
All of us are Gods.

'*Har Har Mahadev*,' repeated Iqbal.

And then there was light.

Someshwar watched the sun, east of the Khuzdar mountains, slowly raise its head and gently peek at the world, illuminating the peak of the tallest mountain. The skies welcomed their fiery star, blushing a deep red.

A scout came riding in. Someshwar knew what that meant. The enemy's cavalry had been sighted cresting the last mountain pass before Khuzdar Valley. They were approximately one hour away.

It was time.

Time for battle.

———◦⦙⦙◦———

'Damn …' whispered Vijayan.

He had been waiting patiently. He had climbed a tree to the east of the farm and enjoyed an unobstructed view of the hedge-fences and the entrance to the estate a short distance away. He was well within arrow-firing range. Amal was stationed on the branch above him. There were ten other Chola soldiers spread across the neighbouring trees. Hidden from view. Armed with bows and arrows, and the critical tactical advantage of holding high ground. Their task was to shoot as many Turks as possible, when their advance slowed down because of the attack from the hedges. Forty mounted warriors were under Pulakit's command, hidden among the trees to the west of the farm, behind the goat pen and cottage. They would ride in at the opportune time to flank the Turks.

And forty Indian soldiers, along with four hundred armed slaves, waited in the barn under the command of Narasimhan. The kill zone.

Dhruv, Pulakit and Vijayan were tasked with slaying as many Turks as possible before they reached the barn. Or at least unhorse them. Then it was up to Narasimhan and his men to slaughter them all.

'The snow?' whispered Amal, answering Vijayan's 'damn'.

Fresh snowfall had just begun.

'Hmm,' answered Vijayan.

'It's not a problem,' said Amal. 'It will cover our tracks and the work we did overnight. Mud on old snow is a dead giveaway.'

'That's true. But the fresh snowflakes will make the hedge slick. That will make it more difficult for our fighters to stab through with their spears and forks. The slaves are not trained soldiers. The Turks, mounted on their horses, will be the most dangerous for us. We need those horses maimed or killed.'

Amal nodded. 'Let's leave it to Dhruv. He has two hundred people with him. More than enough men. I am sure he will deliver.'

'I hope fate has not conspired against Dhruv's mission, that's all.'

'I have faith in Allah,' said Amal. 'He has delivered the Turks here to be massacred by us. It will work out.'

'*Inshallah*,' said Vijayan.

Inshallah was an Arabic expression that meant *with the will of Allah*.

'And with the blessings of Lord Shiva,' said Amal.

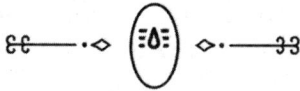

CHAPTER 19

The Battle at Khuzdar

Firdaus's farm, close to Khuzdar, Afghanistan

'AAAAAH! TUUURRRRKKKSSS! NOOOOOOOOOOO!'

A child screamed. Almost melodramatically. As if on cue, the other children also began to cry. And a young woman, the lone adult with them, began herding them desperately towards the farm entrance.

'A little too theatrical,' whispered Vijayan. He had a clear view from his vantage point in the trees. 'They must draw the attention of the Turks and incite them to attack. But this seems overdone.'

The children entered through the farm gate and sprinted down the hedge-bound pathway. Their adult supervisor ran after them, bellowing loudly, 'RUUUNNNN, CHILDREN! RUUUNNNNN!'

'We should cut some of their food rations for overacting,' said Amal, rolling her eyes.

The children giggled and laughed as they ran. At their tender age, even after all that they had suffered, this seemed like a game to them. Many were pushing at the dense morning mist that hung close to the ground, like they were playing with clouds.

Vijayan pointed with his right hand. 'Look.'

Amal turned to look in the direction that Vijayan had pointed. She could see the Turks begin to appear at the top of the distant hill. A massive lone rider up front. And like ghosts, mounted warriors emerged from the thick fog behind him, outlined starkly at the hilltop. The morning mist created an optical illusion, making the arrayed enemy seem like an endless line of phantom ghouls emerging from the foggy miasma.

Vijayan and Amal saw the humongous Turkic rider in the front draw his curved scimitar from its scabbard and hold it high.

The children's screams had worked. They were loud enough for the sound to carry and echo towards the mountains. And the Turks were used to people reacting in terror at their mere appearance.

Abu Q'asim turned to his men. 'Keep an eye out for the girl that the governor-mufti wants,' he warned. 'She is *not* to be harmed. As for the others … no mercy!' He pointed his scimitar forward and roared. 'For the Faith! For the sultan!'

'For the Faith! For the sultan!' boomed the Ghaznavid soldiers.

'Kill them all!' roared Abu Q'asim as he kicked his horse into action.

Abu Q'asim's horse reared its head violently and went up on its hind legs. The front hooves came crashing down on the ground, and the beast burst into a fearsome gallop. In rapid succession, the Turkic horsemen followed their leader and thundered ahead.

'Kill them all!'

They raced towards the farm. They were probably a five-to-ten-minute ride away.

The Turks had taken the bait.

Vijayan whistled a loud birdcall. *They are coming.*

Dhruv, at the hedges, made another birdcall. *We're ready.* Zayn Husayn, behind the hedge opposite to Dhruv, also responded in whistle.

And so did Pulakit, hidden behind the goat pen and large cottage in the west. *We're ready.*

From the barn, Narasimhan whistled a deep birdcall. Almost like the screech of an eagle, the greatest predator bird alive. Delivered in a deep baritone. *Avarkal varattum!*

Narasimhan's message was a colloquial term used by Indians across many defensive battles. When they are trying to lure the enemy into charging to their doom. In Hindi, one said *Aane do!* In Punjabi, it was *Aan deyo!*

Let them come!

—⋅◦⋙◦⋅—

The Turks raced towards the gates of the farm. And immediately hit the bottleneck.

The slave children and their supervisor had long raced into the barn in the southern section of the farm. As ordered by Narasimhan, Dasarna had led the children to the other end where, hidden out of sight, they slipped through the barn's back door. They were received by some women, who led them into the thick forest that lay farther south of the barn. This was where all the children, old men and non-combatant women, numbering a few hundred, were hidden. Along with Someshwar and Iqbal. They had been given explicit instructions: if they thought that the Indians were losing the battle, they should rush to the town and try to blend in there, to avoid being captured by the Turks.

Meanwhile, faced with the bottleneck, Abu Q'asim had ordered his troops to form rows of three mounted riders and march abreast into the farm through the hedgy pathway.

Both Vijayan and Amal had noticed that the Turks were not wearing their leather torso armours. Nor had they strung their bows. Warriors rarely did so unless they were sure of battle since excess stringing of the bow weakened both the recurves and the strings themselves.

Evidently, the Turks had expected to ride to an easy one-way massacre, not serious combat. They had thought their swords and knives would be enough for this tired, cowardly rabble of slaves.

Among the greatest enemies of soldiers is overconfidence. Many battles have been lost due to it.

'He's marching slowly,' whispered Amal. 'Not galloping through the hedgy pathway.'

The passageway between the two hedges was obscured by the thick morning mist, the copious leaves and shrubs of the hedges working practically like an insulation. The mist was so dense that it almost appeared like a cloud had descended on the path. This made it almost impossible for those using the path to see anything from the ground level up to a height of two feet.

The Turks *had* to slow down. They couldn't just gallop through this pathway. What if their horses slipped or tripped on the ground? The upshot was that the Turkic horses crawled slowly and carefully forward, moving three in a row, squeezed together by the hedges on the left and right.

Perfect.

Stabbing would be so much easier.

Amal smiled. *Allah is with us.*

Vijayan whistled a birdcall to his men in the trees. *Wait. No firing yet.*

He wanted the last of the Turks to be inside the gate so there would be no escape.

Dhruv had the same idea. He had given strict instructions that no slave was to make a noise or stab with their spears or pitchforks till they heard the order from him. He didn't want to give any of the Turks the chance to ride out from the back when the attack began.

Dhruv could not see the Turks at all from where he was hiding behind the hedge. He could only hear the horses. He waited for Vijayan's loud birdcall signal.

Vijayan, watching from high up in the trees, with a perfect view of the Turks, saw the last row of Turkic riders finally enter the main gate onto the hedge-bound pathway curving into the farmland in a circuitous route. The first row of the mounted Turkic riders was just a short distance from the other end of the curved hedgy track, about to break into Firdaus's large open farm.

They were all in.

In the trap.

It was time.

Vijayan whispered, invoking his Goddess, 'By Meenakshi of Madurai.'

And the Pandya loudly whistled a birdcall for his comrades behind the hedges, mimicking the sound of a peacock's mating cry.

The Turks should have asked the obvious question: What the hell was a peacock doing in that area?!

But bloodlust and overconfidence had clouded their thinking.

'ATTACK!' roared Dhruv. His order was loud and clear.

Almost instantaneously, Zayn Husayn, behind the hedge line on the opposite side of the path, also screamed ferociously, 'ATTACK!'

The slaves began jabbing forward ruthlessly with their spears. Deep into the bellies of the steeds that the Turks were riding. Dhruv had assumed that since the slaves had never killed anyone, at least not to his knowledge, they may hesitate a bit. Particularly while stabbing innocent horses, whose only crime was being beasts of burden for the monstrous Turks.

Which is why he had commandeered two hundred slaves, so that he had one killer for every horse.

But the freed slaves did not hesitate at all. Years of repressed rage had finally found an outlet. They kept stabbing repeatedly. In rapidly brutal strikes.

Horses neighed furiously in agony as spears and pitchforks pierced viciously into their bellies. The beasts started bucking wildly. The Turks on their backs tried desperately to hold on.

'AMBUSH!'

'AMBUSH!'

The cries rang out from the Turks. But it was too late. They were trapped. Dhruv had already killed the horses and the Turks at the gate entrance. And they had collapsed right there. The escape route from the pathway was blocked.

'KEEP STABBING! KEEP STABBING!' thundered Dhruv.

The horses were desperately trying to move away from the blades goring them savagely and mercilessly. But there was no place for them to escape. The beasts were perilously packed into the narrow passageway. The horses in the right and left rows of the three-column cavalry had no chance. The slaves repeatedly stabbed forward so viciously that many of the animals soon had their bellies ripped open, their intestines slithering out slickly. Some of the slaves pointed their spears upwards, jabbing at the Turks themselves, lacerating them. The Turks had no chance. Their swords simply couldn't reach the slaves who were at least a spear's length away. Many of the Turks fell off their desperately agitated horses and began to get trampled underneath. Blood was splashing in all directions, as the beasts and men fell, and the white snow-covered earth morphed into shades of crimson.

Abu Q'asim, the grizzled veteran of multiple battles, instinctively knew that he had little time left to turn the situation around. He had hurtled impetuously into an ambush.

Overconfidence. The downfall of many generals.

'Forward!' thundered a furious Q'asim. 'The only way out is through!'

'The only way out is through!'

The orders made their way through the cavalry instantly. Every rider hollered it out loud. The finely honed training of the Turks kicked in.

'Forward!'

The Turkic riders in the middle column kicked their horses and started pushing forward, leaving their comrades to the left and right to die. Cantering through the blood-splattered pathway. Not caring for the thick mist. Their commander had ordered it. And they obeyed.

The Turks were monsters. But they were courageous monsters.

'Forward!'

Nearly two-thirds of the mounted cavalry of the Turks had been decimated in the hedgy passageway. But the rest, a little over seventy of them, burst through into the open land of the farms.

'Formations!' cried Abu Q'asim.

But there was such a racket from the slaves screaming as they stabbed forward that not all the Turks heard his command. Some Turks at the head of the line instinctively rode around the hedge to kill those attacking them from behind the green fence, slaying a few slaves who had no chance against mounted riders bearing down on them.

'Formations!' roared Abu Q'asim again.

He expected more traps. He was right.

Before the Turks could gather into formation, a shower of deadly arrows fell upon them from the trees to the east.

Vijayan and Amal. And the ten Chola–Parmar soldiers.

'FIRE AT WILL!' shouted Vijayan.

The Indian archers up on the tree branches had the advantage of being on high ground. This ensured their aim was perfect and true.

They fired ruthlessly in an almost continuous volley.

Practically every arrow found a target. The Turks, without their standard armour protection or the benefit of defensive formations, were pummelled repeatedly. The sharp missiles ferociously slammed into the Ghaznavids, wedging into eyes, cheeks, throats, torsos, legs. Many of the Turks were hit multiple times and looked like human porcupines.

The Turks instinctively turned and started riding to the west of the farm. But their troubles were not over. They rushed headlong into another barrage of arrows.

Pulakit had led his forty mounted soldiers, who were hidden behind the goat pen and the cottage, into battle. Fresh. Untired. And eager to kill. They released volley after volley of arrows on horseback, thundering forward towards the Turks. Killing many more of the Ghaznavids.

By now panic-stricken and unnerved, the Turks, finding ambushes awaiting them at every turn, reined in their horses again, changing direction and riding in desperation towards the south. The only area of the farm that they were not being attacked from.

The arrows from Vijayan's troops on the trees and Pulakit's mounted warriors who were pursuing the Turks continued to fall on the barbarians. Many more Ghaznavid soldiers fell, arrows mercilessly thumping into them.

'To the barn!' A cry arose from the Turkic riders.

The barn seemed empty. There was nobody at the gate. No noise came from within it. It appeared safe. But appearances are, sometimes, deceptive.

'To the barn!' shrieked the Ghaznavids again.

In the confusion and cacophony that abounded in the farm, very few heard their commander Abu Q'asim's order. 'NOT INTO THE BARN! RIDE AROUND! RIDE AROUND!'

Q'asim was right. By now, he had realized that they were facing a brilliant military mind who had planned the ambush perfectly. He expected an even bigger trap to be waiting for them in the barn. He wanted to ride around it.

But only two of his soldiers heard and followed his command.

The other surviving Ghaznavid soldiers—just forty of them now—rode straight into the barn.

Right into Narasimhan's lair, where forty of his soldiers and four hundred well-armed slaves stood waiting for them.

Avarkal varattum!

Let them come!

Let them come! For they will not leave alive!

———⋄⋇⋄———

The forty Ghaznavids who rode into the barn stood no chance. Narasimhan's soldiers had been waiting for them. Straight ahead and along the sides. They were ready with multiple arrows dug into the ground, for easy drawing. And one arrow nocked already in their bows.

The Turks were welcomed with a fusillade of missiles the moment they rode in. Before they could react, each Indian soldier had pulled an additional arrow from the ground and shot another round.

'Retreat!'

Just as the Turks were beginning to turn their horses around, Pulakit and his mounted soldiers rode in behind them. At the entrance to the barn, the Indians took their time, aimed well and fired a perfectly directed volley into the last row of the Ghaznavids. Right at the napes of their necks, where the hairline begins. Each and every arrow found its mark. And all the Turks in the last row fell to their death, arrows obscenely impaling their throats.

The Indians never attacked their enemy from behind, for it was considered adharmic. But the Turks deserved to be treated just like they treated others.

As the wise Vidur, from the epic Mahabharat, had said, '*Shathe shathyam samacharet.*' *The wicked must be treated with extreme wickedness.*

Most of the Turks were already dead. The few who survived had fallen off their horses. The former slaves rushed forward, armed with their spears and pitchforks. They stabbed the Ghaznavids again and again. Some of them ran outside and found Turks lying on the ground. Some injured, some dead. The slaves stabbed them all. Repeatedly. And then they started mutilating the Turkic dead bodies.

In the meantime, Dhruv had led his contingent of freed slaves into the passageway, and they repetitively knifed all the injured and incapacitated Turks they found there. Ensuring they were dead. And despite Dhruv's instructions not to, some of the slaves here too started mutilating the Turkic cadavers.

Narasimhan's soldiers, however, remained with him. Disciplined. They were Indian soldiers. They could be wicked, but never barbaric. They would not mutilate their enemies' corpses.

The Indian soldiers waited for further orders. Their general had still not raised his fist with the victory exultation. The battle is not over till the general says it's over.

Narasimhan looked around. Something didn't feel right. His instincts kept warning him.

Pulakit rode into the barn and dismounted.

'Where's the Turkic commander?' asked Narasimhan.

'I can't find him either, General. He had ridden towards the barn. I had seen him. He should be here …'

Narasimhan quickly said, 'Get the slaves back into the barn. They are not safe till …'

And then they heard the loud screams. From behind the barn. Towards the south.

Narasimhan and the other Indian warriors immediately mounted their horses and started riding. Towards the commotion. Towards the south.

—·◦◦✠◦·—

A little earlier, while the battle was raging in the barn, and the surviving Turks were being massacred in the farm passageway, Abu Q'asim, with two of his soldiers, rode around and behind the barn. Towards the south. He found a dense grove of trees there. He dismounted, pulled his horse down along with him to hide and became quiet as a mouse. He ordered his soldiers to do the same. And then he asked one of them to quietly steal into the grove and report any booby traps he found there.

He planned to escape towards the main Khuzdar town, commandeer the local battalion and then return to the farm to burn everything to the ground. But he expected a trap in the grove as well. And he was naturally being cautious.

Deep inside the dark grove, a petrified Yazadeh could see the three Turks at the edge of the tree line, where the light shone brighter. She recognized the fiendish massive form of Abu Q'asim, the Turkish Butcher of India.

The waif-like young girl sobbed desperately. Her body shaking as terror gripped her heart. She whispered in a panic-stricken voice to her father, 'I cannot go back! I will not go back. That monster … The governor-mufti … He beats me! He bites me! He does dirty things to me … My intestines hurt … I cannot go back alive, Father. You kill me! You kill me now!'

'Hush, Yazadeh!' Arif whispered as he hugged his child. A tear trickled down his cheek. 'The butcher may hear you. But I promise you, we will not be taken alive. I promise you, my sweet child.'

In the meantime, the Turkic scout had returned from the grove to Abu Q'asim.

'No soldiers there, My Lord,' the scout whispered. 'No traps either. Just a few hundred of the escaped slaves.'

'Are the slaves armed?' Abu Q'asim murmured.

'No. Just women and children. And a few old men.'

'Okay. We will ride around and leave for the south.' Even in an absolute military rout, Abu Q'asim's ego was undefeated. He self-identified his action as 'leaving' not 'fleeing'. 'We'll go to Khuzdar and return with their local battalion.'

'My Lord,' the scout whispered. 'I also saw the beautiful slave girl there. Yazadeh. The one we have been asked to bring back to Ghazni.'

A man should know when he is defeated. Because then he will make wiser choices. In a resounding defeat, the key aim should be to survive, not to secure a better option. But how can a man make that choice, if he refuses to control his ego and admit that he has been defeated?

'Alright,' Abu Q'asim said, keeping his voice low. Many options clouded his judgement. Something to show to the sultan to compensate for the loss of Ghaznavid soldiers. A girl to satisfy his lust. A way to hit back against his enemies before escaping. Who knows what drove his decision, but Abu Q'asim seemed interested in trying his luck one more time. 'We'll ride in, grab her and gallop out.'

—·◦❧◦·—

As soon as Abu Q'asim rode into the grove, the slaves started screaming in alarm and panic. He had thought the battle at the barn would still be raging. He didn't know that all his soldiers there had been killed almost immediately. And his enemy, Narasimhan, had grabbed the opportunity and the horses to ride out behind him.

'Not one Turkic soldier should escape alive!' Narasimhan had roared as he rode at the head of his mounted cavalry. 'No Ghaznavid should escape to warn others about what happened here!'

His soldiers were crystal clear on their orders as they had raced after their general.

Abu Q'asim rode hard towards a fleeing Yazadeh, deftly manoeuvring through the slim spaces between the dense trees. His dark eyes gleamed with evil triumph. And lust. He bent low, while still riding his horse, and tried to grab her shining, flowing hair, to yank her onto his saddle. Yazadeh jerked her head. His grip slipped. She screamed and curled into a ball against a tree.

'I will not let you take my daughter, you monster!' cried Arif with desperate bravado, punching the air with his weak fists.

The other slaves were running helter-skelter.

Abu Q'asim stopped his horse and reached down. He grabbed Arif's neck with a single hand and yanked him up like a frail and forlorn rabbit. He thrust his short sword deep into the old man's belly, piercing through the spine, and flung his body aside.

Yazadeh screamed in horror and tried to get up. 'Father!'

Arif fell into her outstretched arms and the girl fell back again, her father's corpse pinning her down.

'Dammit!' screamed Abu Q'asim, sheathing the sword back into the saddle scabbard. 'Cover me!'

Abu Q'asim's soldiers rode in front of him and protected his flanks, as the butcher dismounted. He would have to pull Arif's dead body off Yazadeh to be able to lift her onto his saddle.

One of the Turkic soldiers looked back fearfully at his commander. *This is taking too much time!*

Abu Q'asim effortlessly picked Arif up and threw his corpse away like he was a rag doll. In the meantime, Someshwar had slipped out from behind a tree and approached Yazadeh.

Abu Q'asim, focused on picking up Yazadeh, did not see Someshwar. The Gujarati merchant raised a knife and brought it down with all his might. It sank into the Turkic general's thigh. Abu Q'asim roared in pain and let go of Yazadeh. He ducked, avoiding another swing from the frail Someshwar.

Taking inspiration from Someshwar's valiant act, some of the other slaves gathered and started throwing stones at the two mounted soldiers protecting Abu Q'asim's flanks.

'You will not take this little girl!' the elderly Gujarati merchant yelled.

Abu Q'asim stepped forward and kicked Someshwar in the groin. The old man fell to his knees, groaning in pain. His knife dropped to the ground.

Abu Q'asim drew his scimitar and raised it high with both his hands. He swung it down in one swift motion. A vicious strike. The scimitar cracked Someshwar's skull and split it in two, almost down to his mouth, killing him instantly.

The Turkic butcher tried to pull his weapon from the mutilated body of the originator of the Indians' mission in Ghazni. But it was stuck in the thick skull bone. He glanced at a paralysed Yazadeh, her eyes wide in sheer terror, and grinned. 'Just a moment, you whore. Wait for me.'

The butcher's eyes danced sickly with bloodlust as he moved his sword sideways in a ripping motion to free it from Someshwar's skull bone, cutting through the cheeks. The scimitar was important to Abu Q'asim. Finally managing to free his blade, he slipped it back into his scabbard.

He turned around and picked up Yazadeh.

Just then multiple arrows slammed into the two Turkic soldiers with Abu Q'asim. They fell from their horses. Dead.

The Indian cavalry had ridden in to the rescue.

Abu Q'asim heard a rumble. A low, whirling roar. Like thunder. Like the searing, menacing growl of a waking lion. The hair on Abu Q'asim's back stood stiff like a horse brush.

Two maddened eyes glowed like forest flames atop a rising mountain.

Narasimhan was staring at Someshwar's mutilated body. His friend. He was staring at the little girl. Blood on her face.

His annulus pendant burned into his skin.

It demanded justice.

And sometimes, the only justice is brutal execution.

Abu Q'asim whirled around. A trapped animal who sensed death. He felt an alien emotion.

Fear. Terror.

Narasimhan swung his feet and dismounted easily from his horse. Not taking his eyes off Abu Q'asim, he drew his sword. He turned his head and pushed the thick iron guard on his paralysed right shoulder backwards. The shield was tied to his paralysed right arm, tight and steady. He held the sword slightly away from his body, almost like it was an extension of his left arm.

Pulakit, Dasarna and the Indian riders behind him began thumping their chests and roared.

'Kill! Kill! Kill!'

Abu Q'asim could not move. He was catatonic. In the grove, the chanting reached a resounding crescendo.

Narasimhan stood before the brutish Turk. Abu Q'asim dropped Yazadeh like a twig and almost instantaneously swung his sword. From the left. Hoping to push the gigantic Narasimhan back on his paralysed right side. The Indian reared his right side at the last moment, glancing the ferocious strike from Q'asim aside with his fixed shield, while slicing upwards with his own sword. Narasimhan caught the Ghaznavid's right forearm in the follow-through of his strike, cutting savagely through the extensor muscles and incapacitating it. The scimitar flew out of the Turk's sword arm in a crimson flash, as he lost control of his hand, and blood spurted from his severed muscles.

Q'asim stepped back. His face overcast by sheer dread. He hadn't even seen where the enemy strike had come from.

And yet, the forearm of his sword arm had been cut through fiendishly. He knew ... He knew that he was facing an extraordinary warrior. A lion among men.

He knew ... He knew that he was as good as dead.

The Indians waiting behind continued thumping their chests and roaring, *'Kill! Kill! Kill!'*

Q'asim reached quickly to his side with his good left hand. To the knife on his side scabbard. But before he could even draw it out into battle, Narasimhan, moving faster than what seemed humanly possible, charged forward with his shoulder guard aimed at Q'asim. It came in like a rock missile launched from a faraway trebuchet. The guard hit the Turk on his left shoulder. The bulky iron armour of Narasimhan's shoulder guard smashed Q'asim's shoulder joint at its weakest spot, bulldozing the thick shoulder bone out of its socket. The Turkic butcher's dislocated shoulder slumped like a broken tree branch hanging by a tenuous trunk collar.

Abu Q'asim was shrieking in pain now.

'Kill! Kill! Kill!'

He swung his right arm wildly, in a futile attempt to fob off the mighty Chola warrior, risen like a resplendent phoenix from the ashes of his haunting torment.

The best way to wash off the taint of innocent blood is by shedding the blood of the wicked.

Narasimhan avoided the blows as if he were playing a gruesome wargame with a wounded child. The lion was toying with his prey. The Turk knew his game was up. He retreated like a cornered animal.

Abu Q'asim looked at Narasimhan with murderous hate. He clutched his broken arm and hurled unclear abuses at the general. One word, though, was unmistakable.

Kafir.

Kafir.

Kafir.

The Chola strongman mercilessly swung his mighty sword, cleanly severing the Turk's right arm just above the elbow. Blood burst forth in a torrent through the gaping wound as Q'asim roared in misery. Narasimhan kicked the Ghaznavid hard in the groin. The Turk fell to the ground.

Narasimhan went down on one knee and swung his sword down towards Q'asim's throat. A strike that would have beheaded the butcher. But the Chola general stopped just two inches away from the hapless Turk. Then he looked down. He remembered how the legendary God Narasimhan had destroyed Hiranyakashipu, the disgusting demon who had tried to kill his own son.

Narasimhan. The God he had been named after.

The mortal Narasimhan turned his sword vertical and stabbed ruthlessly downwards, into the belly of the Turk. The strike was so fierce that the sword went all the way through, bursting through the Turk's back, and burying itself into the forest ground.

All around stared, unmoving, arrested by the macabre spectacle.

Narasimhan roared ferociously. He flexed his biceps and pushed the sword in even deeper. With almost divine wrath. Till the hilt cross-guard of the sword slammed into the Turk's abdomen. The sword, literally, couldn't go in any deeper.

The blade, running through Q'asim's belly and buried deep into the ground, had now immobilized the Ghaznavid warrior, nailing him into the earth, like a peg fixes a tent into the ground.

The Chola general looked around and thundered, 'This man will bleed to death! Nobody will show mercy! Nobody!'

Abu Q'asim, the Turkish Butcher of India, kept howling in agony. He would have to keep howling for an hour longer, before he would bleed out and find the merciful release of death.

——◦✦◦——

From Firdaus's farm, the ground crested to a hill towards the south. And then there was a long road to Khuzdar town.

Talib had been on this hill all morning. He had ridden in late at night, turned into the forest that canopied the hill and tied his horse to a tree. Then he had climbed one of the tall trees, to get a good look at the farm.

The local Gwadar merchant who had helped Someshwar was Talib's asset. Why? Because most Gwadaris hated Mahmud of Ghazni. They did not want to be a part of his empire. The Balochs, who were the majority community in Gwadar, wanted independence. This local merchant was someone who acted on his beliefs. Therefore, he usually supported those who worked against Mahmud. Of course, some money to lubricate the process always helped.

The upshot was that Talib got to know of Someshwar's plans. The local Gwadari merchant had assumed that two would be better than one against Mahmud, for an enemy's enemy is a friend. The local Gwadari merchant had assumed right.

Talib had also got to know of the Abbasid medallion that Someshwar had shown to the Gwadari merchant. To showcase the skills of the team he travelled with, to get more weapons support. It had convinced the local Gwadari merchant. It had convinced Talib too, who had decided to travel to Firdaus's farm and seek an alliance with the Indians. As far as Talib was concerned, it didn't matter if it was the Arabs or Indians who assassinated Mahmud, as long as the sultan was killed.

Talib had been watching from the treetop, formulating a plan to approach the Indians without being killed, when he suddenly saw a cavalry unit emerge from the other side of the valley, far in the distance. By the time the cavalry had ridden to the farm, he could recognize the distinctive form of Abu Q'asim.

Talib cursed his misfortune. It seemed that even the Indians, like his vaunted Arab allies, would be murdered by fate. For who could survive an attack by *Turk Kasap-e-Hind*, *the Turkish Butcher of India*?

And then he saw, from his vantage point, the most brilliantly executed ambush he could imagine. The attack in the passageway, the archers in the trees, the flanking cavalry from behind the goat pen and then the massacre at the barn.

Talib was awestruck. He had never seen warriors of this calibre. They would be perfect for his master Ismail's purpose.

When Allah shuts one door, He opens another.

Talib looked up to thank his God. He whispered, 'Mahmud, your days are numbered ...'

Now all he had to do was plan how he would approach these fearsome Indians and yoke their strength to his master's cause.

CHAPTER 20

The Debt of Sins Past

Ghazni, Afghanistan

'My boy!' Mahmud of Ghazni exclaimed with pride. 'My young lion. Conqueror of India!'

'My uncle!' cried Salar Maqsud, nephew to the sultan.

He walked briskly towards Mahmud on the restored floor of the Jama Mosque. The two men wrapped their arms around each other with admiration and warmth. Mahmud kissed Salar Maqsud repeatedly on both cheeks. He looked at him and beamed.

'Uncle, *you* are the Conqueror of India!' Salar Maqsud humbly replied. 'I am only your servant, and I maintain the yoke of control for you in the land of the *kafir*s.'

'The only way to ensure control over those exasperating Indians is to keep hammering them repeatedly! They keep rising in rebellion like bloody cockroaches. They are not like the Persians … They don't stay down once beaten …'

'True … Sad, but true. I have a rule. When in India, every morning, I just get up and randomly thrash some Indians.

Just keep thrashing them till they learn to stay in their place, at our feet.'

Mahmud stared hard. 'I hear there is trouble brewing among the heathens again?'

'Nothing serious … I can handle it,' answered Salar Maqsud. 'Some lowborn Hindu princeling from Shravasti is roaming around with a band of brigands. A minor irritation. I will swat him like a fly, uncle! I am returning to India after the festivities are over.'

'Hmmm …' Mahmud mused. 'What is his name?'

'Suheldev. Don't worry. The sultan of the world, the soon-to-be-caliph, does not need to think about such minor matters. I'll handle this Suheldev.'

Mahmud looked to his side. 'I am hogging you! Your aunt is eagerly waiting to say hello to you. And of course, your uncle, my brother, the governor-mufti of Ghazni!'

'My Lady.' Salar Maqsud saluted smartly and bowed low to Kausari Jahan. The queen nodded gently, a carefully crafted warm smile adorning her regal face. Salar Maqsud turned to Ismail, who stood to the right of the sultan. He bowed low to the uncle he had never met until now.

'My uncle! Finally, back from Guzgan. I presume you had a pleasant stay there.' The young Ghaznavid general smiled with disingenuous geniality.

'Oh, nephew, if only you had visited and given me the opportunity to host you in my opulence,' said Ismail with a laugh. He spread his arms wide with robust warmth. Salar Maqsud walked into the embrace.

'My brother praises you to the high heavens, nephew,' said Ismail. 'The Ghaznavid sultanate resounds with stories of your valour in India. Even the sultan's sons do not enjoy the special place you occupy in my brother's heart.'

'You are too kind, My Lord, Governor-Mufti,' replied Salar Maqsud humbly.

Salar Maqsud gestured towards a shy young man to step up beside him. He had been walking discreetly, two steps behind.

'Uncle, of course you remember Kerim, my right-hand man. Consider him equally responsible for the successes in India.'

Mahmud guffawed. 'Of course! It is hard to mention Salar Maqsud without mentioning Kerim,' he said with a twinkle in his eye. 'A truly fine young man you are, Kerim,' he added as he slowly ran his gaze over the tall, slender and unnaturally fair-skinned Kerim from head to toe. 'Truly fine.'

Kerim blushed.

Ismail awkwardly looked at the queen and found unusual resonance. Homosexual relations were not permitted in their understanding of Islam.

'Indeed, he is, My Lord,' said Salar Maqsud. 'Speaking of good men, I hope I can meet Abu Q'asim before I depart. I hear he is out on a hunt.'

'He is,' said the sultan. 'Walk with me, nephew.'

The two men sauntered towards the main hall of the Jama Mosque. The other three remained behind.

'How did the slaves escape, uncle?' Salar Maqsud asked.

'Nasty business, Maqsud,' said Mahmud. 'My brother recruited some *kafir*s to restore the mosque in time for the ceremonies. They escaped one night, just like that. Several guards died in the melee. Ismail suspects that it was an inside job. Kausari thinks that is preposterous. I love both my wife and my brother dearly, but they sure don't get along.'

'That is no secret, uncle. The entire city knows about the clash between the queen and the governor-mufti.'

'Whose side should I take?'

'I cannot help you with that, uncle.' Salar Maqsud smiled. He looked at Mahmud and added solemnly, 'But yes, it is a fact that the entire administration has become dysfunctional due to their infighting.'

'And in spite of it all, we have accomplished this!' Mahmud waved his hand jubilantly, showing off the grand mosque. 'This is the magnificent place where I will step into my new role—a role that is bestowed upon me from the Highest Authority. Once I become the caliph, I will return to India for another *jihad*. We will quell this upstart prince you talk about. We will destroy the Hindu and Buddhist kings of the land. We will convert or kill them all. I will fulfil the prophecy of *Ghazwa-e-Hind, the foretold conquest of India and the destruction of the* kafirs! We will rule India forever!'

'Or at least north India, for now. We can pick their kingdoms off one by one. They are deeply divided into castes, and many of them believe in non-violence!' Salar Maqsud snorted as he said this. 'And most of the Buddhists actually think that we will be kind to them, because we ourselves were Buddhists until recently.'

Mahmud laughed along. 'They're idiots. They don't understand. We prove our loyalty to our new faith by destroying our ancestors. The ones before us were in *Jahiliyyah, the age of barbaric ignorance.* We are now pure since we have accepted the One True Faith. We prove we are good

Muslims by devastating our ancestral religion everywhere. Buddhism will not be allowed to survive anywhere.'

'True ... But the south will be tougher,' continued Salar Maqsud. 'They are still militantly Hindu ... in fact, very militantly Hindu. They even practise animal sacrifices. And Rajendra Chola is too powerful.'

'Well, I'll have to leave something for the next generation.'

'True that, uncle. However, it is Ghazni's responsibility to bring the One True Faith to India. We will drench their heathen soil in their blood, till they either convert to Islam, or accept their lower *dhimmi* status and pay us *jaziya* in money and their women.'

'*Ameen* ...' said Mahmud, using *the Arabic version of Amen*, which a person of faith says at the end of prayer, asking his God to fulfil his prayer.

'*Summa Ameen*,' replied Salar Maqsud.

—·◦⚔◦·—

Ismail and Kausari stood sullenly beside each other near the mosque's entrance. Kerim, the beautiful young man, had forsaken the baleful duo and gone off to explore the grounds.

The queen turned to Ismail with supercilious eyes, but the angry fire in them was obvious. At least obvious to one capable of noticing subtleties, as Ismail was.

'A fat tub of lard keeps visiting every night and waiting outside my chambers ...' she said, her tone conversational and polite.

Ismail looked at her, a bemused expression on his face, though he knew exactly who the queen was speaking of. 'Fat tub of lard?'

The queen had a slight snigger on her face as she stared at Ismail with disapproving eyes. 'You are not as smart as people say you are.'

To a naive passerby, it would sound as though the queen and the governor-mufti were convivially discussing the weather. But the conversation was nothing short of a sword fight.

'Oh,' sighed Ismail theatrically, and then laughed softly. '*That* fat tub of lard ... You have a good sense of humour, great Queen. I will use this description for him.'

'You still haven't told me what that Persian Waddling Hippo was doing outside my chamber.'

Ismail laughed louder. 'Waddling Hippo. I am going to use that too ... But as for your question, I don't have the foggiest idea. The Hippo has a mind of his own. Who can tell how the brains of these Persians work?'

The queen's expression turned serious. 'Hippos can waddle in any direction ... Depending on who whips the hardest.'

'True. I experienced that when my workforce escaped. I am sure you had nothing to do with that.'

'I am sure that you are sure.'

Ismail smiled. 'And yet, the mosque has been rebuilt.'

'Because I helped.'

'I am sure you did.'

'Once again, I am sure that you are sure.'

Ismail laughed in response and looked away, not caring to respond.

Kausari's eyes briefly flashed fire. 'You have been back a very short time ... Be careful, noble Governor-Mufti.'

'I was born careful, great Queen. But are you ensuring that your Base of Power is careful?'

Kausari kept quiet. Enraged at the fairly obvious reference to the sultan in a public place. But she hid her anger well. *Ismail must be getting really powerful to speak so brazenly.*

Ismail tucked his hands under his long, loose sleeves. 'Allow me to speak plainly, lovely Queen. You know the path that has been chosen is dangerous. No Turk, no non-Arab will ever be accepted in that role. I know you have tried to dissuade him, but your Base of Power didn't listen. If something untoward were to happen, who would you be left with? I have loyalists throughout the empire now. You can count on me ... But for that, you must choose well.'

Kausari Jahan narrowed her eyes. Stunned by the open talk. She glanced around briefly to ensure that nobody was within earshot. She immediately regretted it. She had shown weakness. She knew that Ismail would never have said these words if anyone was within listening distance.

'I can have you executed for what you are implying,' Kausari hissed, her words soft and almost in a whisper.

'And what *was* I implying, My Lady?' teased Ismail, raising his hands like he was showing off the calligraphy on the mosque walls. 'Please do not sully the House of Allah with unholy thoughts ... But we can converse more freely in a more suitable place—my palace, if you prefer. I feel that we can really be each other's strength if we work together. I listen, unlike you-know-who ... I only seek to know you better. *Much* better. Though I know a lot already.'

The queen was taken aback by his insolence.

Furious, she looked away. And saw the sultan and Salar Maqsud walking back towards them.

She smiled and turned to Ismail. 'You get bolder by the day, Governor-Mufti,' she said under her breath. 'There is a very thin line between bravado and stupidity.'

Ismail smiled warmly to ensure that the sultan didn't get suspicious. But his tone was crisp. 'I will never cross that line.'

Kausari looked at Ismail. 'I pray you do.'

---·◦⚔◦·---

Yalan emerged from the servants' rooms in the sultan's palace and tiptoed softly down the corridor. He wore no footwear, his steps light as a feather. It was a couple of hours to sunrise and his nervous heart pounded in his ears.

He had been part of the sultan's kitchen staff for many years. He had been appointed on Khwaja Hassan's recommendation, despite his less-than-honourable background. He always knew that a day would come when he would have to repay that favour. He had been doing undercover work for the Jundiin-ul-Din, the religious police, and had hoped that would be enough. But in his heart of hearts, he knew that the work he did wasn't really dangerous enough to repay his debt to the prime minister. He just wasn't prepared for the heavy risk involved in what had finally been asked of him. However, he had no choice.

In preparation for his task, he had been transferred, just the previous week, to the sultan's personal staff.

The palace was blanketed in sleep, except for the ground staff patrolling the outer periphery. He glanced at the starry sky and walked to the end of the corridor. He placed his hands on the railing, surveying the ground below. A cold breeze stabbed his face like icicles in the air. He watched the two guards turn right to walk the length of the palace.

A six-minute window.

The guards would then turn right again and walk the far length, away from him. Yalan leaned out and turned his head upwards. Sure enough, a faint yellow light emerged from the window above him, a window to the chamber in which his target slept—or more likely, was awake.

Yalan climbed the railing and clung to a pillar. He stretched his left foot and found a foothold in a crack between the sandstone bricks. He extended his left hand and held the narrow drain-ledge. His right hand quickly followed and then the right leg. And now came the difficult part. He placed his left foot on the narrow footing in a wall crack, extended his left arm as wide as he could to hold the column support and ensured a good grip. Then he began climbing. The strain heavy on his back, fingers and legs. His shoulders burned but he continued climbing, till he reached the targeted ledge. Breathing hard, he placed his forearm on top of the ledge and hauled himself up. He crouched on top of the window ledge. On the count of three he half-stood, grabbed the window frame and found his balance. He let go of his left arm and released some tension. He held the frame again.

He heard the strains of an Arabic chant in a low feminine voice. He slowly rose up and peered into the room. The lady sat behind thin gossamer curtains at the far end of the plush royal bedroom. He straightened his legs farther and took a closer look.

The curtain swayed in the night breeze, revealing the queen. She sat on the floor, her back to the window. With nothing covering her head, her shock of auburn hair rolled down her back like stormy waves on the sea and fell in a shining heap on the floor. Her body covered the light-emanating source of her attention.

The soft tinkling chants dissipated almost into silence by the time they reached him. He could make out that it was in Arabic, most probably. He just wasn't sure what the words were. And he knew he had to provide answers.

What are you chanting at this unearthly hour, Queen?

Yalan was startled suddenly.

He felt a cold slithering sensation on his right forearm. He hissed and jerked his arm, almost losing his hold on the window frame. A snail plopped off onto the ledge, flung to a short distance. Yalan held the frame again. Unnoticed until then, the falling snail startled a small bird sitting quietly at the other end of the window ledge. Alarmed, the feathered creature cooed, stretched its wings and flew off.

Yalan said a silent prayer and looked up. And froze.

His eyes locked into the wrathful gaze of the queen, standing at the window now. Her eunuch guard loomed beside her.

Horror. Dread. He was trapped like a whimpering rabbit.

Yalan hastily tried to slip away but Hakeem grabbed both his wrists. He shifted his hands under the spy's armpits and hauled him up like a little puppy.

Kausari Jahan glared at him. She turned to Hakeem and whispered, 'By the Holy Lake and the Sacred Mountain, the timing was just right.'

Yalan was flailing around in Hakeem's iron grip, desperately trying to squirm free. Unable to make any sounds since Hakeem had covered his mouth now with his gargantuan left hand. But he still caught on to the key information. '*The timing was just right.*' *Was she expecting me? Have I been set up?*

'You make a sound, you die,' whispered Hakeem.

Yalan nodded. These words he understood.

The eunuch bodyguard relieved the spy of his *peshkabz*, the *lethal Persian dagger*. And pushed him down flat on to the ground. Kausari Jahan walked to Yalan and crouched next to him. He stared at her. Transfixed by her ethereal beauty, paralysed by the menace in her eyes.

'I recognize you,' she whispered. 'You work for the Jundiin-ul-Din. That snake Ismail has really crossed the line now …'

Yalan was about to say that he was ordered to come here by Prime Minister Khwaja Hassan and not Governor-Mufti Ismail. But he had enough of an instinct for self-preservation to keep quiet. Small men know that they can never truly understand the machinations of powerful people.

'I'm so sorry, My Queen. I was only following orders. I will follow you now. Please tell me what to do.'

Kausari smiled. 'And what will you do for me, silly man?'

'Anything you want, My Queen.'

Kausari raised her eyebrows and laughed softly. She knew, like any truly exquisite woman would, the almost sirenlike effect she had on an ordinary man. But the tone and the words had to be just right.

'Tell me, silly man,' said Kausari. 'What did you hear from outside my chamber?'

Without wanting to, Yalan glanced briefly at the queen's bosom. Many men couldn't control themselves in her presence. She clutched an object close to her heart, blocking it from view.

'I didn't hear anything, My Queen. I could make out that you were praying in Arabic. But I couldn't decipher the words.'

'Hmm.'

Yalan felt even more nervous at the 'hmm'. He blabbered along, trying to prove his usefulness. 'But I can be your spy, My Queen. Get you any news you like.'

Kausari looked at Yalan. A smile on her face. She feigned interest. 'News?'

'Yes, My Queen. News about the sultan. About the prime minister. About the governor-mufti. I will bring you all that.'

The queen smiled. The truly sublime smile she reserved for the one she loved, or when she had to make a man forget he had a brain so he would do exactly what she ordered him to do.

The smile had its effect. Obviously.

'I pledge eternal loyalty to you, My Queen,' Yalan ventured boldly, glancing again at her bosom. 'I will do whatever you tell me to do.'

Kausari Jahan nodded. And then turned to Hakeem. 'Cut off this good man's tongue. Break his bones but keep his face intact. Pick up his family. They will be our guests in the safe house. Set aside one thousand gold coins for them. Prepare to welcome the morning with formal charges slapped upon the governor-mufti for attempting to assassinate the queen of Ghazni at the hands of a Jundiin-ul-Din spy.'

Yalan remained silent. Stupefied by the prospect of the punishment he would receive. No man wants to lose his tongue. But one thousand gold coins meant that his family would be taken care of, forever. No man would pass up an opportunity like that either.

But he didn't have the time to think any more about the offer, to weigh the pros and cons. Because it wasn't really an offer. It was more of an ultimatum. He also didn't have the time, since his thoughts were interrupted as Hakeem boxed him hard with his humongous fist, knocking him unconscious.

The queen stood up and walked to the window. She looked to the sky and saw the moon. She nodded and smiled. Her eyes fell on the snail. It had industriously crawled back to the centre of the window ledge. Like *Kheper*, the *Egyptian scarab dung beetle*.

She picked the snail up on the tip of her right index finger, brought it close to her forehead in reverence and closed her eyes.

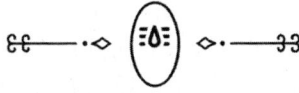

CHAPTER 21

The Man Who Started It All

Firdaus's farm, close to Khuzdar, Afghanistan

Dhruv sat in the snow at the edge of Firdaus's homestead. He did not feel the cold. Warm tears had made thin, smooth grooves in the rugged, snow-chilled face of the desolate young man.

Twenty-four hours had passed since the annihilation of the Turkic hunting team that had pursued the escaped slaves. The hunters had been hunted down to the last man, including the once-feared Turkish Butcher of India.

Victory had been achieved. But the costs had been heavy.

The previous evening, all the Indians had stood respectfully, mourning the gentle Gujarati merchant as a heartbroken Dhruv cremated his noble father, Someshwar, with full Vedic rituals. Soft chants from the Garuda Purana, usually recited during a funeral, accompanied the sombre ceremony. The mission practice till now, of the Indians keeping their assumed Muslim identities front and centre at all times, had been abandoned momentarily, considering the

329

melancholic occasion. But the chanting had been done as softly as possible, so the sound wouldn't carry far.

Dhruv had believed on the night before the battle that fate had reunited him with his father. But how could fate have been so cruel? They showed him his lost heaven briefly, only to take it away again so heartlessly.

Yazadeh cried continuously as a grave was dug for her loving father, Arif, according to Yazidi rituals and he was buried in it. All the Indians and the freed slaves had stood by her, supporting her during the ordeal. Amal had taken the Yazidi girl under her wing like a protective mother.

The brave farm owner, Firdaus, the contact for the Ghazni traitor, had also been killed. One of Q'asim's men had beheaded Firdaus as he had courageously tried to save a slave. Even Iqbal had been injured in the fight, but not too seriously. Firdaus had been buried on the farm grounds with proper Islamic funeral rites, attended by all.

Approximately sixty slaves had died, most at the passageway clash. And eight among Pulakit's men and the Chola soldiers had made the ultimate sacrifice. Narasimhan, Vijayan and Pulakit had ensured that proper funerals were conducted for all, according to the respective traditional beliefs of the dead.

The corpses of the two hundred Ghazni soldiers had been stacked up behind the barn, snow falling upon them. Some wanted the bodies thrown unceremoniously off a nearby cliff, to be eaten by wild animals and pecked at by scavenger birds. Nobody had the energy, inclination or motivation to perform any funeral ceremonies for the monsters. The Muslims among the former slaves, and even Amal, had told Narasimhan that as far as they were concerned, these people were not Muslim. In fact, they were a blot on the fair name of Islam. But Narasimhan had not made a decision yet about the Ghaznavid Turkic corpses. The freezing weather gave him some time since the bodies were not putrefying as quickly.

The armour, weapons and surviving horses of the Turks had been commandeered, to be used by the Indians.

Narasimhan was overlooking the arrangements for breakfast for the vast numbers under his charge when he noticed Dhruv sitting by himself in a far corner of the farm.

Victory had been achieved. But the costs had been heavy.

Narasimhan walked to the grief-stricken young man and sat down beside him. 'Your father was a man of incredible virtue and purpose, Dhruv. He was a true devotee of the Mahadev. He was a great son of Mother India.'

The snow was beginning to thaw slightly under the morning sun. Dhruv brought his hands together respectfully in response to the commander.

Narasimhan placed his hand on Dhruv's shoulder.

Dhruv wiped away a tear that emerged from the corner of his eye. 'What manner of torture is this ... I see my father, just for a little while. Embrace him. Receive blessings from him. Thank my luck that the Gods are finally not against me any more. And the next morning, I see his mutilated body ... The best man I have ever known ... I see him die like this ... Truly, the Lord is cruel to have led my father to his doom. He would still be alive had he stayed in India.'

'But *you* may have died then, Dhruv,' said Narasimhan gently. 'Even if you had pulled off this daring escape from Ghazni, the Turks would have come after you the way they did. Without the timely intervention of our soldiers, who are here only because of your father, there is no doubt that you and all your fellow travellers would be dead by now.'

Dhruv was stunned into silence. He had never looked at it this way.

'Can you consider the possibility that perhaps your father was sent here, along with us, to ensure that you live ... Your father brought all of us here, so that his son would survive the attack by Abu Q'asim. And then, having rewritten your fate, he moved on ...'

Dhruv remained silent. Tears were streaming down his cheeks.

'The question is: What will you do with this second life gifted to you because of your father's sacrifice?'

Dhruv took a deep breath and looked down.

'My emperor, Rajendra Chola, once told me something really beautiful ...'

Dhruv looked at Narasimhan.

Narasimhan continued, 'If the Lord Mahadev can take away something that you never imagined you would lose, then he can also bless you with something that you never imagined you would receive. All you have to do is keep living, keep walking. As the Aitareya Upanishad says, "*Charaiveti, charaiveti.*" Keep walking, keep walking.'

Dhruv looked down tearfully. 'My father had said something similar to me once. I hadn't listened ... I didn't understand ...'

Someshwar used to explain their ancient culture to Dhruv repeatedly. But he was too young and rebellious to ever listen attentively. *I wish I had listened more to you, Father ... I wish I had spent more time with you.*

'Then listen to your father now.'

Dhruv nodded.

'So get up,' said Narasimhan in a strong tone. 'Come back to the land of the living. Honour your father, honour his memory—by being the man your father would have liked you to be.'

Dhruv's tears were flooding out now.

'Your father's soul is still here. He is watching. Make him proud.'

—◦⚜◦—

Narasimhan and Dhruv were walking towards the main farm buildings now.

Dhruv took a deep breath and whispered, 'I am not going back to India, General. I am coming to Ghazni with you. My father brought you this far. I will fulfil his responsibility. I will pay his spiritual debt to the great Mahadev, Lord Shiva … That is, if you will allow me to join your command.'

Narasimhan smiled and patted Dhruv on his shoulder. 'I will be honoured to have you join our troops.'

Dhruv stopped and saluted Narasimhan formally.

Narasimhan nodded. His tone became commanding. 'At ease, soldier.' As Narasimhan turned, he saw Iqbal, Vijayan and Pulakit approach.

Vijayan and Pulakit assisted the aged Iqbal, who moved with slow deliberation, wounds on his left forearm and right thigh. Dhruv broke away from the general and moved towards his father's friend. The old man's eyes sparkled when they fell upon the lad. He stopped and spread his arms wide, a childlike smile upon his tired face. Tears poured out in a rush.

The two held each other without saying a word.

Vijayan and young Pulakit walked over to Narasimhan and stood at attention. The general brought his left fist to his chest in a salute. Enemies once, belonging to warring states in their homelands, Narasimhan and Pulakit looked at each other with respect now. They had both fought splendidly, with courage and skill.

'Namaste, General,' Pulakit addressed the great warrior with a bow of the head, joining his palms together.

'Namaste, Prince Pulakit,' said Narasimhan.

Pulakit glanced at Vijayan and then back at Narasimhan. 'I was told by the brigadier of your ... of your unpleasant encounter with my people before you left our country.'

Narasimhan smiled. 'Your soldiers did what any group of honourable men would do—seek vengeance for the death of their king. And I will say it again, your father was a great man. He fought with honour and *Dharma*. It's unfortunate that we were on opposing sides.'

'We are not on opposing sides now ...'

'We certainly aren't, noble Prince. I am honoured to call you my comrade.'

'And I am proud to call you my ally and commander—if you will have me.'

Narasimhan was surprised. 'Do you intend to come back to Ghazni with us?'

'Yes.'

'But didn't you just escape? Why go back to the hyena's den?'

'I escaped to save the slaves and lead them to freedom. But I must go back to the hyena's den. I must. Why? Because the nauseating hyena is still alive. And lions love to hunt hyenas!'

Narasimhan smiled. 'I see your great father in you … It will be my honour to have you in our team, Prince.'

'Then I present myself, Pulakit, along with the soldiers travelling with me, to your command.'

'It's my privilege to accept your service, Prince.'

'Pulakit …' corrected Pulakit.

Narasimhan frowned.

'I am under your command, General. I am not a prince when you address me. I am your soldier.'

Narasimhan smiled. 'Alright, Pulakit.'

'I have a request, though.'

'Yes?'

Pulakit continued, 'I had promised the rescued slaves that I would get them to India. If I return to Ghazni with you, I will be breaking my word to them. We Chalukyas are *Suryavanshis*, the *clan of Lord Ram*. We would rather die than break our word of honour. Can you help me?'

'No Chalukyan will break his promise as long as I am there to help, Pulakit. I will have a group guide them to Gwadar port. Our ship will dock two weeks from now. So there is more than enough time. The ships will take them to safety, to India.'

Vijayan cut in, 'I suggest we send Iqbal*ji* with them, as their guide and leader. He is injured and should be sent home. His presence will ensure that the ship crew recognizes the freed slaves and allows them to board. And then we can travel with a small team to Ghazni.'

They looked at Iqbal. He didn't object.

'Sounds good,' said Narasimhan. Suddenly, he grimaced as he felt a sharp rise in his ceaseless pain and tried to adjust his paralysed right arm with his left.

Pulakit looked at him with concern. 'If it's alright with you, can I look at your wound? I think I know the weapon my people might have used on you.'

Narasimhan nodded. And they started walking to Firdaus's cottage.

———o✦o———

The brace on Narasimhan's right arm had been removed. As had the bandages. The Chola general turned around and allowed Pulakit to inspect his back. The prince of Vatapi ran his hand over the dark, partially healed wound made by the poisoned arrow.

'How have you been feeling since you were hit, General?' Pulakit asked, narrowing his eyes and examining the raw slit in the skin. 'Tell me about all the symptoms.'

'Dreadful,' Narasimhan answered laconically. 'I feel sickeningly weak when not infused with these cursed stimulant herbs that course through my veins like rivers of fire. The herbs revive me but also inflict me with a new pain to forget the old. And there is a deep, ever-present ache where the wound is … It feels like molten steel is oozing out of the wound. But sometimes there is a sharp, sudden burst of fresh increased pain.'

'Any nausea?' asked Pulakit.

'Plenty,' said Narasimhan, sighing. 'I have vomited three times since the morning.'

'Cough?'

'Yes. Particularly at …'

'Night?' interrupted Pulakit, completing Narasimhan's sentence.

Narasimhan turned around. Surprised. 'You seem to know the symptoms exactly, Prince.'

'Pulakit.'

Narasimhan smiled. 'Sorry … Pulakit. But it seems like you know exactly what afflicts me.'

'I think I do.'

Narasimhan became serious. 'Am I dying slowly?'

'No, I don't think you are,' said Pulakit. 'This particular poison should have killed you by now. It is incredible that you have survived for so long. And what's more, you are not just moving around but are even capable of fighting.'

'What poison is this?'

'My people were perfecting a new *toxin* when I was still in Vatapi. It was a grey substance called *kunati*, alloyed with the brittle iron of an arrowhead or a knife. The smallest dose could make a man suffer and a substantial one could kill instantly. It appears my people have learned to administer just the right dose to prolong a man's suffering before he ultimately succumbs. I am almost certain that this is the poison that entered your body. The symptoms match perfectly.'

'Okay,' said Narasimhan sombrely. 'I am told I fell unconscious the moment the arrow broke through my skin.'

Pulakit pursed his lips. 'Sounds exactly right.' Pulakit turned to Amal, who had also joined them. 'Amal*ji*, did the arrowhead splinter and disintegrate *inside* the wound before extraction?'

'Yes, it did,' said Amal. 'That's why we were unable to extract a substantial portion of the arrowhead pieces from his body. They were so tiny that we would have caused more damage trying to take them out.'

'Hmm …' said Pulakit, 'that was the new technology my people were developing. An arrowhead that is not just *laced* with *kunati* but in fact is *made of it!* The general has a reservoir of poison lodged in his flesh right now and his blood is distributing its contents all over his body even as we speak. Continuously. It's a slow-release poison, among the most lethal toxins known to man.' Pulakit turned to Narasimhan. 'I am genuinely surprised that you are still alive, General.'

'You seem disappointed!' Narasimhan chortled.

Pulakit chuckled, 'Too late now!'

Narasimhan broke into hearty laughter.

'But seriously, we must extract the arrowhead shards from your body. The longer they remain in there, the worse your symptoms will get. I can do the extraction. But the procedure will likely be very invasive and painful, depending on where the arrowhead is nestled. Unless …'

'Unless?' Narasimhan raised an eyebrow.

'Unless we had a lodestone that could pull out the shards once we cut your skin and surrounding flesh wide enough,' said Pulakit.

'A lodestone?' Vijayan remarked.

'Yes, a lodestone. A *magnetized material*. It would attract and pull out the *kunati*, given that the poison is administered through an iron alloy. But this is not Vatapi. We would have had access to all the required equipment there. Where are we going to get a lodestone in this godforsaken land, though?'

Vijayan looked at Narasimhan, his eyes wide in delight. *The miracle has been travelling with us. We just didn't know it.*

Lodestone … The Somnath Shiva Linga was itself a powerful levitating lodestone.

'What?' asked Pulakit, noticing the looks of excitement being shared between Narasimhan, Vijayan and Amal.

'We have a lodestone … In fact, we have *the* lodestone …'

—◦⚜◦—

Pulakit stared in awe.

He was with Amal and Iqbal in the small cabin next to the pigeon coop. There, hidden in a niche, was a precious box that the Indians had always ensured was well protected and away from prying eyes. Amal and Iqbal had taken off their slippers before entering the cabin. As soon as Pulakit realized what it was, he too slipped off his footwear.

Tears came unbidden to his eyes. 'Is this …'

'Yes, it is,' answered Amal.

Iqbal picked up the precious sacred relic from the box with both hands, with the utmost respect. Pulakit bowed his head low and joined his palms together, as if in prayer. Iqbal placed the holy object in his hands.

An electric current ran through Pulakit's body. He started crying. '*Om Namah Shivaya … Om Namah Shivaya* …'

'Jai Somnath*ji*,' said Iqbal.

'Jai Somnath*ar*,' repeated Amal.

Pulakit gripped the fragment of the Somnath Shiva Linga tight in his fist, as fury arose within him. 'Mahmud must die.'

Amal placed her hand on Pulakit's shoulder. 'He will. He will die a dog's death.'

—◦⚜◦—

'Turkic rider?' asked Narasimhan. His right arm had been tied in a brace once again.

The general was surprised at the news that had just been delivered by Dasarna, the loyal Parmar captain. Apparently, a Turk, who had introduced himself as Talib, had just ridden into the farm, asking to meet the leader.

'He specifically asked for Salman, General,' said Dasarna.

Salman was the late Someshwar's assumed Muslim name while in Ghaznavid territory. Narasimhan looked at Vijayan quizzically.

'No idea what this is about, General,' said Vijayan. 'But if he knows the name Salman, perhaps we should meet him.'

'I agree,' said Narasimhan, turning to Dasarna. 'Bring the Turk to the barn. But disarm him first. And check for any hidden weapons.'

'Yes, General,' said Dasarna and saluted.

—◦✦◦—

The barn had been cleared of people. Only Vijayan and Narasimhan were present.

And Talib in front of them.

All sitting on uncomfortable benches. It was a barn after all.

Narasimhan stared at Talib. He was very obviously Turkic. Aged. Hunched back. Small black eyes. But a calm, tranquil demeanour.

Narasimhan liked that the Turk wasn't speaking too much. A foolish man usually speaks excessively in an attempt to impress others. A wise man remains silent till his words are necessary.

Narasimhan's instincts told him that this Ghaznavid was a smart and capable man. Whether he was an enemy or a friend was yet to be decided.

When Narasimhan refused to start the conversation, Talib finally spoke up.

'I believe that it was your fellow Indian, Chanakya, who had said many centuries ago that an enemy of an enemy is a friend.'

Narasimhan remained silent. But he was surprised by the reference to Chanakya.

'You can cross-check all that I am about to tell you with Yazadeh, who I saw in your camp. She knows who I am. And can verify my identity.'

'How do you know Yazadeh?' asked Narasimhan.

'That does not matter. I know of Salman as well.'

'I heard. But that doesn't mean anything.'

'Perhaps Someshwar would mean more?'

Now Narasimhan was genuinely shocked. As was Vijayan. But they kept their expressions deadpan.

'What do you want?' asked Narasimhan.

'Why don't you bring Someshwar in here?'

'What do you want?' repeated Narasimhan.

Talib held his breath. 'He didn't survive the battle, did he?'

Looking at the expression on Narasimhan's and Vijayan's faces, Talib knew he was right.

'That's unfortunate. The Gwadar merchant really liked Someshwar.'

And the paisa dropped. Narasimhan and Vijayan understood the source of Talib's information.

'I'll ask one last time,' said Narasimhan. 'What do you want?'

'The same thing that you want,' answered Talib. 'The death of the sultan.'

Narasimhan and Vijayan leaned forward. Interested.

'My name is Talib. I am a servant of Ismail, the governor-mufti of Ghazni and younger brother of Sultan Mahmud. Lord Ismail was the rightful king before Mahmud deposed him. I had come to Gwadar to receive Arab ambassadors from the Abbasid caliphate, who were to help us assassinate the sultan. I know what happened to them.'

Vijayan kept his expression stoic, but internally he was shocked. *How much does this bugger know?*

'Go on,' said Narasimhan.

'I was assured by the Gwadari merchant that you are all very capable. I saw evidence of that yesterday.'

'Go on.'

'My master does not care who carries out the assassination, as long as it is not him or anyone in his employ. It could be Arabs or it could be Indians. We don't care about the origin of the weapon as long as we have the same target. It seems that a temporary alliance could be possible between us,' said Talib.

'And why should we trust you?'

'For the same reason that I am trusting you. We have no other option.'

Narasimhan grunted, non-committal. But in his mind, he was becoming increasingly convinced. *Yes, of course, the man cannot be trusted. We may be walking into a trap. But what choice do we have? After the death of Someshwar and Firdaus, we have no leverage left. This is our only hope. And maybe the governor-mufti is the royal contact that Firdaus had lined up, in any case.*

'Also, if I was really on the other side, I could have used my master's authority and marched here with the local Khuzdar battalion. Capable as you people are, do you really think you could stand up to a cavalry of two thousand trained Turks? The fact that I didn't do that is in and of itself proof of my intentions,' said Talib.

Narasimhan remained silent. *Good point.*

'All we want from you is that you kill the sultan and his key lieutenants—one of whom, Abu Q'asim, you have already dispatched. We will need his twin sons to be killed as well.'

Vijayan couldn't believe their good fortune. The mission seemed to have become handicapped with the deaths of Someshwar and Firdaus, since nobody had access to the traitor in the Ghazni royal family. But the Gods had placed another man, apparently in the traitor's employ, directly in their orbit.

'You really think killing the sultan is that easy?' asked Narasimhan.

'Yes, it can be. It seems Allah has brought us together. Your mission can be very easy, if you have the sultan's brother willing to help you ... I will take you to Ghazni in hiding. We will shelter you all in a safe house and put you in the right place at the right time, to strike. And in exchange ... what do you want?'

'We want the death of the sultan. And the pieces of the Somnath Shiva Linga that your people have apparently buried under the steps of your main mosque.'

Talib was surprised. 'That's it? No gold? No precious stones? No land?'

'The Somnath Shiva Linga is worth more than all the wealth in the world.'

Talib frowned. *These people are strange.*

He couldn't hear Vijayan's thoughts, which would have clarified his doubts. *We Indians earn wealth. We don't loot it.*

'Do we have a deal?' asked Narasimhan.

'Of course, we do. But ...'

'But, what?'

'We have one additional demand which is non-negotiable.'

'What demand?'

'The slave girl, Yazadeh.'

Narasimhan glanced at Vijayan. This was completely unexpected.

Talib felt the need to explain. 'This would be a personal request. My master is ... he is infatuated with her.'

Narasimhan was aghast. 'But she is a child! No more than thirteen or fourteen.'

'This is non-negotiable. Think it over.'

---◦✣◦---

Firdaus's cottage had been sanitized and converted into a temporary surgery unit.

Narasimhan's brace and bandage around his right arm had been opened. His back washed with clean water and sterilized as best could be done with local herbs. He had been administered some medicines that the Indians had brought along with them, to anaesthetize his back, where the surgery would be done. Pulakit had warned him that they did not have enough medicines to ensure proper anaesthesia and that he would have to tolerate the pain. Dasarna had joked at that time, with an immortal line that was particularly popular in north Indian folk plays: *'Mard ko dard nahin hota!' A real man feels no pain.*

Narasimhan had laughed softly at the joke. He was lying on his stomach and feeling increasingly drowsy. But he forced himself to stay awake, because he had to answer questions from Pulakit about what he was feeling.

'I wonder …' said Narasimhan.

'Wonder what, General?' asked Amal, who, along with Dasarna and Zayn Husayn, was placing the sanitized surgical instruments on a plate for Pulakit to use as the Chalukyan prince washed his hands.

'I wonder … Perhaps … I was not hit by the Chalukyan arrow … to pay for *my* sins …'

'What do you mean, General?' asked Vijayan, as he tied Narasimhan's limbs to the bed with soft cotton cloth, to ensure that he wouldn't make any sudden movements as he felt the inevitable pain once the procedure began.

'Maybe … Maybe I was hit so that my body could transport the instrument … which will make Mahmud suffer for *his* sins …'

'How so?' asked Pulakit, who was standing next to the bed now.

'Mahmud is our *Vishalakshitah* … The *one targeted for poisoning* … Don't throw away the arrow shards which you will extract from me … We will use them … Use them on Mahmud …'

Pulakit smiled and glanced at Vijayan and Amal, before turning back to Narasimhan. 'As you command, General. We will begin now. Ready yourself.'

Narasimhan grinned. 'I was born ready.'

Men, real men, prove their manhood with silly jokes in times of danger. And other men, real men, laugh along with their comrades at such times to cement the male bond.

Pulakit and Vijayan, along with Dasarna and Zayn Husayn standing behind them, laughed at Narasimhan's joke. Amal rolled her eyes and gently touched the back of Narasimhan's head. She placed a short length of rope between the teeth of the general, to ensure that he didn't bite his tongue during the surgery. And then she held his head down gently. The pain would begin soon.

Pulakit splashed astringent on the not-completely-healed wound. Iqbal had found it in Firdaus's stores. The astringent had been heated and distilled further. It stung hard on contact with the slightly open cut that was still on the scar tissue.

Narasimhan's body stiffened. But he didn't make a sound.

'I'm going to cut now, General.'

Narasimhan held his breath.

Pulakit slit through the scar tissue, skin and subcutaneous tissue with the surgical knife. Narasimhan bit hard on the rope, breathing deeper and deeper. He growled as Pulakit began to burrow, deeper and deeper, into the poisoned, unhealed flesh, carefully searching for shards of the *kunati* arrowhead.

He finally found the first traces of black iron in the bluish crimson of the general's poisoned blood that was leaking out. Holding the flesh apart, he held his right hand out. Dasarna handed the holy lodestone relic to Pulakit. The Chalukyan prince inserted its narrow edge into Narasimhan's wound.

Forgive me, my Lord Shiva, for using you like this. But only you can draw out the poison, just as you did during the Sagar Manthan.

The lodestone, with its strong magnetic properties, began attracting the *kunati*-infused iron shards towards itself.

The great Chola warrior screamed loudly. Violent scenes from his life flashed in his mind. It felt as though all his negative energy, all the pain, all the guilt of all that violence, was being pulled out of him. Towards the open wound on his upper back. And from there, it was being sucked out of him, in a divine act of immense grace and kindness.

Narasimhan's mind went blank and he descended, unconscious, into the darkness.

Then, after what seemed like lifetimes, Vijayan and Zayn loosened their hold on his shoulders and arms, but only slightly. Pula held up the piece from the Shiva Linga, blood and splinters of metal clinging to it. He handed the Shiva Linga lodestone to Dasarna, who was holding a fresh clean cloth to receive the sacred relic. It would be washed later and cleaned thoroughly. The *kunati*-infused arrow shards would be stored and refashioned, to be used on Mahmud. And pujas would be performed for the Shiva Linga lodestone fragment to seek forgiveness for the use of the sacred relic in this manner.

'General ... General ...' Pulakit was trying to get Narasimhan to respond.

But Narasimhan didn't say anything. His body was spasming slightly.

'General, there will be pain. But has the feeling of molten steel within your back and shoulder gone?'

Narasimhan was breathing hard, not responding. Pulakit looked at Amal, who poured more warm distilled astringent on to the open wound to sanitize it further and then wiped around it with cotton swabs.

The burning sensation of the liquid appeared to wake Narasimhan, as his head moved a bit.

'General ...' Pulakit repeated. 'Has the molten steel feeling within your back gone?'

'It's ... gone ...' Narasimhan's words were broken. 'The ... feeling ... is gone ...'

Pulakit smiled triumphantly at the others around him and turned back towards Narasimhan. 'The poisonous shards are out. The *Neelkanth* has pulled out the poison once again.'

By 'once again', Pulakit was referring to the *Sagar Manthan*, the *churning-of-the-ocean episode* in the Indian legends, when Lord Shiva had helped both the *Devas* and the *Asuras*, the *Gods* and the *anti-Gods*, respectively, when poison had emerged from the swirling waters of the sea. Poison that would destroy the entire universe. The powerful Lord Shiva had drunk the venom to save all of creation from being poisoned. So potent was the poison that his throat turned blue. That's why he got the name *Neelkanth*, the *Blue-Throated One*. It's a very cool story. If you haven't heard it, ask your parents.

Pulakit efficiently stitched the wound shut with *Guduchi* sutures, a technique known to all Indian soldiers who carried these plant fibres during wartime. Sutures made from this *medicinal plant* had inherent antiseptic properties and dissolved naturally over time. Pulakit then bandaged the wound clean.

Amal, who herself was a medicine woman, looked at Pulakit with admiration. 'You've done a good job.'

'Thank you,' said Pulakit, before looking down at Narasimhan.

The general had stopped moving. No more spasms. Zayn gently pulled the rope out of Narasimhan's mouth. They let him sleep. The danger had passed. Now was the time for healing.

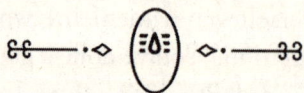

CHAPTER 22

Unlikely Allies

Firdaus's farm, close to Khuzdar, Afghanistan

It had been two days since the surgical extraction of the *kunati* poison-infused arrow shards from Narasimhan's back. He was recovering surprisingly quickly. The pain had reduced dramatically. He was able to move his right arm a bit as well. Pulakit believed that it was only a matter of a week or at most two before Narasimhan had complete use of his right arm and shoulder once again. The cold and dry atmosphere of the mountains would only quicken the recovery process.

The caravan of former slaves led by Iqbal was ready to leave for Gwadar. They would reach the port city well in time to board the ships and escape to India. The slaves had been given provisions such as clothes and shoes, and made to bathe, clean and shave, so that they looked like ordinary citizens. A route that avoided the major population centres had been planned for them.

Pulakit had been extremely unhappy with the plan to take Yazadeh back to Ghazni. She would be the only former slave not escaping to India. But Narasimhan had explained that they had no choice, and had assured Pulakit that he would get Yazadeh out when they escaped from Ghazni after assassinating Mahmud. Narasimhan had sworn this on his own life. He had told Pulakit about the Indonesian princess Odiratna and how he could never again allow a little girl to be hurt on his account. Amal had also sworn on her blood, in front of Pulakit, that she would look after Yazadeh like a younger sister. She would ensure that Yazadeh was with them when they escaped from Ghazni after the mission. After much persuasion, Pulakit had agreed.

What had made it easier to convince Pulakit was Yazadeh's own desire to go back. All she insisted on was that if Narasimhan had even a sliver of a chance, then he must kill Governor-Mufti Ismail as well. Narasimhan was surprised by Yazadeh's demand, for she was still a child. But Amal had later explained to the general that if a daughter were to see her beloved father being killed in front of her, while trying to protect her, she would change completely. She would not turn into a hapless woman seeking a shoulder to cry on. She would turn into Goddess Durga, seeking righteous vengeance. In fact, Yazadeh had asked Amal to train her on the basic stabbing techniques. And Amal was only too willing to teach her, for Ghazni was a dangerous place for all of them.

As Iqbal was preparing to leave, he sought out his friend's son, Dhruv. 'Keep this with you,' said Iqbal, handing over a sealed letter. 'It is a complete list of your father's assets, spread all over the world. It also contains the secret location where you will find the documents of property ownership, besides treasures in gold and precious stones. It's a lot less than it used to be, because your father spent a lot of his wealth on this mission ... But it is still a considerable amount. You will need to manage it once you return home.'

Dhruv smiled. 'You keep it, Iqbal uncle. What if I don't come back?'

Iqbal pulled Dhruv's ear. 'Shush! Don't say silly things to tempt fate. Nothing will happen to you. You will return. And when you do, you will take control of your father's possessions, businesses and responsibilities. My son will be your junior partner, just like I was your father's.'

Dhruv beamed and embraced Iqbal. 'I will need you to train me when I return, uncle. Until then, will you please keep this list carefully, for my sake?'

Iqbal touched Dhruv's cheeks, tears in his eyes. 'Your father's immortal soul will protect you, my boy. I will be waiting for you. We will build even greater businesses together.'

A little later, Iqbal set off along with his large caravan of former slaves. He had been told to inform the Chola ships' captains that there may be delays in the return of Narasimhan and his band. Hence, they should ferry the slaves to India and return, post-haste, to Gwadar. A signed letter from Narasimhan with these very instructions would convince them. Also, Iqbal was asked to use the ship pigeons to send a message to Emperor Chola with an update on the mission.

Early the next day, Talib and Narasimhan were at the gate of the late Firdaus's farm, mounted on their horses. Narasimhan looked behind him. There were around eighty soldiers on horseback, armed to the teeth, refreshed and well fed. The horses and the weapons of the massacred Turks was being put to good use. They were carrying enough dry food and fruits to last the journey. They were set. Set for the assassination mission.

Farther behind, he could see the large barn up in flames. Talib had convinced Narasimhan that throwing the corpses of the two hundred dead Turkic soldiers off a cliff would be a mistake. The unusually large presence of predatory birds in the air may draw the attention of the battalion stationed in Khuzdar town. The dead bodies could be investigated and identified. News of the massacre of the Turks would travel to Ghazni, which would make Mahmud ramp up his security and make the assassination mission difficult. It would be much better if Mahmud believed that Abu Q'asim was still on the hunt for the slaves. And so the Indians had piled up the dead bodies of the Turks in the barn and set it aflame.

To complete the charade, Talib had drafted a message to send to Mahmud in Ghazni. The letter would state that the Turkish Butcher of India had found and killed around two hundred slaves and burnt their bodies where he had found them. Also, that Yazadeh wasn't among the slaves that he had killed. And that the other slaves had likely escaped to Persian lands and Abu Q'asim was riding onwards to hunt them down. Considering that Abu Q'asim would now be in enemy territory in Persia, even if just in the borderlands, he would anyway keep communication to a minimum for safety reasons. To convince Mahmud of the authenticity of the letter, Talib had pulled off a ring from Abu Q'asim's cold dead finger and used it to affix his seal onto the parchment. The letter had then been sent to Ghazni by bird courier.

'Shall we, Nasrullah?' asked Talib, using the assumed Muslim name for Narasimhan. He had been briefed well.

'We shall,' answered Narasimhan. 'Mark my words, the Sultan will be in Dire Straits soon.'

Vijayan, slightly behind Narasimhan, but within earshot, smiled and spoke up. 'I agree. Mahmud will soon swing on a hangman's noose and become the Sultan of Swing.'

Pulakit laughed softly, as he kicked his horse into action. 'Sometimes, a good joke is So Far Away from me, So far, I just can't see.'

Narasimhan glanced at Pulakit and Vijayan. 'True, my Brothers in Arms.'

'Enough!' snapped Amal. 'Let's just ride in silence!'

Vijayan whispered, 'Have you heard The Sound of Silence? An Uncle called Garf wrote it.'

Amal reached out and hit Vijayan on the back of his head, just as everyone broke out in peals of laughter.

—◦✣◦—

Ghazni, Afghanistan

'Where the hell have you been?' hissed Malik Ayaz.

Talib had just returned to Governor-Mufti Ismail's palace in Ghazni, after having settled the Indians in a safe house. Upon entering the palace, he had gone immediately to meet the slave woman Reshma, and she had informed him that Ismail had been arrested around three weeks earlier by the royal guards.

Serious accusations had been thrown at him by Queen Kausari Jahan. He had been charged with heinous crimes, ranging from espionage to an attempt to assassinate the queen to even un-Islamic behaviour. Talib was stunned that such charges had even stuck. Because overwhelming evidence would have been needed for an arrest warrant to be issued on the powerful governor-mufti of the realm. And that too, just a few days before the anointment of Sultan Mahmud as caliph. Before Talib could even process this information, Malik Ayaz had landed up at the governor-mufti's palace to interrogate Talib about his absence during this time of peril for his lord and master. Talib had told Reshma to stay in the servants' quarters and flee the city in case the conversation with the King of Lahore didn't go well.

'How did you know that I had returned, My Lord?' asked Talib, trying to delay the obvious questions, so that he could formulate lies that would hold. He did not want to reveal anything about the conspiracy with the Arabs.

'I had informers placed outside here, obviously!' Ayaz seemed livid. 'Was it you who provided evidence against my father?'

'Of course not, My Lord,' shrieked Talib. 'How can you even accuse me of that?'

'The fact that you were conveniently absent when this storm hit my father, is very, very suspicious.'

By now, Talib was fearing the worst. Would Malik Ayaz give Talib up to save his father, Ismail? He knew that the politics of people at the top was always utterly ruthless. They never hesitated to surrender a pawn, no matter how loyal, to save themselves or more important players.

'I had been sent to Gwadar by the governor-mufti himself, My Lord,' cried Talib, quickly taking out a document that was stamped with Ismail's seal for entry into Gwadar port to receive some important state guests.

Malik Ayaz grabbed the letter, glanced at it and looked around. 'So where are the important state guests?'

'Umm … My Lord …'

'Alright. Let me clarify further. Where are the Arabs?'

Talib was shocked. He had been told not to speak of the Arabs to anyone, including Malik Ayaz. 'Uhhh …'

'They better be here, or you are dead, Talib.'

Talib realized that it was time to come clean. To save his own head. Perhaps, Ismail himself had told Malik Ayaz of the secret plan with the Abbasids. So Talib sang like a canary. He told Malik Ayaz everything. About the Arabs being killed by the Indians, of the massacre of Abu Q'asim and his men at the farm outside Khuzdar, and the recruitment of the Indians to their cause.

'Farm outside Khuzdar? What farm?' asked Malik Ayaz.

'Some man called Firdaus had a farm there. Maybe the Indians had threatened the poor man and taken over his property. But I can't be sure since Firdaus had been killed by the time I reached the place.'

Talib thought he saw Malik Ayaz inhale sharply at the mention of Firdaus but didn't think much of it. 'What do we do, My Lord?'

'Where are the Indians?'

'In a safe house.'

'In Ghazni?'

'Yes, My Lord.'

'Nobody else knows the location?'

'You will know it soon, My Lord … So, nobody besides you and me.'

'Do you know you were followed by Prime Minister Hassan's spies?'

Talib blanched. 'I saw them on the outskirts of Ghazni, My Lord. But they lost sight of me at the suburb outside the inner walls. I am sure of it. Nobody else saw me.'

Malik Ayaz looked at Talib, shook his head, then turned towards the wall. He stared at it, smoking the hookah.

'My Lord?'

'Quiet! Let me think …'

'Yes, My Lord. My apologies …'

Malik Ayaz sat in silence for a bit longer, then appeared to make up his mind. He turned to Talib. 'Maybe, this will all be for the good, after all. We can still save my father.'

Ayaz then explained the plan to Talib, who had many questions—like how in God's name did they find the evidence to arrest a man as powerful as Ismail? Everybody in Ghazni knew of the feud between the queen and the governor-mufti, but what had been done to Ismail seemed unbelievable.

Ayaz told Talib that the evidence appeared irrefutable. An undercover member of the Jundiin-ul-Din religious police called Yalan had been caught peeping into the queen's bedchamber in the dead of night, and everyone knew that the religious police was headed by Ismail. Although Yalan's tongue had been cut off as punishment for trespassing, the man had repeatedly, and vehemently, pointed to Ismail in the courtroom when he was asked who had sent him on this strange mission.

Talib was surprised at the name and raised the obvious suspicion: 'What kind of a name is Yalan?'

'Exactly!' Ayaz said. 'The name itself is a clue that there is something wrong.'

And then Malik Ayaz went on to explain how it turned out that Yalan had been transferred to the sultan's domestic staff just the previous week.

'The prime minister …' whispered Talib.

'Precisely, only Khwaja Hassan could have issued such an order. But he swore, under oath, that the governor-mufti had forced him to do so, to either assassinate the queen or to generate fabricated evidence against her. The fact that spies had filed reports earlier, of the governor-mufti and the prime minister meeting regularly outside the palace of the queen, made the evidence even more damning!'

Talib was flabbergasted. 'My God! That witch has been planning this for months!'

Ayaz lowered his head and stared at Talib. The silent message was implicit but clear. *Know your status, slave. Even if it is true that Kausari Jahan is a witch, it's not your place to say these things.*

Talib immediately realized his mistake. 'My apologies, Sire. My sincere apologies.'

Ayaz took a breath, forgiving Talib silently. 'But your return, with the Indian assassins in tow, has turned the tide. Maybe my father's penance helped.'

At the confused look from Talib, Ayaz explained that Ismail had sworn off meat, wine and women the day he had been arrested. He had promised that he would follow these self-imposed rules as penance till Allah freed him from these unfair charges.

'It looks like when all had turned against your father, God came to save him,' said Talib.

Malik Ayaz nodded. 'But first, let's ensure that he doesn't get executed and get him out of jail. Then we will implement the rest of the plan.'

—·◦⸎◦·—

'Talib has come to meet us with another man, General,' said Dasarna.

Narasimhan and his brave eighty had entered Ghazni the previous evening. Talib had led them to a strange safe house. A safe house that was so overt that it was covert.

A high-end brothel.

Hiding in plain sight. Smart.

The brothel was so exclusive and expensive that no common man visited it. And the rich nobility usually asked for home service, so they didn't frequent the establishment. Unknown to all but a handful, this brothel was owned by Ismail—behind the cover of a few 'nominal proprietors', of course.

'Who is it?' asked Narasimhan.

It had taken the Indians particularly long to reach Ghazni, since they had taken unfrequented and longer routes to avoid unnecessary attention.

Along these isolated routes, they occasionally passed magnificent uninhabited ghost towns with the remnants of ancient architecture that could be traced to civilizations driven to dust by the Turks. Grand cities built by the Hindu Shahi Pathans and Buddhist-Hindu Balochs that had long been abandoned as the people who populated these vibrant civilized towns had either been massacred or ethnically cleansed. Many modern Indians didn't even know that the new name for the Uparisyena mountains, the *Hindu Kush* mountains, actually meant *the place of Hindu slaughter*, just like *naslkush* meant genocide and *khudkushi* meant suicide.

'Apparently, Malik Ayaz, the King of Lahore, has come with Talib,' said Dasarna. 'But whatever his grand title, he is more of a governor and spends most of his time here in Ghazni.'

Narasimhan had insisted that he and his troops be housed in an unused part of the brothel. That meant they were cramped in, with an average of eight persons to a room. But it also meant that they had no risk of being ambushed at night by strangers and neither would any of his men be in danger of being seduced by the usual inhabitants of the building into doing something that would put them all in danger.

'Hmm. It's strange for someone from the Turkic nobility to be up and about so early in the morning ...' Narasimhan straightened his thick fur coat, for it was too cold for him. 'In any case, it's not like we have much of a choice ... Let's meet him.'

A short while later, Malik Ayaz and Talib walked into the chamber where Narasimhan stood, waiting for them. Along with Narasimhan were Pulakit, Vijayan, Amal, Dhruv, Zayn Husayn and even Yazadeh.

Malik Ayaz nodded at Yazadeh. He didn't recognize Pulakit, Dhruv or Zayn, obviously, since they had been lowly slaves during their time in Ghazni. And he was meeting the rest for the first time. The King of Lahore looked at Narasimhan and considered him.

Narasimhan noticed that Yazadeh did not seem too uncomfortable in Malik Ayaz's presence.

'Sit, please,' said Ayaz after a long period of silence, taking a seat himself.

'Thank you,' said Narasimhan, as he sat down. He noticed that Malik Ayaz's tone was deep, measured and calm. He was a serious man.

The rest of the people remained standing.

The King of Lahore looked around. His eyes rested on Amal, and he smiled. Women have a sixth sense about a man with 'clean' eyes that are devoid of lascivious intent. It makes them feel safe. Malik Ayaz had clean eyes. 'We have women warriors in my native land, Georgia, as well. They fight under the banner of the great Mother Mary.'

Narasimhan frowned. 'I thought you were Muslim?'

'My father is Muslim. My late mother was Christian.'

'Some Indians find Jesus Christ very inspiring as well. His message of love for all is a lot like what the noble Lord Mahavir, the Jain Tirthankara, spoke of.'

Malik Ayaz smiled. 'Hmm. I find Jainism very inspiring too.'

'Perhaps I will take up that path,' said Narasimhan, 'when I am done with this martial life. Non-violence and vegetarianism are good for the soul.'

'Hmm … But some souls are meant to suffer for others … Because you can be non-violent only when you have someone else standing in front of you, willing to be violent to protect you.'

Narasimhan smiled.

Nobody around them expected a conversation of this nature. Not at this time. Malik Ayaz stated the obvious. 'Let's talk about what we actually came here for.'

'Yes, of course,' said Narasimhan.

'You must have heard about governor-mufti.'

'Yes.'

'He will be released tomorrow. And he will come to my mansion.'

Narasimhan was surprised, but did not say anything.

'You have Yazadeh with you, so there's no point hiding things from you that you would find out from her anyway. Governor-Mufti Ismail is ... very important to me.'

Narasimhan nodded, wisely not making any comment.

'You will sit tight here for a week to ten days. I will arrange for you to be physically near the sultan when the time is right. Then, you will assassinate him, and escape from here with your team. I never want to hear from you or your people ever again.'

'Of course.'

'But ... I have one condition ... None of you will kill Governor-Mufti Ismail.' Malik Ayaz looked around as he said this, then turned back towards Narasimhan. 'Give me your word in your God's name. I know Indians will never break their word if they have sworn on their God.'

Talib looked at Malik Ayaz from behind him. With admiration. Not for the first time did he feel guilty that he couldn't tell the King of Lahore the truth, that his father, Ismail, did not care for him at all.

Narasimhan pulled out his knife, cut his palm and swore a blood oath in his assumed name in a slightly louder voice. 'I, Nasrullah, swear on the name of the Mahadev Himself that neither I nor anyone of my troops will kill Governor-Mufti Ismail.'

Malik Ayaz seemed satisfied. He turned to Yazadeh. 'I will come to take you to my mansion when my father returns. Do not worry, no harm will be done to you. I just need you to keep him calm and stable until the assassination. And you too can escape after that.'

Yazadeh, to Narasimhan's surprise, nodded.

But Narasimhan hadn't realized what Yazadeh was thinking. She was not one of his troops since she had not pledged loyalty to him.

'I will come along for her protection,' said Amal. She had personally sworn she would protect Yazadeh.

Malik Ayaz nodded his assent. And then clarified, 'But you will have to come as a servant. And remember the vow that your general ... What was the name I was supposed to say ... Nasrullah? ... Yes ... Remember the vow that your General Nasrullah just made.'

'I will honour Nasrullah's vow,' said Amal.

Ayaz turned towards Zayn, suddenly speaking in Arabic. 'Are you an Arab?'

'Yes, Lord,' answered Zayn, instantly replying in Turkic to the question asked in his native tongue.

'And you are with the Indians? Why?'

'I was a slave here.'

Ayaz was genuinely surprised. *An Arab slave? That could only mean one thing.* 'What's your name?'

'My name is Zayn, Sire.'

'Your full name.'

Zayn stiffened.

'You are not in any danger, Zayn of Arabia,' said Malik Ayaz. 'What's your full name?'

'Zayn Husayn.'

Malik Ayaz leaned back. Like he was pondering something. Narasimhan didn't understand.

'You are Shia,' said Ayaz.

Zayn nodded.

'Your Arab identity can be useful,' said Malik Ayaz. 'But do not use your full name where I will send you.'

'Yes, Lord,' said Zayn.

Malik Ayaz stood up suddenly and looked at Narasimhan. 'Our business here is done. I will see you all soon.'

Narasimhan too stood up, smiled and spoke to Malik Ayaz with respect. 'Yes, King of Lahore.'

—⋄⁂⋄—

Vijayan was miserable as he nudged Amal's lose hair behind her ear. 'I am not happy about this.'

'Valeed,' said Amal, 'I am probably safer in King Ayaz's palace than all of you on your assassination mission. It is me who should be worried about you!'

Vijayan laughed softly. The first sign of courage was a sense of humour in the face of danger. He had always admired his beloved Amal's valour.

'Valeed, we have sworn to protect Yazadeh,' continued Amal. 'We cannot go back on our word. I must ensure that one of us is present to get her out to safety once Mahmud has been assassinated.'

Vijayan nodded.

'I don't have a choice …'

'I know,' said Vijayan, miserable. 'The logic is undeniable. But that doesn't mean I have to like it.'

Amal laughed. 'I will see you at the meeting point outside the city when all is done. You make sure that you remain alive and meet me there.'

'Yes. Because who will rescue me and take me home to India if I miss my rendezvous with you!'

'Precisely!'

Vijayan and Amal laughed and held each other. They embraced tightly. Their strong love drowned out their concerns.

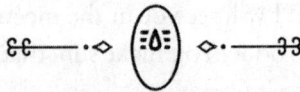

CHAPTER 23

Court of Illusions

Ghazni, Afghanistan

Ismail stood in the middle of the court chamber, facing the sultan. Mahmud of Ghazni sat at the head-end of the chamber. Seated beside him were Kausari Jahan, Malik Ayaz and the Persian prime minister, Khwaja Hassan. Other senior Ghazni nobles were also in full attendance.

Everyone expected the governor-mufti to be awarded the death penalty. There was just too much overwhelming evidence against him. The only doubt was regarding the date and perhaps the manner of execution.

Ismail too expected to be given capital punishment. He was also sure the actual execution would take place after the anointment of Mahmud as caliph. Ismail knew his elder brother well. He could guess that Mahmud wouldn't want anything to interfere with the glory of what would be the high point of his life.

Ismail had prepared his mind and heart for the worst. He was in for a surprise. Not just because of the pronouncement that was made but also because of where it came from.

Kausari Jahan spoke crisply. 'My Sultan, My King, I am the one who has been hurt by this awful man.'

Ismail looked at Kausari with a deadpan expression. *Yeah. Yeah. Don't bore me. Get on with it.*

'I have every right to demand righteous vengeance and justice,' continued Kausari. 'But ...'

Ismail frowned. *But?*

'But however much I may hate Governor-Mufti Ismail, I love you more, my liege, Sultan Mahmud of Ghazni. I love you more than life itself.'

Mahmud looked at his wife with tenderness and then glared at his younger brother, Ismail.

The exquisitely attired and coiffured Malik Ayaz, who was slouching on his grand chair till now, sniggered softly and rolled his eyes.

A few other nobles noticed the gesture of the King of Lahore. And most had the same thought. *Of course ... the gold-digging Kashmiri witch loves the sultan ... Which idiot would actually believe this?*

Kausari continued like she hadn't noticed anything. 'And therefore, in my unbounded love for you, my dear husband, I entreat you that you spare your younger brother, Ismail, from the death penalty.'

Ismail was stunned. *What?!?*

The governor-mufti looked at Malik Ayaz, his secret illegitimate son. Malik Ayaz had an expression of complete shock on his face. But Ismail knew what a good actor his son was. *Has my son worked out a deal?*

'But to ensure that there is no risk to either your person or me, I entreat you that the governor-mufti be placed under house arrest for some time,' said Kausari.

'The queen is merciful and wise,' boomed Mahmud loudly.

'Glory to the queen! Glory to the sultan!' said Malik Ayaz loudly, looking like he was struggling hard to control his shock. The entire court resounded with the same cry. Nobody wanted to be on the wrong side of the mercurial Mahmud.

'I agree with the queen,' said Mahmud. 'The governor-mufti is placed under house arrest at the palace of the King of Lahore, Malik Ayaz. None of the governor-mufti's staff will be allowed to be with him. We shall revisit this matter in another month. So it shall be written, so it shall be done.'

Mahmud raised his hand, and his scribe came hurrying with a parchment that had already been written on. Bizarre, considering the judgment had only just been pronounced. Mahmud affixed his seal on it and gave it to Malik Ayaz. 'Implement this, Ayaz.'

'Your will, My Lord,' said Malik Ayaz, bowing low and saluting, though his expression left nobody in doubt about what he apparently was thinking: *Why has this become my headache now?!*

Ismail, though, had caught on to something else that Mahmud had said. *In another month? He will be caliph in another two weeks. He won't need a grand mufti in another month. As caliph, he will be above any mufti anywhere in the world. I will still be killed. Mahmud will just keep me alive till he becomes the caliph. Oh God ... I am not safe yet ... I am not safe yet ...*

By this time, Malik Ayaz had already walked up to Ismail. Ten soldiers, who were under the command of Ayaz, had marched up too.

Ayaz spoke with a lazy air of effeminate exasperation. 'Come with me, Governor-Mufti.'

And so, the surprisingly short court proceedings came to an end.

—·◦⟨⟩◦·—

'What just happened?' asked Ismail. 'Did you get it done, my son?'

'A deal was struck, Father,' said Malik Ayaz, entering his mansion. His tone and demeanour completely different now.

'But I will still be killed.' Ismail's voice had become high-pitched, which happened whenever he was nervous. 'He is just waiting to become the caliph.'

'You are alive for now, Father. Focus on that. A lot can happen in a month.'

'Yes, a lot can happen. Don't you remember what happened to the previous grand mufti of the Jama Mosque? Do you actually believe that he fell down the stairs of the mosque minaret by accident?'

'Then, may I suggest that you don't climb any minarets for now?' Malik Ayaz laughed softly.

'This is no time for jokes, Ayaz!'

'Calm down, Father. There are no mosque minarets here. And you are alive for now. We have a month to come up with a plan.'

'What was the deal that you struck?'

'Nothing that you were not going to do in any case. You will give a *fatwa*, an *opinion*, with as many references as possible from the Holy Quran and the Hadiths, to prove that a non-Arab can also become a caliph, provided he has achieved what Sultan Mahmud has.'

'In my opinion, it is not possible. Only an Arab can be a caliph.'

'Do you want to live, Father?'

Ismail remained silent.

'Then make sure that you issue a *fatwa* that a non-Arab can become the caliph. I know you were working on this, in any case. You just stopped in the last three weeks. Restart that work, and I will ensure that my father remains with me forever.'

Ismail took a deep breath. 'Can't I go back to my palace?'

'It's one of the conditions of your release, Father. You can't go back to your palace, and none of your old staff can meet you. You have to stay in my mansion and be served only by my servants.'

Ismail harrumphed. His nervousness was decreasing. And he was beginning to negotiate.

'I have found Yazadeh. And I will bring her here.'

'You have!' Ismail's mood suddenly lifted.

'Remember your vow.'

'Of course! I will honour my vows of celibacy and remaining a teetotaller till I am completely free of these vile and false charges on me. But it will be good to have Yazadeh around. Just to see her.'

Malik Ayaz smiled.

—·◆·—

The Indian warriors waited three whole days at the gaudy safe house, guarded by a few men of the Jundiin-ul-Din who were still loyal to Governor-Mufti Ismail. On the afternoon of the fourth day, Malik Ayaz and Talib visited them.

Narasimhan stood up as Malik Ayaz entered, welcoming the King of Lahore with respect. Following the lead of their general, Pulakit, Vijayan, Amal, Dhruv, Zayn Husayn and Yazadeh stood up too.

'Welcome, noble King,' said Narasimhan.

'Namaste,' said Malik Ayaz.

The word sounded very different in the Turkic accent, and so Narasimhan took a moment to comprehend what Malik Ayaz had said. As soon as he understood, the Chola general smiled warmly and joined his palms into a namaste.

'Please sit ... um ... What was your name supposed to be ... Nara ... Nari ... Nariman ... no ... Oh yes, Nasrullah,' said Malik Ayaz, as he took a seat, smiling mischievously.

Narasimhan smiled and sat down. 'Congratulations on the release of the governor-mufti.'

Malik Ayaz smiled and nodded. 'But that is only the first step.' He turned to Amal and Yazadeh. 'Among the terms of Governor-Mufti Ismail's release is that he can only remain in my mansion. And no member of the governor's household staff is allowed in to serve him. So it will only be my staff in the mansion. Talib won't be there. I hope that's alright.'

Amal turned to Yazadeh. The Yazidi girl nodded. She didn't seem too troubled.

Malik Ayaz's eyes stayed on her for a moment, then turned to Narasimhan. 'I hope your people will remember their oath.'

'They will,' confirmed Narasimhan.

Malik Ayaz nodded and looked down, like he was thinking about something.

Narasimhan asked, 'What's the plan, Lord?'

'Who …' Malik Ayaz hesitated. He breathed deeply and stared at Narasimhan. 'Who among you will do the actual killing? I will not be able to get more than one person in at the right time.'

Narasimhan understood the implication. And he didn't need to think any further to make his decision. 'It will be me.'

Malik Ayaz bent forward. He was a smart man, the King of Lahore. Brave, even. But his courage lay in the domain of intellect and royal intrigue. He did not have the raw physical courage that only warriors possess. And like any wise, confident man, Ayaz admired those who had abilities that he didn't possess.

'Are you sure, General?' asked Malik Ayaz. 'It could be a one …'

'… a one-way trip,' said Narasimhan, completing Ayaz's statement.

'It doesn't have to be, but it most probably will be …' answered Malik Ayaz. 'Are you sure?'

All eyes in the room were on the general.

Narasimhan's face had a cold expression. Stoic. Impenetrable. His voice was a soft whisper, but the tone was hard as steel. He quoted a poet he loved, a European called Babington, who had written a poem on an ancient Roman war hero. 'How can man die better, than facing fearful odds; For the ashes of his fathers and the temples of his Gods.'

Malik Ayaz smiled. He was well-read. '"Horatius at the Bridge" …'

Narasimhan nodded. 'Yes. It's from that poem.'

'Most men will love that poem. But very few men can actually live it.'

'There is no greater honour than to live those lines …'

Malik Ayaz nodded. 'You are a remarkable man, General. Alright … I will ensure that you are in the right place at the right time. It will be around ten days from now.'

Narasimhan nodded.

'What is your choice of weapon?' asked Malik Ayaz.

Narasimhan turned to Pulakit. The Chalukyan prince reached into the folds of his robe and pulled out a small, crude fish-knife. It had a wooden handle fastened to a small shard of *kunati*-infused metal.

Malik Ayaz smiled. 'It will break inside?'

Narasimhan was impressed by Ayaz's deduction about the weapon despite not being a warrior. 'Yes.'

'Good poison?'

'The best.'

'Only the best for the sultan,' chuckled Malik Ayaz.

Narasimhan laughed. As did the others.

'You don't happen to have another such knife, do you?' asked Ayaz.

Narasimhan shook his head. 'I'm afraid not.'

'That's too bad. This could have been useful for me too …' Malik Ayaz turned to Zayn. 'I want you to inscribe something in Arabic on the handle: "Only an Arab. Always an Arab".'

Zayn smiled. 'Smart.'

Narasimhan looked at Malik Ayaz. 'I have heard that many Turks themselves don't believe that a Turk should ever become the caliph … That only an Arab should be the caliph.'

'True. Let them think that the Arabs agree with them.' Ayaz turned to Vijayan, the obvious second in command.

'For the rest of you, I will send instructions in due course, including on how to recover the sacred relics of your God from the mosque.'

'Thank you,' said Vijayan.

'For now, all of you stay in this building. You are safe here. I will not come here again. From now on, all news will come from Talib. Trust only the instructions that he brings you.'

Talib, standing behind Malik Ayaz, smiled. Narasimhan and his followers nodded.

Malik Ayaz stood up and turned to Amal and Yazadeh. 'And now, ladies, I hope you are prepared to accompany me to my mansion. It is time.'

Yazadeh's nervous heart picked up pace. She glanced at Amal. They had been informed earlier. They were prepared as well. But no matter how prepared one is, the moment of truth always brings some hesitation. And the best way to defeat this hesitation is to move ahead immediately, before indecision starts clouding the mind.

'Let's go,' said Amal.

—◦✦◦—

'Finally, my son ... After all these years,' said Ismail.

Ismail had been at Malik Ayaz's mansion for a few days. He had initially been uncomfortable ... After all, it was a new place, an unfamiliar bunch of servants, a different chef ... But Malik Ayaz had been trying to make his father feel at home. Some of the furniture from the governor-mufti's palace had been brought into Ayaz's mansion to give Ismail a feeling of familiarity. Ayaz's servants had been instructed to be as obsequious as possible. The chef had been instructed repeatedly to learn and recreate the foods that the governor-mufti enjoyed. And the chef was trying very hard because, clearly, it mattered a lot to his master, the King of Lahore.

But Malik Ayaz had returned with one more gift to help his father relax more. However, the gift had not been revealed, yet. 'I know, Father. Finally, the sultan will pay for the sins he committed against you.'

'I am amazed by the way destiny works.' Ismail smiled affably. 'Mysterious … The slaves who escaped from me have led my brother's assassins to me! Truly remarkable.'

'The Lord works in mysterious ways, Father.'

'True that,' said Ismail. He turned serious as he said, 'But … the sultan's sons … They should also be …'

'Yes, Father. It has been arranged. Don't worry.'

'And there should be no evidence …'

'There will be no evidence.'

'Well, Nasrullah will die along with the sultan … And his comrades are under our control,' said Ismail with a wink. 'Once Mahmud falls, we will round up these "suspects" and do to them what Kausari Jahan did to my man.'

Malik Ayaz just smiled. Silent.

Ismail chuckled and continued. He was in a happy and talkative mood. 'The Indians have brought all the "evidence" with them, in any case: the stolen garments and armour of Abu Q'asim and his men.'

'Father, there is no need to talk about these things. Even the walls have ears.'

'Of course. You are right.'

'But remember what we decided about the queen. It's very easy for men to slip when it comes to her.'

'I won't!' said Ismail, irritated. 'It's almost like you think I have no control over myself.'

Ismail did not speak his mind openly, though. He wanted nothing more than to subdue the feisty Kausari Jahan in his bed. But that could wait.

'Well, in any case, I have a gift for you, Father.'

The King of Lahore clapped his hands, and the door to the chamber opened. Ismail held his breath, a beatific smile on his face, as Yazadeh walked in. Amal waited at the door behind the curtain.

'This reward will be yours in ten days, for you cannot touch Yazadeh at all till then,' said Malik Ayaz. 'Mahmud may be anointed the caliph then, but the gifts of the Almighty are all reserved for you, Father.'

Ismail giggled like a little child who had just been reunited with his favourite toy.

---◦✄◦---

'I can understand you helping us assassinate Mahmud, Zayn,' said Narasimhan. 'His army enslaved you and some of your tribe. But why are you helping us recover the sacred relics of the Shiva Linga? Doesn't this go against your religion?'

Zayn and Narasimhan were in the safe house. Breakfast had been eaten. The day's physical exercise had been completed. They could not step out. All they could do was talk. So that's what they were doing.

Zayn smiled. 'Do you know what my full name says about me?'

'Yes, I remember what Malik Ayaz said … It means that you are a Shia Muslim, right?'

'Yes. Shia is short for *Shi'at Ali*, or the *followers of Ali*. We are those who follow Imam Ali, who was also a caliph. We are different from the Sunni Muslims. The Turks are all Sunnis.'

'Amal told me about that. She also told me she is a Sunni Muslim, though she is Indian. You don't have a problem with her, do you?'

'Of course not. Amal is a good and kind woman. However, the main difference between the Shias and Sunnis is that we Shias follow the lineage of the family of Prophet Muhammad, peace be upon him, while the Sunnis say they follow the *Sunna*, or the *traditions and examples of the Prophet*.'

'I understand. But why should this lead to you having a problem with the Sunnis?'

'I don't have a problem with the Sunnis. I am not helping in the search for the sacred relics of the Shiva Linga because you are an enemy of an enemy.'

'Then why are you …?'

'It's a long story.'

Narasimhan laughed. 'You have someplace you need to be?'

Zayn laughed as well. 'Alright, let me tell you the story, in brief. It begins in a place called Karbala.'

'Where is that?'

'In the Arab lands, to our west.'

'Alright. What happened there?'

'Over three hundred years ago, a great battle took place in Karbala, and our Imam Hussain, the son of Imam Ali and grandson of the Prophet Muhammad, peace be upon him, was unfairly killed by the soldiers of Caliph Yazid of the Umayyad dynasty.'

Narasimhan's mouth fell open in shock. 'What are you saying? A descendant of your Prophet? An Imam? And an Arab Muslim caliph had him killed?'

'Yes. We Shias consider the killing of Imam Hussain as the greatest tragedy for humanity.'

'This is terrible. And it's outrageous that a Muslim ruler got this done.'

'We mourn the sacrifice of Imam Hussain to this day.'

Narasimhan nodded in sympathy.

Zayn continued, 'What many in India don't know is that there is a tribe of Indians called Mohyal Brahmins who ...'

'Mohyal Brahmins?' interrupted Narasimhan. 'I haven't heard of them. Where are they from?'

'From the region of Punjab, in the northern parts of the Indian subcontinent.'

'Okay. So what do the Mohyal Brahmins have to do with this tale?'

'History tells us that there were some Mohyal Brahmins in the Arab lands when the battle of Karbala happened. They fought to defend our Imam Hussain. Many of them died in that battle. They were proud Hindus, but they died to defend our Imam.'

'I didn't know this ...'

'Not just that, some members of the Prophet's family had to escape due to the continued attacks mounted by the Umayyad caliphate. And they were given refuge by the Hindu king of Sindh, Raja Dahir.'

'I had no idea about this either.'

'Many of us Shias who know this, believe that it is our duty to return the favour. Hindus fought to defend and protect the family of our Prophet. What kind of Muslims would we be if we did not return that kindness? We therefore fight to defend Hindu Gods and Hindu beliefs. That is the way we repay our debt to your community.'

Narasimhan smiled and embraced Zayn. 'Thank you, my friend.'

CHAPTER 24

A Twist in the Trail

Ghazni, Afghanistan

Malik Ayaz had assumed that Mahmud would be delighted with this Arab support for his anointment as the caliph, but the sultan seemed suspicious. Even the mighty Mahmud was beginning to feel nervous as the biggest day of his life approached. He was seeing threats everywhere.

'Your Majesty,' said Malik Ayaz, speaking calmly and softly, 'for an Arab from the Abbasid court to even be present here during your anointment is a strong statement. But what Zubair Usman is offering is that he will himself read all five prayers of the day in your name. And that too from the rebuilt Jama Mosque. This is like an open Arab endorsement of you taking up the role of caliph.'

Zubair Usman was the suitably Sunni Muslim name by which Zayn Husayn had been introduced to Mahmud. The sultan of Ghazni had met the Arab briefly and was initially extremely excited about the presence of someone from the court of the Abbasids during the ceremony. He had carefully examined the medallion hanging around Zayn's neck. It was a circular golden medallion emblazoned with the round, black seal of the Abbasid caliphate—clear evidence that the person who wore it was a senior officer in the court of the Abbasids. This was the very medallion that Vijayan had grabbed while killing the Arab ship captain during their battle at sea.

But now, after a few hours of mulling over it, Mahmud was re-evaluating the decision in his private chamber. He seemed unsure.

'My Sultan,' said Kausari Jahan, 'it is rare that I agree with the King of Lahore. And you know what my views have always been about the risks of you being declared caliph. But on this occasion, I agree with Malik Ayaz. I think the presence of someone from the Abbasid court will only make your anointment as caliph more compelling in the eyes of the common people and, more importantly, the nobles. Remember, we want all members of the Turkic nobility and even the tribal elders to pledge their loyalty to you as caliph. That will cement your new role. The presence of an Abbasid representative only aids that.'

Malik Ayaz looked at Kausari. She looked tired, with dark circles under her eyes. Like she hadn't slept in days. He could understand why. 'Thank you for your support, great Queen.'

Mahmud laughed. 'Strange to see the two of you agreeing with each other.'

'Whatever my differences with Ayaz,' said Kausari Jahan, smiling, 'we both want what is best for you, husband. Because we are nothing without you.'

Mahmud nodded. 'That is true …'

Malik Ayaz smiled.

'But what about Zubair's request, asking me to help free the Abbasids from the Persian Buyid oppression?' asked Mahmud. 'What do you both think about that?'

'I say it's an opportunity, Your Majesty,' said Malik Ayaz. 'The Arab has a letter from the Abbasid Caliph—the soon-to-be-ex-caliph, actually—inviting you to invade his territory and defeat the Persian Buyids. This gives you a legal excuse to invade their lands.'

Of course, Mahmud didn't know that the supposed letter from the Abbasids was a forgery.

'We can decide later what to do with that invitation, My Sultan,' said Kausari. 'I wouldn't attack the Arabs just yet. They want to be free of their Persian overlords—that's understandable. But what's in it for us? The Persian Buyids are strong. And we have too many Persians in our own administration, not least of all Prime Minister Khwaja Hassan. We can never truly trust their loyalty if we invade the Buyids. These Persians always stick together.'

'Hmm,' said Mahmud. It did not escape his notice that Malik Ayaz seemed unhappy with this opposition from his queen to the war against the Persians.

'The time for all that will come, my husband,' continued Kausari Jahan. 'But for now, I think, having the Arab read prayers in your name at the Jama Mosque when you are declared caliph is only to your benefit.'

Mahmud turned to the King of Lahore. 'Well, Ayaz, it seems that my wife has convinced me to go with your idea. I hope you are grateful to her.'

Malik Ayaz started laughing, the lazy arrogance of a dandy on his face. 'I am sure that the queen and I will find other reasons to fight each other soon. But for now, we are both committed to your anointment as caliph, My Sultan.'

Mahmud laughed, clapping Malik Ayaz hard on his back. This caused the slender Ayaz to lose balance temporarily, which made Mahmud laugh even more loudly. Kausari joined in too. And Mahmud could see Malik Ayaz glare at Kausari in barely disguised irritation, before the King of Lahore also laughed along good-naturedly.

—◦◦🗡◦◦—

'About time!' hissed Faiz, the Jundiin-ul-Din guard. 'We have been waiting for you since the afternoon!'

It was late at night and the deserted street where the brothel stood was as asleep as asleep could be.

The replacement guards, who had come to take the place of the stationed guards, did not even deign to respond. One of them just lazily held out his hand. Faiz looked at his fellow guards, cursed and handed over the signed warrant. The replacement guard looked over the document. It all seemed in order; they could use this warrant to check anyone who wanted to enter or leave the high-end brothel.

Faiz and his colleagues immediately began marching out. Eager to get home. They were already delayed.

As they turned into a small alleyway that led off the street, they were stopped by a massive African-origin man. At least six feet three inches in height. Gargantuan, with rippling muscles that filled out his Jundiin-ul-Din uniform to bursting point. The marks on the uniform clearly showed he was a captain.

Faiz saluted, too much of a disciplined soldier to ask the obvious question: What was a Jundiin-ul-Din captain doing in this deserted alleyway by himself so late at night?

But there was no further time for the obvious question to arise. Five soldiers emerged from the shadows, bearing heavy clubs. Faiz and his colleagues were bludgeoned heavily from behind. Straight on their heads. Their skulls battered into pieces, slivers of brain oozing out like thick pinkish-grey paste.

All dead. Minimal blood. Almost no sound.

'Nicely done,' whispered the giant African-origin captain to his men, adjusting his clearly ill-fitting uniform that was a few sizes too tight.

'Thank you, Captain Hakeem.'

Hakeem peered from the corner of the alleyway at the door of the brothel safe house where Narasimhan and his band lay hidden.

There was nothing untoward. No sounds. Nobody there, except for the queen's guards in stolen Jundiin-ul-Din uniforms. They now controlled the only entry and exit into the safe house. Hakeem's soldiers would rotate as the replacement guards as well, since no Jundiin would receive fresh orders to come to the safe house—as the queen's guards had possession of the signed warrant. Using similar tactics, they had replaced many of the Jundiin soldiers earlier at the slave camp as well; the command-and-control systems of the religious police were not as good as those of the army or the royal bodyguards.

Hakeem nodded again. 'Nicely done.'

He turned to his men and whispered, 'Strip these men of their uniforms. Throw the bodies in the city kiln at the edge of the inner wall.'

As his soldiers obeyed, Hakeem started walking back to the palace. To immediately report the news of the operation to his mistress, Queen Kausari Jahan.

—◦✦◦—

'All okay?' asked Malik Ayaz.

'Yes, Sire,' whispered Talib.

Talib and Ayaz were in the outhouse of his mansion, strictly following the sultan's command that nobody from Ismail's personal staff would be allowed inside the mansion where Governor-Mufti Ismail had been put under house arrest.

'Has everything been delivered?'

'Yes, My Lord.'

'Nothing untoward?'

'No, great King,' said Talib. 'Nasrullah and his team remain steady, training in their free time. The Jundiin-ul-Din guards are rotating regularly and are always alert.'

'Good.'

'Do I need to bring anything for Zubair?' asked Talib, using the assumed name for the Arab Zayn.

Zayn had been staying at Malik Ayaz's mansion, per Mahmud's instructions.

'No,' answered Malik Ayaz. 'All under control here.'

Talib nodded and rose to leave.

'Also ...' said Ayaz, raising his hand casually.

'Yes, Lord?'

'Stay at home till day after tomorrow morning,' said Malik Ayaz. 'Till it is all done. Do not meet anyone. Do not speak to anyone.'

Talib was a smart man. He understood. So it would all happen the following night. Logical. Mahmud would be anointed caliph the next day. By the evening, the entire city would be celebrating and partying. And the sultan would be partying the hardest. Security would be lax.

'Tomorrow is also just a day before the moonless night, Lord,' said Talib. 'It will be a dark night. The timing couldn't be more perfect.'

Malik Ayaz smiled. 'Take care, Talib.'

The test had been set. Whether Talib would pass it, or walk into a trap, would be known by the afternoon of the following day. *Let's see.*

It was late in the afternoon the following day.

'We are finished!' shrieked Ismail, as he burst into the mansion with Malik Ayaz. The governor-mufti was furious. In a state of panic, like a cornered animal.

Mahmud's anointment as caliph had gone flawlessly. Ismail had delivered his *fatwa* in the Jama Mosque square, as he was supposed to do, opining publicly that a non-Arab can become the caliph. And then all the other ceremonies had been conducted by the priests and tribal elders present. The Arab from the Abbasid court, reading the prayers in the name of the sultan, had made a huge impression on the public. Mahmud couldn't have been happier. Celebrations had already begun in his palace.

Malik Ayaz didn't react at all. He glared at his servants, who rushed away, deep into the inner chambers of the mansion. Ayaz led Ismail calmly to his private chamber. And only then he spoke. 'You must learn to keep your emotions in check, Father. I have told you so many times, the walls have ears.'

But Ismail was beyond reason. 'Did you give the correct instructions to Talib? And to the Indians? I wonder if you were on top of everything. I had specifically said that …'

'I had given all the proper instructions, Father,' said Ayaz firmly, interrupting Ismail. 'Do not say or do things in anger which you will regret. You have a tendency to do that.'

Something in Ayaz's tone made Ismail step back. He started breathing deeply. Fear still strong in his heart.

'I'm sorry, Son. But … but you had told me that the assassination will take place just outside the mosque this afternoon … When his security would be the weakest … Mahmud is back in his palace now … He is the caliph now … What … What happened?'

'I don't know. I have to find out.'

'I am sure it's that Talib's fault! He is an idiot! That fool can never be trusted!'

Ayaz breathed deeply. For he was sure now. Sure that Talib could be trusted, because he had not passed on the information. 'Talib has been loyal to you for decades, Father.'

'He's an idiot! I'm telling you, he's an idiot!'

'Ups and downs are a part of life. You must learn to breathe deeply, stay calm, roll with the punches and hit back when the time is right.' Malik Ayaz had just quoted what his beloved mother had once told him.

'I don't need self-help lessons right now, Ayaz!'

'Stay calm, Father. Let me find out what happened.'

'I am dead … I tell you … I am dead …'

'Nobody will do anything to you, Father. Not as long as I stand in front of you.'

'I am dead …'

Malik Ayaz turned to leave.

'Where are you going?' Ismail screeched in panic.

'I have to go to the palace, Father. The sultan will be expecting me there.'

'Go to the safe house before that. Find out where those cowardly Indians are! You can't trust these Hindu eunuchs! They are born cowards. Kill them before they spill any secrets.'

'I cannot go to the safe house any more, Father. You know that. Do you want me to be spied upon and get into trouble myself?'

'No, no … Of course, not … You are the only one I can trust.'

'But I will meet Talib before I go to the palace.'

'Kill him! Kill that idiot! It's all his fault!'

Malik Ayaz nodded. He knew what he needed to do with Talib.

'Get me out of Ghazni, my son,' pleaded Ismail, holding his son's hands tight. 'Please … Before the sun rises tomorrow … Otherwise, I am dead … I am dead … Mahmud is now the caliph. He is the head of the state and religion. There is nobody in all Islamdom who is more powerful than he is right now. He doesn't need a grand mufti any more. I am dead … I am dead …'

'You are not dead yet. Stay calm. I will return soon.'

'Get me out of Ghazni, my son. Please … I beg you.'

'Father …'

'Please! Get me out of here. Please …'

Malik Ayaz finally appeared to relent. 'I will arrange for some soldiers to slip you out of the city when it is dark and safe. I will meet you at a rendezvous point outside.'

Ismail almost jumped in relief. 'Thank you! Thank you so much, my son!'

Malik Ayaz turned to leave. 'Now, stay here. I will send someone with my ring. He will take you out of the city.'

'And Yazadeh too,' said Ismail, negotiating already, since the immediate danger was under control in his opinion.

Malik Ayaz sighed theatrically. But he knew this would happen. He knew his father. That's why Amal and Yazadeh had been brought to the mansion. Also, their selfish interests aligned with his. Because unlike anyone who had family in Ghazni, Amal and Yazadeh could never be swayed by anyone loyal to the sultan. Malik Ayaz knew that. And they would deliver his father where he wanted them to. 'Not just Yazadeh, but Amal as well. But you stay here till I send the men who will take you out of Ghazni.'

'Alright. But I will be alone here. What if some …'

'I am leaving my guards at the door,' said Malik Ayaz, interrupting his father. 'Do not step out of this chamber. Stay here, where you are safe. Safe, till my messenger appears.'

'Send him quickly …'

'I will. But it cannot happen before nightfall. Let me go now.'

—◦⚔◦—

'Is everything set, My Lord?'

Talib was surprised that he had been called to this meeting. It had been just a few hours since the anointment of Mahmud as caliph. The sun had still not set. And Talib was under the impression that the assassination would take place later at night, in the palace.

'Everything is set, Talib,' answered Malik Ayaz, at ease on his comfortable sofa. 'Just a few hours more.'

Still standing, Talib looked around. The rest house, close to the outer wall, was small and nondescript. A perfect place for a covert meeting. He did not know that this house was secretly owned by Malik Ayaz. 'Why was I called here, Lord? Do you need me to do something?'

Malik Ayaz's words were soft and calm. 'I need you to leave the city.'

Talib frowned. He was about to ask something. But he hesitated.

'You are a smart man, Talib. You should know what is good for you.'

'Yes ... yes, Lord.' Talib was still trying to work out the implications. He was sure that Mahmud would be assassinated. Otherwise, even Malik Ayaz, and Ismail before that, would be fleeing the city. And when Mahmud would be killed, Talib would certainly have a role to play. He would be useful. Unless ...

Malik Ayaz suddenly got up and handed a pouch to Talib. The servant dithered, unsure whether to open the pouch.

'You can look inside.' Malik Ayaz's tone was kind.

The gentleness in the king's voice intrigued Talib. He opened the pouch and found a *hundi* inside. A promissory note. For money. The number written on it stunned him. This was an amount of gold beyond his wildest dreams.

Talib's mouth fell open in shock. 'Lord?'

'My men are waiting outside,' said Malik Ayaz. 'You will leave immediately. They will escort you on your journey for a day. After that, you will go on to Lahore. The *hundi* will be redeemed there. And then you will disappear. Change your name and appearance. I never want to see you or hear of you ever again.'

Talib could not understand the generosity. This was a blessing far greater than he had ever imagined. There was only one thing missing … Could he live without … But did he have a choice?

Malik Ayaz answered the questions running silently in Talib's mind. The King of Lahore's voice was tender but his face was expressionless. Stoic. 'Reshma is waiting with some of my soldiers, an hour's ride from the city gates. If you leave now, you will reach her easily before nightfall.'

Talib's overwhelmed heart couldn't bear it any more. All his dreams, in fact fantasies, fulfilled. In an instant. He started crying and fell at Malik Ayaz's feet.

Malik Ayaz had a mock grimace on his face, like most good men do when confronted with anyone too grateful. He pulled Talib up. 'She is too young for an old man like you, Talib. But if the both of you are happy, then who am I to complain?'

Talib was still stunned. How did Malik Ayaz even know of his love for the slave woman Reshma? Even his own master, Ismail, had never divined it. The King of Lahore was intuitive beyond belief. Like he had been brought up to be that way, trained to be that way. It almost seemed as if …

And then the veil lifted.

Talib finally understood.

Understood why he couldn't be in the city. Why he had to leave. Why it had to be at this very moment—not earlier, not later.

He finally understood why Malik Ayaz was doing what he was doing.

Ya Allah …

Talib's eyes teared up again. Not from gratitude for the blessings he had just received. But because of the sympathy he felt for his benefactor. He reached out and held the hands of the King of Lahore. And breathed deeply. Nodding in compassion. In understanding.

It has to be done. It is the only path to justice.

Two very smart men. With the wise intuition of the Feminine. And the righteous desire for justice of the Masculine.

'My Lord …' said Talib, crying now. 'I … What you …' Talib took a moment to compose himself. 'What you are doing … What you are about to do is justice. It is justice.'

Malik Ayaz took a deep breath. And then he whispered, as tears flooded his eyes, 'Her name was Sara.'

Talib cried even more. *Sara.* Aramaic for *noblewoman.* It made sense.

'Sara … May Allah bless her … May Allah bless her, My Lord.'

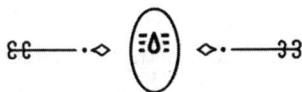

CHAPTER 25

The Sacred Pact

Ghazni, Afghanistan

Malik Ayaz laughed playfully and stumbled out of the sultan's bed holding a cup of wine in his unsteady hand. His feet were wobbly.

'Oops.' Some wine fell on the expensive carpet.

It was an hour and a half to midnight.

'Come back … you … rogue …' Mahmud teased his lover. 'Come … ba …'

Malik Ayaz stood still. Suddenly alert. His drunken stupor almost instantly disappeared.

'Sultan?' asked Malik Ayaz.

Mahmud snored loudly. He had been drinking, dancing and lusting for many hours now. Even a man of Mahmud's voracious appetites could be dulled by satiation, alcohol and tiredness. The quality and quantity of the sedative that Malik Ayaz had mixed in his wine was also just right to push him over the edge.

'Caliph?' Ayaz called, louder now.

Mahmud's snoring continued unhindered. He was certainly knocked out. The sedative's effect would last for a couple of hours at least.

The King of Lahore dressed hastily. He walked quickly to the door of the inner chamber, unlocked it gently and stepped out. He then walked towards the entrance of the main chamber and swung open the door. He recognized the guards. New guards. Suitably loyal to the emerging regime. 'Two of you, wait at the inside door. The rest, wait outside the main chamber.'

'Yes, Lord,' answered the tall soldier.

'Nobody is to enter or exit. If the sultan stirs, one of you will come running to find me.'

'Yes, Lord.'

'Where is she?' asked Ayaz.

'In her chamber.'

Malik Ayaz nodded and began walking quickly. Time was of the essence.

—◦❀◦—

Hakeem recognized the form of Malik Ayaz walking towards him from a distance. It was dark and late on this near-moonless night. The fire torches blazing in the hall niches spread some light, but not enough. Malik Ayaz's gait was instantly discernible, though.

'My Lord,' said the loyal Hakeem, bowing his head.

Malik Ayaz stopped, with a surprised frown on his face. 'You have never called me that before, Hakeem.'

Hakeem bowed his head even further. 'The time wasn't right till now.'

'And now it is …'

Hakeem agreed. 'And now it is, Lord.'

'She's inside?'

'Yes, Lord. She is praying.'

Malik Ayaz nodded and walked quickly into the chambers of the queen of Ghazni.

—◦◦✦◦◦—

Malik Ayaz could hear soft chanting as he went deeper into Kausari Jahan's chamber. He had never been inside before. There had been no reason to. But he knew exactly how the chamber was structured and laid out. He knew every detail. He had been told of it many times. His steps were therefore confident and sure.

He walked past the cushions and the sofas, towards the alcove in one corner of the inner chamber. The light satin curtains swayed as the night breeze wafted in from the window to the south, cooling the room even further.

Ayaz walked up to the alcove, where the chanting seemed to be coming from. He could see the gorgeous queen, seated on the ground in a meditative posture, her wavy auburn hair cascading down her back. He noticed an Islamic prayer mat rolled up neatly and laid respectfully against the wall. Unlike the extravagant and gold-lined prayer mat of Sultan Mahmud, this one belonging to the queen was simple and austere, the kind that devout peasants had. There was a niche which Kausari Jahan was facing. It was usually covered with a sliding wall that lay flush against the surface, such that, when the wall slid close, it was almost impossible to even notice that there was an opening there. But this time, the sliding wall was open. And the small hidden niche behind it revealed a tiny idol. One that was, appropriately, facing south.

The *Dakshinamurti*. The south-facing idol.

Kausari did not turn. She would not be disturbed when she was praying. Malik Ayaz waited politely. Listening to the soft incantation. He knew what it meant. But had never heard it in the traditional chanting form before. Kausari kept her voice almost to a whisper. She had to. But the King of Lahore could hear her voice clearly.

'*Om … Namah … Shivaya …*'

'*Om … Namah … Shivaya …*'

'*Om … Namah … Shivaya …*'

He knew that she had to complete the chant one hundred and eight times. He would have to wait. And then he noticed the other person in the room. A giant hulking presence. Slightly bigger than the fearsome Abu Q'asim, the Turkish Butcher of India. For a moment, Ayaz's heart skipped a beat in fear. And then, almost immediately, he realized who it was, and smiled.

The giant whispered softly, 'Greetings, King of Lahore.'

Malik Ayaz nodded and murmured, 'Namaste, Nasrullah.'

Narasimhan had been secreted here into Kausari's section of the palace with the help of Hakeem's guards, who were stationed at the safe house, disguised as Jundiin-ul-Din.

They stopped speaking as they heard a movement from the alcove. Kausari Jahan bent forward, touching her head to the ground. She touched the feet of the idol, her eyes still closed. Finally, after a few moments, she rose and turned. And smiled at the two men.

'Namaste, *benitath*,' said Malik Ayaz, using the *Kashmiri term for elder sister*. He walked up to Kausari Jahan, bent down and touched her feet, showing respect for the traditions of the queen's native Kashmir.

Kausari placed her hand on Ayaz's head. 'Live long and prosper, *dzmao*,' she said, using the *Georgian word for brother*.

Malik Ayaz smiled. 'The night is finally here ...'

'The night is finally here ...'

'It couldn't be a better night,' said Narasimhan. 'The monthly Shiva Ratri.'

The greatest festival for devotees of Lord Shiva happens on the fourteenth night of the waning moon of the Indian *phalgun* month. That night is called the *Maha Shiva Ratri*, literally, *the great night of Shiva*. This is well known. Less known is that there is a monthly Shiva Ratri as well. The fourteenth night of the waning moon of every month is celebrated as the monthly Shiva Ratri by those who are fierce devotees of the Mahadev.

Malik Ayaz asked what he had always wanted to. And he knew he would not get a chance again after this night. 'Great Queen, you are a devout Muslim. I know that. Then why do you worship Shiva as well?'

Kausari smiled. 'My full name is Kausari Jahan Mattoo. My father converted to Islam. But we Kashmiri Muslims are clear. We only changed our religion. We didn't change our ancestors. I worship both Allah and Lord Shiva. All forms of the Divine are one.'

'The Turks don't seem to agree with that,' said Narasimhan.

'These Turks don't understand Islam,' said Malik Ayaz.

'Is our man asleep?' asked Kausari Jahan, focusing on the work at hand, for time was short.

'Yes,' said Malik Ayaz, before turning to Narasimhan. 'Are you sure?'

Malik Ayaz and Narasimhan had had an extended debate on a specific tactic. Ayaz had suggested that Narasimhan kill Mahmud while he was still drugged asleep. Narasimhan had flatly refused. Being a dharmic warrior, he would not attack an enemy while he was sleeping. Also, Narasimhan had been instructed by Rajendra Chola to deliver a message to Mahmud about why he was being killed. So the sultan had to be awake.

'Yes. Absolutely sure.' Narasimhan was crystal clear. 'I will wait for him to wake up. You had said he always wakes up a few times at night to go to the toilet …'

'Alright. The guards will let you in.'

Narasimhan nodded.

'He is a loud screamer.'

Narasimhan frowned at the seemingly useless information.

'Make sure you break his jaw first,' clarified Malik Ayaz. 'His sounds will carry far this late at night.'

Narasimhan smiled slightly. 'You think of every detail.'

Malik Ayaz grinned. 'Those with raw physical power can afford to just wing it. But those who rely on their wits, like me, must think through every detail, so that we are not confronted with a challenge that is beyond our physical capacity.'

Narasimhan smiled fully now.

'And tell Emperor Bhojadev Parmar, the friend of your Emperor Rajendra Chola,' said Malik Ayaz, 'that the Caucasian has repaid his debt now.'

Narasimhan's mouth fell open slightly, as he finally realized who Bhojadev Parmar's contact was in Ghazni.

The Caucasian … It had never struck him before. It was so obvious. Georgia is in the region of the Caucasus Mountains.

Narasimhan smiled and said, 'Thank you, Lord Ayaz.'

'Thank you, General Narasimhan,' said Malik Ayaz, grinning as he used Nasrullah's actual name.

Narasimhan laughed softly. Both men turned to Kausari Jahan solemnly.

Malik Ayaz knew what the answer would be. But he had to ask. He had to. 'My Queen, are you sure? There are ways that …'

Kausari Jahan interrupted the King of Lahore. 'Don't start this again, Ayaz … I … I don't want to carry on … My mind … and my heart are made up.'

Kausari Jahan Mattoo was already married when she was kidnapped by Mahmud of Ghazni. Married in Kashmir, to Firdaus Mattoo. She would never forget him. He could never forget her. When she was kidnapped by the Turkic emperor from Lohkot in Kashmir, during one of his raids into India, Firdaus had tracked and followed the Ghaznavid army as Mahmud's *jihadi*s returned to their homeland. Firdaus settled down close to Khuzdar, having bought farmland there with the money he had raised from selling his properties in Lohkot.

Kausari and he established a secret encrypted pigeon communication system. They worked slowly over many years to find warriors who could assassinate Mahmud, so that Kausari would be free to return to her true love. This is why Kausari established a secret alliance with Someshwar; she was the 'traitor in the royal family' who had anonymously promised to help the Gujarati merchant in his mission for vengeance against Mahmud. While Kausari's initial aim was to return to Firdaus, she also came to understand the

Turks deeply while in Ghazni. She realized that seeing only Mahmud as monstrous was an inadequate understanding of the situation. There were many more like him in Ghazni, particularly among the elite. They were like rabid dogs who knew only how to bite. Killing Mahmud would only mean that another rabid dog, just like him, would take his place. And if the suspicion for the assassination fell on Kausari, she knew that the Ghaznavids would burn down her beloved Kashmir in vengeance. Therefore, her calculating mind had told her that the only way her land would be spared was if she was also found assassinated along with the sultan. When she found out about Firdaus's death from Malik Ayaz just a few days prior, her pining heart agreed with her calculating mind.

'This is the best way … This is the only way … It is not possible to negotiate with rabid dogs. It is not possible to instil fear in rabid dogs. It is not possible to civilize rabid dogs with the benefits of education and culture. The only way to stop them from attacking you is to make them turn on each other. That is precisely what the plan was. To trigger a civil war.'

The previous grand mufti of the Jama Mosque had agreed with Kausari's analysis of the Ghaznavids. That is why he had agreed to join the conspiracy against Mahmud. It was his seal on the letter that Someshwar had shown to Rajendra Chola, along with the royal seal that Kausari had inscribed. This was before the previous grand mufti was killed and Ismail placed in that role.

'This is the best way …' agreed Narasimhan.

The trio held each other's hands.

This would be the night when they would all wreak their righteous vengeance.

The wife.

The son.

The devotee.

All three would finally get their justice.

—◦✦◦—

'We are the all-conquering Turks,' the Ghaznavid soldier grumbled. 'Why do we have to listen to these locust-eater Arabs?!'

The Jama Mosque was practically deserted. It was an hour before midnight. The ceremonies of the day and the celebrations that followed had left most of the mosque staff tired. A skeletal security team of five soldiers remained. They had been ordered to help the Arab-led delegation as they conducted some prayers at the mosque. The Arabs claimed that this was the standard ritual at a mosque where a caliph had just been anointed. And no Turk could argue with them, since none of them was sure what the Arab rituals really were. But reactions to this differed among the Ghaznavids. Some respected the Arab right to conduct the rituals, since they were the original Muslims—the first Muslims, after all. But some others, like this Ghaznavid soldier, resented the unnecessary respect being given to the Arabs. Because the Arabs were hardly a warrior race now; they were more interested in science and culture. And most Ghaznavid Turks respected one thing and one thing alone: the fine art of conquering and killing.

'Quiet, Daud,' another soldier whispered. 'They may hear you.'

'They have fifty of the Arab's soldiers here.' Daud continued grumbling. 'Why do they need us? Let us go home.'

'Daud!' A distant order fell upon their ears in the quiet night.

Daud sighed and saluted, then marched slowly towards the Arab. The other four Ghaznavid soldiers followed.

'I need all of you in the inner quarters,' said the Arab. 'Some arrangements need to be made for a ritual. This is the last one … Then you all can leave.'

'Your will, Lord Zubair,' said Daud, delighted that he and his friends would finally be relieved from duty and could go home.

Zayn Husayn nodded. He turned and began leading the Turks towards the inner quarters, to the side of the main structure of the mosque. This was where Mahmud had waited, earlier in the day, while the ceremonies were being prepared for his anointment. The Ghaznavid soldiers thus had reason to believe that maybe the Arabs had some work to do there as well.

The door was already open. There was a flaming torch at the far end of the wall. Zayn waited at the side, outside the doorway, and let the Ghaznavid soldiers pass him to enter the room.

That was the first mistake the Ghaznavids made. They should have become suspicious. They weren't women being waited on by a gentleman, who would let them use the door first. They were soldiers following their commander. A commander never stops to let his soldiers pass. A leader always leads. You don't lead from behind.

The second mistake the Ghaznavids made was to not be on their guard and look behind the door upon entering. Standard soldier training dictates that you always check and clear the area behind the doors as soon as you enter a dark room. You don't want to walk inside and then be ambushed from behind.

And that is precisely what happened. A swift ambush. Each Ghaznavid marked by two Indian soldiers. The killing was rapid and efficient. Quiet. Effortless. Almost too easy.

Vijayan turned to Zayn waiting outside the room and whispered, 'Done.'

Zayn entered immediately and pulled out a parchment from the folds of his cloak. The contents had been discussed with Malik Ayaz and Narasimhan earlier. The document was pasted on the far wall of the room. A simple message was written on it, in both Arabic and Persian.

Always an Arab. Only an Arab.

All true Muslims, be they Turk, Persian or Arab, know this to be true.

Those who disagree are Murtad.

And a Murtad deserves just one punishment.

Death. Death. Death.

Those who follow Islam are willing to kill or be martyred for what is Islamic.

Witness the proof of Islamic Justice.

Murtad was the Arabic word for *apostate*. But the clever word that was used in this public missive was 'martyred'. In both Arabic and Persian, the word for *martyr* was *shahid*, which was also the name of the elder twin son of Mahmud. All knew that Shahid was the most religious person in the royal family. The younger twin, Mohammad, was much like his father Mahmud in terms of tastes and addictions, and everyone knew that he was loyal to the sultan and his queen, Kausari Jahan.

Perfect.

Let people interpret that perhaps it was the deeply religious and fanatically doctrinal Shahid, who had been offended by his debauched father's bid for the caliphate and had allied with the Arab Abbasids to get Mahmud killed. Shahid in Arabic also meant *witness*, besides martyr. This was not the case in Persian. Hence, the use of the word 'witness' in the last line made the conspiracy even clearer.

The hope was to trigger a civil war between Shahid and his younger twin brother, Mohammad.

'And now, to the Mahadev,' whispered Pulakit.

'Yes,' said Vijayan softly. 'To the Lord …'

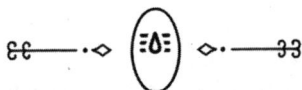

CHAPTER 26

Retrieving the Lord

Ghazni, Afghanistan

As commanded by Vijayan, thirty soldiers, led by Zayn and Dasarna, were stationed at the Jama Mosque's main entrance gate, to shoo away any passersby. But nobody came to the mosque this late in the night. Most were sleeping. And those who weren't were celebrating and engaged in distinctly unreligious activities, far away from the long shadows of the mosque.

Vijayan and Pulakit, along with twenty soldiers, were in the mosque's main courtyard, at the western end of the main staircase leading out of the courtyard towards the main prayer hall, the central pool where devotees performed their ablutions right behind them. The instructions from Malik Ayaz were clear. Ismail had overseen the rebuilding project. He knew all the architectural designs and the smallest details. Ayaz had got the information from Ismail and relayed it to the Indians.

'Sixth step from the courtyard,' Vijayan whispered as he led his team.

They climbed six steps.

'Fifteen paces to the right.'

The Chola–Parmar squad followed him, their hearts racing.

A low drone had begun among the soldiers.

'*Namah Shivaya* …'

'*Namah Shivaya* …'

'*Namah Shivaya* …'

Pulakit and Vijayan reached where they were supposed to and immediately took a step back. They couldn't be standing over the hallowed ground. Pulakit held out his hand behind him, and a soldier gave him a stout steel crowbar. He looked at Vijayan, whose wet eyes said more than any words could. Vijayan nodded. Both Pulakit and he touched the marble slab with the crowbar. And felt a slight magnetic tug from below.

The lodestone …

Pulakit's mouth fell open as he gasped audibly, his emotions getting the better of him. Vijayan went down on his knees and touched the stone slab with his hand, offering respect.

Lodestones always attract steel. And the Mahadev always attracts men of steel.

Vijayan looked at his men, tears swimming in his eyes. 'The Lord … He is here …'

'Hurry,' whispered Pulakit.

The Indians thrust their prying instruments in the tiny gaps in the large marble slab and the supporting masonry of the step. The soft chanting continued as they worked assiduously and carefully.

'*Namah Shivaya* …'

'*Namah Shivaya* …'

The recently laid mortar binding the two layers gave way and the slab came loose to reveal the hollow dark space beneath. Vijayan thrust his hand into the darkness. Tears flowed freely and blinded his eyes. His fingers felt a smooth surface. Using both hands, he flexed his biceps and pulled out a dark stone, similar in texture to the relic that had been in Someshwar's possession.

All the men fell to their knees and prostrated before the broken sacred piece of the Divine. But they all stood up almost immediately, wiping their eyes dry. There was work to be done.

A few men pulled open fresh cloth bags. And Vijayan carefully placed the sacred relic inside.

'*Namah Shivaya* ...' Pulakit said reverentially, as he pulled another piece of the hallowed Shiva Linga out from the cavity and placed it gently into the cloth bag.

The work continued. Without any other noise but the sounds of soft chanting.

'*Namah Shivaya* ...'
'*Namah Shivaya* ...'
'*Namah Shivaya* ...'

Soon, all the sacred relics had been safely transferred inside the two cloth bags. And then the Indians, continuing to work silently, covered the dark hollow space with the marble slab and pushed the mortar back in place, leaving the step looking practically undisturbed.

'We don't want to attract any attention when we walk out of the mosque and into the city. We must appear normal, like soldiers carrying out some order, indistinguishable from others. Bury your emotions deep. Calm the mind. Still the heart. No tears.' Vijayan's order was soft but firm, for any signs of excess emotion on the faces of the men would attract suspicion.

Prince Pulakit added, 'We are the followers of Shiva. We are men. We show no weakness on our faces.'

All nodded.

'Let's go,' ordered Vijayan.

They marched out of the mosque calmly, with sure steps.

—·◦❦◦·—

Malik Ayaz had been galloping hard for over an hour. It was nearly midnight. He was well outside the city now. He had ridden these lands for years and had planned on this being the rendezvous point for nearly as long. He could find his way easily, even on a night that was very dimly lit by a tiny sliver of the moon.

He recognized the spur on the rocky outcrop. He manoeuvred his horse around it, through the narrow passage that existed between the two rocky protrusions. The passage was so narrow and short that it would have been missed by most, even during the day. Once one went past the passage, the area opened into a large, flat enclosure, surrounded by tall, craggy ridges. An open area surrounded by high stony bluffs. It was almost impossible to find unless you already knew that it was there.

Perfect.

Perfect for what Malik Ayaz wanted to do.

He reined in his horse, jumped off and hobbled his mount. And then he whistled loudly. A long, clear, sharp whistle.

And he heard another whistle in response. Almost an exact copy of his.

'Bring him.'

And he was brought.

Ismail. Younger brother of Sultan Mahmud. The former governor-mufti of the capital city of Ghazni.

Malik Ayaz's father.

Led by Amal. Six soldiers accompanied them. And following the soldiers was Yazadeh.

'My son!' exclaimed Ismail. 'My gratefulness to Allah that you are here. This idiot Amal is not listening to me! And all the soldiers are following her orders, not mine!'

Malik Ayaz turned to Amal. His voice firm and deep, dramatically different from how he sounded when he was in Mahmud's palace. 'What happened?'

Ismail cut in to answer. 'I told this imbecile that we must keep riding, to get as far away from Ghazni while it is still dark. Before my absence is noticed. I was only thinking that because ... because it may get you into trouble.'

'I know how much you care about me,' said Malik Ayaz.

Ayaz's tone caused Ismail to grow more nervous. And whenever Ismail grew nervous, his voice became shriller and he tended to overspeak, using verbose babbling to calm down a tense, hysterical heart. This time was no exception.

'You don't understand, my son,' said Ismail. 'These fools ... Amal is an idiot. And the soldiers are even bigger idiots for taking orders from her ... I was only thinking about you ... I don't want to cause any trouble for you, my son ... That's why I was saying that we should keep riding ... But she kept insisting that we have to wait ... that we have to wait for you ... I know ... I know why you didn't get any Turkic soldiers to help me escape ... They could betray us due to their loyalty to Mahmud ... But these ...' Ismail screwed up his face in disgust as he pointed at the soldiers with him. 'These Zoroastrians and Greeks and *Abdis* ... They can't think … They're genetically idiots … Even worse, they were listening to a woman's orders … She may be a Turk, but she is a *woman*!'

Ismail believed that Amal was a Turkic woman, for she did look it.

Ayaz looked at the six soldiers who guarded Ismail. Among them were Zoroastrian Persians, Christian Greeks and African Muslims. African Muslims were called *Abdi*s by the Turks; *Abdi* was the *Arabic word for slave*. Malik Ayaz hated that term.

'If these Persians, Greeks and Africans trouble you, I have other nationalities here as well,' said the King of Lahore. Malik Ayaz whistled in three short bursts. Loudly. Around ten soldiers rode in almost instantly, like they had been waiting at the passage entry. 'Here come the Indians.'

The soldiers dismounted quickly, hobbling their horses and getting into formation behind Malik Ayaz.

'Welcome, Dhruv,' said Malik Ayaz. 'Are you carrying the extra clothes for me?'

'Yes, Lord,' answered Dhruv, bowing his head. 'You think of every detail.'

Ismail looked confused. He was becoming increasingly terrified. 'What's going on, my son?'

Malik Ayaz didn't answer his father. He turned to Amal. 'Perhaps you should take Yazadeh away.'

Malik Ayaz had told Amal what he was going to do. He had trusted only two women with his deepest, darkest secret. Kausari Jahan and Amal. He had to tell both, because he needed their help. The conspiracy couldn't have been pulled off without Kausari. And he knew that he could count on Amal to deliver his father to this spot. Her selfish interest was aligned with his. He had heard about her warrior capabilities from Talib. That's why he had agreed to take her to his mansion from the Ghazni safe house.

Amal knew what Malik Ayaz was going to do. And she also knew what Yazadeh would want. She answered almost immediately. 'She should stay.'

Ayaz insisted, saying, 'She's a child. There are some things that children should not see.'

Amal held her ground. 'There are some things that should never have been done to children. You have no idea of the crimes that have been committed on Yazadeh, King Ayaz. Trust me. She would want to see this.'

'See what?!' shrieked Ismail. He was convinced now that he was in danger. Serious danger. But he still held on to hope. Almost foolishly so. 'My son … My son … Let's leave quickly … I have enough money salted away … We'll be safe together …'

'Her name was Sara.' Malik Ayaz was teary-eyed as he said this, his voice hoarse and emotional. His fists clenched tight.

Ismail was confused. 'What? Who? Whose name was Sara?'

'The one whose painting I had shown you.' Ayaz's words burst from his gritted teeth like whiplash. 'The one whose painting you found beautiful.'

'My son … I … I don't know what you are talking about … We will always have time to talk later … Even about Sara, if you want … But let's get out of here …' Ismail tried to push his way forward, but he was held back by the soldiers.

'I was a little more than three years old,' said Malik Ayaz. 'A toddler. Nobody remembers anything from when they are that young … But I do … I do … I remember every detail …'

'Son … We'll talk … Later … But let's get out of here …' Ismail was still trying to leave.

'SHUT UP!' shouted Amal.

Ismail finally shut up.

Malik Ayaz spoke again. 'You had returned to Tbilisi after four years ... My mother believed that you would accept me, since I was born of your flesh. She believed that even if you didn't accept her, you would at least accept me, your child. And if you did, my life would be made. So she naively went to meet you at your palace. In your private court, when you were with your friends. There were ten of them, I remember. She told you who I was. Your son. And you laughed. And then you beat her. I remember ... I remember ... I was cowering against the far wall. You beat her till she bled. And then you raped her. And then you beat her again. And then you had your friends rape her ... All of them ... Taking turns ... You beat her between every time. I watched it all ... I was crying continuously ... I watched it all ...'

Ismail genuinely didn't remember this. He had done such things so often. And *kafir* women were fair game. He sincerely believed that his religion said that it wasn't wrong to rape or beat *kafir* women. But he had the sense to keep quiet.

Yazadeh was glaring at Ismail. Fists clenched tight. Body shaking in fury. He had done the same to her. Beat her and then raped her. Often.

'My mother survived that night ...' continued Malik Ayaz. 'She brought me up ... She never hid anything from me ... She toughened me up ... She taught me everything I know ... She sacrificed everything for me ... Her memory is my God.'

Ismail tried to say something. But no words emerged.

Malik Ayaz was holding the pendant, shaped like the Christian cross, hanging on his neck now. Tight. His knuckles were white. It was hers. It was his mother's pendant. 'Her name was Sara.'

Amal was crying. In sympathy. But the men around her had one emotion. And one emotion alone. Rage. Pure untainted rage. For what is a man worth, if he cannot avenge the woman who gave birth to him? What is a man worth, if he cannot get justice for the woman who brought him up? What is a man worth, if he cannot fight for the honour of the greatest woman he would ever know?

'I have been waiting ... For decades ... All your friends are dead ... You are the last one ... Mahmud didn't release you by himself ... I convinced him to release you ...'

Ismail's heart was beating hard. He was still hoping for mercy. Somehow. But even his thick skull could not stop the thought that was forcing its way in. This was the end.

Malik Ayaz drew a short sword from his scabbard. It had a vicious, irregular serrated edge. The kind that would cause immense pain. 'You can scream all you want. These rocks around us ... No sound escapes from here.'

'Ayaz ...' Ismail finally whispered. 'Listen to me ... I am ... We can ... You are my son ... I am your father ...'

'You are not my father!' roared Malik Ayaz. 'You are only the man who raped my mother! I am not *your* son! I am my *mother's* son!'

Ismail tried to run again. But the soldiers surrounding him held him back.

It was time to settle a mother's debt. And Malik Ayaz began settling that debt. With blood and pain.

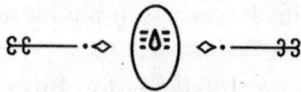

CHAPTER 27

Vengeance

Mahmud's palace, Ghazni, Afghanistan

It was half an hour past midnight.

Narasimhan had been waiting patiently in the sultan's chamber. By the inner wall close to the bed, where Mahmud slept bare-chested and in loose silk pyjamas.

The breeze flowing in from the east-facing window was very cool, considering the month. The heavy linen drapes blocked most of the draught. But some of it got in through the space where the curtains were slightly open, cooling the room down. There was very little light that filtered in, though. The moon was just a little sliver this night. Even more, it was on the other side of the palace. It was after midnight and the moon was already in the western sky, while the windows in Mahmud's chambers faced east. This meant that, besides the tiny flame lamp on the side table of the sultan's bed, there was virtually no light in that part of the chamber. Of course, if one moved farther away from Mahmud's bed, closer to the main door where the sofas and cushions were, the standing lamps provided ample light.

Narasimhan was close to where Mahmud was sleeping. And he was virtually invisible.

He was sitting on the ground, cross-legged, against the near wall. Hands resting on his knees. Like a yogi. Awake. Alert. Breathing calm and slow. Waiting for Mahmud to stir from his deep drunken sleep.

He had decided that if Mahmud didn't wake up an hour after midnight, he would wake him up. He couldn't wait forever. Sunrise would occur around six hours after midnight.

Luckily for Narasimhan, it didn't come to that eventuality.

Mahmud shifted in his sleep. A low-pitched, feral sound was heard. 'Mmm ...'

Narasimhan stood up instantly.

Mahmud's eyes opened a bit. Still groggy. 'Hmmm ... Water ... Ayaz ...'

Narasimhan, whose eyes had adjusted well to the dark, walked up to the large marble table by the wall and saw the lodestone, a piece of the Shiva Linga that he had placed there earlier—as a witness to what his devotee was about to do. He touched the sacred relic, then picked up a silver jug nearby and poured water from it into the silver cup by its side. He then walked over to the bed.

A bleary-eyed Mahmud turned his head towards the gargantuan Narasimhan walking towards him in the dark. His eyes half-drooping, vision still foggy. 'Hmmm? Abu Q'asim ... When did ... you return?'

Narasimhan stood right next to the bed. He did not answer.

Mahmud propped himself up slowly on his elbows. 'My goddamned head hurts ...' He held his hand out for the glass of water.

Narasimhan handed Mahmud the glass and stepped back. Into the shadows. He immediately reached for the small cloth bundle tied to his waist. And pulled out a large precious stone. Almost as big as a rock.

A diamond. From the mines of Golconda. A gift from Kausari Jahan. Only the best for Mahmud.

Diamonds are the hardest naturally occurring substance known to man. Far stronger than rocks.

This particular diamond was massive and had been cut exquisitely, a large head tapering to a flat concentrated base.

The instrument of the Lord's vengeance.

In the meantime, Mahmud had finished gulping the water down, though much of it trickled out from the side of his mouth, on to his neck and chest. He flopped his head back on the pillow, closed his eyes and held out his hand. For the glass to be taken from him.

Narasimhan didn't respond.

The sultan shook his hand that held the glass and grunted impatiently. 'Hmmm ...'

Narasimhan didn't move.

Mahmud opened his eyes and shouted in anger. 'Abu! Take the glass!'

He's awake now.

Narasimhan, despite his enormous frame, moved as swift as lightning. Quick steps forward on his toes, light on his feet. He brushed Mahmud's right hand aside with his left, and the glass went crashing to the floor. Almost simultaneously,

Narasimhan swung forward, flexing his powerful shoulder and back, bringing his right arm down brutally, in a ferocious strike. His hand holding the solid diamond aligned perfectly for the blow.

A direct hit. On the mandible. Narasimhan couldn't have executed this blow any better.

Among the first things boxers are taught by their coach is how to protect their faces during a fight. Tuck in your chin, keep a defensive fist up and clench your jaw. This ensures that the lower jaw is not fractured by the opponent at its weakest point, the joint of the mandible bone structure. Tight muscles keep it stable.

Mahmud hadn't clenched his jaw. He didn't know that he was about to be pummelled. Even worse for him, his tongue happened to be between his teeth.

Narasimhan's perfectly executed blow not only fractured Mahmud's jaw but also caused his crashing teeth to slice neatly through his tongue.

The sultan's hands shot up to his mouth in immense agony. He was trying to howl. But no coherent sound came out. His tongue was cut. And his jaw broken.

Narasimhan stepped back. Into the shadows.

Mahmud sprang out of his bed. Despite the grievous pain he was in. He heard a deep menacing growl emerge from the shadows.

'You are a rabid dog,' snarled Narasimhan. 'But a courageous rabid dog. I will give that to you.'

A furious Mahmud, blood dripping from his mouth, reached under his pillow and pulled out the short scabbard. A fighter is always ready for battle.

Narasimhan glanced at the scabbard tied to his own waist and then stared at Mahmud. He stepped back, deeper into the shadows. 'Let's make it fair. I'll not use my knife for now ... We are dharmics, not cowardly *jihadi* hyenas like you, who attack people without warning. But I had to break your jaw when you weren't ready, because I couldn't have you screaming and calling others to your aid. So to make up for it, I will let you fight with a knife. While I am armed with a gift from one of the greatest women I have ever met.'

The Indian stepped farther back, where the light from the standing lamps behind could reach and illuminate him a little. He raised the diamond that had been given to him by Kausari Jahan. 'Remember this? It used to adorn the main wall of the sanctum at Somnath*ar*. The mighty Chalukyas had donated this diamond to our Lord Mahadev. You stole it when you desecrated the temple. And gave it to ...'

Mahmud kept edging forward. Furious rage coursing through him. *Kausari ... I'll kill her ...*

'Yes ... You gave it to your wife ... And she gave it to me to use against you.'

Mahmud kept stepping forward, towards his attacker, being drawn away from his bedside by Narasimhan. The Chola general knew of the other blades hidden beneath the bed.

'Our Lord Shiva forgives and forgets easily,' said Narasimhan. 'But His followers don't. We remember. And we avenge Him.'

Mahmud tilted his head to the left and made as if to step leftwards. And then, all of a sudden, using his left foot as a spring, he lunged forward and to the right, swinging his knife sideways. It was a good move. Against any good warrior. Or even an exceptional one.

But Narasimhan wasn't just an exceptional warrior. He was one in a billion.

Narasimhan swerved to his left, easily avoiding the strike. As he stepped back, he sniggered. 'Come on … You are the famous Mahmud of Ghazni. You can do better.'

Mahmud tried to roar as he lunged forward, but his mouth could only muster a grotesque inarticulate gabble. Narasimhan stepped back, effortlessly dodging the blow once again.

Mahmud kept rushing forward and swinging, trying to push Narasimhan farther back, in the direction of the main door of his chamber. Narasimhan easily side-stepped every strike and continued to step back. They slowly moved into the light shed by one of the standing lamps. For the first time, Mahmud could see Narasimhan clearly. And make out that he was Indian.

Mahmud breathed heavily as he lunged over and over, unsuccessful each time. And then Narasimhan heard a sound that could not be mistaken for anything else. A strong hiss. He glanced at Mahmud's blue silk pyjamas which were getting rapidly drenched from the groin downwards, as urine escaped in torrents down Mahmud's legs.

Narasimhan laughed. 'Don't worry … I won't tell anyone … I know it's your age, not your cowardice …'

An enraged Mahmud slashed angrily, trying desperately to deliver a strike on the fearsome Indian warrior. But Narasimhan continued toying with the sultan as he swerved and repeatedly avoided the blows, floating like a fabulous butterfly that could never be caught.

But through these movements, Mahmud had managed to come close to a table. He deliberately pushed a vase off the counter. As the vase crashed with a loud noise, Mahmud glanced towards the door.

This caused Narasimhan to chortle, 'Nobody is coming from there, you fool. The guards at your door are ours ... You are going to have to make a louder noise. Maybe to attract the guards patrolling the gardens below ... They are still yours.'

Mahmud pivoted with his right arm in a broad arc, trying to force Narasimhan to his left so that he could sidestep the Indian to reach the standing lamps. They were built like chandeliers, with many kilograms of crystal glass. They would certainly make a noise loud enough to reach the guards on the ground, two floors below. But Narasimhan was too quick for the sultan. He leaned back, easily evading the latest swinging strike from Mahmud. And in a simultaneous motion, which would have been almost impossible for any other warrior due to the angle at which the back needed to be bent, Narasimhan brought his left arm up with incredible speed. He grabbed Mahmud's wrist with almost superhuman timing, just as the knife had moved harmlessly ahead. And he held on tight.

Mahmud struggled to free his arm from the vice-like grip of the Indian. But the fearsome Turkish warrior, known across the world for his strength and brutishness, could not succeed. Narasimhan stretched Mahmud's arm further back. And struck ferociously with his right arm, walloping him with the diamond again. Almost perfectly at the junction of the shoulder bone, fracturing the collar bone cleanly and dislocating the humerus bone in the upper arm from the glenoid socket joint. Mahmud howled, or at least made a poor attempt at it with his broken jaw, as he collapsed on the ground, the knife falling free from his hand. Narasimhan kicked the knife away.

'I have been told that this is the shoulder you had flexed to swing the hammer at the Somnath*ar* Shiva Linga,' snarled Narasimhan, as he went down on his haunches to get a better look at Mahmud's face. 'It had to be broken. I'm sure you understand.'

Mahmud tried to slither backwards using his good left arm and hand.

Narasimhan got up, swift as a panther, steady as a bull. He stepped across Mahmud's supine body and turned. His feet at Mahmud's left shoulder.

The sultan of Ghazni stared at Narasimhan with pure terror in his eyes. He was experiencing levels of panic that he had never felt in his entire life. Raw, primal fear.

'This hand,' said Narasimhan, pinning Mahmud with his knee and rendering him immobile. He pointed to Mahmud's left hand. 'This hand had held the hammer ... Had it not?'

Mahmud was shaking his head desperately, his body convulsing fearfully, struggling to escape. For he could guess what was to come.

Narasimhan bent his powerful back and smashed Mahmud's left hand with the diamond. Repeatedly and ruthlessly. Like a blacksmith hammering on iron. Pounding well-aimed blows on the wrist, palm and fingers. There are twenty-seven bones in a human hand. Narasimhan ensured that every single one of them on Mahmud's left hand was fractured. Some were even pulverized into tiny fragments.

Mahmud's body was trembling and spasming hysterically. Tears were pouring down his cheeks. The suffering was beyond breaking point. There wasn't too much blood, for

Narasimhan was not cutting Mahmud's muscles to pieces, but bashing the bones in. There wasn't too much noise either, for Mahmud's mouth was incapable of producing much sound. It was a silent demolition.

Narasimhan suddenly rose. 'Oh yes … You had held the hammer with both hands … Hadn't you?'

The Indian stepped over to the other side, bent down as before and bludgeoned Mahmud's right hand into pulp.

'I was told that you had also rested your filthy left foot on the base of our sacred Shiva Linga … That criminal foot must be crushed … But we cannot allow the precious diamond to touch your feet. So I will crush your left knee instead. It's a fair trade, don't you think? A knee for a foot?'

Narasimhan walked over to the supine Mahmud's feet. By now, the sultan's body had surrendered. He didn't even try to slide back or escape. He knew it was pointless. He just kept shaking his head, voicelessly pleading for mercy. His broken jaw and sliced tongue ensured that whatever he tried to say came out as gibberish. Not that Narasimhan was even attempting to decode what Mahmud was trying to communicate.

The Chola warrior went down on one knee and raised his arm, allowing the diamond to be clearly visible to Mahmud. And then he got to work. Hammering on the left knee. The first blow caused multiple fractures on the kneecap. But Narasimhan didn't stop there. He kept beating and bashing at and around the left knee of Mahmud. Again. And again. And again. The femur, the tibia, the fibula. Large and powerful bones of the thigh and shin. All of them converging at the knee joint. All of them fractured. Crushed. Splintered.

Finally, Narasimhan rested. Seemingly satisfied with his work. He looked at Mahmud and rolled his eyes. The sultan had fallen unconscious.

The gutless wimp can't take what he used to dish out to others.

The Indian walked over to the side table and placed the blood-smeared diamond on it. He fetched the silver jug and poured some water on Mahmud's broken face, forcing him out of his comatose state.

Keeping the jug aside on the floor, Narasimhan went down on his haunches and whispered, 'You need to be awake, Sultan. This was only *my* punishment. Now I will carry out my emperor's punishment.'

Mahmud lay on the ground with scalding tears, mixed with water, streaming into his hairline. Silent sobs. Silent screams. Silent dread.

Narasimhan delicately pulled out a slim knife from a small scabbard.

'We Hindus believe that the eyes are the window to the soul,' continued the tormenting Narasimhan. 'So you must see everything that will happen to you now. If you close your eyes, your soul will miss its lesson for the next birth.'

A petrified Mahmud shook his head from side to side in terror. His eyes shut tight. He could guess what was to come. Narasimhan clicked his tongue in irritation and held Mahmud's head tightly with his gigantic left hand. The sultan squealed. His body stiffened. He kept begging incoherently for mercy.

Narasimhan held the knife delicately, his pinkie finger raised. And very carefully, with surgical precision, cut and peeled off both the eyelids of Mahmud. He then flicked the skin off the knife. He stared at his handiwork. There were no eyelids, but there was no damage to the eyes at all.

The Indian nodded. 'Now you cannot shut your eyes to the truth.'

The Chola general tucked the knife away and then pulled out the *kunati*-infused blade that was tied to the other side of his waist. He had memorized the message from his emperor and memorized it well. And the time to recite it had finally come.

'Mahmud Ibn Sebuktegin,' said Narasimhan to the *barbarian*. 'Filthy *mleccha* wretch. Hear this truth from my emperor, Rajendra Chola. Remember this truth from the pride of the Tamils and the defender of the Indians, Rajendra Chola. Know this truth from the servant of Lord Shiva, Rajendra Chola. We Hindus have long memories. We will remember. We will wait. But we will avenge. The time will be of our choosing. The place will be of our choosing. But we will avenge. If you attack our Mother India. If you desecrate our Gods. We will avenge. There is no place on earth where you can hide. There is no place in the three worlds you can escape to. Because we will avenge. For we Hindus always pay back our karmic debts. You help us, we will help you. You hurt us, we will make you feel pain in ways you did not even think possible. We Hindus *are* the law of karma. For we will always give back to you what you give to us. Do not shut your eyes to this truth.'

Narasimhan raised both his arms, holding the *kunati* knife tight.

And he remembered his crime. His karmic debt. To Princess Odiratna.

The best way to wash off the taint of innocent blood is by shedding the blood of the wicked.

Narasimhan flexed his back and shoulders. His arms came down like a hammer. The knife plunged in. Deep. Into the belly of Mahmud. Straight into his liver. But not deep enough.

The Indian giant then twisted the blade in a circle inside the flesh. Mahmud kicked and writhed, though not so violently now, for he was losing strength rapidly. Blood was bursting out in torrents. Narasimhan sliced the knife through the abdominal cavity, lacerating every major organ there. Kidneys. Stomach. Intestines. Letting pieces of the *kunati* spread all over. With every major organ pitilessly cut up, there was no chance of Mahmud surviving.

The strength in the struggling sultan slowly waned, as blood pooled around him.

Narasimhan pushed the blade in deeper and snapped the hilt of the embedded knife.

Mahmud lay on the ground. Conscious. Trembling. Quivering. In intense pain. In unbearable torment.

'You will bleed out. But not immediately. You will live for a short while. And suffer. And with each moment of that suffering, Mahmud of Ghazni, you will remember that a Hindu never forgets.'

Narasimhan rose. He walked to the table and pulled a cloth out of the bag there. He wiped the blood off the diamond. And then wiped the blood off himself as best he could. He tied the pouch around his shoulder and across his chest now. He then brought the *ansh*, or *portion*, of the Shiva Linga, the lodestone—which had been lying on the table all this time—to his forehead with respect and then slipped it safely into the pouch. He quickly slipped the now-clean diamond in as well.

Then he pulled a parchment out of the pouch and pasted it on the inner wall closest to Mahmud's dying body.

A simple message was written on the paper, in Arabic and Persian.

Only an Arab. Always an Arab.

Narasimhan looked around. Everything was as it should be.

He walked to the east-facing window in the sultan's room, climbed out and descended into the darkness.

Narasimhan moved like a stealthy cat. He flitted across the royal courtyard, avoiding distracted guards on their night rounds, guards who were still in a celebratory mood due to the anointment ceremony earlier in the day. He reached the boundary wall and hid his frame behind a patch of damask roses planted on a high platform. He recognized the marker. He climbed the high wall with ease. He found the large curved tray that had been placed there, containing a particular mix of chemicals. Narasimhan had not fully understood the chemistry when Malik Ayaz had explained it. But he remembered that there was perhaps some rubidium in there. He knew what he had to do. He reached for the small container he had carried in his pouch. And edging back, poured some water on the chemicals. He then moved back even farther and looked up at the palace. High. To a particular window. Queen Kausari Jahan's lit window. A slim delicate form was silhouetted against a dim glow—an angel with a red vital aura.

Thick violet fumes began to emanate from the tray on to which Narasimhan had poured some water.

The signal had been given.

Mahmud was dead.

He knew that, by now, the queen would have given her precious *Dakshinamurti* of Lord Shiva and her Islamic prayer mat to her loyal bodyguard Hakeem to immerse in the River Arghandab close by. All Indians did that to their sacred and hallowed objects, when they could not use them any more. There was nothing else that was sacrosanct to the queen now. Not even her own life.

'Die well, My Lady,' whispered Narasimhan. He thought he saw the queen nod. But he couldn't be sure from this distance. He touched his heart, bowed his head towards her, turned around and clambered down the wall.

He nimbly wended his way through the dark alleyways of the sleeping city. He knew where he had to go. Where his comrades were waiting for him.

As he turned a corner he stopped suddenly. Beggars. Sleeping on the streets. A woman and a child. The child, no older than four or five years. The mother sat up with a start and shielded her little girl behind her. This was a cruel city. Full of malicious men. Many of whom had a taste for small children.

A tough city for mothers.

She locked eyes with the giant. Defiant. Protective.

The best way to wash off the taint of innocent blood is by shedding the blood of the wicked.

No ...

That is half the truth ...

An even better way to wash off the taint of innocent blood is to protect another innocent ...

Yes, a dharmic warrior must punish the wicked. But even more importantly, he must protect the weak.

For *Dharma* states that far greater than the Apex Predator is the Apex Protector.

The Apex Predator flees from the strong and hunts the weak.

The Apex Protector punishes the wicked and protects the weak.

Wash off the taint of innocent blood by protecting another innocent ...

The gold annulus pendant did not burn on his chest any more.

May the Mahadev always bless your noble soul, Odiratna.

The Chola general sat on his haunches and snapped the golden annulus pendant dangling from his neck. He held it out.

'Take it,' he whispered. 'Take it and get your child off the streets.'

The beggarwoman hesitated. She wondered what the catch was, for it was, clearly, a very valuable object, a large amount of gold.

'Take it and rid me of my guilt,' said Narasimhan. 'Please take my charity and save me ...'

The woman seemed to understand. She stretched out her trembling hand and took the gold bangle. She smiled.

'May Allah shower his blessings on you,' she said softly. Tears poured down her face. 'You are a good man ...'

Narasimhan, the hardened warrior, the killer of the wicked, the battle-scarred giant, started crying at the words that were kind beyond measure.

'You are a good man …'

Narasimhan reached out and gently touched the child on her head. Then he quickly got back on his feet and walked away.

A commotion seemed to be erupting in the palace complex he had left behind. He looked again at the tall palace. Easily observable on the hill that was visible from all parts of the city. He stared at the far window where he knew she was. Smouldering flames were raging there in myriad colours. Orange. Yellow. Red.

Narasimhan placed his balled fist to his chest and bowed his head, saluting a remarkable woman, for one last time. 'Die well, My Lady, Kausari Jahan …'

And then he whipped around and darted into the darkness.

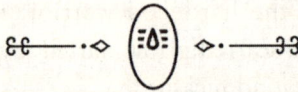

CHAPTER 28

A Time to Rebuild

Gwadar Port

A hooded man climbed up the rope ladder suspended from the front deck of the ship. It was an hour before sunrise.

'It's him!' cried Vijayan. 'It's the general!'

Narasimhan climbed up easily, followed by around fifteen soldiers who had rendezvoused with him outside Ghazni's city gates and ridden with him to Gwadar.

'Took you long enough, Sir!' said Brigadier Vijayan, as he stretched his hand over the rails towards the hooded man. Narasimhan grabbed the outstretched hand and heaved himself on board. He threw back his hood and engulfed Vijayan in a tight embrace. The two men thumped each other's backs with joy and relief.

'Thought you had lost me, didn't you?' asked Narasimhan with a twinkle in his eyes.

'Not a chance,' said the Pandya, his voice jocular but his eyes emotional. 'You've been through worse and survived. That barbarian Mahmud could never be your undoing!'

'I know, I know!' Amal walked towards the two men. 'He sounds so certain now. You should have seen him pacing the deck, day and night, looking at the docks for any sign of your return. I was jealous to see him pining for you!'

Vijayan laughed, embarrassed, while Narasimhan smiled warmly. He looked around and saw the joyful faces of Amal and her brothers—Aamir and Altaf, who had returned to Gwadar after dropping Iqbal and the former slaves in India. On the far side, Pulakit, Dhruv, Zayn and Dasarna rushed forward, their faces suffused with happiness. Each of them greeted the great Chola hero, one after the other.

'I'll return in a moment,' said Amal, turning to leave.

'Sure,' said Narasimhan.

'Congratulations, General!' said Pulakit. 'Mission successful! The entire land is rife with rumours. Some say the sultan was killed by Prince Shahid, in alliance with the Arabs. Others say that the sultan died from some strange affliction.'

'Strange affliction?' remarked Narasimhan. The Chola general and the platoon travelling with him had, in abundant caution, circumvented all major population centres between Ghazni and Gwadar. They had avoided talking to the locals as well. The result was that they had not heard any of the rumours swirling around in the Ghaznavid empire. 'What affliction? Syphilis?'

Pulakit and Vijayan laughed. Syphilis was a sexually transmitted disease that usually afflicted debauched men and women. And as all knew, the Ghaznavid Turks could be disgustingly debauched, with Mahmud being the most degenerate of them all, literally at the apex of this pyramid of perversion.

'No, no,' said Vijayan. 'Some are claiming it is malaria.'

'Malaria? How can he contract malaria high in the windy mountains of Kandahar? There are no mosquitoes in this season.'

'So the word on the streets of Gwadar is that the malaria story has been propagated by Prince Shahid, since he doesn't want those people who are more loyal to Mahmud than they are to the original Arabic interpretation of Islam to go against him. And the idea of the "Arab assassination plot" has been spread by Prince Mohammad, since he wants the Turks to rise against the "Arab bigotry and hatred" towards them.'

'Perfect … So the religious zealots among the Ghaznavids will gather behind Prince Shahid and the Turkic racists among them will gather behind Prince Mohammad.'

'Yes,' said Zayn. 'The Arabs are also delighted with this outcome. Because our people are too civilized to win against the barbaric Ghaznavid Turks. And some of us Arabs are actually afraid that the Turks want to take away control of our Islam from us. Let them fight each other, I say.'

'It's happening already,' said Pulakit. 'The initial killings have already begun. It's a matter of a few weeks before full-blown civil war breaks out among the Turks.'

Vijayan added, 'It is rumoured that Salar Maqsud—the sultan's nephew—is hurriedly returning from north India. The rabid dogs of war are turning on each other.'

Narasimhan smiled. 'Our work here is done.'

'General,' said Amal, who was walking back towards the men, along with Yazadeh, as two soldiers carried a heavy trunk to the deck. The trunk was enveloped in a silver casing. A third soldier placed a foldable table on the ship deck, and the trunk was placed on it. Narasimhan could guess what was in the trunk. He slipped off his shoes.

The trunk was carefully opened by Amal. Inside, the comfortable base was lined with a satin saffron-coloured cloth. On it, in as close an approximation as possible with all the broken pieces, was the reassembled Somnath Shiva Linga. Narasimhan reached into his pouch and pulled out the *ansh* that was with him. He quickly estimated where the piece should go and placed it in position. Then he touched the stones with his hands and brought his hands to his eyes.

Narasimhan looked at his comrades with moist eyes. '*Har Har Mahadev.*'

An ancient Indian cry that went back to the dawn of time. One that always electrified their souls. *Har Har Mahadev* … All of us are Mahadevs … All of us are Gods …

Amal, Vijayan, Pulakit, Dhruv, Dasarna and all the others present chorused, '*Har Har Mahadev.*'

'You know, General,' said Zayn, 'Malik Ayaz's instructions were perfect. We found the sacred relics very easily.'

'He's a good man. Is he still in Ghazni?'

'No,' said Pulakit. 'We've heard that he has slipped out to Lahore. Waiting to find out who wins the civil war.'

'And maybe hoping to declare independence, perhaps …' said Narasimhan. 'He's a good man. And a smart man.'

'We certainly couldn't have done it without Queen Kausari Jahan,' said Vijayan. 'None of us saw that coming … That she would end up being on our side. We heard of her sacrifice from the advance scout you had sent.'

'She was a good woman …' said Narasimhan. 'May the Gods bless her so that her next life is less tragic and grief-stricken.'

'*Ameen*,' said Amal.

'*Summa Ameen*,' said Vijayan. 'May Allah and Lord Shiva bless her noble soul.'

'Have Iqbal and the rest of the former slaves reached India safely?' Narasimhan asked Altaf, Amal's brother.

'Yes, General,' answered Altaf. 'We returned immediately after dropping them safely in Gujarat. And waited here for Amal *aapa* and Vijayan*ar* to return.'

'And we also decided to ask Yazadeh to come to the Chola lands with us, General,' said Vijayan. 'Maybe she can set up a Yazidi temple in Tamil territory.'

'Why not,' said Narasimhan, smiling. 'Our heart is always open to all who respect India, including the Yazidis.' Then the Chola general took a deep breath and spoke loudly. 'Well, we cannot keep the emperor waiting. You all know our destination. Let's go! Cut the mooring lines!'

—◦✦◦—

Somnath, Gujarat, India

It had been six months since the death of Mahmud. The civil war still raged strong in Ghazni. The Turks were gorging on a frenzy of bloodshed, as brother clashed with brother. All the others around them, including the Indians, had a period of respite from the endless violence of the Turks.

The assassination mission had succeeded spectacularly.

The great emperors of the Indian subcontinent had gathered at the Somnath Temple. Rajendra Chola, of the Chola dynasty, the most powerful man in the world, who ruled much of south India, east India and Southeast Asia. Emperor Bhojadev, of the Parmars, who reigned over much of central India, with most of Madhya Pradesh and parts of Chhattisgarh, Gujarat, Rajasthan and Maharashtra under his administration. Emperor Jayasimha, of the Chalukyas, who ruled most of Karnataka, Maharashtra and Telangana. And Emperor Bhimdev, of the Solankis, who presided over most of Gujarat and parts of Rajasthan. The Somnath Temple technically fell within the territory of the Solankis.

All these empires may have been Indian, but they had all battled with each other at some time or the other in the past. While they may have had past enmities, what united them was their devotion to Lord Shiva. And they had come together to the ruins of the Somnath Temple to contribute resources and also finalize the plan to rebuild the temple.

'If only we had been united,' said Rajendra Chola, 'that barbarian Mahmud would never have dared to lay his filthy hands on our Lord's temple.'

All the emperors and their empires had fought the Turks in their own ways. To defend their lands, their people and their Gods. But they had always fought separately. Never under one flag. Never.

'I agree,' said Emperor Jayasimha. 'If our ancestors had got together and supported the Hindu Shahi Pathans and the Buddhist-Hindu Baloch, who protected the borders of the Indian subcontinent, then the Turks would have never had an inroad. We must fight our actual enemy, rather than battling each other.'

While Emperor Bhojadev had sent soldiers to support the Hindu Shahi king, Anandpal, against Mahmud the Turk,

Anandpal's immediate neighbours had not. A similar situation had plagued the Solanki kings in Gujarat as well. The fact that Jayasimha, the Chalukyan emperor, had separately sent his soldiers to fight the army of Ghazni, and the Cholas and Parmars had sent another mission, was clear evidence of the Indian kings having the right aims, but not working together. For none of these missions were joint efforts.

'True,' agreed Emperor Bhimdev Solanki. 'Our lack of unity makes us easy prey for our enemies.'

Many under the command of the different emperors, who had got to know each other during the Ghazni mission, had met each other already at the gathering. Narasimhan, Pulakit, Vijayan, Amal, Dasarna, Dhruv, Iqbal, Yazadeh, among others. Catching up on old times. Renewing past bonds. All had congratulated Vijayan and Amal on their recent nuptials. Dhruv was about to embark on his maiden trade voyage, with Iqbal and his son. Emperor Jayasimha had thanked Rajendra Chola and Bhojadev Parmar for their soldiers saving the life of his younger brother, Pulakit.

The priests and their helpers were almost done with their preparations for the *shilanyas*, a *ceremony for the laying of the foundation stone*, for the new Somnath Temple. The emperors would be carrying out the rituals, under the guidance of *purohits*, or *priests*.

'I only partially agree on the unity point,' said Emperor Bhojadev. Everyone listened. For Bhojadev Parmar was not just a great emperor and fierce warrior like the other three with him. He was also a scholar. He had written eighty-four books on subjects as varied as astronomy, medicine, chemistry, metallurgy and architecture, as well as philosophy and poetry. A true polymath and a genius. 'All of us have fought the enemies of India, the Turks. And yes, we fight each other too. So you can say we suffer from a lack of unity. But don't the Turks keep fighting each other too? And their internal battles go to extremes that we cannot imagine here in India. Sons torturing and killing their fathers. Brothers publicly skinning brothers alive. Men murdering women and children, sometimes from their own extended families. If there is a lack of unity among us, one can argue that there is an even greater lack of unity among the Turks. And yet they often defeat us Indians. I don't think our lack of unity is our key weakness. It is a weakness, yes, but not our key weakness.'

The three emperors were silent. They had never thought of it this way before. They had always assumed that it was the lack of unity among the Indians which caused them to lose wars. An official came up to Rajendra Chola to inform him that the preparations for the ceremony were complete. But the mighty Chola gestured to him to wait and give the emperors a few moments of privacy.

'Then what do you think is our key weakness?' asked Rajendra Chola.

'*Shatrubodh*,' said Bhojadev Parmar.

'*Shatrubodh*?' asked Bhimdev Solanki.

'Yes. *Shatrubodh*. *Knowledge of the enemy*. The great Acharya Chanakya had spoken of this. A young scholar called Pankaj who studies at Bhojpal University has also written about this. What I am telling you is based on his theory. We think of the Turks as imbecilic barbarians, only capable of fighting like dumb brutes. And nothing else. But I say that they are smarter than us in one department: *Shatrubodh*. They have complete clarity on their enemies and their ways. They understand their enemies well. They study our way of life to know how to defeat us in ways that ensure we will stay defeated. Why do you think they destroy the idols of our Gods and not just steal them for ransom? If they were just thinking about money, then ransom is far more profitable, right? But they are masters of *Shatrubodh*. They break the idols of our Gods, to ensure that our spirits are broken.'

Bhojadev Parmar continued, 'They even have a hierarchy of enemies. At the lowest level, their primary enemies are Hindus, Buddhists, Jains and even Yazidis and Zoroastrians, because they see us as idolators. We are the worst of creatures on their list of enemies. There is nothing we can do to make them not treat us like enemies. Our very existence is offensive to them. To a lesser extent, they see Indian Muslims, and also Jews and Christians, as enemies. Because they have a racist hatred towards the Indian race and deeply hate Jews and Christians who have not updated their religion to the "correct version". At a better position than this group are the Persian Muslims. Because they follow Islam, and the Turks believe the Persian race is better than the Indian race. In a more favourable position than the Persian Muslims are the Arab Muslims, because they are thought of as the original Muslims. And at the apex are Turkic Muslims. This, in summary, is the Turkic outlook.'

'Hmm,' said Rajendra Chola. 'That's an interesting insight. Perhaps our fault is that we think all religions are the same, all cultures are the same, that all people want to love each other and it's just politics that divides them. We live in this la-la land where we think that all we need for a better world is love and fresh air. But the Turks are clear and ruthless, particularly when it comes to their in-group and their enemies.'

'Also,' continued Bhojadev Parmar, 'whatever their internal fights and civil wars, they will never support an enemy against one of their own. Never. For example, they will never support an Indian in a fight against a Turk, even if the Indian has accepted Islam. They are perfectly certain about who their in-group is and who their enemies are. We are not. We think of the Turks as just another group of people, no different from us Indians. *Vasudhaiva Kutumbakam.* We believe *all of humanity is one family.* Some Indian kings think there is nothing wrong in allying with a Turk against a fellow Indian. That displays a lack of *Shatrubodh.* A lack of understanding about who your true enemy is.'

'So what do you think is the solution?' asked Jayasimha Chalukya.

'We must deeply learn the knowledge and philosophy of *Shatrubodh.* I am building a great temple complex called Bhojeshwar. It will be one of the biggest in the world. And we will have a colossal temple to Lord Shiva at its heart. But we will also establish an institute within the complex, teaching the philosophy of *Swayambodh, Shatrubodh, Parabodh* and *Yugbodh.* This is a time of significant geopolitical shifts taking place all over the world. A period of chaos. The old global order will collapse during this chaos, and a new order will emerge. If we Indians are not adept in these four critical fields, we will be among the losers in this era,' said Bhojadev Parmar.

'You must build this complex, my friend,' said Rajendra Chola. 'It will be for the good of India.'

'I am also tracking the career of a prince called Suheldev, from a small kingdom called Bahraich. Very smart young man. He seems to have a lot of clarity on *Shatrubodh* about the Turks.'

'Suheldev,' said Jayasimha. 'I will follow his story with interest. For one can certainly assume that when their civil war is over, the Turks will turn their attention to us once again.'

'They certainly will,' said Bhojadev Parmar. 'We can only delay their attacks, but not stop them altogether. Because whenever they get a chance, they will invade us—that is who they are. We must remain eternally vigilant against enemies like them.'

There was a whisper from a Chola official, for the auspicious time for the *shilanyas* ceremony was upon them. 'Your Majesty …'

'Yes, yes.' Rajendra Chola nodded. 'Come, my friends. Let us lay the foundation stone together for a great temple to our Lord. May it stand forever.'

Jayasimha, the great Chalukyan emperor, looked up at the evening sky. A splash of red was streaked upon it, as the sun sank gently into the horizon.

He softly chanted a *shloka* or *verse* from the Shri Rudram hymn from the Yajur Veda scripture, which was dedicated to the Mahadev, for one of His names was Rudra.

Asau yastAmro aruNa uta babhruH sumaNgalaH |
ye chemAM RudrA abhito dikshhu shritAH sahasrasho
vaishhAM heDa Imahe ||

He is red while rising, He is golden-yellow later,
He dispels darkness, He is auspicious,

His other forms spread in all directions like rays of light,
He is Rudra,

And one of His Forms is the Glorious Sun.
We bow to Him.

The other three emperors smiled at Jayasimha's perfect enunciation of the shloka. And stared at the gentle rays of the sun in the distance.

The sun may set regularly. That is the unbreakable cycle of *ruta*, the *principle of the natural order of the universe*. But equally so, another unbreakable law of *ruta* is that the sun always returns and rises regularly as well.

The Gods may retreat at times. And at such times it may appear to their devotees that their world is coming to an end. That the Gods have abandoned them. But it is the sacred law of nature, that when the time is right, the Gods always return.

Have faith.

Because without the Gods, the existence of the devotees is meaningless. But equally so, without the devotees, the Gods lose Their purpose. Perhaps the greatest love story is the one between the devotees and their Gods.

The emperors joined their palms and bowed towards the Sun.

Reminded of their greatest love. Their supreme subject of devotion. Their finest source of wisdom. Their utmost source of strength.

Shiva.

And then they looked at the ruins of the temple. There was work to be done.

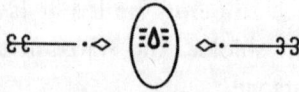

EPILOGUE

A Prophecy

Kanchi, Tamil Nadu, India

It had been one year since the death of Mahmud. The Ghaznavid empire was still convulsing and wobbling, brought to its knees by a brutal civil war. Meanwhile, in western India, the Temple reconstruction at Somnath*ji* was proceeding quickly and well.

Prince Rajadhiraja, the son of Rajendra Chola, and Prince Jaya, the son of Bhojadev Parmar, had arrived at Kanchi on a special mission. For a crucial matter related to the Somnath Temple. They had been accompanied by Prince Pulakit of the Chalukya dynasty and General Narasimhan as well.

'But I didn't understand, noble Shankaracharya*ji*,' said Rajadhiraja Chola. 'Are you saying that we should not use the shattered pieces of the lodestone Shiva Linga in the rebuilt Somnath*ar* Temple?'

Adi Shankaracharya, the *first* Shankaracharya, who lived about three hundred years earlier, had harmonized many of the schools of *Dharma*. Some claimed that Adi

Shankaracharya had lived much earlier, nearly one thousand four hundred years earlier. Whether it was three hundred or one thousand four hundred years that was the true antiquity of the great Adi Shankaracharya only the Mahadev would know, but there was no doubt that in the minds of most human beings, he was considered to be one of the greatest Hindus and finest Gurus ever. He had established various Shankaracharya *peeth*s, or *monasteries*, across the Indian subcontinent. These were located in Dwarka in the west, Joshimath in the north, Puri in the east and Sringeri in the south. These monasteries had been established to preserve and propagate Vedic knowledge and guide the dharmic way of life through challenging times. But many said, there was a fifth *peeth* as well. In Kanchi, deep in the south of India, in Tamil lands, close to the Palar River. Where, it was rumoured, the first Shankaracharya had spent the last days of his mortal life. But here too one found the traditional dharmic comfort with multiple truths, because others claimed that Adi Shankaracharya had left his body close to Kedarnath*ji*, far in the northern parts of India, nestled in the high Himalayas. It seemed that, even in death, Adi Shankaracharya had sought to unite the different regions of the Indian subcontinent.

Each of these monasteries established by Adi Shankaracharya was headed by a Shankaracharya, who was regarded as a successor to the first Shankaracharya. And the spiritual status of these living Shankaracharyas was second to none in the eyes of most Hindus, particularly those who worshipped Lord Shiva.

'No, you shouldn't, my child,' answered the Shankaracharya of Kanchi.

'Respected Shankaracharya*ji*, I know that the Mahanirvan Tantra principles speak of how *khandit murti*s must be submerged in water and not worshipped,' said Jaya Parmar, since he had learnt about the proper rituals regarding *broken idols* from his scholarly father. 'But many rituals also hold that if the original *murti* was very powerful, we can repair all the restored pieces and perform a special *Pran Pratishtha* again, so that the devotees can worship the same *murti* once it has been repaired.' *Pran Pratishtha is a ritual in which the life force is invoked and established within a murti, essentially bringing it to life as a deity.*

'You can do that,' said the Kanchi Shankaracharya. 'But you should not.'

'But why?' asked Pulakit Chalukya.

The Shankaracharya leaned back and took a deep breath. He glanced at Narasimhan, the oldest among the four men who had come to meet him. The general had lived long, seen the highs of success and the depths of grief. Every person will experience rock bottom, the lowest point in their life. When everything seems to go wrong. If you survive those terrible experiences, you will emerge a different man. Fundamentally different. Like how Narasimhan was now. There are some things that only time, life and trauma can teach you. The energy of youth has to be tempered by the fire of pain to mature into the warm glow of wisdom.

And as with men, so with civilizations.

'There is a cycle that most civilizations go through, my children,' said the aged and wise Shankaracharya to the four men. 'They rise, they soar, they stumble, they fall. And often, they never recover. They die in endless decay, buried beyond redemption in the sands of time. The mightier their achievements, the more colossal their wrecks. It happens to most civilizations. But some are different ... They fall, but they don't die. They get up, dust themselves off and rise once again. The truly mighty are not those who soar high at the peak of a cycle and expect to remain forever on a pedestal. The truly mighty are those who come back from the depths of despair and destruction. The truly mighty are those civilizations that can come back from the dead. The pharaoh Ozymandias may have been the king of kings, but he didn't know it. His great culture of Khemit, ancient Egypt, is dead and is probably never going to recover. But our culture, India's culture, is still around. What is truly special about us is not how high we soar, but that we recover from death and are reborn. It has happened many times. The last death for our land was during the great war of the Mahabharat, which ended the peak of our Vedic culture. But we recovered ... We came back from the dead ... And we erected something equally extraordinary over the last two and a half thousand years, which built on our Vedic past, but added so much more ... The world admires us as the greatest culture in history, the magnificent land of Bhaaratvarsh.'

'But what does this have to do with the Somnathar Temple, great Shankaracharya?' asked Rajadhiraja Chola.

The Shankaracharya noticed that Narasimhan was not asking questions. It was almost like he had understood the message already. The younger men, however, suffused with the youthful energy that makes growth possible, but without the knowledge of what or indeed where they should be growing, needed answers to their questions.

'The destruction of Somnathar was a message to us,' said the Shankaracharya. 'A much clearer message than the fall of the Sun Temple at Multan three hundred years ago at the hands of Muhammad bin Qasim.'

'What message, great Guru?' asked Jaya Parmar.

'That tough times are upon us. Our decline has begun.'

'But we just won, respected Holiness,' said Pulakit Chalukya, confused. 'We killed Mahmud, and our vengeance is complete. And when the Turks come again, we will beat them once more.'

'We will beat them at times, but we will also lose at times,' said the Shankaracharya. 'I have studied the stars. I have perused the charts and the signs. We Indians have a difficult one thousand years ahead of us. Every civilization that rises will experience this decline. And as I told you, we have been through these cycles many times. We are entering the declining phase of this particular cycle. We will see one thousand years of constant attacks in three phases. The first phase has already begun. The Turks will keep coming back. And there will come a time when they will conquer, even rule, much of India. In the second phase, a race of pale-skinned European men, from even farther west, will invade and conquer us.'

The three royals stiffened. In their mind, India was unconquerable. They couldn't imagine foreigners ruling India.

The Shankaracharya continued, 'These foreigners will rule us for nearly one thousand years. The north of India will keep fighting. And the bravery of the north Indians against the foreigners will help keep the south Indians relatively safe. Because the foreigners will be too busy fighting the north to have the capacity to invade and devastate the south. The farther south you will be in India, over the next one thousand years, the more of our ancient culture you will be able to keep alive. Practically all our ancient temples in the north will be destroyed. But the temples in the south will remain standing. So the pieces of the shattered Shiva Linga must be kept secure here, as far south as possible, during this oncoming thousand-year period of chaos and violence. I will tell you about a group of Tamil *agnihotri* priests who will continuously perform all the rituals necessary on the pieces of Somnath*ar*'s Shiva Linga, to keep the energy strong in the fragmented pieces of the *murti*.'

'But those who worship broken idols suffer spiritually,' said Rajadhiraja Chola. 'Won't the Tamil *agnihotri*s suffer?'

'Yes, they will. And that is a price that their community is willing to pay. For Lord Shiva. And a thousand years later, when the time is right, they will take these pieces to a Tamil sage called Shankar. Who will reconsecrate the Shiva Linga pieces again. That is when the Somnath*ar* Temple will be truly restored. That is when the decline of India will end. And we will start rising again. Until then, one small piece of the broken Shiva Linga can be kept at Somnath*ar*, buried under a Bel tree, so that it provides spiritual sustenance for the repeated revival of the Temple.'

'How will we know when the time is right?' asked Pulakit Chalukya.

'The time will be right when Ram returns to Ayodhya.'

The princes were confused. Rajadhiraja Chola asked, 'But Lord Ram is in Ayodhya. His greatest temple there, the *Ram Janmabhoomi*, stands strong.'

The Kanchi Shankaracharya smiled sadly. 'We have a lot more suffering ahead of us, my children. You will not see the day when Ram leaves Ayodhya. But your descendants will.'

The princes stayed silent. They couldn't even begin to imagine Ayodhya without Ram.

'But he will return. Ram *lalla* will return.' Kanchi Shankaracharya's voice shook with emotion as he spoke of Ram as *a little child*, for that is how his *murti* was consecrated at the Ram Janmabhoomi Temple. 'We Indians will bring him back. A thousand years later.'

'We will suffer for that long?' asked Jaya Parmar.

Shankaracharya sighed, for he was old enough to see the silver lining rather than the dark cloud. 'Mother India will only suffer. But the other ancient cultures will all die out. After one thousand years, the only pre-Bronze Age culture that will still be alive will be ours.'

'Will our rebuilt Temple of Somnath*ji* be destroyed again by some other invader?' asked Pulakit Chalukya. He had caught on to what the Shankaracharya had said about the 'repeated revival' of the Somnath Temple.

'Yes, it will.' The Shankaracharya's eyes had teared up a bit. 'But we will rebuild it again. And again. And other temples too. This will be a fierce resistance mounted by us, indigenous Indians, against these foreigners. We will suffer tragic defeats. However, we will also win many battles. And most importantly, we will never surrender. Our Motherland, our dharmic culture, will survive. And a thousand years later, the rise will begin.'

Narasimhan finally leaned forward and asked a question for the first time. 'Great Guru Shankaracharya*ji*, you initially spoke of three phases of attacks in the thousand-year period of decline. The first will be by the Turks. The second by some pale-skinned Europeans. Who will attack us in the third phase?'

The Shankaracharya smiled. Trust the wiser older man, who has suffered in life, to ask the most pertinent question. 'The third phase will be the most heartbreaking one. Because in the first two phases, the ones attacking us will be foreigners. But in the third phase, it will be our own people, some of our fellow Indians, who will attack us.' The Shankaracharya raised his left hand. 'These people will be our own, but they will mentally and emotionally secede from Bhaarat. Hating everything about us. Always siding with foreigners. Attacking every fault in our civilization as if we are uniquely flawed, as if every other civilization is perfect. This will be the most difficult phase.'

The Shankaracharya raised his right hand. 'Difficult because the people who love India will not be able to battle these self-haters. You don't strike your own body because a part of it has contracted some foreign infection. The India lovers must not attack the India haters but attract them back to loving the Motherland.' The Shankaracharya held his left hand with his right, almost like the right was comforting the left. 'Those on the other side are our own people after all, even if they are lost. We must not hate them, even if they hate us. We must bring them home with love, kindness and understanding. It will be a difficult struggle, but our India lovers will ultimately succeed. The India haters will be brought back into the family.'

'But why must we go through this decline?' asked Rajadhiraja Chola.

'Because that is the law of nature. Everything that rises must also fall sometime. And more importantly, you learn much more from your defeats than from your successes, you grow much more in grief than in happiness. The Indians who will populate our land a thousand years from now must analyse the one thousand years of decline. They must understand why their ancestors lost, so that they don't repeat those mistakes. And they must learn what is special about Indian culture that it survived a thousand years of unrelenting martial, intellectual, financial and cultural attacks. When they draw the right conclusions and learn the right lessons, they will manage the next rise so much better.'

Narasimhan smiled slightly. 'That's a big task for our descendants.'

'Yes, it is.' The Kanchi Shankaracharya then looked across the humongous gulf of time and space, across one thousand years. He looked at you, dear reader, and whispered, 'One thousand years are nearly over, my child. It is time for Mother India to rise. It is time for *Dharma* to rise ... Get to work.'

Om Namah Shivaya.
The Universe bows to Lord Shiva. I bow to Lord Shiva.

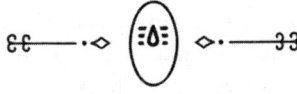

References

Prologue: The Last Stand at Somnath

1. Firishta. 1829. *Tarikh-i-Firishta (Gulshan-i-Ibrahimi).* In *History of the Rise of the Mahomedan Power in India,* trans. John Briggs. London: Longman, Rees, Orme, Brown, and Green.
2. Quran.com. 'Tafsir Surah Al-Anfal - 41'. Accessed 30 July 2025. https://quran.com/8:41/tafsirs/en-tafsir-maarif-ul-quran.
3. Islam Q&A. 'What Is the Ruling on Intimacy with Slave Women?' Accessed 30 July 2025. https://islamqa.info/en/answers/13737/what-is-the-ruling-on-intimacy-with-slave-women.
4. Oxford Reference. 'Ghanimah'. Accessed 30 July 2025. https://www.oxfordreference.com/display/10.1093/oi/authority.20110803095850460.
5. The Urdu word 'ghanimat' (غنیمت) is derived from the Arabic word 'ghanimah' (غَنِيمَة), and both words share similar meanings related to booty, plunder or spoils of war. *See* Rekhta Dictionary. 'Maal-e-Ganiimat'. Accessed 30 July 2025. https://www.rekhtadictionary.com/meaning-of-maal-e-ganiimat.
6. Joukowsky Institute for Archaeology and the Ancient World, Brown University. 'Dar al-Islam/Dar al-Harb, Islamic Archaeology Glossary 2007'. Accessed 30 July 2025. https://www.brown.edu/Departments/Joukowsky_Institute/courses/islamicarchaeologyglossary2007/4005.html.

7. Quran.com. 'Tafsir Sūrah AlBayyinah - 98:6 to 98:8'. Accessed 30 July 2025. https://quran.com/al-bayyinah/8/tafsirs.

8. Facchine, Tom, and Zohair Abdul-Rahman. 'Why Idolatry Is the Greatest Evil'. *Dogma Disrupted* (podcast). 11 August 2023. Yaqeen Institute for Islamic Research. Accessed 30 July 2025. https://yaqeeninstitute.org/watch/series/why-idolatry-is-the-greatest-evil-dogma-disrupted-podcast.

9. Muhammad, Abu Salman, and Adnan Chishti Attari Madani. 'What Is Shirk'. Islamic Beliefs and Information. *Safar-ul-Muzaffar* 1442, October 2020. Accessed 30 July 2025. https://www.dawateislami.net/magazine/en/islamic-beliefs-and-information/what-is-shirk.

10. Islam Q&A. 'Obligation to destroy idols'. Accessed 30 July 2025. https://islamqa.info/en/answers/20894/obligation-to-destroy-idols.

11. Nazim, Muhammad. 2014. *The Life and Times of Sultan Mahmud of Ghazna*. Cambridge: Cambridge University Press. (Originally published in 1931.)

12. Munshi, Kanaiyalal Maneklal. 1952. *Somnath: The Shrine Eternal*. Bombay: Bharatiya Vidya Bhavan.

13. Majumdar, Asoke Kumar. 1956. *Chaulukyas of Gujarat: A Survey of the History and Culture of Gujarat from the Middle of the Tenth to the End of the Thirteenth Century*. Bombay: Bharatiya Vidya Bhavan.

Chapter 5: Two Emperors and Their Lord

1. Islam Q&A. 'Obligation to destroy idols'. Accessed 30 July 2025. https://islamqa.info/en/answers/20894/obligation-to-destroy-idols.

2. SurahQuran.com. 'Surah Kafirun aya 6, English translation of the meaning Ayah'. Accessed 30 July 2025. https://surahquran.com/english-aya-6-sora-109.html.

Chapter 7: Plans and Pilgrims

1. Khosa, Aasha. 'Foreign rulers, Ulema, Syeds played key role in keeping Pasmanda on the margins'. Awaz: The Voice, 31 May 2023. Accessed 30 July 2025. https://www.awazthevoice.in/opinion-news/foreign-rulers-ulema-syed-played-key-role-in-keeping-pasmanda-on-the-margins-21774.html.

2. Fyzie, Faiyaz Ahmad. 'Pasmanda Muslims are using social media to counter those defending the medieval Taliban'. ThePrint, 14 October 2021. Accessed 30 July 2025. https://theprint.in/opinion/pasmanda-muslims-are-using-social-media-to-counter-those-defending-the-medieval-taliban/749708/.

3. Sangam Talks. 'Pasmanda Muslim bigotry: An Ashrafia threat | Faiyaz Ahmad Fyzie |'. YouTube, 30 September 2021. Accessed 30 July 2025. https://www.youtube.com/watch?v=TavDzjCus0o.

Chapter 12: The Price of Escape

1. Pulitzer Prize–winning American historian and philosopher Will Durant wrote in *The Story of Civilization, Vol. 1 (Our Oriental Heritage)* (New York: Simon & Schuster, 1935), on pp. 459–60:

'The (Turkic/Persian/Arab) Mohammedan conquest of India is probably the bloodiest story in history. It is a discouraging tale, for its evident moral is that civilization is a precarious thing, whose delicate complex of order and liberty, culture and peace may at any time be overthrown by barbarians invading from without or multiplying within. The Islamic historians and scholars have recorded with great satisfaction the slaughter of Hindus, the forced conversion of Hindus, the abduction of Hindu women and children to slave markets, and the destruction of temples carried out by the warriors of Islam during AD 800 to 1700. Millions of Hindus were converted to Islam by the sword during this period ... Taxes raised from infidels were spent at pleasure by the sultans ... Those who survived were left in poverty, humility and despair.'

The same section, on p. 459, states: 'For the first time, says Lane-Poole, we see a Mohammedan government supporting itself by a systematic oppression of non-Moslems.' This was cited within Lane-Poole, Stanley. 1893. *Medieval India under Mohammedan Rule*. London: Methuen & Co., on p. 205.

2. Belgian Indologist and historian Koenraad Elst, in *Negationism in India: Concealing the Record of Islam* (Delhi: Voice of India, 1992), says the following about foreign Islamic (Turkic, Persian, Arab) invaders:

'The Islamic reports on the massacres of Hindus, destruction of Hindu temples, the abduction of Hindu women and forced conversions, invariably express great glee and pride. They leave no doubt that the destruction of Paganism by every means was considered the God-ordained duty of the [foreign invading] Moslem community ... Rape and abduction of women and children and the destruction of their idols, acts which have been recorded with so much glee by the Muslim chroniclers, [were] not restricted by social status; upper-caste kafir or low-caste kafir suffered alike.'

Elst contends that the ideology viewing Hindus as 'kafirs' provided the religious justification for such acts of destruction, forced conversion and enslavement, making violence against non-Muslims—including the sexual enslavement of women by the conquerors—an accepted element of strategy rather than isolated crimes.

Chapter 16: The Price of Justice

1. Barani, Ziauddin. 1867. *Tarikh-i Firoz Shahi*. In *The History of India, as Told by Its Own Historians*, trans. Henry Miers Elliot and John Dowson, ed. Zafar Hasan. London: Trübner & Co., pp. 105–10.

2. Badauni, Abdul Qadir. 1898. *Muntakhabu-t-Tawarikh*, Vol. 2, trans. George Ranking. Calcutta: Asiatic Society, chapters 10–12.

3. Firishta. 1829. *Tarikh-i-Firishta (Gulshan-i-Ibrahimi)*. In *History of the Rise of the Mahomedan Power in India*, Vol. 2, trans. John Briggs. London: Longman, Rees, Orme, Brown, and Green, pp. 80–85.

Chapter 20: The Debt of Sins Past

1. Sunnah.com. '(41) Chapter: The Battle Expedition of India'. *Sunan an-Nasa'i* 3175, The Book of Jihad. Accessed 30 July 2025. https://sunnah.com/nasai:3175.

2. Islam Q&A. 'Hadith about the conquest of India'. Accessed 30 July 2025. https://islamqa.info/en/answers/145636/hadith-about-the-conquest-of-india.

3. Rekhta Dictionary. 'Gazva'. Accessed 30 July 2025. https://rekhtadictionary.com/meaning-of-gazva.

4. Rekhta Dictionary. 'Hind'. Accessed 30 July 2025. https://rekhtadictionary.com/meaning-of-hind-1.

Chapter 22: Unlikely Allies

1. Ibn Battuta's statement about the meaning of 'Hindu Kush' can be found in the authoritative English translation by H.A.R. Gibb—*The Travels of Ibn Battuta*, Vol. 3, works issued by the Hakluyt Society, second series, No. 117 (Cambridge: Cambridge University Press, 1971), p. 580:

'After this I proceeded to the city of Barwan, in the road to which is a high mountain, covered with snow and exceedingly cold; they call it the Hindu Kush, that is Hindu-slayer, because most of the slaves brought thither from India die on account of the intenseness of the cold.'

Books by Amish

The Shiva Trilogy

The fastest-selling book series in the history of Indian publishing

THE IMMORTALS OF MELUHA
(Book 1 of the Trilogy)

1900 BCE. What modern Indians mistakenly call the Indus Valley Civilization, the inhabitants of that period knew as the land of Meluha—a near-perfect empire created many centuries earlier by Lord Ram. Now their primary river Saraswati is drying, and they face terrorist attacks from their enemies from the east. Will their prophesied hero, the Neelkanth, emerge to destroy evil?

THE SECRET OF THE NAGAS
(Book 2 of the Trilogy)

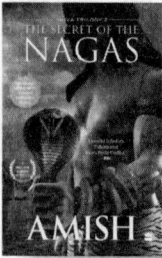

The sinister Naga warrior has killed his friend Brahaspati and now stalks his wife, Sati. Shiva, who is the prophesied destroyer of evil, will not rest till he finds his demonic adversary. His thirst for revenge will lead him to the door of the Nagas, the serpent people. Fierce battles will be fought and unbelievable secrets revealed in the second part of the Shiva Trilogy.

THE OATH OF THE VAYUPUTRAS
(Book 3 of the Trilogy)

Shiva reaches the Naga capital, Panchavati, and prepares for a holy war against his true enemy. The Neelkanth must not fail, no matter what the cost. In his desperation, he reaches out to the Vayuputras. Will he succeed? And what will be the real cost of battling Evil? Read the concluding part of this bestselling series to find out.

The Ram Chandra Series

The second-fastest-selling book series in the history of Indian publishing

RAM: SCION OF IKSHVAKU
(Book 1 of the Series)

He loves his country and he stands alone for the law. His band of brothers, his wife, Sita, and the fight against the darkness of chaos. He is Prince Ram. Will he rise above the taint that others heap on him? Will his love for Sita sustain him through his struggle? Will he defeat the demon Raavan who destroyed his childhood? Will he fulfil the destiny of the Vishnu? Begin an epic journey with Amish's Ram Chandra Series.

SITA: WARRIOR OF MITHILA
(Book 2 of the Series)

An abandoned baby is found in a field. She is adopted by the ruler of Mithila, a powerless kingdom, ignored by all. Nobody believes this child will amount to much. But they are wrong. For she is no ordinary girl. She is Sita. Through an innovative multi-linear narrative, Amish takes you deeper into the epic world of the Ram Chandra Series.

RAAVAN: ENEMY OF ARYAVARTA
(Book 3 of the Series)

Raavan is determined to be a giant among men, to conquer, plunder, and seize the greatness that he thinks is his right. He is a man of contrasts, of brutal violence and scholarly knowledge. A man who will love without reward and kill without remorse. In this, the third book in the Ram Chandra Series, Amish sheds light on Raavan, the king of Lanka. Is he the greatest villain in history or just a man in a dark place, all the time?

WAR OF LANKA
(Book 4 of the Series)

As Raavan kidnaps Sita, Ram seethes with rage and grief. The war of Lanka is imminent; it's a war for Dharma, after all. Will Ram defeat the ruthless and seemingly invincible Raavan? Or will Lanka fight back like a cornered tiger? And, most importantly, will the real Vishnu rise? In this fourth book of the Ram Chandra Series, the narrative strands of Ram, Sita, and Raavan crash into each other and explode in a slaughterous war.

The Indic Chronicles

LEGEND OF SUHELDEV: THE KING WHO SAVED INDIA

Repeated attacks by Mahmud of Ghazni have weakened India's northern regions. Then the Turks raid and destroy one of the holiest temples in the land: the magnificent Lord Shiva temple at Somnath. At this most desperate of times, a warrior rises to defend the nation. King Suheldev—fierce rebel, charismatic leader, inclusive patriot. Read this epic adventure of courage and heroism that recounts the story of that lionhearted warrior and the magnificent Battle of Bahraich.

THE CHOLA TIGERS: AVENGERS OF SOMNATH

Mahmud of Ghazni believes he has crushed the spirit of India—the Shiva Linga at the Somnath Temple lies shattered and thousands are dead. But among the ashes of destruction, five people—a Tamil warrior, a Gujarati merchant, a devotee of Lord Ayyappan, a scholar-emperor from Malwa and the most powerful man on earth, Emperor Rajendra Chola—resolve to strike at the heart of the invader's kingdom. From the grandeur of the Chola empire to the shadows of Ghazni's bloodstained court, *The Chola Tigers* is the untold story of vengeance that became Dharma.

Non-fiction

IMMORTAL INDIA: YOUNG COUNTRY, TIMELESS CIVILIZATION

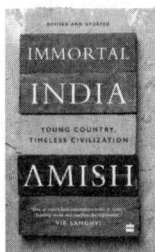

Explore India with the country's storyteller, Amish, who helps you understand it like never before, through a series of sharp articles, nuanced speeches and intelligent debates. In *Immortal India*, Amish lays out the vast landscape of an ancient culture with a fascinatingly modern outlook.

DHARMA: DECODING THE EPICS FOR A MEANINGFUL LIFE

In this genre-bending book, the first of a series, Amish and Bhavna dive into the priceless treasure trove of the ancient Indian epics, as well as the vast and complex universe of Amish's Meluha, to explore some of the key concepts of Indian philosophy. Within this book are answers to our many philosophical questions, offered through simple and wise interpretations of our favourite stories.

IDOLS: UNEARTHING THE POWER OF MURTI PUJA

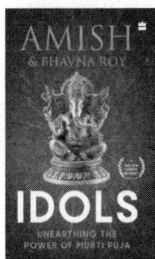

In this companion volume to the bestselling *Dharma*, Amish and Bhavna tackle burning questions about idol worship through simple, varied and astute interpretations of myths and religious texts. They unearth the symbolic essence of *Ishta Devata*, dive into the benefits of *bhakti* and tackle the importance of religion for people and society in this insightful and thought-provoking book.